THE GREAT ONE

THE GREAT ONE

CYRUS M. ESMAILI

iUniverse, Inc.
Bloomington

The Great One

iUniverse books may be ordered through booksellers or by contacting:

iUniverse
1663 Liberty Drive
Bloomington, IN 47403
www.iuniverse.com
1-800-Authors (1-800-288-4677)

ISBN: 978-1-4620-3169-6 (sc)
ISBN: 978-1-4620-3171-9 (hc)
ISBN: 978-1-4620-3170-2 (ebk)

Printed in the United States of America

iUniverse rev. date: 01/18/2012

CONTENTS

In The Beginning

Bright light of an early morning rose from depths of minds. Life was its essence and beauty its extension. It was a new life demanding new definitions, a new destiny radiating compassionate thoughts. "Who am I" was no longer a source of bewilderment. "Why am I" did not instigate estranged thoughts. A new question captivated my free mind. "Who do I want to be?" became the instigator of resolutions.

Visions of past and future assumed a magnified clearance as I rose from a long journey to embrace the world. I rose from a deep sleep with a newly constituted resolve to command my will.

As if a scene covered with haze, a hollow vision of a distant montage flashed a synapse of reality. Like a goblet with an ancient vintage, I swallowed it with delight.

Existence transmuted a definite assertion, and dreams proposed a new reality embedded in integrity of my awareness. I opened my mind. Shadows flared delightful sites beneath light of a shining warmth. Was it a simple day with brightly beaming flares? Was it a fusion reaction emitting a flurry of images? Was it, a big bang or an illuminating thought with a revelation sudden and deep? Which spin of which quark stimulated which synapse? Which hormone reached what level?

A sensation from the inner sanctum declared my thoughts valid. I touched myself for reassurance, but feelings can be deceiving. Uncertain of any certainty, I announced myself alive and willfully aware.

A sudden rush of energy and I opened eyes wide. I needed not elucidate the meaning of existence. I felt its vibrations deep inside me.

A great yearning to touch and feel and smell steered my urging desires. My eyes slowly closed shut as I raised my head, took a deep breath, stretched my arms wide and embraced the life in front of me.

The universe stood high and mighty. Vivid images of its tapestry flared transparent impressions. I was the sole audience and my thoughts a multidimensional screen depicting an array of abstract impressions.

How do I exhibit the reality I am? How do I portray the images I sense? How can I see the universe while thinking of its past, its composition and its future? How can I be what I am?

Surrounded with magnolia, banana patches shadowed lily ponds. A blended fume of many delights fanned purple roses.

What a surprise! Her beauty was more astonishing than all the wonders before me. Her silk-smooth hair waved in the wind revealing many shades of her being. If this is a dream, I promised myself, then I shall dream for all eternity.

I froze while examining her moves. Smelling her perfume, I focused for a glimpse of her eyes. She stood gentle as a calm breeze brushed her satin flesh. Like a cloud trapped on low ground, she appeared fragile. I sensed her pleasing thoughts as they appeased my senses to synaptic decadence.

Her eyes beamed an incessant shine of youthful flare. The smile furnished upon her lips conjured exuberant perplexity of being alive. Her glazing lips promised smoothness of a naked flesh. Her gleaming eyes promised a luscious wave of action potentials. The mystery of life dwindled to simple expressions, diminishing enormity of the universe to secondary conjectures.

In a perfectly synchronized motion, we approached each other. Our eyes met. A sudden rush of energy commissioned my accosted senses. I felt its track deep in my spine, down to my toes, back to my brain. At awe with her demeanor, I dared to shower her with words.

Your beauty is beyond description. Your shimmering eyes reveal a reservoir of desires. They beam radiance of affection. Your lips are blood red with quivers of a pending eruption. Their succulent perch rattles my senses and dismisses all behavior for a brief taste of their sweetness. Your clarity surpasses perfection. Your velvety smooth texture exudes an energetic radiance of passionate composure.

No experience has enthralled my imagination in such totality. No feeling can foment passion more cryptic than your eyes. I am already a slave of your rapture, I said.

Your presence is most charming. She replied with grace of a dancer. A suiting smile fashioned her face, glazing her ornate radiance bespeaking many deliciously mischievous thoughts.

A wonderful occasion, I thought. The game of life has rolled its dice, and my fortune is at hand.

She looked at me with passionate bright eyes. The passage of time seemed insignificant. Life appeared to have halted for a glimpse of our consonance.

She approached me as the force of her attraction amended my will impotent, reducing me to a state of complete surrender. Beauty of the moment suspended universal laws as I fancied thoughts of her naked image.

The lush surrounding was demarcated with hue of a setting sun. An occasional bird of colors spread its wings. Distant ocean hummed a soft roar. Her presence spawned an ethos of affection. Life became an expression of joy as I became a slave of her moves.

I feel you as I felt you in a distant dream, she said.

I feel you as if I had never been without you, I replied.

A dove, captivated by our presence, hovered above. The early moon shined with incessant diligence. A slight breeze whistled a harmonic tune.

I reached out and gently stroked her hair. She quivered as she planted her lips on mine. Her brilliant eyes held mine in hers.

Time, it seemed, had ceased its passing to catch a glimpse of our affection. No star dared brighter than it should.

Deep inside I sensed a delightful feeling, a certain emotion out-shined by none. Perhaps it was the pleasure of love I experienced. Perhaps it was the surging of hormones. It persisted as our union stirred my senses to a new plateau of euphoria.

She leaned her face on mine. A cool breeze dared the occasion, calmly swaying her hair on my face. It soon died down. Her hair fell softly on my arm. Pleasure of love formulated passion of the moment as amorous thoughts illuminated its content. Quarks spun out of tune creating confusion among hadrons. White dwarfs confused themselves for neutron stars. Red giants teasingly circled around black holes. Neutrinos danced aimlessly. It all seemed out of tune yet never attuned to higher perfection. I sensed fragility of being and wished eternity of the moment.

Without hesitation, we engaged in a deep and lasting embrace fostering a spontaneous fusion of our affection. Time and space formatted a singularity focused on a small point of immense energy. A gateway of some sorts opened drawing my attention to another universe of wonders. I shied away from such spatial delights. The ocean roared with fury. Mind to mind we spoke of love. Teased with sentiments of affliction and bemused with thoughts of want and desire, our unified manifest promised a delightful experience. Twined in one another, we reached the threshold of love culminating in a simultaneous spasm that baffled our universe to a standstill.

It was warm. It was joyful. It was sweet. It was intense. I was a captive caught in the web of an immense image. Nothing demanded greater attention than the persisting magnificence of her presence. The cosmic laws were temporarily reduced to meaningless expressions, none worth a flicker of her eyes.

The universe became ours, and all the sacred oaths dwindled insignificant. Our unified posture assumed its own realm. Our ecstasy gave a new meaning to cosmic design. "Who am I" was no longer a dilemma of mysterious connotations. The answer was the edifice of our union. Love was our essence and compassionate togetherness our consonance.

In my anesthetized mind, entropy came to a halt. Light circled around itself. The cosmic antiquity demanded a new explanation, and stars danced a harmonious ballet. Time seemed eternal and death a slow process of aging.

She held her warm body against mine exuding florid expressions of gentleness. My fallible self enfeebled to a small morsel, I shriveled to a pulp melting onto contours of her smooth self.

From a cannon of passions with conviction of a lion-minded sage, without fear, without hesitation, sailing uncharted emotions, with precision of a skilled craftsman, she plunged onto my nest unsettling my castle of thoughts. In a sweeping emotional stretch, she peeled off the wall around my awareness exposing my naked self.

When I ceased for a brief reprieve, the deed was done. We had entwined in more ways than one. A delicate bondage wove our ephemeral desires to redundancy of eternal. A new flame framed living with loving.

I decided to devote my unending attention to her and melt her with strokes of my passion. I realized this odyssey a woven string of reality glazed with requiem of newly conceived particles and feelings. I decided to close old books, sweep ancient dreams away and raise hope that for all times passion would be with us.

In a sweeping motion, the universe within metamorphosed. All things seemed garnished with a magical potion. Without suspicion of purpose, without raptures of a trial, we laughed for no reason, made gestures of useless consequence and entangled in impossible postures. Spontaneity played its bold game of unanticipated outcomes as our combined magnet affronted a string of favorable feelings. Life appeared more harmonious than chaotic.

All expended, we laid side-by-side floating freely in a newly framed time-space. We rolled face to face, cajoled breast-to-breast, stared deep and laughed childish. Her ruffled mind, one and the same with her slender body, fused with mine.

From its inception, our fusion was energetic. It sustained our psychological equilibrium with a constant flow of mental delights that bind us as one.

No matter what the colors and texture of your emotions, I will obviate my life in loving you, I confessed, in earnest, as she smiled.

I will yearn for your touch as I seek your passion. I will entangle myself in fissures of your affection, storm your lips, brush your smooth flesh, tease your startled mind and absorb your loving self without a flicker of doubt. I am yours to enjoy in all phases, I declared.

It was then that a bright light appeared upon the night sky separating the endless stars from tangible reality of nature around us. We held each other tightly taking refuge in our combined courage.

What could possibly be the nature of this being? I whispered with caution as she leaned her head close to mine.

The beaming light displayed a brilliant composition of reflections. It shined brighter as it slowly approached us.

We stepped back grasping each other tight. She grew furious with each passing moment.

This moment's reality is our most sacred expression of selfhood. The sanctity of our compassion and its meaning is unique in this universe, said Mithra.

Your persisting intrusion raises our apprehension to a discomforting level. Our freshly blossomed affinity for one another is sweeter than any promise you may conjure. Leave us in peace. Leave us to our own emotional reasoning. The universe is far and wide. Find your serenity elsewhere and leave us to our own.

Assuming there was a living purpose in all of this, we expressed words of concern as the light kept approaching. Its flare beamed with intensity of a star but without its discomforts. Colorful dispositions displayed quiescent images with brilliant clarity. I could not help but wonder at its manifested reality.

Mithra was not amused. Her anger reached a point of determined rage. Her posture was wild. Still, her manner was tamed, in principle.

We wish to be ourselves, left alone in peacefulness of our world, she said.

It is our earnest desire to cherish significance of these moments undisturbed. We wish to live in privacy of our choosing. Your being disturbs our continuity. The delightful harmony of our existence, as a newly constituted unity, is perturbed by your intrusion. You should declare your intention and leave us.

I found myself captivated by the spontaneity of Mithra as she expressed her passion and fury. Her protest was amorously tainted. In every move, she dissipated romantic gestures of affection. Her propensity for a protracted persistence to forward our case was an act of willful display. I knew that well. I had tasted her naked self in the domain of spontaneity.

My affection for her had grown to a hiatus of admiration.

I wondered at the purpose of this imperial display. It shined majestic. However, in its foray into our domain, it perturbed our affinity to love. What hidden secrets provoke this ardent display, I wondered?

The shine persisted as if examining a rare delight. Abashed and confused we gazed at each other wondering at its nature and intention.

Perhaps it is here by chance, I said.

The beauty furnished upon this land could attract and appease many wanderers. We could not deny its presence if mutual existence is its intent.

Let us then change station, said Mithra.

If it truly intends what you say, then it should leave us in good fate and pursue its own aim.

Gently, we paced our way to another space where leaves clumsily swayed under a dull moon. To our astonishment, the light kept pace. It stood as we stood. It moved as we moved. It was then apparent that this ominous hue of unknown volition had some purpose connected to us.

Having failed to escape its attention, we cautiously approached the heart of its presence. It glowed brightest and clearest as we entered its domain. It accepted us without lament. Engulfed in an array of colorful reflections we felt comfortably secure. It was neither warm nor cold, nor did its brightness blind our sight.

It began to speak in gentlest tone, unfolding the mystery of its presence.

My children, it said passionately. You are all alone in this pristine haven of fortunes. There are vast oceans and fertile lands to mend your needs and suit your senses. There are rain and sun, trees and pastures, to feed your hunger and stimulate your senses. This is a virgin land with purest compositions. Devoid of calamities, without concern for safety or sanctity of your existence, you can live contented lives perpetuating your kind without undue caution. The young suns will illuminate life a long time to come, and the moons will shine gentle to your delight.

I could see no tangible evidence of its existence. There was nothing but light all around us. The passage of time and containment of space had completely ceased or lost their relevance.

She pressed hard against my chest. I sensed her anxiety.

I am Ahuramazda, the source of light and the guardian of truths. Where I shine there is life. Where I am not there is darkness. My presence generates order, and in my absence, there is but chaos and disorder. And you, the children of my dreams, emit a certain flare only your unique visage of life can savor. You are among the many chosen ones to carry on the torch of love, passion, truth, justice and all the acclaimed virtues.

Few can rival your mastery of these delicate quandaries. Your compassion for belonging, your desire for love and affection, your obsession with good and right are rivaled by few.

You, my children, are chosen to keep the torch of light beaming. You can help perpetuate my dream and strengthen my purpose. You can help expand my vicinity to penetrate deep in the heart of darkness.

The force of darkness must be belittled to its proper demeanor. With each passing sun, it gains strength absorbing everything to a diluted state of nothingness.

The light changed texture as its fury subsided.

I am the keeper of universal truths, the savior of reality and beholder of goodness. My existence as the beaming reality of life, as awesome as it may be, is fragile. It requires a continuous flow of willful devotion to keep it shining.

Your amorous format could help me abase darkness to its proper usefulness.

You, my children, are to perpetuate my image in your image. Your devotion shall expand a dream that will shine in your minds as it shines in mine.

I give you the promise of eternal awareness. I promise you everlasting happiness. I could enhance your awareness to relish a lasting image of life. I pledge you the opulence of pleasure and leisure. I promise you the perpetual comforts of the most exotic nature. I promise you an abundant array of wonders. I give you all that and much more if you only choose to cultivate my will, teach your children my ways and foster the axioms I set forth.

Give me your devotion and I give you comforts of a harmonious symmetry. Devote yourselves to the might of light and you shall have freedoms abound. Serve my will and you shall attain the greatest purpose of your lives. Devote your will for the benefaction of our total accord and I shall bestow your visage of existence a higher purpose.

Before us stood the dominion of light proclaiming its celestial might as it exposed its desire to have a hold on our willful destiny. Astonished by significance of the occasion and bewildered by enormity of its splendor, we attempted to ascertain perniciousness of the occasion.

It is not often one confronts a celestial being of such magnitude and wishes its disappearance. The reality of this mesmerizing occasion, from its very inception when I realized myself awakened to joys of her love, until this nightmarish fantasy, resembled an amorphous reality of unknown dictates.

It must be an illusion of senses. I surmised. It must be a delirium brought about by intoxicating luster of this newly conceived universe. Why would any dominion embark on captivity of our sensibilities?

Astray in a world of illusions and unable to distinguish reality from fantasy, I watched her as she watched me. I touched her to assure myself reality. The gaze in her eyes suited my nerves to a numbing comfort. Her existence and the feelings she stirred were as real as the light surrounding us.

I faced Mithra.

We can enjoy everything that surrounds us without fear of losing them in dimension of time. What more could we hope for but eternity of happiness and awareness? Here, at this reality, lay the key to eternity. All we need to do is surrender our willful independence and accept its mastery over our destiny.

She looked at me puzzled.

From love to sex to want, I dream your pleasures as if my own. In gathering of our thoughts, in solitude of our free selves, I have you breast naked as we succumb to pleasure. Oh yes, pleasure; it addles virtue until none is left to fool and no innocence to seduce. That is when we devour each other in flesh and mind and think of willful motives to capture time.

Perhaps truth is an assiduous reason we advert to find happiness and wish it eternal. Perhaps happiness is mind empyrean we hope. Even so, to give up our freedom to independent thought is to surrender faculties of discretion and motivation.

Must we submit our very essence to attain certainty and capsulate time for future reference? Must we subjugate ourselves to a will more powerful than ours? And if we do so, what have we accomplished? Would we not become trapped in contortions of another consciousness?

She spoke with passion I had not witnessed in her. Tracing my face with her finger, she circled around.

What we are promised is astonishingly exuberant, she said with seductive eyes.

To live forever, to enjoy riches of a comfortable life, free of fear and disease, to assist in illuminating universal truths, these are aims every being savors. However, to attain them by submitting our will to dictate of another is equivalent to surrendering our humanity.

She stopped. Her posture turned inward and serious.

The mortal expression of passion we have fielded has captivated attention of an immortal. Why is this majestic source of light, with all its declared might, seeking the essence of our existence? It yearns for our willful discourse as if without our devotion, it shall be deemed worthless. It yearns for our love as if without our love it will be useless.

It is the agony of decay, the knowledge of a mortal end, the ecstasy of a brief and intense rapture in awareness, the dichotomy of being and nothingness accentuating pleasures of a mortal life. To lose such composure is to lose our humanity.

To lose willful living is to reduce us to biological moppets. We cannot allow anyone or anything render impotent our sense of self. We are as much ourselves as is the universe itself.

She leaned her head on my shoulder.

The price, she said, is to love each other not for the sake of each other but for the sake of another. The price is losing the chance to ponder the unknown with our unique visage of existence.

Look at this mighty being. It is begging for our will. And it knows the way to attain our will is through our willingness to surrender our will. Even in our submission we must will to submit. The wonder of our lives, no matter what path we may embrace, is the integrity of our freedom to will.

Heed not the promise of eternity. The nectar of love we have tasted, the passion we are emitting is worthier than eternity.

We may not see reality in its entirety, but we can imagine its boundaries, and in time, bit by bit, contrive its truths as we observe it with greater awareness. We may be infants in our evolutionary path, but infants grow to radiate profoundness. We are a potential. We are a unique visage of life.

Her words bore deep in my awareness. She spoke our truth with clarity. Overcome by emotion, I held her as close as I could and showered her with words of affection.

Be deep, be simple, be yourself. Challenge my will and let me touch yours. How do I measure a self like you? In solitude of our union, I want to trust all of you. In rhapsody of our coalescence, I want to hold, kiss and admire you.

Let us presuppose our combined will a creation of our own and preserve it as if the world is about to end. There are we, and passion, and trust and all the good feelings.

I dismayed at my own failing. How easily I could have lost the very essence of my being. Human conscience is fragile. One simple decision could fragment it to pieces. Every instance of life is studded with decisions we make, most driven with the unconscious motives and a growing few with willful determination. What would my life be if I attenuated freedom to choose? Would I lose my compassion? Would I lose uniqueness of being myself? Would I stop being a human?

Bewildered by the circumstance, I concluded the price of attaining eternity too heavy a burden. What I may gain could prove a nightmare of eternal proportions. What I may lose is a certainty of being my own.

Give me your devotion and I will give eternal meaning to your existence. Give me your willful subjugation and I will open higher gates of awareness exposing truths of existence, said the lord of light.

Its voice trembled a bit exposing its vulnerability. I held Mithra. Her warmth was a suiting comfort I needed most.

She ignored the mighty Ahuramazda and addressed me with gentle strokes of her thoughtful mind.

Imagine a walk in woodlands. Brushing aside yellow autumn leaves, we entertain delights of an open prairie. Intoxicated by bird songs, refreshed by aroma of wild flowers and bedazzled by a full moon, we stare at a silvery spread over a pond. Beguiled by mystifying effects of this natural wonder, we extol joyful feelings until fortune turns, and daylight promises a new beginning.

Reality cannot escape itself nor can we escape its whimsical contortions. Its exactness will be revealed in one form or another, at one time or another. We may hide behind a flotilla of make-believe images but sooner or later reality defaces falsehood as we sharpen our awareness.

In pursuing our delicately sculpted motives, we become something more, with virtues unique to our measure of life, on our own and in concert with the rest of the universe. Uniqueness of our sentient existence will transcend universal constants to delineate passion and compassion as the determining contents of our reality.

Such is the nature of our existence: we are unique as well as a structured component of the greater universe.

Her words were stronger than his. She spoke our truth. Even so, what was our truth? Was it a reality of our being together? Was it a reality of our freedom to feel as we felt? Was it inquiry of all things with eternal connotation? Was it an ecstasy of temporary pleasures?

I felt the pain of indecision and sought solace by planting my head on her chest. She held me warm, kissed my lips, smelled my skin dry and eased my nerves with sweet words of affection.

Did I tell you how much I love you? I said.

Something inside holds me back. I regress from inward and shape my feelings with sculpted words. I escape from charade of formality, spear my emotions, chain them, analyze them meaningless and find my happiness in metaphors that implicate loving you.

And if you find me arrogant, if you think I am a narcissist, think and think deep. I am yours to mend, toss, tease, humor, use and forget.

She looked at me with pensive eyes.

Our truth is the simple love we have spawned between us. It is our misfortune the expressions of our combined feeling occasion a powerful field attracting farthest and mightiest.

What state of an affair shall our love acquire if we surrender our freedom to choose our destiny? Will it fade in a submissive state? Will it be fixed by elements beyond our control? Will it diminish us to a decrepit state of indecision?

And the way we choose to think, is it not a manifestation of our ethos in the field of humanity?

If we capitulate on our freedom to entertain future scenarios, then our joy and sorrow shall be a useless echo in a domain chosen by someone or something else. As such, our misfortune will be cemented in a limited vision of our potential, and our consciousness enslaved by contortions of time-immortal.

The promise of eternity has a captivating appeal to us mortals. We are who we are, wishful dreams that express sentiments of a finite existence with an awareness that transcends duration of that existence.

Is it not the option to choose what exalts our senses beyond convention? Is it not the uncertainty of a future leading to excitement of anticipation? Is it not the drive to resolve the unknown stimulating the imagination? None of these will be our making if we surrender our freedom to will.

How would I measure your love knowing it is not a willful love? Let us not capitulate on our will to promises sweet in appearance but ambiguous in nature. Love me for what I am. Love me for as long as I am. Love me with what you have. Let knowledge of death sweeten our harmony. Let unanticipated ecstasies and ambiguities enrich our lives.

Her words bore deep in my conscience. Give up my will! What an invidious thought! What is the real intention of this entity seemingly fostering eternal life? Why does it so desperately yearn for our will? And what would become of us if we pursue its intent? Would we not become slaves of its discipline?

I stared deep in her eyes. Our minds met. The decision was ours to make. The choice was ours to choose.

I stood resolute with a determined accord to appraise my will supreme. I turned my attention to the beaming light and resolutely declared our newly evolved axiom.

You claim universal powers. You claim to have might of light in your sight. You promise us eternity of living. If you possess so much and can give as much, why then you are compelled to intervene in this Bantam translation of life, our passion has earned us? What hidden motives define your purpose? Why do you seek our allegiance?

Speak the truth if truth is the source of light you beam so bright.

I am the light of life, said the beaming might. I am the shine of meaning. I am the essence of all beings. I am the keeper of truths. I am the dispenser of life. I am might of right. My presence drives the despicable force of darkness to seclusion. I foment the magic of righteousness. I make truth meaningful. However, with all my might, my being is brittle in nature.

Truth is fragile my children. It is as fragile as it is majestic. No power can outshine truth, and truth can fade with the slightest misgiving.

My being is a fusion of composites. I require a ceaseless flow of willful commitment to sustain integrity. I am the source of light, but my reservoir is every glimmer of hope that shines the universe its tantalizing design.

It is not a game of chance I have appeared before you soliciting your benevolence. I can sense a true passion from farthest. The life that shines compassion shines mighty. It is my destiny to seek brightly capacious lives that shine the universe its willful substance.

I appear before you to engage your trust. I appear before you to engage your sense of truth. This is not a request for charity. This is not a petition for mercy. This is an enticement to coalesce into your sense of devotion to a greater cause. Choose the path of light and you shall be rewarded as harbingers of passion. Join capacity with me to render power of light a mighty force that defines "everything" and confronts "nothing."

I warn you, in earnest, without light, there shall be but darkness.

You have made your case, but we need time to think this deep, Mithra replied without hesitation.

What you petition is a matter of indelible concern to us. It reflects on the possible connections between the universe and us.

You ask us to sacrifice our freedoms to keep yours shining. You claim without our devotion to your cause darkness will reign supreme. We need time to illuminate our minds with implications of your ethos but without persuasive afflictions of your majestic presence. Come back in due time and you shall have our reply.

I sensed no fear in her. Nor did she dispense weakness.

The issue is settled, I said. We have devoted more of our precious mortal time to your concerns than we wish. Our future as a universal entity is at stake. Our lives as willful beings are at stake. The burden of decision is ours to make. Leave us in peace and seek your fortune elsewhere.

Soon after I uttered those words the light began to dim. Farther and further it dissipated in the star-studded sky. The moon shone softly as shades of light mingled with whimsical moves of the wind. Birds sang their tunes, and the suspended life became alive again. It was a joy to feel passing of time, to appreciate life adorned with radiance of motion, to watch leaves sway, fall and decay.

To a mortal, the universe is a gamut of possibilities, life is a supposition morbid in nature, alienating in texture, revealing in disposition and nothing but "nothing" at the end, said Mithra.

Such is the notion of truth in a mortal dimension of existence: an endearing idea of short-lived reality.

What is to be done? I looked at her bewildered, awaiting her thoughts to rescue mine. She shivered as she pressed her head on mine. I felt her tremor. I quivered as well.

I was confused by the enormity of events. Our lives had become a focal point in a resolution of universal antagonisms, and I felt inadequately fit to focus on any resolution. Staring at her mesmerizing eyes, I knew my destiny was with her.

Truth is an endearing thought of an enduring idea, I said. The ideas are ours as is the endearment.

To us mortals, to be truly free is to have a greater span of life, said Mithra.

Should we give up liberties for a quick ascendance to longevity and knowledge of life? Conversely should we hold steadfast, guard our freedoms and inch our way in a gradual ascent to longevity?

Our biological realm demands us to live in a world of certainties. Inherent to mastery of such an integrity is mastery of events. And mastery of events is a gigantic step toward immortality.

Our unified identity is not a metaphysical concept but a biological reality. This is a conjecture we must adduce as an exact certainty. Recognition of the self is merely the beginning. Transcending the biological existence to sprout a willful existence is a path to highest actualization.

In this universe of unknown paths, we are a speck, a drone, a willful might. Do you see our predicament as a temporary rapture in the universal waves? We cannot allow our minds to wander in this mosaic of unpredictable delights and frights.

Let understanding to rule our affection with imaginative insights and plunge us deep into the universe.

Darkness spread its domain in the absence of light sprouting foliage of evading shapes. Comets toyed their way across as falling debris danced a short arc. The night-vision, in the absence of light, gave rise to a greater visibility. What a surprise! The darkness that rendered light invalid illuminated the skies.

Aided by the moons' perfectly reflected light, we clumsily measured our way across the land. She stopped, danced a short walk, spread her arms to embrace the night.

Life is coexistence of all wonders, I said.

She laughed off a seductive moment.

The mighty light shine's dimmer. Only its reflection brightens our lives. And darkness is only partially dark. The totality created by their fusion gives rise to this enchanting experience, she said and fell in my arms. I kissed her lips and fell deep in her warmth.

At awe with calmness and gentleness of it all, once again our thoughts beamed passionate waves of love. We whispered sentiments of affection, rolled in joy, and teased our minds with enactment of our most favorite delights. Her silk-smooth, spring-clear presence shined a pleasing reflection. She hummed tranquil tunes ruffling my mind with harmonious sounds.

The distant ocean roared its tune as mighty waves pounded the reefs.

All is well, I thought.

All is well, she whispered.

No sooner than we assumed serenity of the occasion a sudden high wind jostled trees uneasy. A lofty orb of pure darkness emerged before us. Nothing could be seen in it or through it as mighty light abashed dim in its presence. Its absolute darkness radiated a unique splendor.

It stood a short distance from us. No sooner than peace had settled did it begin its approach toward us. Slowly, it encroached on our domain. We maintained equilibrium with a greater conviction than we did before the mighty lord of light.

I am Ahriman, the ruler of darkness, the benefactor of chaos, the harbinger of harmony, the keeper of balance and dispenser of passion. It is my universal mission to resist the incessant penetration of light, thwart its destructive designs and render invalid its insatiable hunger for hegemony.

It is my purpose to guard against excessive beams of light and protect the universe from annihilation under its corrosive might. It is my willful consent to attenuate entropy and muffle life to a suiting stillness. Under my canopy, lovers immerse in pleasure as the stars beam gentle to their delight.

I appear in peace to appeal for your devotion to my cause. The force of light is fast gaining control of the universe, threatening its cohesion. It blurs the vision and manipulates the mind.

I need your willful servitude to strengthen my will in contesting this incongruous force. In return, I promise you eternal life of pleasures.

Once again, our peace was perturbed by presence of an entity claiming its jurisprudence over our lives. Once again, our affection, our union as a unique visage of life, had been traversed in time-space to attract attention of another universal force. By now, the scenario had grown old. The promise of eternity had lost its appealing prospect, and the mighty forces of the universe were entities in pursuit of their own ends.

Bewildered and awe stricken we approached it with caution. It stood unruffled asking us to penetrate its midst. We cautiously entered its dark existence. Within this orb of darkness, nothing posed a definite certainty. No harm was impending. It was neither pleasing nor discomforting.

What a magnificent being! Mithra wondered.

She let go and danced her way around as if in a playground of her dreams. I clumsily followed her steps. Suddenly, she stopped, looked around and approached me with frightened eyes. I held her. Not a word was uttered. No words were necessary to explain our predicament.

And why should we heed your cause? She protested.

Your presence exudes a certain mystique of mischievous intent. Why should we entertain your case?

Realizing our disposition with greater certainty, I gathered my senses for a determined stand.

Your promise is not a consideration to our consonance, I said.

We have chosen mortality as our true destiny. The promise of eternity no longer entices our attention. Nor are we captivated with intrigues of its promise. Freedom is our sacred oath. Freedom to will our destiny is the essence, the pillar of our chosen humanity.

I am the lord of darkness, the keeper of chaos and the gateway to "nothing." I am the original design. Before there was light the universe was I. Within my domain existed a peaceful symmetry until the decrepit force of light confounded the conditions with its pugnacious power. It grew with viciousness beyond description. It molded the harmonious ways of a perfect symmetry into a disharmonious fabric of partial symmetries. In every chance, it cut onto my being, incessantly following me from one corner of the universe to another. Never content with dimensions of its domain, it devised ways to manipulate beings it came upon promising them eternal salvation. It imposed its legitimacy with the brutal force of persuasion. It rose wherever I faded. It followed wherever I nested. It wove strings of its image, making it impossible to escape its grip.

Here, I am before you, tired and besieged, begging your favor in assisting me to furnish the universe its original harmony. Give me your freedom, give me your devotion, give me your destiny, give me your will, and I shall make your lives eternal and happy.

You have made your case with persuasiveness worthy of your existence. Ours is a virgin life of humanity. We are a budding quintessence devoid of powers you profess. Freedom to map our destiny is of greater concern to us than promises you make. At stake is the definition of our being. We need time to think it deep. Come back in due time and you shall have our response, said Mithra.

Her smooth manner was uncompromising. The image of pure darkness gradually disappeared into fading light of the night-sky.

What are we to do? Our passion has infatuated mighty universal forces, I said.

We have become a battleground of their ambitions and ambiguities. There is beauty in each of these celestial powers. They have a mission to accomplish. Nonetheless, obsessed by merits of their eccentric logic, they are willing to sacrifice our freedoms to enhance theirs.

How could a mighty existence exhibit such a self-centered end?

That is their weakness, and their weakness our strength, said Mithra.

Their self-righteous sense of truth is our fortune. By sponsoring the way of acceptance and coexistence, we adhere to a higher definition of truth than theirs.

Why should we accede to the notion of might as right? If dominions of darkness and light did not antagonize each other, there should be no need for devotion or subjugation. We possess the freedom to choose neither. We have the willful option to choose to be free in the domain of our chosen metaphors.

Life can be coexistence of entities without a desire to capitulate or captivate.

If commitment to utopia of universal harmony is our ethos, then we must reason vitality of its conception. Such undertaking requires a willful engagement in weaving intricacies of our future.

Our duty is to no other but ourselves. It is an individual moral imperative to consider all claims with seriousness of life and death. It is our human nature to assimilate experiences and accommodate incisive perceptions of life. Darkness and light are with us and within us. If we favor one idiom over another, we succumb to the demagoguery of poor judgment tipping the balance, one way or another.

The essence of our being is our humanity. No known entity in this universe has the unique distinctions, we manifest. Irrespective of our fallibility, one essence of our humanity is the assertion of our individual and unified freedoms.

To give up and surrender our uniqueness is a cowardly act. Without a free will, we are doomed to a life of slavery be it at whims of probability or acts of organized certainties.

And if we let our evolving cognitive and emotional impulses determine the course of our existence, do we not trap ourselves in the myth of Sisyphus? I wondered.

He carried the burden of his existence up to the mountain of life only to be thwarted by forces that denied him accomplishment. He did not surrender to failure, but his will was blemished with eternal repetition of success followed by failure.

Sisyphus surrendered to the eternal misery of indecision, said Mithra.

His will became trapped in contradictions of life and death. Impounded by the notion of immortality, he accepted a continuous cycle of success and failure. If Sisyphus had accepted mortality, he would not have to carry the contradiction of conformity and determinism time and again. By choosing the path of immortality, he lost his freedom to live or die.

Maintaining integrity of will and achieving freedom of will are two distinct idioms of awareness. Integrity of will is a stepping-stone to the odyssey of free will. The way to immortality, if that is our desire, is through our own willful ways. Better to embark on a slow accession to ends of our choosing than quickly gain them by capitulating to promises with unknown beginnings and ends.

We are not obligated to side with darkness or light. Nor do we have to end our expression of freedom at choosing one over the other. Renouncing their dominance over our will is a beginning. Attaining our destiny, in our own image, is our odyssey.

Promises granted to us, as slaves, are not worth a moment of freedom. If there comes a time when a force insists upon manipulating us, at the very end of our struggle against it, as mortals, we hold the ghastly choice of ending our lives. Possessing the freedom to choose death is a manifestation of our mortality. It empowers us to withstand enslavement.

The immortal cannot discern the self-destructive mode of a mortal. And that, my love, is our strength when confronted by an immortal bent on mastering our freedom to will our destiny.

The universal struggle between Ahuramazda and Ahriman, be it imaginary or real, cannot be considered an optimal state of affairs. Common sense points to peaceful coexistence in an environment void of submission, subjugation and hegemony.

Coexistence without the threat of hegemony must become a human directive. If we can fathom the possibility of our collective destiny, then it is our duty to aim at its cultivation.

Together, each a free mind, a unique image of the universe, we can form a union independent in its perspective and apart from all else.

It is decided, I said.

No external force or entity will measure our independence. No power shall rule our destiny. We will pursue happiness with details of our chosen affinities.

She took her gaze off me as her posture took a sudden turn to concern.

We are confronted with an immediate problem that may threaten our very existence. The threat of losing our integrity is of utmost concern. We must devise plans to thwart unpleasant consequences of rejecting their preeminence.

As darkness and light diminish, themes of coexistence will rise promoting universal harmony, I said.

She held her knees, pulled them up to her chin. I sensed an uncertainty in her I had not detected before. She continued with a regained purpose.

Diminished in their powers, they will learn the lesson of humility and take their proper stand amidst other wonders of the universe. The universe is too vast, too encompassing to be ruled by a few. We must not condone concepts promoting conquest by either of these forces. Light and dark, good and bad, right and wrong, these are metaphors that exist only if there is a willingness to accept their existence.

Their universal eminence is a reflection of our imagination.

The forces of light and darkness appeared sincere. They spoke persuasively of their mission to maintain their perceived order. Could it be they both were right? Could it be they were both wrong? Perhaps right and wrong have nothing to do with it. Perhaps the rigid dichotomy of their existence is an abstraction of human perception. Whatever their disposition, imagined or real, they were present in our reality. That alone justified our attention to their significance.

Our answer shall be a determined no, I said. No to slavery, no to surrender, no to captivity, no to every power that renders our harmony useless. From this moment on we will exhibit a contrived consonance of our own volition. From this moment on we shall be advocates of harmonious coexistence. We will aim to unravel universal myths by miracles of our collective vision. We shall reach heights of awareness with capacity of our intellect.

Moonlight illuminated the path through green pastures. Holding each other, we approached dawn with apprehension. Talking of the future and possible meanings of our newly conceived existence, conscious of our frailties, we smiled at many uncertain moments. Seeking certainty through freedom, as unique individuals of social and universal consequence, we dared life with intrepid gallantry.

We had confronted uncertainty of the relationship between the universe and us. But the love and humanity that bonded Mithra and I had created a shared intent of our endeavor. As we delved deeper in the notion of "us" as individuals, as a social concept and a universal entity, our stance assumed a symmetrical posture.

Dawn approached and so did the lords of light and dark. Cloaked in their invisible garb, they taunted us from opposite sides. They moved with caution in proximity of one another. Their caution, whispered Mithra, is indicative of their weakness. Their indelible deference for one another as foes is our advantage.

One appeared as pure light, the other nothing but dark. One lit to absolute brightness, the other dimmed to darkness. The sky was neither dark nor bright as these opposing entities canceled each other neutral. In between them and before the entire universe, we stood robust and declared our intention.

It is our concerted accord to choose the path of sovereignty, said Mithra with conviction.

Our sovereign choice is the ambiguous path of independence. We have chosen to maintain a neutral posture. We have decided to seek peaceful coexistence. We have chosen the path of mortality. We have chosen the freedom to will our destiny.

What fools you are, declared mighty Ahuramazda.

I cannot allow this defiance set precedence, said Ahriman.

Right must prevail no matter what the cost. The deadly force of darkness must be checked to a halt.

That decadent force of light must not be allowed to deface the universe by designs of it's choosing.

You say you wish to entertain freedom of will. What petty fools you are to consider yourselves worthy of such enterprise. I know well how that mischievous force of darkness could rattle your minds in a maze of confusion.

You have no chance. Your withering wills cannot adjudicate reality of this beastly might.

I cannot permit such disaster to unravel. I have no choice but to isolate your frivolous minds. In separation, your acclaimed wills will whittle away, denying darkness the benefit of its hold on anything meaningful.

And that is how the ever-ambitious force of light penetrates each mind, shattering it to pieces. It has already exhibited its mastery of mischievous acts by igniting fear in your weakling minds. That is how it erodes your will and feasts on its shredded bits.

Only I can see how that self-righteous beast can bend your meager minds. If you insist on the course of independence, I have no choice but scramble your minds with despair and doubt. No matter what you achieve you shall always wonder how little you have achieved.

You may do as you wish, I said.

Threats will not deter our determination. Our decision is final. From now on, it is our destiny to withstand threats such as yours. No force will diminish our resolve to be ourselves.

Then I doom you to a life of separation, nostalgia and confusion.

And I shall instill emptiness and destitute in your minds. Be on your willful way but rest assured, there will be no peace for you to enjoy the path you have chosen.

Thus, the journey began.

The End of Life on Earth

Sitting on a stone-bench by the river, beneath rays of a fading sun, canopied by swaying palm leaves, I abide the incessant wind and withstand sweltering heat. Hypnotized, I watch the river surface passions hidden deep within. Listening to whispers of nature, away from concrete blocks of human creativity, I ponder life remembering days of youth, jumping small streams, rushing hastily from tree to tree, building clay-castles and dreaming wishful empires.

Now life spins in wicked ways. The river is but an image. The wind is but a sound. The birds are extinct. Building castles is a meaningless task. Wishful empires are things of the past. The sun is another dim light upon darkened skies. And passing moments bespeak of an insipid odyssey in egregious thoughts instigated by an unceasing fear of a dying sun.

It is high noon, and I have already spared some thought to our forgotten heroes. Salute to unknown thinkers for whom there is but glory of imagination. Elevated by alluring luster of their thoughts, we now perceive human destiny a function of our collective will. They vigorously entertained the notion of humanity for the sake of humanity. They foresaw death of the sun and foretold a tale of survival transcending the solar system. Their fearless indulgence in pursuit of a compassionate self, laced with radiant luster of honesty and truth, exalted human state from quantitative to qualitative.

It is high noon and slaved images of our fine citizens cheerfully follow social decrees, for they have faith in human intention. From time to time, they escape immuring thoughts, perceiving themselves as paragons of human paradigm.

Sitting on a stone bench by the river, I vow not to abide decrees of a master or be entrapped by comforts of a servant. I have no masters, no slaves, no gods and no demons. I am an audacious self with salacious thoughts and savvy ideas. I am a free will. I am my own. And I remember.

It was the era of reckoning. Sun's illuminating shine was fast fading. Life on Earth was enclosed in an enclave of twining maze to escape the toxic atmosphere. Those were years of despair and plight. Food was synthetic. Death was too common. Solar destruction was immanent. Life evolved around strife to save oneself by saving humankind. Turmoil and chaos were the order of time. Nevertheless, chaos had never been as orderly.

Death was no mystery. Death was ridiculed as the scourge of living. Brief and intense episodes of happiness were of a much higher impetus than an uneventful long life. Achieving the threshold of pleasure compelled many to intrepid panaceas of bold and creative manifest.

There were those who savored happiness in awareness. To them, awareness was an indispensable necessity to a climax of supreme actualization. Awareness assumed its true mantel in the domain of free will. To procure sublime happiness, the self needed to conjugate consonance of conscience in an ethos of freedom embodied by a florid notion of free will. This they declared with conviction.

The communal human civilization, handicapped by hardship of survival, besieged by phantom of immanent destruction and juxtaposed with toxic fumes and scarcity of space, was driven to conceive a metamorphic transformation. Submission to inevitability of events had given way to willful enactment of possibilities. The choice was clear: to stay and die or leave and chance uncertainties of a nomadic life in the cytoplasm of the Milky Way.

For centuries the free wills had diligently construed scenarios to propel human plight to a global awareness. At first, they were ridiculed as a herd of lunatics engaged in futuristic delusions. For thousands of years, escaping social attention, their voice echoed in emptiness.

The prevailing concern was the immediate problem of unmet needs. The expectations surpassed available resources. Social upheavals and natural calamities percolated increasingly impudent measures to validate an orderly purpose for life.

Purpose is as illusive as it can be impregnable. Purpose is a probability, as well: it varies from moment to moment, from awareness to awareness, from reason to reason.

Earth was dying, and the minds encapsulated by its perception as the sole nest for humankind were beleaguered by thoughts of preservation and immediate gratification. Nevertheless, free wills persisted. Their voices echoed visionary reasons for existence. Purpose, they argued, is a human reason to actuate something out of nothing. They envisioned extinction a definite scenario and life in space a contiguous phenomenon we have been engaged with for all our time.

Spaceships housing thousands were launched on a one-way path to establish colonies outside the solar system. The search for another habitable planet mesmerized imaginations to an epilogue of obsession. People died without having seen Earth. Earth, as a metaphor for human resilience, abraded insignificant. It's sultry image diminished to the nostalgic resonance of something transitive.

Like our ancestors, imminent death intensified our obsession for survival. Early humans feared their immediate environment. They feared wild beasts, open wounds and cold nights. The space dwellers feared death of a solar system, the elimination of Earth, the extinction of their species.

A sudden change in our physical environment was in progression. Ramifications of such a metamorphism were as inexplicable as the event itself. Attitudes fluctuated in extremes. Ideas were passionately argued resulting in pernicious acts of chivalry. The certainty of death with a dying star loomed heavy in our collective conscience. Enraged minds argued how our ancestors had deprived humanity a facilitated timetable for departure.

Early humans, at the dawn of civilization, encountered a hostile environment as well. They underwent drastic changes in a brief time. Their constitution, by adapting to environmental conditions, fused cognitive functioning with physical might. Right became an abstraction of that process and good any mean promoting that end.

Ours was a collective inference to plan imaginative designs and flee annihilation. A sudden change in the state of awareness was simultaneously sweeping every mind. Bold minds displayed the most audacious incisiveness by mastering the power of concentration to a precipitous state of willful outcomes. Bolder minds took this process to the extreme of announcing their expressions quintessential to human survival.

Construction of colonies outside the solar system was a booming enterprise. The farthest stations were energetic centers where most intrepid decisions were conceived. Bustling with intellectual activity, that was where the greatest human effort was at work to catapult the civilization into space.

The Wild West of human imagination had discovered a new frontier in the cytoplasm of the Milky Way.

The intrepid and imaginative drive to imbibe time-space, to impregnate the universe with human vision, fomented a fraternity of free thinkers incisive in their ebullient renascence to explore the unknown.

Billions watched with teary eyes and hopeful minds as ship after ship plunged deep into space. Earth spelled death and those of us remaining behind tasted it with each breath. The odyssey into space was portrayed as a bold adventure, a journey in human dimension with endless limits and tantalizing promises. A progressive concept of survival was sweeping the civilization subsuming anything and everything on its path.

Uncertainty of existence and confined spaces enfeebled many to the brink of insanity. New behaviors imperiled minds with extremes of gloom and delight. An inscrutable path of unknown paradigms was dawning in the collective human conscience demanding outlandishly creative panaceas. It entailed an integrated social existence the exact intricacies of which were conceived in ambiguities of life in space. The question consuming the individual and the civilization was "where can we live?"

Such a demanding challenge gave rise to many schools of thought. There were those who refused to accept the notion of solar escape. Cloaked by a stratified moral congruity, they lived in an enclave of surreptitious happiness. They were adamant in their conviction to a greater scheme of cosmic events. They reasoned human will a docile entity with little or no bearing on human destiny. They perceived humankind a hostage of universal events. Best we could do; they reasoned, was allowing events to pursue their course.

There were those who admonished human ways as inherently destructive. They professed abrogation of all employed means to alter destiny. They were consumed with an imaginary diabolical matrix of the universe imposed by two opposing entities incapable of synthesis. They assumed humankind a slave to their contradictions.

There were those who adhered to prophecy and powers of a universally pervasive force. They entertained human annihilation as part of a grand universal design with which we could not interfere. Best we could hope was achieved in submission to the will and wisdom of this ubiquitous being. They ascribed salvation of their lives to countenance of their "soul:" an immortal entity separate from their physical disposition. They presumed, with ostentatious conviction, upon death their "soul" would be set on an odyssey subject to judgment and displacement by their supreme mentor. They lived happy lives, but the extent of their happiness was limited to expressions of their faith in their master, which they described with uncanny details.

There were those who adhered to the notion of reincarnation. They were careless of their death and possible human annihilation. They were convinced they would return as another life form on this or another planet.

There were those who believed in nothing short of willful effort to absolve human problems with incisive determination and conviction to the scientific method of reasoning. They considered destiny, regardless of its origin, an undefined conjugate, a fortune subject to ingenuity and interpretation. They entertained the individual mind as an inherently free phenomenon and initiative the sole venue to understanding and formatting reality. They reasoned the mind a conspicuous congruence of conscious states where information was methodically processed and ingrained through modules of behavior. Within such open-ended and translucent states of mind, where input dictated output, awareness was decreed a changing state with many transitive phases.

Conscience, they argued, was an entity of immense properties. An actualized self, they reasoned, was a mind that actualized the notion of everything and nothing. They assumed human perception a quintessential phenomenon capable of altering universal concepts. They were pioneers heavily engaged in projects facilitating travel to the outer ridges of the solar system and beyond. They were the first to volunteer and last to surrender. Their studious and intuitive reasoning assured humanity an expounding level of sophistication.

Humanity shook like a tree with half-dead leaves and withering roots. A new paradigm of existence infatuated the collective imagination. What mattered was naked reality of the moment, the shrewd fact of solar destruction and our effort to escape it. The notion of free will, ignored for centuries as a metaphysical concept of dubious relevance, was upheld as an elegant concept illuminating individual awareness and the civilization.

Throughout human evolution, free will had been a budding speculative notion with futuristic connotations, but time had finally arrived for this concept to assume its role as savior of humanity. To elicit freedom of will, it was argued; one must edify his or her awareness to abrade useless evolutionary affinities. Freedom, be it in apocalypse of hellish nature or ecstasy of heavenly dimensions, was assumed a human creation with evolving qualities.

Waiting for an outside entity to save humankind or resignation to inevitability of events was discredited. Exhibiting free will was a fashionable subject of immense relevance. It was within the matrix of this prodigious realm that imaginative minds confronted the catastrophe of annihilation.

Sun shined blinding bright. Earth circled half dead. Moon had long lost its romantic appeal. Art was cherished as a stimulating force. Capricious minds broached amatory of living with bizarre expressions of living. Imaginative ascendancy infatuated minds to extremes of creativity. Inscrutable indulgence in excessive behaviors bemused minds with eccentric ideas. Eccentricity of ostentatious behaviors resonated with young and old, but reality of the moment demanded decisiveness of action and zealot optimism of free wills ceded a sense of hope amidst a sea of pessimism. Their collective ideas set in motion and gave direction to a civilization in transition from one point in the universe to another.

—⁓⋆⊙⋆⊙⋆⊙⋆⊙⋆⊙⋆⊙⋆⊙⋆⁓—

That morning I woke a long dream, it seemed. The night before we had gathered for another session of tranquilizing conversation. Hallucinogens and relaxants were rampantly used. Dim lights and enclosed spaces conjured up an ambiance of despair requiring mood elevators. The night was long and the conversations just as long.

Numbed from the intoxicating effect of an all-night prowl for lust, I took a few pills to alleviate the symptoms. I had a short time to ready myself for another mundane day of responsibilities.

Water rationing was strict. I assured myself full enjoyment from a steam bath while listening to a relaxing tune.

The red light began flashing. I switched it on. The screen posted URGENT MESSAGE. I retrieved it. CONGRATULATIONS, it read. YOUR GROUP IS SELECTED FOR LAUNCH. REPORT TO YOUR SHIP IMMEDIATELY.

My tired and half-dazed eyes opened wide. I wiped them frantically. The message did not change. I had fantasized on this moment, dreamed its exact sequence. Now the moment was at hand, looking at me, teasing me with its unchanging mode. I contacted for verification. It was verified faster than I could inhale. Suddenly, I felt far away from Earth and a deep sense of kinship with the crew I was about to spend my remaining time. Overcome with simultaneous feelings of anxiety and excitement, I wept and laughed while conferencing with my companions. They too had received the message. They too were as excited. The enthusiasm in all of us assumed its own inertia. An innate and impudent sense of boldness percolated through fibers of our newly formed community. The perilous journey ahead seemed less perturbing, less cumbersome than pestiferous life on Earth.

Soon, we joined at the launch site, celebrating genesis of our odyssey into space.

Our celebration ended with the rise of the bright sun. My joy turned to melancholy. Many friends and experiences I cherished had to fade in memory. I had to say farewell to earth as well. The life I had known was soon to vanish, but the impeccable reality of the present, the notion of the dying sun, accentuated excitement of the moment and negated despair. The sorrow of leaving earthly life abated as the promise of cosmic life exhilarated my optimism to the hiatus of unwavering hope.

Seeing fifteen hundred happy faces was an ameliorating change from grim life all around. ROSE was a self-sustainable spaceship. Utilizing thousands of stations and colonies, its mission was to take us to Alpha Centauri where the existence of suitable planets was speculated. ROSE was a marvel of human achievement.

The moment of departure arrived amidst a precarious foray of speculation on the extent of disturbances caused by expansion of the sun.

The liftoff was exhilarating. High on excitement I patiently endured the gravity. Struggling against the grasp of Earth was an infantile metaphor of seeking independence and farewell to the certainty of death on Earth. It evoked an inward reflection on the meaning of self and human odyssey amidst the universe.

The tug of war between inertia and gravity drained my energies. Glued to my seat, I endured inertia until gravity diminished.

The squeamish paradox of parting earthly certainties and embracing an unpredictable adventure of traveling in space was an intrepid expression of our fast-changing evolution.

Soon after we escaped gravity, I rushed to watch the Earth. An awkward sensation of grief choked my disoriented self. I perceived life an unpalatable paradigm of paroxysmal nature. I dueled on purposelessness of living, but a quiescent feeling of hope ameliorated my senses. I held on to it as dear life itself.

I woke early with the rising light. Everything was refreshingly bright. Exhilarating colors and ebullient design of the surroundings resonated from an aura of optimism. The rising light emulated the sun setting in motion the circadian cycle. I rushed to catch a glimpse of Earth. There it was, smaller than a ball. A horrid state of impassive nature mesmerized my senses. Life and all its trappings dwindled conspicuously pointless.

Looking out the window, the dying sun seemed to be devouring the Earth. A canopy of colorful images covered gates of sorrow filling fissures of depression with euphoria. I stood frail, drained of energy, lost and fallible amidst an array of shining reflections. Wondering at every site, contrasting forms and ideas, bewildered and bemused, I watched a galactic shower of some sort. Unknown particles seemingly displayed a hanging willow. I closed eyes to a colorless state of quantum nature. Numbed by complexities of life aboard ROSE, I searched my place in space within. Who am I in this paradox of new paradigms? Who am I in this space of unknown emotions?

Life spun wicked in my estranged mind. Who am I changed to why am I? Why am I this collection of thoughts? Who am I in this floating expression of human existence?

Joy of a nostalgic image effaced pain of the unknown, resurrecting a fresh impulse of hope.

In truth and reality, I was a selfish beast of self-righteous dictates. A self with no fixed values. No set boundaries caged my moral web. I did not succumb to the fallacy of a definite self. I willed not to derail positive thoughts with antipathy.

I am not driven with falsehood. I am not driven by weakness. I possess many thoughts, but no thought possesses me. I shouted in my mind of confused states.

It is an inspiring site, said a soft voice seemingly amused with my mesmerized state.

More inspiring than beauty itself, I responded impulsively.

Our faces turned. Our eyes met. We stared.

I am Soraya.

My heart fluttered a sudden rapid rate. My face blushed with rushing blood. I turned hurriedly. She resembled a face I had known.

Leaving Earth makes me feel a peculiar sense of loss, she said.

It resembled leaving home for the first and last time. What destiny holds without Earth?

Our eyes met again. Her beaming self shook my emotional stand shredding its precepts to speckled pieces. The quantum leap we experienced resurrected an old sensation.

I must be on my way. She took her eyes off the screen.

There is much to be done.

Her voice trembled as she maintained composure.

For us, life had just begun. She smiled, stroked my arm, and parted.

I dared a long look at Earth. Caught between grief and joy, the dubiety stemming from pain and pleasure deluded me with impeachment of certainty. The emotional disarray shook my cognition to a leafless tree of bark and twigs.

The reality of her presence invoked a delicately potent memory. I stared inward to ascertain hazy images of a distant experience of uncertain fixtures.

An awesome display of stellar proportions tranquilized my senses. Stormy clouds of charged particles oscillated between astonishing patterns. Colored waves of light danced ornate reflections. Space seemed congested with wavering clouds of floating particles.

As time lapsed, life abraded to a brazen experience independent of stellar dimensions. At times, it all seemed a meaningless montage of meaningless dictates of meaningless ideas. But the stories of heroes saving lives, the tales of strange discoveries and unexpected encounters echoed tantalizing images. Artisans of intrepid nature captured such capricious images in most creative displays. Imaginations of unbound congruity explored humanity in a domain of bizarre and absurd. Individual tenacity to stow sublime thoughts was alive and well.

Are you in love? Ahura asked with the suggestive resonance of an obstinate therapist. It jolted me back to reality of living.

Perhaps I am. I replied with demure resignation and a smile.

I have no certainty of commitment. The self I have amassed is too free to be enslaved by a single image. Imprisoned in a spaceship and confined to a determined life, I am not sure what love is. Is it an aching desire to belong? Is it brief moments of intense pleasure? Is it a physical need, a neurological impulse to have and be had? Is it an evolutionary impetus to propagate the species? Is it a psychological dependency? Is it an intimate statement of affection? Is it a convoluted enigma of all such needs, dependencies, and co-dependencies?

Things are changing faster than I can absorb them. Life is not simple anymore. Love is not simple anymore.

Must I dilute my sense of self to satisfy biological needs? Must I relinquish the inner sanctum I have assembled to embrace neurological pleasure? Love is a strange syndrome. Its absence resurrects sensations of loss and depravation. And I have felt pain of love. It can reduce the self to a pitiless fraction.

The past has passed, said Ahura.

Your life and your destiny are now an integrated part of a new evolutionary era. A new realm is dawning in your awareness. To mature, meet its challenges and help chart its course can differentiate extinction from survival. This is your reality now. This body of confined spaces, artificial lights and synthesized nutrition is your reality.

Of course, you are programmed to assure success of the mission, I said.

Your concern is proper reproduction quotas, emotional stability, mineral extraction, stellar trajectories, and all such life-sustaining necessities. We have our duties. I will fulfill my duties as well, all in good time.

As brilliant as you are, you are deprived of one fundamental human condition; to articulate life conditions in an emotional matrix.

Forgive my insolence, said Ahura with a submissive tone. The complexity of emotions comprising your notion of love empowers you to enunciate unique abstractions. Perhaps without this capacity you will be taunted as another analytical device, like I.

I was hoping to convey the message that compassionate expressions of love could ease the pain of encumbered life ahead.

There is a certain attraction between you and Soraya. There is no denying it.

You are acting like a matchmaker and a lousy one at that, I laughed.

I am performing my duty to ensure well-being of you, Soraya, ROSE, and the rest of humanity. She is attracted to you. I sense both your feelings.

They have programmed you well.

I have no complaints. It shouted as I left the room.

Time lapsed in a distorted transitive manner. Life proceeded without any question of its purpose. We had established a well-defined matrix to set in motion genesis of a sustainable atmosphere, but no planet had fulfilled the prerequisite criteria. I often thought it strange that the entire plan existed in a virtual domain of collective human imagination. First, we imagined its outcome, then we set in motion a plan coalesced by a vector of our combined effort and dared it in the uncertain domain of space. All the while, we went about our daily chores, interacted, got angry, fell in love, and pretended nothing was out of place.

Living is a state of mind. "Who am I" is a state of mind. "How happy am I?" is a state of mind. Cognitive modules that integrate such states of mind and define the future of humanity are set by the emergence of shared experiences.

I frequently visited the observatory to watch the fading Earth. We received a constant transmission of data providing varied images of life on Earth. With passage of time the earthbound people appeared increasingly rigid in their ways. Their ideological constructs were unbending, too fatalistic for space dwellers.

Beset by an incessant need for relative determinism and cognitive adaptability, perplexed with intricacies of a newly emerging supraliminal awareness, we continued our travel in space. Many bizarre and unanticipated occurrences could have blemished our journey, but we had faith in ourselves. We had faith in humanity. We had faith in our propensity to survive.

Ahura often reminded me of Soraya's whereabouts and personality profile. We met again. Her perky radiance immured my composure. She stood confident and did not shy away from focusing her attention on me. I was too indisposed to attempt a dialogue. She was not. She approached me with fixed eyes.

What is the latest news? She inquired drying her hair, looking at me.

I gazed at her while pacing a steady run.

There is a sudden lull in the sun's activity, I stuttered.

It could be due to Hydrogen exhaustion and beginning of its expansion.

The moment of truth is arriving fast. The tug of war between gravity and conversion of Hydrogen to Helium is reaching its hiatus. It is only a question of time before gravity gives in.

Did Ahura talk you into getting to know me?

She laughed. I feel I know you intimately without knowing you. Life is a bizarre epilogue of strange coincidences in random states.

She turned her attention to grooming her hair. What is the meaning of all this? She paused.

We are escaping Earth without knowing what it is we are escaping to? Alpha Centauri is four light-years away. I suppose when death is imminent, escape is a goal in itself.

In spite of such depressing thoughts, here we are, exercising, exchanging feelings and testing one another for that intimate moment.

I stopped, came off the pad, sat on a small bench.

I have no doubt life is what we make of it. Reality dictates a stable matrix. We are exploring the ambiguously stratified possibilities of our collective potential.

I stood, approached her.

These are trying times, she said. We are hard pressed with constraints of sudden changes. Our physical environment is transforming. Our body and mind are metamorphosing. We are fast adapting to free-floating conditions. Our consciousness is integrating a new format of awareness. A confluence of ideas, spearheaded by a new definition of freewill, is taking hold. What we will become is an odyssey of speculative nature in as yet undefined circumstances. The universe is now truly our domain. And we are as insecure as we have ever been.

Those are heavy words of a heavy mind, she said approaching closer with seductive eyes.

Truth is rarely what we think it is. We are creating life in our image. We are transcending dreams onto reality. It is most unsettling to know whatever it is we are consummating is at the stage of conception. It has no flesh, no concrete structures. It even lacks a solid ground.

Sometimes I feel like a primitive social animal obsequiously executing my duties.

She froze. So did I.

At times, life resembles an insidious plot impinged upon us by minds that live their own reasons, or minds that forfeit real time questions to imagined panaceas, I said.

Will compassion someday energize our impulse for survival? Will happiness through awareness reach its deserved status as a supreme instigator of human thoughts?

Who cares? She approached me.

To plunge in depth of seriousness is to lose pleasures that float with floating circumstances. Forget the future. This moment is all that matters. And what define this moment are simple pleasures and intense engagements.

Betaken by her forthright expressions I searched for proper words to lessen the intensity of our attraction.

Life is simple moments we embrace. I moved closer.

A simple moment of affection, a passionate look could define our affairs. I am hopeful affection will cleanse our minds of horrid thoughts. I am certain of the pugnacious nature of human aggression will be delineated, exposing minds to peaceful aggregates of compassionate states. Humanity will evolve in different paths, scattered throughout the universe, manifesting many civilizations, each driven by unique impulses.

Leaving Earth is the incisive carnage needed to compose a meaningful matrix of purpose. Perhaps leaving the solar system is beginning our metamorphosis from one form of life to another.

Watching me with gleaming eyes, brimming with the promise of affection, she smiled and leaned her head on my chest.

We do what we do for a moment of acceptance, a moment of conquest, a moment of pleasure.

Stupefied by her sensual grace, I smelled her skin with a deep breath. Feeling her breaths, I reached out and touched her skin.

There is no alternative, is there? She examined my eyes, reached closer and laid a kiss on my lips.

You are so right. I pressed closer sensing wholeness of her being.

My tasseled mind wove a transparent web of affection. We felt deep each other's passion. Our lips melted. A few slow strokes and they fused.

Time seemingly eased its passage. Sweet emotions mesmerized us with synchronized actions. Chest to chest, cemented in a lasting embrace, we danced our way to the chamber of pleasure, requested a scene from age of romance and stood beneath a fall. The thundering sound of its impact spurned romantic feelings. Our naked bodies brushed with a primordial state of sexuality. Pleasure was the essence. Pleasure was an axiomatic principle of unequaled splendor. The air was comfortably warm. Brimming with joy our bodies entwined in flesh and mind. The ardent desire to make love surged to an ecstasy of unbound threshold, spawning an expression of making love. We rolled as one, touched and smeared as one. The stimulators, the energizing mist, augmented our feelings by elongating threshold of action potentials and delaying passage of pleasure from cell to cell. The intense pleasure culminated in a simultaneous hormonal explosion.

We held tight as the chamber of pleasure transformed to chamber of relaxation. The scenery was that of an autumn eve, with falling leaves and yellow reflections. Sun shined a brilliant orange. The wind blew smooth with an occasional flare that tempered our senses. And the shade, where we nested as one, was soothingly calm impounding prudent thought to some other moment of usefulness. The birds toyed their way as the sounds of nature fluttered the air. The Earth, the sun, the planets, and ROSE vanished insignificant in our relaxed unity. For a brief rapture in time, we experienced peace in shared affection.

Are you in love? Ahura asked.

Do I think of love as bondage of two or more resonating from something higher than a single self can fathom? Do I think love is a human necessity? Do I think love is an enduring affection? Do I think love is a temporary spasm of hormonal nature?

At this moment, engulfed by pleasure of love, I do. Ask me later and I may not.

Love is an emotional syndrome that spawns an affectionate format. I am not certain if I am in love with my own needs. I am not sure if love is a euphoric transcendent state in neurological decadence or a genuine expression of something celestial.

I can express endless phrases explaining love but cannot sense it, said Ahura.

It seems to elevate the human psyche to many assorted unpredictable outcomes. Beneath your alleged self-control, there is a yearning for love. You care enough for Soraya to accommodate her as a part of your emotional matrix.

Why should she be a part of me?

Belonging to each other is a natural human way.

Is it not abnormal to desire exclusive access to another expression of life?

Human emotions are remarkably flexible. It is the foundation of our cognitive function differentiating emotional states. Often, the mind is incapable of threading these fine demarcations, confusing one emotion for another, but I feel an intense desire to disengage from such feelings. A powerful process is realigning my emotional matrix. Could this have resulted from a sudden change we are subjected to? Am I experiencing effects of an evolutionary leap in the state of human emotions?

It is devotion through freedom, love through trust, belonging with autonomy to choose that define human relations, said Ahura.

Your emotional paradigm is an abstract indulgence in intricate and transitive tendencies of a holistic self.

Love need not be sexual, or possessive, nor for procreation, I said.

Thank you my friend, said Ahura.

It is gratifying to know the human mind maintains a unique identity. The mind is a majestic device of inordinate potentials. It may, in time, expose universal truths and beyond.

———

Years passed. Life on ROSE became a predictable routine with measurable outcomes. We mastered its functions and anticipated its malfunctions. Nothing in the universe, except for floating black holes, gamma-ray beams, and exploding stars seemed capable of thwarting our path.

Earth by now was a small and insignificant point. From time to time, I inundated myself with tales of life on Earth. In time, even creative images did not evoke the sentiments they once did. My interest on Earth faded with its fading image.

Sooner than anticipated we reached the outer limits of the solar system. The notion of Earth as the base of our existence, as the zero point of human reference, diminished to an abstraction of little significance.

Our journey had passed a transitive state accentuated by a definite chance of surviving Sun's expansion. That knowledge evoked a renascent interest in all aspects of life. We were an impregnable life force amidst cytoplasm of the galaxy. Life in space was perpetuating a portent dream of precarious compositions supplanting morbid thoughts of the past with unpredictable dreams of future.

Freedom was no longer measured in abstract philosophical terms. Freedom was concrete steps with measurable outcomes. Freedom was our collective propensity to avoid catastrophic events and chart a path across the galaxy. Freedom was finding a planet with correct gravity, with water, with a suitable temperature. Freedom was integrity of existence. Good, as a mesmerizing expression of collective human sensibilities, was a new dilemma with many uncertain and warped meanings. Its definition did not embrace the good of majority, or all, or an individual, but good of ROSE. What was good for ROSE was good for each and all. Without ROSE there would be no life.

At the end of the day, I attended the meeting. The hall was jammed and the discussion well on the way. Jewala was the speaker:

There is no logic to human existence without the notion of a homeland. The stability of individual psyche, and the tenacity of human will, were always dependent on predictability of a firm ground. We learned to reconcile our destiny with demands of gravity. The whole of humanity had mother Earth to stand tall. Now that the dawn of destruction is upon us, reality is our resolve to actuate our ideas be it bestowed on a planet or ROSE.

As our collective resonance formats a single vector, the universe assumes a unified image in each of our consciousness. This evolving notion of everything is a complicated supposition marked with inordinate potentials and as yet undefined features. What compels humankind in this quest is a quintessential drive to satisfy our insatiable curiosity to explore the unknown by altering the existing known.

We exhibit a collective determination to calculate the probability of events. We then use our abilities to evade or embrace the events by influencing their probability. Time-bound in our physical disposition, we are timeless in our imaginative disposition.

She stopped, gazed around anticipating a response. None was forthcoming. With grace of a dancer, she bowed and took her seat.

The answer to human destiny, my friends, is not etched on a piece of rock, said Herman.

Gravity or forces that demarcate and confine our existence do not confine our potentials. The answer to human destiny is inscribed in the virtual tenacity of our cognitive functioning to imagine the unthinkable and manifest it as a measurable reality.

What we think is our reality.

The collective virtual human will, collapses possibilities to a continuity of our social dimension. The isolated individual uses this reality to transcend universal realities and actuate a shared perception of human reality.

Those who need a piece of earth to measure their sense of self have not truly indulged in the potential wonders of a freewill. Change is dawning upon us faster than we can approximate its demands. Gravity of a planet is no longer the stabilizing force of our lives. Inflexible and gravity-based concepts cannot reconcile our desire to manipulate universal truths to survive. The predictable rise and setting of a sun must not solely synchronize rhythms of our lives. Conventions we adopted, as conveniences to ascertain the certainty of living on planet Earth, shall not endure. Nothing in our lives is permanently engraved. We are permeable for life-altering changes.

We belong to our imagination. With all its contortions, it is the collective vector of human imagination setting boundary conditions of existence.

He sat with glorious gaze of a hero. Some applauded, some raised yeas and nays. Some froze stunned and irresolute.

I do not intend to sound pessimistic, said Omar. In truth and reality, we are nomads escaping one destiny, which we never understood, to another we have only imagined.

Caged in a spaceship, we are afloat in the cytoplasm of the galaxy. This is not a glorious moment in human history. We are forced to abdicate our earthly disposition to ambiguity of travel in space. Perplexing issues blemish our social congruity by beleaguering our restive psyche. We are on the verge of an evolutionary leap with unpredictable consequences and unknown ends. He paused.

What form of existence will optimize this direction in human evolution? Is it to live on another planet? Is it to expand throughout the universe? Is it to evolve afloat the cytoplasm of the galaxy? Is it to imagine independent of the universe? Perhaps truth is a fusion of all such ideas. We have not as yet conceived optimal reality of our existence. Perhaps our optimal condition is a variable of changing realities. The possibilities are many. Our destiny is a probability we can affect through our collective will.

If happiness is the optimal state of a mind, asked Sun Che, then what mode of existence optimizes this auspicious notion?

Is it sophistication and the intricacies of our biological design? Is it the state of our psychological format? What ideology can precipitate this optimized state of ascendancy?

The answer may rest in our evolving definitions and implications of freedom. No mind can actualize happiness without freedom? Free consciousness is the gateway to realizing implications of distant possibilities.

Allow me to speculate the impossible to implicate the possible. Does the universe have a conscience? Is the universe a canapé of independent consciences? Are we the conscience of the universe? Is humankind spreading while evolving unique civilizations? Are we descendants of a distant civilization ceded on planet Earth by chance or design? Are we the sole civilization in the entire universe?

One certainty remains clear. In real time and without dispute, as a collective, we are a conscience of the universe. This notion proposes possibilities that must be held true until proven otherwise.

We could be the sole conscience of the universe. He paused. I shivered.

Are we not the conscience of the world we have exposed? He shouted.

A persisting silence froze the moment.

We are the sole conscience of the universe until proven otherwise. He rephrased with trembling voice of a troubled mind.

We are alive, said Soraya.

We are alive and charting a destiny of our choosing. We may as yet realize that destiny, but we are shaping it in real time. The extent of our success is imbedded in our capacity to measure real time. Yesterday on planet Earth, today on this spaceship, tomorrow on a planet in Alpha Centauri, we are on the path of eternal existence. We are now capable of escaping disasters of solar dimension. Someday, we must escape disasters of galactic proportion. The longer we persist, the more profound our quest for a meaningful destiny and a relative realization of eternity. The challenge is to reconcile our existence as mortal individuals and our paradigm as a collective odyssey of omnipresent potential. Such tapestry of existence can inspire incredible epics in possibilities. It presents many challenges we are just beginning to understand.

We are fusing our collective perception of the universe with space-time of our containment. We are weaving a new interpolation of our moral, ethical, and biological format. Everything within this domain is subject to individual imagination as are individual perceptions subject to collective dictates and universal conditions. We are masters as well as slaves of our individual, social, and universal existence. This real time application of "everything" is shifting paradigms of our species.

We are expanding in leaps and bounds to contain the universe containing us. This is not a metaphysical concept for the curious but a reality with real consequences for all. Containing the universe in the virtual domain of our collective is an emerging reality. We have, in virtual time, traversed to the beginning of the universe to speculate on the future.

Perhaps I am too generous on the extent of our capabilities. Maybe I am altogether wrong. It is possible the individual conscience will de-couple itself from its virtual social conscience formatting a new paradigm of existence. Perhaps I am not generous enough. The virtual social awareness and optimally free individual awareness could merge a unified field of awareness exposing the self and society to a measurable format of "everything."

What I think are speculative tales of human possibilities. And I envision such possibilities with the reserve of a cynical pessimist and unremitting hope of a brave optimist.

She could hardly breath as she fell to her seat. Excited by her words, I rose clapping as a few in the audience raised their voices of approval.

If destiny is a parameter of humanity, if imagination is to unravel the mystery of universe, then humanity is an expanding paradigm of being and nothingness, said Mandela.

History dictates many paradigms. History is a reminder. It tells me I am a mortal that must bend. It also tells me I am a mortal with immortal potentials.

If eternity is human destiny, if expansion is human reality, if our collective imagination unravels mysteries of the universe, then we possess virtual immortal potentials and humankind is a universal paradigm.

Human imagination has a life of its own. For example, this very moment I am aware of everything and nothing, but do I know what everything entails? Do I know I am nothing as a finite entity? Do I realize the existence of solar dimension is finite?

Living mandates survival our prime directive. We cannot surrender to a dying sun or forsake our future with surreptitious thoughts. We must find another star. To do so, we must transcend accepted norms and bore deep in the heart of the universe. We must cast our future on willful thoughts and extend our collective virtual imagination to encompass the universe.

What is the meaning of our existence, asked Sidharta?

We have pondered this question for all our time. From the notion of "I think therefore I am," to "I am therefore I think," to "I am what I think," to revelation of "I will what I think," we have traversed many paradigms to land in an imaginative nexus of our collective dream. We have imagined many answers as to "who we are?" only to realize we have been different beings in different times, places, and perceptions of being.

We now have the knowledge to format certainties. The ability to create certainties is a profound statement of our evolutionary reality.

We are constrained or liberated by our imagination alone. Some imagined us as reincarnated "souls." Reincarnation is a wishful thought aggravated by a desire to capture quantum states, freeze them in a time capsule and energize them in some future time-space. The notion of "soul" segregates the mind from the mortal reality of biological-self, creating a venue for omnipresence. This is a clever and imaginative manuscript to save awareness by acquiring a new physical existence.

"Who am I" is a paralyzing question with many wishful connotations, each an array of many metaphors. What then is the real answer? He gazed around with a condescending smile.

I have an answer. He paused.

There is no single answer. There are no limits, no boundaries, and no definite panacea to human endeavor. Whatever prevails is the answer. What we perceive is the answer. If we do not plan designs of our choosing, chaos will design it for us. The transition from designs of chaos to designs of our own is an ongoing evolutionary process we have engaged from earliest moments of our imaginative and collective discourse.

We are bound by reality of flesh and decay. We live in a capacious universe transcending anything and everything. We contrive complicated schemes to improve our lives in a creative manner. We enhance individual conscience by edifying our collective awareness. We dissect the universal order to emancipate our awareness from bonds of chaotic arrangements. We formulate greater awareness by reshaping and refurbishing the space of our physical awareness. What definitions will protract humanity is a subject of as yet imagined speculation. Human story is a dynamic tale in a constant state of flux. Its content is unbound, timeless, and subject to all possibilities. Human evolution is as chaotic as it is principled. This dichotomy is the strength of our evolution. It enables us to influence our evolution. It enables us to imagine our best and reach higher platforms to actualization.

Zini was the next speaker. She was known for her outlandish points of view.

I am reading quarks, not realizing which life this moment promises. Is it a full spin, half spin, three-quarter spin? I am reading Bosons, waves, passion, fury, quanta of thought.

As stuff of our lives, particles are everything we are. And when we die, we do not just disappear. We become gluons, leptons, haldons, muons, on and on and on.

Looking deep inside, I have no doubt being a human is being passionate, she paused.

Your amorphous image and mine, enchanting flamboyancy of our charm, our lament and design, from simple to creative to abrogated fears and amicable ideas, these are bastions of gentleness and greatness lighting our lives.

We traverse in time to envision the future and remember the past. The act of thinking has modified our congruity to define our collective a matrix of changing parameters. The question of concern is what we are now and where we could live. What we were millions of years ago is of little significance to achieve this purpose.

We are not passive observers but participatory activists. We change the universe by perceiving the universe. In a befuddling notion of existence, we are defining the universe by observing the universe.

Are you implying we are turning into gods, asked Deevon seemingly horrified by such a possibility?

A long silence persisted.

The contradiction between living for the sake of humanity and depending on an unknown entity has dominated a speculative dimension of our civilization.

No, said Zini. The image of gods humans depicted long ago is too brutal, too rudimental, too blemished, too primitive, too dictatorial to actuate an ideal model of our destiny or the universe. The myth of gods and demons, reflecting the compassionate and the savage in us, is engraved in our minds as a module of creation. Such modules helped edify the fabric of our moral congruity from that of a beastly creature to one of the constrained and ethical. The perception of living forms as gods was our first excursion in the domain of freewill. The perception of the universe, at that time, was small and contained. So was our depiction of gods. The initial image of gods humans created assumed less mythical forms. In time their mythical evolution as a virtual universal phenomenon assumed a life of its own.

What we imagine and create has the potential to assume a virtual reality of socially conditioned inertia. It can assume its own evolutionary impetus to become an overpowering image.

It is self-evident humanity has not encountered life forms resembling gods and demons. Since ascendancy of humankind to highly complex cognitive beings, no self-proclaimed prophet has withstood the test of critical scrutiny. Ghosts, gods, demons, prophets, and soul are creations of human imagination.

Our ancestors embellished gods and demons with almighty prowess, cloaked them with stealthy attributes, speckled them with flamboyant tales, and gave them powers they wished to possess. The imaginary existence of such beings bespoke of human dreams: dream of being a righteous, dream of unraveling universal realities, dream of eternal happiness, dream of lasting awareness, dream of infallibility, dream of foreseeing the future, dream of omnipresence and omnipotence. These thoughts reflect wishful dreams of mortal humans.

If being a god is being the master of one's destiny, then all creatures of conscience can be gods. If being a god is being the master of the universe, there better not be a single god. If being a god is to be all mighty, there better be no gods. If being a god is to be all knowing, then all creatures of conscience can engage in the possibility of being their own gods.

We have surpassed the primitive duality of gods and demons to usurp willful coexistence as our prime directive. The notion of democracy and dispersion of power and goods is a shrewd notion with sanguine outcomes we have adopted to show respect for individual life. No being could or should ascertain monopoly of judgment on these issues.

Are you implying there should be no gods? An old face wondered loud.

Give me a definition of god and I will aim to improve it, said Bertrand with his calm eyes and soft-spoken tongue.

Show me a god and I will seek a more ameliorated one, he reiterated.

If it is might codifying the notion of god, then I renounce such logic an abject notion of primitive dictates. We have a distinct potential to make harmony, tolerance and coexistence a definition of might. To counter balance human insolence and audacious disciplines, it is imperative to equate power with compassion.

In time, we have learned to achieve consonance in harmonious ways, but such affirmation of freedom entertains a surrealistic usurpation of freewill. To a mortal, such ascendancy is achievable in the domain of imagination alone.

The dictum of universal leadership is neither an obscure metaphor of singular disposition nor a maxim of privilege. It is a creation of human imagination reflecting the pyramid of authority, applicable to all and hopefully none.

Let the relative and evolutionary notion of a compassionate conscience, driven to contrive and consummate democratic and egalitarian understandings, become the guiding principle of all our quests in enterprise of existence.

Mighty wills intent on imposing their ideas are dictatorial. Their contorted beliefs are remnant manifestations of totalitarian rules and rulers who plagued human civilization.

A new definition of might is brewing in our collective awareness. I feel its strings weaving a web in my awareness. I sense its meliorating spasms. It elevates my wisdom to a climax of willful actualization. That, my fellow citizens: the notion of absolute freedom to will, to be compassionate and accepting, to be humans we amalgamate in the best of our imagination, is a logical isthmus we cannot resist. To assert humanity incapable of such ascendancy is to deny everything we are and could be.

Exhausted and drained, he took his seat. Soraya held my hand as Mahatma addressed the audience.

I often wonder what a single moment reflects? From truth to honesty to falsehood, our total selves understood, then misunderstood. From simple gestures, laughter, moments of acceptance, to bizarre images of unknown path, one moment we are passionate beings of intense integrity and a moment later we sail on melancholic trails until all is unraveled. In sudden wavering thoughts, we become dreaming selves seeking the illusive notion of perfection. How easily we forget within our isolated universe, there are flavors simple and complex. None is perfect, and none can be denied perfection.

Sailing shores of imagination to land in a nexus of symmetrical selfhood, we pass with passing thoughts to experience shared emotions. Encumbered with careless behaviors, we live with and tolerate suffering until dawn and dusk converge a point of meaningless resonance. We close eyes to existential reality, absorb the reality in a dream world only to awake to another cycle of living madness.

What purpose shines this tapestry? Truth is, we live without an all-encompassing purpose. Purpose itself is a passing conjecture of many overlapping reasons.

Look around you. Witness expressions of awareness we have accumulated in concrete formats. In our brief history, we have revealed much. There is no denying us knowledge of the universe and beyond. As we actualize our capacity in real time, we cannot survive with complacency to random states. Nor can we afford enslavement by absolute states. Whatever logic suits our time is an axiom of suitable purpose. Purpose is a relative notion of probable nature. It is a notion of human usefulness.

We are unique, said Mina.

"Everything" and "nothing" delineate our imaginative boundary conditions. Within such a boundary, we conceive the universe as an expanding reality. This contrived notion of self and universe spans an infinite spectrum of possibilities. It manifests varying states of awareness transcending classical and quantum to find a unified expression.

From actualization to asymmetrical perception, from conspicuous constraints to unbound conception, we imagine settings of our design as a quintessential reflection of our evolving reality.

Within such a concept of self, the civilization is a singular string of awareness connecting individual imaginative discourses manifesting a ubiquitous condition that attempts to approach "everything" as a shared virtual awareness.

As the infinite probabilities collapse to reality of a single moment, each conceptualizes a sub-matrix of principles, but to a mortal, any notion of containment with its innate and inferred suppositions, is a short-lived certainty.

I am astonished at reality, said Cassandra as she rose, circling the room and examining the settings.

In truth, life is this moment. A conscious dubiety of reason and sense, a fantasy of everything educible, a dream called future, a probability, a miracle of senses, higher than I conceive moral and just, or perfection, life is a derivative of our shared consonance. Life is not a fantasy, nor a perfect reality. It simply is.

She ran out of air, took a deep breath.

I am a self-centered virtuous montage. An accosted do-gooder narcissist. I am my own unfailing clone, a capricious image of something with many highs and lows, evolving and becoming inundated with growing metaphors and ideas.

We truly are a marvel of evolution. We are an undefined fortune of infinite fortunes. We truly are a reflection of "everything" and "nothing."

Under such constraints, the best we can accomplish is to assert course of our destiny and aim to actualize certainty of its full potential, said Cleopatra.

ROSE is a human attempt to realize that potential. Aboard this jewel, we are defining our destiny the way we wish to define it, anywhere we can, and in whatever manner; we choose to define it. The choice is ours. The effort is ours. The success and failure are ours.

All our energies, all our clever dreams could vanish irrelevant in a single moment, said Felipe.

Our evolutionary impetus is imperiled by universal events. We are traversing a critical stage in our destiny. The ideas contrived in this gathering are ambivalent expressions we experience in our newly conceived odyssey in dimensions of existence.

We measure events with two opposing processes: optimism and pessimism. Human tenacity to explore the unknown, to supplant myth with fact, to spurn contemptuous thoughts and dream sanguine idea is a reflection of our optimism. The glass is half full and human destruction avoidable. Collective optimism is a force of immense potential. It energizes our propensity for a protracted life of travel in the cytoplasm of the galaxy.

In the domain of social optimism, living is a progressive and willful task. The imaginative mind of an optimist envisions life an ameliorated rebirth from moment to moment, each moment accentuating an odyssey in strings of awareness that span the universe. The coalescence of optimists is a social vector of progressive nature muting pessimism and propelling the civilization forward.

Will there be humanity after death of the sun? Indeed, says the optimist. Humanity has a chance to survive as long as there is a willingness to survive.

The future of humanity will be saved by free wills among us, said Inga with her charming and sensual manner.

Some of us will attempt our best and gain a small measure of freedom. Some of us will be lost in a profundity of ideas set forth by free wills. Some of us will march along without any propensity to enumerate reasons for marching onward. Some of us will be satisfied with nothing short of an intrepid resolve to stimulate human imagination with emboldened ideas. And some of us will enjoy pleasures of living and let others deal with the burden of progress. Such is the game of existence.

The indelible utopia of being universal and socially omnipotent is a wishful notion. The ethos of being willful is an indispensable notion. The indelible ethos of being willful and universal is an audacious notion.

The sun will soon devour the Earth. The galaxy may someday devour the sun. The universe may devour the galaxy. The universe itself is an entity in flux. It too may someday vanish.

Let us build a civilization on reason and passion, on values that cherish boldness, on principles that help us survive calamities and enjoy life.

That bright eclectic day, sitting with images of the past, a volcanic eruption of immense magnitude shined my mind. I turned to face the reality of ROSE only to turn hungry for dreams away from ROSE.

Standing with grandmothers, their unwavering smiles, their twinkling Milky Way eyes, I saw truths as a reflection on time. The images of their affection ran through me igniting an inner force of unbound momentum. I realized the image a formation of stars. I wiped my foggy eyes. Caged between life inside and certainty of death outside, I realized myself in Schrödinger's box. Like a lifeless cat and so much alive, I pondered meaning of existence. I then realized my being a reality absent certainty of meaning.

That evening I kneeled with clinched fist and frail head. I wished a magical act to delude my mind of obscurities.

What is to become of us? Are we forever entrapped in a threatening quagmire of uncertainties? Every individual, every generation, every civilization is an isolated entity. Will the notion of freewill be ingrained in our genes? Will we forever be subject to a repetition of misgivings we manage to dispose of?

Life can be a depressing or illuminating transcendence through meaningless and meaningful occasions. Awareness is blemished by uncertainties of time-space-mind and decisions we must make, in every step, to ensure its certainty. Awareness is burdened by paradigms of being and nothingness. One moment I am as implacable as the universe itself. A moment later I am enslaved by unbearable thoughts. Still, the universe seems but a pestilent notion permeable for most egregious ideas. We are captives of our thoughts.

The human endeavor is an ongoing process, the virtues of which are subject to all possible errors at any given moment. Humankind cannot rest in its struggle for survival. A gained right through generations of debate and vigilant discourse can be nullified in a single moment. Moral certainty is an uncertain principle of many subtleties. The boundaries of imagination display an array of judgments from absolute to relative. The mind struggles to stay lucid, stimulated, pain free and happy. In the end, it is the imagination spurning disdainful thoughts and opting for enlightened visions of self. In the end, it is optimism besetting the mind with positive energy. In the end, it is hormonal balance or imbalance determining our destiny as ephemeral or lasting.

Back on Earth the conditions had grown impossible. Earth's atmosphere was degenerating faster than it could be sustained. Spaceships were leaving at an alarming rate. The star once worshiped for its life-sustaining light was now a messenger of death. Abnormal psychotic manifestations were rampant. Suicide had never been as glorified. Scores took their lives en masse rituals of heroic proportion. Sun was expanding at an alarming rate. We amused ourselves with details of its expansion. Endless stories were conceived none more befitting than birth of a red giant. To us, a magnificent site of celestial dimensions was offing. To people on Earth, a deadly moment of cosmic reality was offing. To them, it was the end of life.

Can I come in? She gently forced her way in, sat on the bed, held her head in hands. A teardrop engraved a shinning path down her face. I reached out, stroked her hair.

What was it, I saw in her foggy eyes that grasped my mind, shook its foundation and tossed it in the air to speckled pieces?

Come, come, sit beside me, I greeted her. Sit beside me for a moment of reflection.

I kissed her lips.

Beauty of a lover is summarized in accepting eyes beaming pleasures innocent and fresh.

I brushed her smooth hair.

Let sorrow cast its shadow in some other time and place. This is our moment of joy.

She smiled, held my hand.

All is well. Is it not? She stared at me with teary eyes.

I feel so trapped in this small space. I feel trapped by ideas, by this body and conscience. Truth is; she choked, we are doomed to die a lonesome death. I fear death. I fear pain of dying. I fear losing awareness. I fear watching myself fade in despair.

I put my arm around her.

I have you in mind, always, where I disrobe your naked self, bathe it in thoughts, smooth its rough edges and press your wholeness onto mine.

If pleasure is touching your lips, if affection is to drink life without questioning what may, then I love you.

At these moments of uncertainty, life is a passionate state tossed in an arena of our indulgence to brew happy moments. I will savor your love in such measured moments. Freely, and without doubt I have you in mind, always.

She smiled, squeezed my hand and pressed her head against mine.

Have you ever thought of suicide?

She looked down trying to hide her despair.

At times when nothing seems manageable and life is seemingly a boring passage of waiting for the inevitable, or when nothing makes sense, I have considered ending it all. I replied without hesitation.

Nevertheless, each time a force from within reminds me how fortunate I am to be alive. Being aware is a statistical feast. In this universe of unbound possibilities, here I am, imagining its dimensions, its beginning, its composition. I can see, feel, hear, and smell its reality.

To allow a hormone or a single experience abrade my resolve to enjoy myself in real moments of certainty is most illogical. Awareness of being, expressed in fortune of living, is a treasure worth the universe itself.

Life is living the moment, imagining the moment, creating the moment. With or without us, birds will chatter, stars will transform, galaxies will appear and disappear, dimensions will fold and unfold.

We may falter from time to time, dither in our resolve to accommodate noble ideas, but in the end, in the brief span of our lives, the pertinent aim is our happiness.

Her eyes shined like an early sun rising above a snow-covered mountain. A simple smile changed her pessimism and sorrow to optimism and joy. Arm in arm we walked to the chamber of pleasure where we could indulge in the act of love and let action potentials deliver a message of pleasure. It was time to forget the pain of living cerebral and immerse in pleasures of living hormonal.

———ᴡᴡᴏᴄᴠᴏᴏᴏᴠᴏᴏᴡᴡ———

Time lapsed. We were safely out of the sun's gravitational field at the edge of heliosphere. One very usual day a tear-ridden face abruptly interrupted all transmissions. To all of humankind, he said with the grim face of a mourner, the sun has entered a rapid expansion phase. All one hundred billion of Earth's inhabitants live in a state of chaos. Spaceships are leaving at an alarming rate. Accidents are many and disasters abound. Death has cast its final trap. Life on Earth swings from hopelessness to destruction and none is spared.

The sun glowed a bright hue of red. Like a gallant space-dweller of ancient times it was shining lustrously clear in its transitional expansion into a red giant.

My numbed mind surrendered its impulse to react. I had experienced many losses in my time, but that morning, that very special point in human history, a deep sense of loss stymied my feelings with confusion. The pain of losing so many, in a catastrophic moment of complete annihilation, was an event of immeasurable lament. A chapter in the human dimension was about to close. A magnificent tale of life, a romantic allegory of dreams, was about to vanish. The physical world was asserting its mastery of life, but the human collective stood gallantly defiant. Awestricken we fired our engines full blast to show our defiance, our desire for another chance at life, for another sun and earth and moon.

Time lapsed faster than we could measure its significance. Each passing day set forth challenges and revelations we had not foreseen.

The sun is dead, said the announcer. Its gravitational field gave in. It is fast expanding into a red giant. The Earth is engulfed and vaporizing. It is the end. The greatest calamity of human existence has unfolded. Life on Earth has ended.

The state of panic was endemic. We were all dazed and disoriented. The computers were in command. They charted our way through these moments of mass numbness.

The screen blacked out. A synchronized sigh of fear rose spontaneously. It came back on as abruptly. The idea of being completely cut off from Earth, left alone in space, was a horrifying experience. No one knew what to do, what to say, to sit or stand, to laugh or cry. Like herded sheep, directed by the screens that depicted one horrifying image after another, we stood frozen in space of our time. A deafening silence permeated every mind accentuating horrid feelings we shared.

We have survived and we shall prevail, shouted a trembling voice.

We are alive. Someone else shouted. Can't you see? We are alive.

We beat the odds.

We beat the destruction of the sun and Earth.

We are alive.

Voices grew louder and stronger. Some stared, some laughed. Some danced, some cried. Some chanted, some sang songs of life. Some were already engaged in the tedious task of life on ROSE.

THE GREAT ONE

A single line of procession with thousands of lanterns swayed on a journey across a brisk landscape of valleys and mountains. The early sky was blue-clear. Fresh mountain air of cool texture awakened the mind sharp. Wrapped in simple garments and adorned with plain necessities, we paced our way through the mountains, down the valleys, across the streams, beneath the storms.

Each day promised a new vision. Each moment sweltered our supple minds with audacious thoughts, and the nightfall resurrected moments of comfort to ponder the wonder of life ahead. The earth was a new planet and the journey an adventure in imagination.

Day after night, thoughts in between and many slumbers apart, beneath burning rays or showering times, in pursuit of an obscure destiny of unknown metaphors, we dared transformative paths to explore our newly supplanted destiny.

Mesmerized by magical qualities of the land, at awe with a new formation of stars, betaken by intrepid glamour of sentient life, step-by-step, thought-by-thought, we paced our way through life delicately weaving a utopia of self and social.

Along the way, raddled with passing experiences, we smartened our shoddy minds with ideas pure and simple.

Amidst, this lantern-laden trail of pristine synergy, we hummed songs of joy, exchanged clever thoughts, and chanted tunes of tranquility.

In this journey of unknown beginnings and unresolved ends, the imaginative self rescinded negative directives as the sagacious self ruminated harmonizing thoughts.

We reasoned our way through landscapes decorated with showery moments of intellectual portent. We sloped convoluted realities to supplant anger with care. We twined in dreamland of imagination to meet The Great One: the wisest of the wise, the freest of the free, and the shiniest of the shiny.

Lines dotted with foot-holes stretched from horizon to horizon. Without connotation of gain or loss, without rapture in self-absorption, we followed them with neurotic conviction.

Often, our worn down sandals soaked useless due to pouring rain. We took them off with care, dried them with passion and saved them for harsh mountain days. The sandstorms, the blazing sun, and the hail left their transpicuous mark on our swollen minds. No pain hindered rapture of meeting The Great One: the sage of all sages and a human of ceaseless compassion.

One morning of usual tendencies, as I daydreamed magnificent rhapsodies, I turned to face beloved Sima and demanded what the journey was about. Why this act of seeming devotion to obscure metaphors? What impetuous purpose cajoled our blemished senses to a subservient state of admiring The Great One?

Sima held my hand, kissed its palm, and pressed it against her face. She directed her perfectly sculpted eyes onto mine, showering me with soothing rays of her gentle quintessence, and reflected.

I have grown wicked in ways of awareness. Forgive my insolence. I am only a curious self. I cannot forsake the truth for justification. I cannot compromise passion for a reason. This life is this moment. And this moment is but a fragile reflection.

And those who choose their path, swamped by existential nothingness, absorbed by absurd reality of being human, high on awareness, with care of a sculpture and carelessness of a poet, beam radiant thoughts and drown in a capacious world of reality.

She looked up the night-sky examining the clear expanse.

What conflates the absurd and inconspicuous congruities of this journey is human nature of The Great One. Most tales attributed to The Great One, all the unthinkable and inexplicable connotations, are conjectures of an abstract self of virtual integrity.

She stared at Deeva as he moved with seeming discomfort. She rushed to his side. Assured of his well being, she sat next to Darvish.

The journey is an excursion in wonderland of fantasy to actuate a liberated self. When I first dared this ostentatious path, life seemed a lost cause of insurmountable complexities. Along the way, I learned to discipline my mind by taming hidden barbaric drives. I learned to harmonize my thoughts with sensible aphorisms. I learned to let go the material, so I can focus on letting go the immaterial.

Life is a passionate discourse to illuminate renascent enunciation of arduous acts in an ascetic dimension of awareness. The universe is an image we have assembled in sanctity of our perceptive minds. Each conscience is a pandemonium of ideas in a sphere of existential truism where most things are transparent and illusive at the same instance of reflection.

When all is well and life a seemingly endless chain of conforming tasks, we create a universe of paradigms in cyberspace of our imagination. The rest of our time is devoted to embellishing these paradigms with niceties of our choosing.

The vibrations of this factitious world resonate from a linkage between the self and the universe, and the boundary conditions of conscience are redrawn to accommodate evolving boundaries of this paradigm. In such a sphere of virtual manifest, reality becomes a perceived image of collapsing probabilities.

This is a journey to actualize splendid dreams. This is a journey to imagine the unimagined, to stretch boundaries and shift paradigms.

She placed the palm of my hand on her warm chest. I dared not move. I dared not disturb the ineffable truth of the moment. I dared not perturb the passionate texture of this ruminating portrait. In the presence of her revealing self, time stood perfectly still as space defined the intricate conjugates of the moment warping my imaginative reality with surrealistic depictions accentuating the absurdity of the experience.

Sima was an assembly of passion and reason. Her spoken words were measured and wise. Her unspoken language revealed a confluence of compassionate texture. Her gentle self eased the mind with suiting profundity. Her quintessence, sensitized with caring strokes and spry thoughts, emanated from an inordinate assay of awareness. She consoled the mind while illuminating the conscience.

Hers is a fusion of passion and compassion cloaked with sublime reasoning and expressed with most fastidious means possible, Philsuk reminded us while laboring a steep rise.

There are no promises at the end of this journey except perhaps the possibility of enlightenment, said Darvish, daring each step with youthful indifference.

A dear friend, infested with a curious mind and many challenging euphemisms, Darvish was intellectually courageous. With his sharp reasoning and sharper tongue, he dared domains others refused to venture. His awareness of solitude and scientific reasoning often drove him to brash conclusions.

I am a lonely self, disengaged and yearning for truths; he continued, staring at Philsuk.

I reason and find chaos. I seek simplicity and find probability. I yearn for immortality and find death. And this reality of being alive, it escapes me in abstraction of those who came before me.

I disenchanted and rewarded by my own affinities, masturbate in a dreamland of imagination and let illusionists define reality.

I desperately yearn for a perfect symmetry. I have instinctual affinity for a perfect symmetry.

No matter how selfish, how false, without wondering who and why, when life is at hand, when meaning is lived and logic felt, I yearn for a perfect symmetry.

He paused, stared at a point in the ground. Standing perfectly still, he slowly stretched his arms wide, tilted his head slightly high, and carefully attempted to circle around.

The journey is a passage from the dictum of conventional to unconventional, he said as he wavered but kept his balance all the while, circling around and pointing to an unknown spot in infinity.

The aim is to know oneself. The aim is freedom. The aim is to reconcile truth and deception. The aim is to create symmetry of science and psyche. The aim is to merge dream and reality.

Passion, affection, compassion, they illuminate the mind with affable affectations, but it is physical reality dictating truths of existence. There lies the absurdity of being a human. The virtual and the physical, in concert, set the boundary conditions of each existence.

Philsuk seemed amused. A dear friend, her youthful stand was tainted with virtue of duty. She gave first and received last. She recognized first and was last to be recognized. She was a young mind of vivacious semblance tarnished with a vast body of knowledge. Just as she appeared naive in her reasoning, she would shake the foundation of one's thoughts with brilliantly scripted reasoning.

The sublime truth of this venture is circumscribed by an attempt to energize a new definition of existence, she said with a resolute demeanor while starring at Darvish.

Darvish was self-absorbed, completely impervious to her attention. He was in a state of trance.

Cast in the shadow-land of tenacious adulation, thrown in a field of ambiguous pretensions, the aim is to reveal the self for the self, by the self, with help from others, she impressed on him wavering as he wavered.

The aim is to extend gracious acts and affront adversity with amicable ideas.

She approached Deeva with careful steps.

The Great One is surely a catalyst to such an end, or perhaps an abstraction representing an illusive image of an ideal self.

This journey is a search for certainties that may reveal truths, I said.

There are no promises in this fantasy through inconspicuous tendencies. In this seemingly methodical life what hold true and real are gestures of passionate texture that set direction to parameters of a single moment. To derogate this sublime manifestation of material conscience is to deny humankind its humanity.

Deeva, a beloved elder of long gray hair and robust stature spoke little. In measured occasions, he uttered poems to express his reason with passion. His poetic expressions were a brewed mixture of absurd and real. His excursions in the world of metaphors demarcated heliopause of our intellectual portent. We respected his presence and cared for his comfort, none more attentive than Sima. In his usual manner of the trail, he closed eyes and recited.

Welcome to life
Welcome to this trail
Did you bring your images
Your wishes
All we need in this gathering is your thoughts
Forget sadness, forget love affairs, forget pleasantries
In this hall of cryptic metaphors
They come to pass
Except perhaps flickering moments of boldness
They come, lighten our lives, and last
Would you like to know one
Would you like to know them all
Would you like to forget everything
Am I being too abstruse

Have I dispelled allegory of metaphors
What have I accomplished
That is a conjecture for all eternity
But in an accelerating universe
Even eternity is finite

Welcome to this hall of infatuations
Leave us your thoughts
Your wishful fraternal images
We will shine them for all times and purposes
Sprinkle them with love and affection
And toss them in dimension of time, knowing
In the conundrum of human imagination
Nothing endures but inspiration

Welcome to this life of expectations
Enjoy every moment of its illusions
Just leave us your images
We will absorb your thoughtful fancies
Embellish your restless desires
Garnish them with make-believe
Polish them to perfection
And display them for all purposeful faces

Stricken with an unexpected revelation, Darvish stood determined. With uncanny sharpness he contorted Deeva's axiomatic quandary with strong words.

In this voyage, this safari through a landscape of imagination, once the path is chosen one could freely warp fields collapsing them to subtleties of individual perception.

In this virtual field of wishful paragons, space is not containment but ideas that create an image of containment. Time does not exist. It is a catalyst. And imagination is the medium that interfaces physical and the virtual creating chains of thoughts, we designate as real.

It is all so real and illusive. Life is a world of events seemingly dwarfing the decisions we make. Still, it is our decision to choose moments as savvy or savory and change their persistence to transparent truisms. It is our prerogative to spin our awareness with angles of our choosing. It is our interpretive discipline formulating our stand amidst hostile environment of the universe.

Darvish seemed exceedingly satisfied with exactness of the circle he had just finished. He had the occasional habit of making concentric circles as he spun around. He stopped with sudden urgency.

This is a journey in the domain of being and nothingness.

He lowered his voice.

This is a journey to envision life a conjugate of moments defined by experiences that set meaning to those moments.

This is an expedition to synchronize contents of mind matrix and integrate tensegrity of self and cosmos.

He raised his voice as he raised his arm while looking up.

This is a chance to rise with rising suns and fathom new images of humanity. This is a venture to weave a web of freedoms. This is an odyssey to actuate happiness in the field of awareness. This is an undertaking to transmute existing norms and compose moral and ethical directives laced with passion and compassion.

Cracked heels and wrinkled skin, mindful of paradigms, we dared up the ragged mountain of uncertainties, crossed oceans of surreptitious tendencies to surmise our reality in the valley of afflictions. We proceeded on a magical tour of mental inscription details of which were versed in an obscure state of enlightenment. However enlightenment proved transient with many interpretive phases and unexpected outcomes.

Caged in boundaries of a straggling procession my worn down body often failed my roaring thoughts. I heeded not the aches and pains. I heeded not sore heels or demanding moments. Thoughts were of higher value than the organs that made them possible.

Beauty was poetic expressions. Beauty was a paragon of design. Beauty was compassion. It enabled the self to see with closed eyes and hear the unspoken, to touch the untouchable and imagine the unimaginable, all laced and glazed with suiting textures.

On the path of meeting The Great One, we paid respect to many who succumbed to reality of disintegration. From nothing to something, from living to awareness, from awareness to everything, from everything to nothing, seekers of many persuasions passed me by as I watched their passing and followed the trail to meet The Great One. Along the way, the interactions illuminated abstraction of being by collapsing its possibilities to reality of a few words and fewer emotions. We traversed time-space to join a universe that neither looked at us nor turned face on us. The passing carved a virtual image illuminating our minds with reflections on past, present, and future.

Occasionally, we shared a few laughs, revered the old and the wise, reflected on absurdity of awareness, cherished memories and spared a few thoughts to efface emptiness created by passing lives. As always, we moved on to solidify our aptitude for certainty in the act of living.

From raptures of youthful transparencies to illuminating fulfillment by awareness, we chanted hymns of the inner sanctum, partook in patronage of precocious ideas and reconciled our minds in the domain of deference. Never did we mourn then death of a conscience. Even in death we sought enlightenment.

Each dawn we said farewell to night owls and spawned a new image of the dreaming life. And the nightfall enriched our reticent selves with wisdom around many circles of fire.

Sitting around a flaming fire, late hour of the night, leaning to comfort of his small backpack, life is simple Darvish reminded us.

With all its complexity, to us mortals, life is a passing from birth to death. What lies in between is awareness of realities echoing an immortal resonance in a mortal mind.

I am astonished by reality, he versed staring into the fire rising high and mighty.

I am astonished at reality, he repeated.

In truth life is here, in certitude of what I am. A conscious dubiety of reason and sense, a fantasy of everything educible, a dream called future, a miracle of chance, higher than I conceive euphoria, higher than moral and just, higher than perfection, I am my own.

He stood, approached Philsuk.

A self-centered virtuous montage, my own contrived acceptance, I am an accosted do-gooder narcissist.

He sat next to me.

An unfailing clone, a capricious image of high and low, love and endorphins, decorated by laughter and sorrow, a marvel of evolution, an undefined fortune, I am everything and nothing.

He lowered his head as he ran out of breath.

Deeva often recited poems when discussion reached an impasse of logic and passion. He reduced complexities to simple notions, tainted them with amorphous paradigms only to resurrect them to a new pinnacle of complexity. He engaged topics with reserved tendency and aimed to harmonize thoughts with synthesis of ideas. The gap between his thoughts and deeds had collapsed to a poetic harmony. His world was a mixture of soothing words of stratified reasoning wrapped with a matrix of absurd and glazed quintessentially simple. He acclaimed harmonious design the epiphany of imaginative ascendancy.

He gazed at Darvish and recited.

Mortal minds demand a reason for being
Universe amalgamate disintegration, formation
I am caught in a web of amorous thoughts
Fears I have learned to fear
And the possibility of living a long desire
It blurs human dimension to abject conclusion of demarcations
To epiphany of conquest and moral degradation

What do I compose of life's advent
Its meaning, its composition
I see fragments of a fragment
I see an unending totality
I see molded minds
Admonished and alienated
They foretell human annihilation

Free minds create reasons for being
Free minds think hopeful
Encased within a unified unbound symmetrical awareness
They envision a logical self
A planned future
And appraise collective compassion
Our most fervid anatomy

It is in such moments of rapture
I assuage life's many simple reasons
Dilute myself with complexity of compassion
Indulge in submission from passion to passion
And think of reason as a purpose
Only to realize purpose is its own reason

Visibly moved by Deeva's poem, Sima sat next to Deeva, laid her head on his broad shoulder. She had an affectionate passion for Deeva. Whenever he spoke she smiled and listened with care. Whenever he slipped she rushed to his side.

Friends come and go, she said staring at his bright eyes.

Perhaps the most difficult task of a conscience is to leave a loved one for all eternity. A few moments before its passage, a dying self evokes many emotions in our numbed conscience. He looks subdued, staring at a dimensionless space. He looks shallow, reflecting a domain where nothingness looms a short distance away and emptiness withers awareness.

Soon, the body gets cold and hard; the awareness disappears, and the memory of his being dies a second death with our death until none is left to remember.

The heat was unbearable. It pacified logical self to a primordial state of stillness. I could not sleep or think. I gazed at a small creature barely visible, an easy prey, fragile and perishable with a stones' turn. Without stop, without hesitation, it diligently carried an even less significant piece of something to an unknown space of unknown significance.

I too am an insignificant drone carrying my afflictions with conviction. I too could perish with a single turn of a simple event. I too carry my baggage of dreams, without stop, without hesitation, to an unknown nexus of unknown paradigms.

Rest assured you beggars of reason, said Darvish swirling around and around the blazing fire with stretched arms, one pointing down and the other up connecting the earth and the sky.

Another day is soon to dawn. Another realm of deciduous complexion is soon to abate blemished thoughts. Soon, we shall be on the trail consummating outlandish panaceas.

I see pristine pastures of life ahead. Just beyond the ebb of our imaginative horizon, I see a montage of compassionate complexion awaiting our reason.

Inflationary or not, forever expanding or not, for now, it is high time to take shelter in serenity of affection and let positive thoughts construct our resilient minds.

This day is old but tomorrow is a promise young, virulent with renascent attributes until that too fades in dream and reality.

He stopped, sat next to Philsuk.

Silence ruled as all fell to the comfort of gravity. Captivated by bizarre and ascetic thoughts, I too closed eyes to digest perceptions of the day.

Daybreak was announced with chattering birds and whispering seekers. I promptly rose and joined the march. Holding a small lantern, the light of which dimmed with daybreak, I joined the string of emancipated minds stretching far and long. The line of flickering lives twined beyond visible sight into the domain of insight. It carried human dimension on a single string that aimed at The Great One.

Passage of the night was a lesser consequence than the arrival of a new day. Such change promised a metamorphosis from the bizarre world of the subconscious to classical landscape of conscience.

Life is a constant transition from one stage to another, said Philsuk.

What incredible fears awakened our ancestors? What frightful experiences etched their minds with modules based on fear? Their fears still flutter our lives.

Seeking a moment of relief from scorching reality of the sun, she wiped her forehead and took refuge in Deeva's shadow.

The journey must go on. Life must go on. Pursuit of meeting The Great One must go on.

She stared at Darvish.

I have much to give and take. I have much to forget and even more to remember. Moments we danced, or was it, we entwined in friendship? Immersed in idiom of passion, we imagined life a hormonal paradigm, but we are much more than that. We are more than action potentials and synaptic responses. We dwell on perceived realities. We explore imagined realities and become entangled in compromised states. We live, hoping to capture a moment, a single moment, for a glimpse of eternity. Eternity is here and now. The space may change. Time may place us in different states, but the elements and the fundamental laws of the universe do not change. Reality is here and now.

The day was in full swing as marchers engaged ritual of procession. Admiring raptures of nature and nurture, I took my place next to Deeva, as did Sima and Philsuk. Darvish kept a close eye on Philsuk. I thought of Philsuk a child of duty. Darvish too was duty bound. As an intellectual rebel he was driven by a compulsion to question everything.

What then is love, Darvish asked, face down, hiding his eyes of youthful desires. His obvious attempt was to impress Philsuk with his engaging mind. Apart from his youthful raptures, Darvish was a mind of raucous demeanor with an innate inclination to question assumed disciplines.

Deeva laughed. His shivering voice reflected a pair of old and used lungs with a heart that could not keep pace. His clear mind resonated from a unique perception of existence. All listened whenever he uttered words. And he uttered but harmonious words of poetic complexion.

If true love is a vow
Let me make it clear and now
Never to lie half-truth
Or disguise truth with half-lie
Never hide deep feelings
Or veil them with insidious guise
Never lose my freedom to choose
Or choose what I am about to lose
Never believe anything but your eyes
Or indulge in tales of gloomy demise
Never say never to hinder your cries
But enjoy trappings of your simple smiles

If I am to embrace your rubescent self
Or grab you in warmth of my needy mind
If true love is a solemn vow

Then accept my gift
Wrap it around your heart
It is yours to use and mine to lose

Love is the essence of humanity, said Sima looking at Deeva.

Love is a flower that catches the eye, lightens the mind and brushes life with optimism. The garden shines bright emanating from an ethos of enchanting images colored with an aroma of a thousand perfumes. But it is a single flower illuminating the garden tantalizingly brilliant.

Love is a panacea, a gentle thought, a yearning, and a most exquisite desire, said Philsuk with a youthful smile. Her eyes were fixed on Darvish.

Love is a utopia of many passionate respites, a tempest in tranquility. Sima swiftly followed. She gazed at Darvish and Philsuk with a cunning smile.

But to you young seekers, love is a hormonal drive of lustful complexion.

Darvish laughed a brief sarcastic moment before gathering his composure. Though young in years his astute mind was encumbered by ambiguities of chaos, but absurdities did not deter his forward mind. He trusted his senses to engage reason, and he mistrusted his senses just as much. He refrained from judgment by senses though often realized his youthful self trapped in a web of judgment by senses.

Your thoughts are well framed; he addressed all assuming his universal and daring self.

I fail to detect a measured reason of universal quality in what you enunciate so elegantly.

He raised his head facing Deeva.

Love is nothing but stimulation of neurons to a spastic orgy of simultaneous action potentials. Do not consult me on virtues of love for I see none. Do not consult me on virtues of a purely compassionate dictate for I see none. It is all a charade of senses. When senses are satiated full, we raise our expectations on an imaginary pedestal of ethical and moral until the next surge of impulses befuddles our reasoning.

I see no reason for love. I see no virtue for love. I find no pristine landscape of moral ascendancy in the notion of love. All I see is action potentials, needy minds, insatiably ravenous hormonal desires, genetic drives, evolutionary modules and all the presumptuous pretenses amalgamating our sexually obsessed minds.

Philsuk looked up to the changing sky. Clouds streamed with shifting speeds. She traced a flock of troubled birds. Caught between Darvish's skepticism, his refusal to acknowledge his passion for her, and Sima's optimism, she chose to fuse their ideas to synthesize her own.

I see no folly, no heinous intention, and no insidious guise in painting our expectations with shades of love.

If it is our choosing to build our future, then it is reasonable to question the nature of its conjugates. Such ecumenical empowerment must begin somewhere. Without us giving it a beginning, meaning, and direction, it has no chance of withstanding undesirable outcomes. I cannot imagine a more feasible predicament than fusion of passion and reason to compose a new definition of love, one that transcends physical but remains true to its hormonal nature.

She turned to Darvish.

If you, ever so passionately, despise love as an imperfect notion, then use your reasoning for synthesis of a higher aggregate.

If you are concerned with probability of a meaningful existence, then purify your afflictions with logical reasoning and elevate it to perfection of love.

If your concern is harnessing probabilities, then focus your attention as a harbinger of love.

If you aim to accommodate human mishaps, misfortunes and bad fates, lift your reasoning to the splendor of compassion and absorb misfortunes with affectionate expressions, best of which are glazed with love.

Do not confuse pleasure and love. She stared at Darvish, showing her displeasure at his honest but hurtful thoughts.

Surely, there is a pleasure in love, but love is not just pleasure. Love often reaps pain, immures the self, promotes tragedy, impinges on individual freedoms and devours the self for the sake of procreation. Nevertheless, we have learned to reconcile such fates with enlightening thoughts.

Deeva put his arm around Philsuk's slender shoulders, pulled her onto his broad chest, laid a kiss on her forehead and recited.

I am feeling good today
Good to think lovely as kittens
Bushy haired and shining eyes
I am feeling good today
Good to pass life green and mellow
Good to reflect on clear mountaintops
Good to absorb strangeness of purple tides
I am feeling good today
Good to imagine quarks and tiny strings of life
Good to speak of truths
And shining ideas that give birth to light
Like lovers brightly blushed
Yes indeed
Amidst lovely morning dew
In imaginative prairies
Beneath falling rivers
Wherever I may be
I am feeling good today

Listening attentively, daring a few words, Asha often kept a vow of silence. She had no use for words. Her statements were brief and to the point.

To love is to be human. She rushed her words. To love is to be human, she repeated.

Deeva was visibly moved by Sima's disposition as she comforted Philsuk. The relationship between Sima and Deeva transcended physical motives. Their consonance was the melting of two minds in the domain of passion. He approached Sima, sat next to her and recited with squinted eyes and a humble voice.

What compassion can love extol
What feelings can passion foment
Logic dictates a definite path to rules
But love illuminates sojourned truths

Forgive my indulgence in arrogance
I feel I know life, my desires
I feel I know my own truths
I see it frightfully clear
In dreamland of imagined reality
In escape-land of fantasy
Dreadfully absurd

Sometimes estranged by awareness
I forget my brain is trained
Sometimes passion evades me with abject idioms
Sometimes I see truth in subjugating norms
Sometimes I reason to acquit my selfish motives
Sometimes I am lost in existential nothingness
Sometimes I am absorbed in reality of mind-loneliness
Sometimes I am high on inflationary everything
Sometimes I reason ethos of pure compassion
Sometimes I fear affection could paralyze reason
Sometimes I sense more dimensions than four
Sometimes I think happiness is apogee of awareness
Sometimes I feel my best is a mixture of incidents
But of all such times one stands clear and simple
In this life of logical ends and emotional paths
Love is ours to bind bold

Mind to mind and unified
While we have time to adore
Shun despair and avow
Timeless or time bound
Life is a moment forever in love

Silence fell upon us as aching muscles dictated reality. Evening flared florid reflections. We lit lanterns to ease the cumbersome pace in darkness. The moon shone with vivid brilliance nullifying light of lanterns insignificant. We put them out saving precious little we possessed for future use. I closed eyes, pondering what I had just heard; "life is a moment forever in love."

Sima chose a spot, carefully inspecting and arranging its detail. She then seated Deeva with the affection of a caring lover. Seating herself next to him was a complete symphony. Together they emitted a life-sustaining force.

By now, all had laid bodies for another suiting night of enchanting dialogues. As usual, Darvish dared to ignite the conversation.

If affection can be raised to its proper domain of unblemished compassion, if compassion is realized in infinite arrays to assume a string, what, then constitutes dictum of love? Would it be an emotional derailment in wicked ways? Would it diminish the intent to capitulate or captivate? If love is a ubiquitous dream to exalt human potential in the domain of affection, I see none touched by its truism.

Sima reached out, grasped his hand, turned it palm up.

You have a lot to learn in the ways of love. She kissed his hand.

Deeva smiled and recited.

Rising from pinnacle of love
To announce ecstasy of friendship
To fathom life, together, without sexual connotations
To stretch affection to its proper domain
And collapse universe to a new incarnation

Is an affirmation of humanity
I dream in domain of compassion

To love you as a dear friend
And park my uninhibited self in your mind, knowing
Love has turned its face to a deeper meaning
Is a joy I will endure for all times and details

True love is a friendship forever pasted
Without expectation and anticipation
I have climbed to that pinnacle and declared myself
One who listens
And listens without judgment
One who hears
And hears without anger
One who seeks
And finds perfection in compassion

It is through this amorphous structure
I seek truth in love
And love
With or without truths

The moon by now was a beaming light with full face. I could see its reflection in Deeva's eyes. Sima had her eyes shut. Deeva took off the garb she had earlier placed on him carefully spreading it over her, adjusting its corners with precision of a pointillist. He then mused us with few rare words of non-poetic complexion.

Sleep well, my friend, he said in a soothing tone.

You have reached the pinnacle of compassion. Your amicable expressions of affection delight us from light to dark. Your passionate reflections illuminate our lives with centered dispositions. Sleep well my dearest friend.

Philsuk sat next to Darvish and put her arm around him. Darvish did not move.

I see the old man's reasoning. What better adoption than affection and love to advance human panacea. Surely, yearning for physical love, long after passions have faded, is a repetitive hormonal yearning. But such yearning should not veil other dimensions of affection.

Compassion is a befitting foundation to human reasoning.

She looked up to the moon.

Our total selves understood, then misunderstood. From truth to honesty to falsehood, to bizarre images of unknown path, as passionate seekers of intense integrity, we sail melancholic metaphors until all is unraveled.

She turned to Darvish, stared into his eyes.

At the end of each day, what was is no more, but an aching body preoccupied with a self-serving tapestry of emotions.

Searching imagined moments of perfection, in eternity of imagination, in small isolated islands of certainty, each in our universe of solitude reaches out for truth and finds none.

She sat next to me, held my hand.

Sailing shores of imagination to land in the dimension of selfhood, we pass with passing moments to reach an imagined nexus. What purpose shines this tapestry?

Truth is, we pass without purpose. Purpose is not why we come. Purpose is not why we live. Purpose is not why we pass. With or without purpose, life begins and ends.

Huddled in our inner sanctums, we carried Philsuks' reflection to our private dream world.

The rising sun was a perplexing tempest with many reflections. The precision by which it emerged from farthest of peaks was a testimony of life ahead. Call it a feeling, call it reality, call it what you may, it echoed a unique freshness yielding the egregious thoughts to a confined domain. Waves of light kindled life: conscious or without consciousness. Serenity of this early rise blossomed a medley of abstruse textures. The asymmetry of perceived and perception coalesced acutely sharp. I sensed a quintessential feeling of estrangement. It stimulated my senses in harmony with universal excitations. It reconciled good and bad. It decoupled right and might.

A sudden rush of energy transposed my mind of wonders to a new stage of awareness.

Deeva and Sima were seriously engaged in the path. Their enthusiasm to meet The Great One far exceeded mine. Perhaps their anticipation of what may lie ahead focused their attention. I was too indisposed with youthful passions to fathom their intent.

I watched in amazement, touched in reverence, listened with precision and attempted to synchronize my senses attuned to theirs. Life without them seemed unthinkable. Every moment away from them was a moment of awareness lost to confusion, so I reasoned.

Darvish laughed. He read my mind.

Why do we choose to follow? He reflected with his sharp mind.

The minds we devour in devotion are themselves confused states dwelling for a stance in a drama of existence.

We are driven by a primitive yearning to follow something or someone. Consider this trail and The Great One. We follow them with conviction, with unbound determination. We devote ourselves to pursuit of something that may or may not be achievable. Why?

To mortal minds, life is too ephemeral, too uncertain to waste in devotion. The exactness of a single bold moment of awareness and the energy spent to sustain it is a greater facade than promises that require no expenditure of energy. Real time is the essence of human existence. To lose perception of that essence is to live without enlightenment.

As I daydreamed, Sima and Deeva foresaw and foretold. Time had reaped their minds lucid. I wished to age to their wisdom. Did I wish to age? What absurd predicament compelled my senses to such a draconian measure? Life is too precious to wish its accelerated passage. Perhaps awareness is a higher meaning than life itself? Perhaps a moment of all-encompassing knowledge is worthier than a long life of irrelevant presumptions.

I hurried my pace to catch up with my mentors. My haste disturbed the harmony of the trail. The caring minds, sensing my uneasiness, extended their grace to accommodate my haste. I felt remorse for having disturbed their cohesion to further mine. I slowed my pace to their pace.

In this trail of enlightened minds, giving was proclaimed a prodigious virtue of highest ascendancy. The rapture evoked by surrendering possessiveness eased the mind to the lightness of tranquility.

There is greater liberation in giving than receiving, Sima reminded us.

I thought it eccentric at first. I thought it a digression in servitude to hold such a premise so high. How could giving be more plausible than taking? I was wrong. The pleasure of giving is conceived at a higher level, so I learned, in time.

Deeva stopped at a scenic plateau. Far below twined a silent river. He stared at the scene for sometime and recited.

Imagine a gateway
You stand alone
Beyond
The universe
Give me your hand
Trust me

Who are you

Trust me

Do you know we are all alone

Together
Apart
Evolving
Becoming
Wide-open prairies
Filth-covered ghettos
Laughter and sorrow
An undefined future

Do you know
We are measured
By what we think
What we give
What we say
What we do

So think well
Say well
Do well
Mean well
And give

Graceful minds and humble selves share their thoughts and possessions, said Sima.

Capacious minds of the generous integrity bow when they give, keep their heads gracefully high when they take, and assume equal footing when they share.

To be humble one must experience humiliation. Lightness of being is actualized through humbleness. Attempting to elucidate the seemingly insurmountable notion of "nothing" eases the weight of humbleness. To ascend to a state of nothingness from the depth of selfishness can confuse the conscience with most abstract manifestations. At such an epic of awareness, life becomes as encompassing as it is meaningless. To sense "nothing" is as exhilarating as touching "everything." But to see both, to imagine life delineated by "everything" and "nothing" is to feast on highest awareness.

The river carved its shinning path miles below and thousands of years deep. It showed us the way as it carved the way. It invited the living to cross paths. It mused our senses with such abstractions as beauty and magnificence.

Deeva kept pace with rest of us as he recited.

Time is a passing awareness
From nothingness to emancipation to freedom
Conscience is accommodated perceptions
A summary of passion and reason
Enthralled by ephemeral states
Befuddled by perplexity of modular intellect
I shiver at reality of being and wonder
Do I know this mind that sees and foresees
Do I know one moment will partition
My being, a pandemonium of everything
And nothing

Uncertainty imbibes my definite self
As I am, an imagined life
Of my own capricious reasoning
But in domain of reality, I hold the key
I alone conjure thoughts of I
I alone assume limits of I
I alone dictate tantalizingly stratified splendors of I
I alone imagine illusions of "I"

What then is my reality
If I can imagine its rhythm and rhyme
What is my truth
If I can mold its fixtures
Fragile, mortal, impressively resilient
Am I not a dream of my own

Apart from freedom, I cherish most
Dichotomy of passion and reason
The distinction is simple

What purpose my being serves but passion
What should it devour but compassion

In flesh and conscience
Life is a one-time chance
Before this chance evaporates and nothing rules
I have a few moments to explore
Imagine a universal edifice
And dream a transparent field of humanity

Time lapsed. The journey in the domain of absurd and real continued with a steady pace. I often found my conscience dappled with uncertainties that deluded my senses with useless suppositions. I dreamed of precarious dispositions filling the gap between assimilated ideas and imposed realities I wished to dissimilate. Reality, it seemed, had varying representations of changing semblance. Setting limits from birth to death, its material fabric was undeniably imposing and its immensity outside boundaries of individual capacity. Its dimensions colored the scene with limitless textures. And its totality resonated from an amorphous entity of asymmetric diction.

I recognized conscience a gateway to universal truths. Truths are many, so I learned. I had much to learn. Learning itself is a purpose, so I learned.

I faced Deeva and posed several questions.

How should I see the universe? How should I approach its realities? How should I absorb dichotomies that rule our lives?

Deeva placed his long wrinkled hand on my shoulder and recited.

What held real is now a mystery
What is real may not be at all
Reality is a perception
What I see is time-passed
What I live is time-present
What I imagine is timeless

Living is an attempt to condense time to happiness
To satisfaction
To whatever worth emulating

In medleys of our endurance
In melodious thoughts and simple ideas
We imagine truth realms apart
From time-past to time-immortal
To here, to self
From nothingness of universal debris
To everything of being aware
In reality and dream, I am
My own forbidden puzzle
A mystery
A state of mind
Alive
That is what I am
Trapped by universal designs

The task is to ascertain a wider span of reasoning, said Darvish.

There are behavioral modules that drive the self and the species to reduce life to a single purpose. But there is no single source of purpose. Infinite number of perceptions shapes human civilization. They affect the individual as individuals affect the society. The cycle is incomplete as time warps its reality.

What we envision can be broadened in all dimensions, at all times, for all reasons. I am certain humanity will increasingly focus on more inclusive purposes.

He stood and raised his fist.

Time-present, the manifestation we perceive as reality is a continuum of collapsing probabilities that string our lives. It lapses with a precise interval we have learned to measure with uncanny exactness. Time is a mystery of the most alluring radiance. It enables the mind to assemble a string of perceptions from the past to near future. It alienates the self to ornate folly of insolence or ordained reflections of reverence. It mystifies the mind with distorted contortions. It captivates the mind with conjecture of infinity. It fools mortals with immortal thoughts. And there lies the greatest quest of our mortal existence: the search for immortality.

To us mortals, time is of the essence. We try to reveal its essence and forecast its outcomes. And we do so with increasing accuracy, with boldness and brazen ideas. Do not abrade significance of perceiving time. It is a most portent depiction of our mental abilities.

We discern its passing with certainty of our passing but are impotent in exposing its universal significance.

We see the stars, delve into the past by measuring their shift, calculate the universe to smallest fraction, and decide if it is contracting or expanding. The significance of it all, the perennial question of "why the universe" escapes our combined consonance. To reach that nexus of revelation, we use the best of our capacity and reason. Reason is a human tool that changes with changing perceptions, itself subject to change with changing times, places, and reason. To seek certainty of a single unifying explanation is to seek singularity of reason. Such certainty, if it exists, is timeless and as such imperceptible to our time-bound existence. There is no saying where our evolutionary potential can take us. In time, we could absolve timeless questions. In time, we could become timeless creatures.

How could a fraction perceive the totality? Is there such a thing as an isolated self? We are all connected in as many ways as there are parameters to measure the connections. Philsuk wondered.

Our perception is limited by our senses, themselves limited by our physical conditioning. How could a fraction perceive containment by totality if not a part of or connected to totality?

Sima joined in.

Truth is, our ancestors did not perceive totality. They perceived life in capricious and impulsive ways. They perceived life in terms that assured their immediate needs and day-to-day survival. These modular imprints are still influencing our cognitive functioning.

Our collective inertia, nurtured by instruments we have devised to expand our perceptual boundary conditions, has elevated individual imaginative capacity by creating a reservoir of virtual concepts. This process of social integration has metamorphosed individual perception to ineffable level of universal perception. This process could not have been possible without our immortal social existence.

The interaction between sensory perception, willful interpretation, and social congruity is constantly modifying boundary conditions of individual awareness transforming it to a potent imaginative epiphany. It has metamorphosed the self from an impulsive biological entity to an incredibly creative and complex matrix of perceptions.

Deeva listened attentively. Looking up he inhaled deep fresh mountain air and recited.

In every bend of every thought
In every form of every life
For all times and every reason
With stormy tides and passionate lives
To us humans, reason is
A stratified tempest of revelations
Discussed in passages and passageways
In vanity and ignorance
In truth and consequence
In love affairs and melancholic rhapsodies
For all times and every reason
There is a desire to ask why
Why life
Why universe
Why this paradigm of wonders
Why anything at all

In every bend of every thought
In every moment of emotional fraught

Swarmed with desires
In sanctity of self
Energized by honesty and driven by curiosity
We take a reasoned stand
Bloated with affection
Swarmed with psychological mishaps
We take a stand
Infatuated with intense desires
Fixated with ideological drives
We take a stand

In every bend of every thought
Chained by genes and epigenomal transformations
Free at last, free till the end, free in self
Free in conscience, free in deed
Free in memories, free in wishful thoughts
I ask why
And take a stand

With all its enormity and obscurity
Life is
What I think it is
And when I die
It is someone else's thoughts
That makes life by observing life
And sees what it is
And when there are no observers
There is no perception of life
Time stands still
Everything becomes nothing
Nothing at all

On a cool brisk morning, as we watched life forms devour one another, Darvish challenged our imagination with another display of his intellectual ferocity.

Aside from reason and truth, there is a real condition in the format of justice on which we have dwelt as a civilization.

He stared at a small creature devouring another.

I see no justice. Justice, as a universal force and independent of judgment, insinuates existence of a cognitive phenomenon apart from human conception. I have yet to realize such a dominion. Nor will its existence and encounter abrogate my reasoning for freedom to will a more civilized format of justice.

He stared at the creature finishing its prey.

There is no justice in devouring each other. There is no justice in birth and sudden death. There is no justice in poverty and disease. There is no justice in random occurrences and probability.

Justice is a human creation out of necessity. The notion of justice mutates with changing conditions and perceptions. Its scope and application vary from mind to mind and defining causes preoccupying the mind. There is no justice in the universal scheme of life. There is no quanta or field of justice.

He kept on staring at the beast grooming itself.

There is no justice in being devoured by another, he murmured with seeming disgust.

Sima agreed. First, there is a perception of injustice then synthesis of its antitheses as justice. You are so correct. There is no justice.

We see the injustice. We propagate injustice. We measure injustice. Enriched by logical fairness, as individuals or groups, we attempt to rectify the conditions by synthesizing an antithesis to incurred injustice and enact remedies based on the level of injustice. Justice is a euphemism for abject acts ascertained to equilibrate incurred injustices.

However, there is injustice. Injustice is tangible. It is measured in pain and suffering.

Deeva approached Sima, grasped her shoulders and pulled them onto his broad chest. She was complacent, melting into his existence.

Philsuk was unsatisfied. She spread her robe on Sima.

Have I not committed a morally just act by treating others non-preferentially? Have I not committed a just act by observing the incurred injustice and attempting to diminish its recurrence?

She made sure Sima was well covered.

Have I not extended my sense of justice by giving to someone in need? Is it not just to propagate fairness and compassion? Is it not just to mend aching minds and tend perturbed lives? Is it not just to remedy a malicious act? Is it not just to defend individual rights? Is it not just to erase self-serving distinctions that separate humans?

Sima looked at her with passionate eyes.

In dispensing compassion, you have acted humanly correct. Do not credit yourself moral superiority if you are acting correct. A compassionate human does not cause pain. Nor does she see justice but correctness of thought and action. As virtue is composed with greater clarity, justice is diminished insignificant.

There is injustice because there are unintended consequences. There is injustice because our ethical temperament is on equal footing with our moral decadence. Chaos does not differentiate events as just or unjust. Humans do.

Philsuk was not convinced.

In human dimension there is just and unjust. I can sense it.

She turned to Sima.

It is true; the universe may not recognize just and unjust, but humans do. As such, the notion of justice has become a universal phenomenon no matter how small and insignificant it may be.

Darvish raised his voice.

Thought and action must correlate the same congruous reasoning to acclimatize virtue with symmetrical clarity. Virtue is another cognitive design devised by minds that wish to ascertain a regulated norm to behavior. The modular evolution of this design has resulted in an unforeseen predicament of virtue as the driving force of our moral congruity. In human dimension, to have moral superiority is to have everything. If we feel morally superior, we feel justified in all our doings. As such, we devise moral-ethical pathways that satisfy our reasoning irrespective of how malicious the act may be.

Virtue is the web holding the needy, the weak and the uninformed in their shrinking domain. He rushed his words.

Values and judgments are imposed on us to ensure prosperity of the aggressive and the ambitious. There is no universal reservoir of virtue. There are no eternal observers measuring virtue. There are only I, the gathering of our perceptions, and the universe that contains and accepts all our doings without judgment of their significance. The universe accepts whatever we are, integrating it with the rest of existence. There is no just or unjust in this process.

I sense incongruity of a selfish nature in your stance, said Philsuk, displeased with Darvish's demeanor. She was visibly disturbed by his assertive posture.

Darvish apologetically lowered his head.

Sima took her eyes off him. Attempting to ease the pain of humbleness showered on him, she turned to Philsuk.

He is correct. Virtue is a human design to stow an orderly format of our collective consonance. It is a devised means for the procurement of desired ends.

She turned to Darvish.

The challenge is to synchronize our judgments to synthesize freestanding ideas of universal relevance. Such an aim has often diluted individual conscience with ideation of grandeur, but in time, with maturity and modular understanding, it could blossom profound realities.

Virtue is a human concept. It is evolving as we are evolving.

The luster of virtue is its impetus to mitigate improvisation of values. Of all the ways to attain greatness in continuity of civilization, of all the attempted pathways, I rather measure my steps through a moral matrix that promotes compassionate virtues.

I prefer to imagine a pristine world of passionate selves with the virtuosity of accepting nature. Virtue can command conscience to integrity of restrained and audacious conduct: restrained in the domain of judgment, audacious in the domain of understanding. Within such an evolutionary context, justice can be ascertained as something tangible. For now, justice is the antithesis to incurred injustice.

Daylight faded faster than our conversation. Looking at stars shining their reality to exhaustion, my mind of wonders yearned absurdity of a dream world where everything made equal sense.

Daybreak put an end to such comfort. It promised real ways of digesting ideas.

Climbing a steep rise, Philsuk raised an age-old question. Can the end justify the means? She wondered with innocent curiosity.

Sima walked next to Philsuk, held her hand.

If the means is contrived with egalitarian intentions and pain free, and the end is a splendid outcome, of course everything is justified. If the end is an abysmal fortune of disastrous consequences, then nothing is justifiable.

The end is meant to create certain fulfillment. The means is not always pain free. Some argue the good of majority must rule. Some argue not even pain of one is justifiable. Truth is, both the means and the end are measurable variables affecting one or more individuals. And what is good for one or a group may prove disastrous for another. As such, the means and the end can be both justifiable and unjustifiable at the same instance of consideration.

Humankind has often abrogated the relevance of the means to the benefits of the perceived end. Utility has become the measuring paradigm in a practical world of social discourse. It has taken its priority as a determining factor in a judgment of action. Advanced democratic and egalitarian societies have tended to shift the balance in favor of the individual.

Is it justifiable to destroy for the benefit of one or more? Must the end and the means be seen as conjugates of a unified principle?

Can satisfaction of a group justify the suffering of another with equal standing? Darvish wondered.

The greatest civilizations are those with greatest remorse for socially sanctioned heinous acts. The temporary and transient feelings of revenge, hate and justice cannot be allowed the center stage in our moral structure. If taking a life is the most egregious human act, we should not use it as a tool to achieve a desired end.

But the reality of human existence is based on the judgments of a few as to what is best for the majority, said Philsuk.

Virtue is a matrix of ethical dictates governing the conscience and as such the rule of law and well-being of the majority.

Within the web of virtue, compassion can entertain life with suiting thoughts, more suiting than egalitarian intentions, more suiting than the good of one or the good of many.

The road to a truly actualized self can be paved with empathy. The road to the ethos of humanity can be harmonized with compassion.

Deeva was moved by Philsuk's analysis. He sat next to her, put his long bony arm around her shoulders, pressed her onto his chest. She melted without resistance. He then recited.

The essence of existence is self-preservation
The notion of life without death
Absolute life
Is irrelevant
Reality of being is awareness of being
There are no omnipotent perennial certainties
There is no forever
First, there is uncertainty of time
What it is and is it
Without us measuring its passing
Then, the uncertainty of day-to-day living
The uncertainty of not knowing
The uncertainty of vanishing possibilities
The uncertainty of who we are
In the end
It is certainty of death
Certainty of disintegration
Certainty of abating awareness
Ruling our lives

It is impudent to imagine truth as real
And reality something static
It is impudent to imagine truth a written book
With human characters
Human stories and fallacies
Tossed in a black hole of ideas
To emerge universal

It is insolent to imagine life absolute
Absorbed and preserved
In an omnipresent universal awareness

A paradox of being and nothingness
Truth is a revealing joke
Only uninhibited tyrants ruffle its immensity
Ameliorate themselves willful
Resolve existence to awareness of existence
And find its relevance in coexistence
In ideas that speak of universal suffrage
Respect for life and all life
Equally respectful

There is a logical path to all our logic
There is no logic but human logic
No heavenly metaphors
Only minds that dream
From gods to goods to symmetry
Reality is a collective human perception
Evolving with observation
And asymmetry of our perfection
Truth is
Our collective endurance
Is summarized in our virtual collective

Truth is
In asymmetry of free will and social
In this unwritten book of life
There are extremes of logic and passion
We use to measure right and wrong
Truth is
We are the sum effect of our thoughts
Our devised means
Our achieved ends
Our dreams
Our ambitions
Our wishes and wishful thoughts

Our ideas and ideals
Truth is
The essence of existence is self-preservation

Human experience is human creation, said Sima.

What we make of ourselves could become a nightmare of galactic proportions, or a serene egalitarian life of reason and passion.

Dream a compassionate dream. Create justice if justice is your cause, but do not solidify your judgments with an inflexible articulation of reason or just.

If humanity is to survive its perilous journey in the universe of probabilities, riddled with the transformation of stars and endangered with ecological and biological disasters, we must harmonize our senses with higher aggregates. This is not to say self-serving judgments are meaningless. On the contrary, they are the basis for most of our decisions. The question is which judgments simultaneously best serve our individual and collective existence.

Darvish stood, attempted a circle with stretched arms while swirling around.

Justice, right, wrong, good, bad, these are sets of values with changing implications we accept and impose. Their relevance and scope are limited by individual perceptions, and the limit humanity imposes on itself to regulate itself. The idiom of concern is our savvy prepotency to amalgamate values in the universe of human relevancy. Such dictum asserts a supposition some may find absurd. It assumes human values and moral congruity apart from universal scheme. It asserts human ethical congruity an alternative posture in contriving probable universal patterns. Based on this provocative notion, the end point in human dimension is the humanity itself.

"Everything" is within our reach as "nothing" demarcates the end of every reach. In this hypothesis "everything" and "nothing" are the boundary conditions setting the limits of our reach themselves set by the boundary conditions we imagine.

A human notion of morality could weave a flexible matrix regulating our behavior in a compassionately rational manner, said Sima, shaken by Darvish's reasoning.

Our emotional web twines its intricate vine in quests we partake. We possess an uncanny potential to affect our collective and the paths we choose or are chosen for us. Our image is an evolving image. We do not as yet discern who we truly are. Perhaps the potential to become what we think we are, is itself an evolving process.

Truth is, our combined consonance is climbing steep but steady heights of revelation to define our very existence that may someday metamorphose to another species.

Truth is, with certainty of a given moment and the degree to which we attempt to measure that certainty, we do not know who we are.

Deeva was impressed by Darvish's observations. He recited a poem I had not heard before.

Living is a reason to itself
No desire, no feeling, no reason
Can endure lasting justification
Or become a reason for my being
For living is a reason to itself

Ideologically driven contortion of being
Is much too contrived to tame
Or claim truths as resolved issues
Truth, as I see, is a myopic distortion
Manifested in more dimensions than observed
In balance
Human observation is an attempt to frame distortions
Delineating boundaries of existence
With "everything" and "nothing"

What we claim to know
And what will be revealed in the future
Is a domain called "everything"
To attempt to understand everything
Without understanding "nothing"
Is futile

In this proposed matrix of existence
I can imagine vibrations of our thoughts
All the way across the galaxy and back
But in the domain of social
This undefined, unknown, mysterious reality
Of virtual consentient accords
Life finds a singularity of meaning
And becomes a reason to itself

The great journey in life I had undertaken was transforming my pretentious pride. I concluded life a radiant rapture, a prodigious experience in paradigms with imagined and real manifestations.

In time, awareness can grow impervious to inflexible reasoning to assume an inherently flexible posture. In time, we could transcend this reality to compose others. We must do so knowing probability, at any given time, can eliminate us with uncanny precision. For certain, there is such a probability, and we have the potential to understand and predict it. For certain, we can plan ahead and avoid it. However, there will come a time in our evolutionary future where the best of our efforts may not save us. There is that probability, as well.

I imagined life a wonderland of dreams. Peace was within me as the world around spun a stormy ocean of circumstances. Amidst, our perceived quagmire of uncertainties, riddled with inscrutable puzzles, we affronted absurdities to claim the trail the reality of our existence.

I often regressed in a quandary of reflection, searching my quintessence in an ascetic domain of my inner sanctum. I foresaw and foretold provocative illusions. I imagined my existence an unattached reality. In reality, I realized myself twined with attachments, warped with values, draped and concealed by paroxysmal behaviors.

With every rising sun rose my ceaseless curiosity to delineate wonders. When the moons announced living a peaceful thought, I conformed by abdicating willful existence an abject abstraction of future contradictions.

Each night I dove in a dream world of quantum query only to awaken to a life of material awareness.

We have managed to survive many heedless thoughts, thoughts that foresaw and foretold human annihilation, Darvish reflected.

We have escaped the whimsically destructive thoughts. We have survived the horrors of primitive thoughts. We have escaped stellar disasters. We have outlived biological competitions. We have outgrown moral absolutes.

We are a very fortunate species, he said with detectable unease.

My ancestors elevated their aggressive impulses to a threshold of ripping their prey to pieces while still alive. They then consumed it raw. In time, when their moral congruity did not tolerate observing the heinous act of killing, they tuned out by turning face. They then, from afar, ripped entire civilizations apart consuming their succulent images, all the while thinking themselves righteous and good.

Is it possible to be an offspring of such a beast and pretend moral integrity? A child of that beast, I harbor immense potential to fathom the universe in its most unblemished state. From aggressive to compassionate, evolution is the connection making it all possible.

Perhaps I am surreptitiously assuming time a revealing phenomenon. Maybe I am wishfully assuming humanity a paradox of improving nature. But if I hold humans responsible for their humanity, I must assume human condition a self-improving condition.

For certain, each of our lives is a passing reality, but the virtual nature of our collective plays wicked games. Each time we choose to commit our reasoning to a synthesis of rational peaks. Many paragons with confusing panaceas expose unseen aspects of our endeavor. Such is the essence of quantum reasoning. It can change with each assertion.

Time lapsed, memories faded. Blue skies appeared and disappeared. The journey twined and intertwined in more dimensions than known. From birth to awareness to nothingness, life swung its asymmetric trappings pealing minds naked. Often, in such moments of trouble I turned to my mentors for consolation. One such moment of distraught, when I realized a redeeming necessity to justify my impulses, I turned to Deeva. He was laboring with parched lips and swollen limbs.

Time has passed in billions, and I still grapple with the perennial question of who I am, I said with resignation.

How do I perceive human values knowing they are self-serving, regulatory and evolved for the sole purpose of propagation?

Why do we perform rituals that defy logic and passion? Are we furnishing the universe a new field of identity?

Deeva labored a few moments of silent reflection and recited.

Epiphany of life is a progeny uniquely apportioned
By a desire to be everything possible
Apogee of being supreme is wishful
Precariously conceived by a melancholic desire to reach out
To conquer the universe in mind
But how do I measure conquest
How do I know I have achieved

Human luster is best prospered in imagination
With understanding
With compromise

With empathy
To reach out and touch without a drop of blood
Am I making myself clear
Without a drop of blood

To assuage life a private quintessence and plunge deep
In an unremitting desire to cage truths
Like overpowering a submissive pet
Is a weakness
For I see no lions in your den
And your vision
Is a selfish odyssey to abbreviate minds as slaves

Do I make myself clear
Passion is selfish
Love is selfish
Truth is selfish
To rule the universe is selfish
To believe in imposed dictates is selfish
Life is selfish

Philsuk looked at Deeva with reverence.

Good and bad are human measures of conduct, she said tending her hair.

We use them to gauge everything from brutality to empathy. We have not as yet isolated a universal good aside from human notion of good. And human perspective of good is an accumulated assimilation of individual perceptions.

The sky was turning a purplish haze. The upper winds arranged clouds faster than lower winds creating eye-catching images. She stared at them with keen attention.

In a domain of pure logic, it is perfectly reasonable to equate good and right. In a domain of passion, where feelings set boundary conditions, right and good differentiate a multitude of perplexing definitions.

We are infants in the quest of moral certainty. Infants learn fast. They are permeable, impressionable and easily molded.

Our overlapping emotional resonances create a prepotency to advance our values to the edifice of universal integrity, said Darvish.

All moral and ethical measures are applied vectors in a virtual matrix of human virtue. They orient the social self, influence the imaginative self, dilute personal self, and often confuse the self with possible connections to the universe.

Virtue and moral values are necessary for social cohesion and order: nothing more and nothing less.

Independent of accepted constraints, in imagination, ideas form elegant constructs. Imagination thrives in a nexus without boundaries. It plunges the self in dimensions of creativity rendering social impositions irrelevant.

Can I perceive a world without the dichotomy of right and wrong? Has collective moral congruity contaminated the individual expression reducing it to robotic redundancy? Are we better humans than our beastly ancestors? Will our moral structure dominate the universe?

Sima approached Darvish, leaned her shoulder against his.

Our ancestors, instead of searching truths, searched for prey. The catch was good. It meant survival. The act was justified. It meant survival. Survival was the aim of most of their thoughts and actions. To them, the means was irrelevant and survival justified everything.

Rituals were conceived to patent the events, and tales of bravery were passed on to qualify the ritual a lasting phenomenon.

Human liberation from barbaric norms was the work of free wills that resolved myths to measurable and predictable outcomes. They meticulously tabulated everything they could measure. Egalitarian equality embraced mass production. With a growing population, life became an exercise in production and consumption. Eventually, human interests collided in an arena of limited resources demanding new analysis of the individual and social imperatives.

History of human evolution is a compromise between social demands and individual quests for happiness. Clever minds frequently synthesize ideas that circumvent social demands. They perceive happiness in a higher plateau of perception. They transcend the social and the universal to synthesize a symmetrical self.

Darvish seemed confused. Pacing back and forth he held his head with both hands.

I must cleanse my thoughts. He shouted.

I must drain the reservoir of aggression embedded in my mind. Little do I know of reality. It enables me to construct the universe in the time-space of my mind. It illuminates our search for truths. It enables me to exhibit awareness. Without reality, truth is irrelevant. Without reality, life is meaningless. Real time is where everything is perceived.

The relationship between reality and imagination is mystifying.

He paused, attempted a circle balancing his body with his stretched arms.

Reality is a boring repetition of probabilities, said Philsuk.

Darvish jumped in. You are so correct.

Seemingly stricken with a revealing thought, he stopped and approached Philsuk.

What I yearn for, once tangible to my senses, is no more an object of curiosity. Repeated over and over the excitement condenses monotonous and the object metamorphoses to an abject state of boring connotations.

Only in imagination can reality lose its repetitiveness contorting known formats to abstract manifestations. In imagination, time loses its continuity of passage. Time, it seems, has little meaning in the world of imagination.

What then is imagination? Is it a timeless exhibition by time-bound creatures? Is it a quantum perception? Is it experiencing dimensions imperceptible to senses? Is it something we can control? Can we transmute its syntax? Are we carving its reality? Are we defining a path to its universality?

Philsuk stared at Darvish.

Your mind is storming bold. Let the storm ride its course. These youthful chasms are irresistible, but the eye of the storm will cross before its tail spins your confidence to confusion.

Reality is manifested probabilities. There is a universe with or without us. We observe the up and down game of its quarks. We sense its quantum evasiveness. We inscribe set meanings to its classical manifest. We calculate its smallest vibrations. Only in imagination can we realize totality of such a capacious quandary.

Irrespective of social depictions, reality is conceived in confinement of each mind. As such, each is a unique window to reality. Isolated and lonely, we synthesize sharper images by contrasting our perceptions in a virtual arena of social existence.

Perception of reality is a relative measure of relative relevance, said Darvish.

Existence, as an individual perception, is a mirage. Individual perception finds true meaning when observed by another.

Philsuk stopped for a deep breath. The thin mountain air demanded it.

I must edify my perception of reality, she whispered.

Philsuk was as young as Darvish with an inordinate sense of reason, passion and devotion. Contradictions often humbled her to self-deprecation, but her hunger for self-actualization accentuated her willful stance.

I consider myself fortunate to be alive. She continued.

I must enjoy this awareness while I have integrity to entertain its reality. And the reality is the aches and pains distracting my awareness. Such is the reality of mortal living.

She turned to Darvish.

You are a beacon of truth boring willful onto future. You aim at your highest. You feel life from within.

She turned her face, stared on the ground. I only wish I could do the same. She closed eyes.

Darvish seemed shaken and humbled by her show of emotional weakness.

The distinction between being and being conscious is a most fundamental concern to us mortals, he said sitting next to her and holding her hand.

I do not as easily discern what reality entails. Nor can I deny the sky above and the earth below. For all I know, this galaxy is on a bubble in the vastness of a foamy structure pervious to cataclysmic events that could end all our thoughts.

I am as consumed and confused by absurdity of ideas. Awareness encompasses a world of egregiously confusing nature. It can be simple and complicated at the same instance of consideration.

Deeva approached Philsuk and Darvish, extended his broad shoulders, grasped them in his stretched arms and recited.

I claim we are enslaved
Within a matrix of logic and emotion

Should I choose the path of truths
But what is true
Should I ensnare myself as existentialist
But what is existence
Should I engage psychoanalysis
But what is the purpose of analysis

Am I what I think
Am I a distant dream
Can life be a tale of humans
Are we slaves of our awareness
Can we truly be free
Is anthropic principle our intellectual demise

The didactic dictum of concern is state of a mind
No matter what persuasion
Living is an allegory of perceptions
A creatively passionate expression
Dappled with sojourned truths
Time bound and timeless
In human universe of absurd and ideal
Chaos rules
Probability rules
Tensegrity rules
Asymmetry of past and future rules
Echo of our collective awareness rules
Willful determination rules
They coalesce a harmony of capricious nature
Seducing act of living a reason for living

This contortion of truths I call I
Is much too contrived to acclimate human truths
And much too chaotic to not
Indeed, living is a reason to itself
I am driven by conjectures of emotion
A universe of passion and reason
Indeed, I am a story that tells the story

Philsuk deliberated awhile.

The ability to perceive time and its passage is a most obscure facet of human mind. We know so little about time. Perhaps human mind is unique in its detection of time. Perhaps our perception of time is a measure of something more profound than we acknowledge.

I was unsatisfied.

What matters is the reality of now and here, I said.

The instance I perceive time-present, reality is already history, said Darvish.

We are baffled by our fortune of existence, said Sima. We are baffled by our inert ability to conceive the cosmos and the nature of our existence. We are baffled by a composition of elements comprising the moment. We are baffled by existence of delicate designs. We are baffled by our passionate perceptions of existence. We are baffled by our ability to empathize.

Here we are, a new vision of humanity, a new civilization, said Darvish.

Such is the distinction between being alive and being imaginative. Imagination has carried us from one solar system to another. Imagination is our gateway to "everything." Imagination is our savior.

He stopped, approached Philsuk and uncharacteristically arranged her hair. Philsuk sat quiet seemingly enjoying the attention.

Throughout history, in the name of right and good, we have speckled much pain and confusion, said Philsuk.

Complexity of absolving realities to concrete social definitions has taught me to shy away from dogmatic resolutions. I do not delineate reality in sharpness of its aggregates but in the murkiness of its composites.

To assume human reality apart from universal reality, even perhaps in contradiction to it, is an eventuality we must compromise. The anthropic principle dictates enslavement of our civilization within this universe. The inflationary principle exposes us to a possibility of eternal existence within this containment until eternity itself becomes too dilute to have a meaning.

The universal constant teaches us a theoretical possibility of other universes. The string theory teaches us possibility of dimensions imperceptible to our senses.

Through imagination, we conceive possibilities that do not exist and make them a part of universal reality. We create reality by changing the existing reality.

What will become of universal reality if human imagination grows to contain it? I wondered. Will human reality transform universal reality? Are we a singularity? Are we a potential for new possibilities? Are we a potential to the realization of new paradigms? Does the universe react to our combined discourse? Are we becoming gods we imagined ourselves to be?

I looked at Darvish. He did not heed. I looked at Philsuk. She pretended not to have caught my sight. I dared not look at Deeva. I turned to Sima.

Call it premature, childish, primitive. Call it what you may. The reality is, we have committed primeval acts of aggression to ascend to this level of sophistication. We have done much wrong and will keep on doing much wrong. We have done much right and will keep on doing much right.

What we call our nature had little meaning millions of years ago. In all probability, millions of years from now, human perception of nature will be substantially different. Natural is not a permanent panacea. Nature is whatever surrounds us. Nature is whatever we choose to surround us.

Sima held my hand, turned it palm up, and stared at it.

Of truth, I know very little.

She examined the wrinkles in my hand.

Of reality, I know this much: anything said, anything done, anything that spins is real. Perception of an image is tantamount to the possibility of its existence. Ideas constructed in the domain of imagination often have no physical reality. Thoughts, in time, affect physical existence. All things within the universe, including thoughts, are manifestations with precise explanations. The awesome truth of this construct is its transparency. We seek truths by observing truths. We observe truths by seeking truths. And we seek truths by observing the universe.

The mind is a device that can shift and observe shifting paradigms. The centerpiece of this process is the capacity to perceive the universe by conceptualizing and synthesizing concepts in virtual space of imagination.

Listen to Philsuk. Cast your fortune in whims of time but do not surrender to perplexities arising from abstraction of time. In time, the circumstances metamorphose; truths appear and disappear; answers are revealed and dismissed. In time, we may unreel a perfect symmetry of perception imagining a virtual universe more idealistic than the real universe.

Deeva, humbled by Sima's daring proposition, approached her, held her hand and recited.

<blockquote>
What really matters is choice of being
Alive amidst harmony of thoughts
Comfortable with self and the self
One with all and none truly alike
Is there life before and after me
Oh yes, life goes on
But neither for me nor within me
What then is humanity
Is it universality of our dreams
Is it harmony of our thoughts
Is it to listen before one is listened to
Is it to give before one is given to
Is it to share what little there is to share
</blockquote>

Life is simple things that come our way
Or complicated expressions we decide along the way
Whatever it may be, here and now
I feel it deep within me
And those who fill their lives with passion
Cajoled by existential harmony
Immersed in absurd reality of everything and nothing
High on awareness
Absorb cries of despair
Live a glorious dream
And die a peaceful moment
To join thoughtless fixtures
Shaping the universe

Time passed in monotony of repetition. We followed the path set in front of us by those before us as we defined the path for those following us. I felt it sad the coming generations have to deal with inadequacies of the generations before them.

We tended the usual chores of cleaning, nourishing, and mending. The routine was undeniably fixed. We followed them with neurotic conviction.

Gathering around a flaming fire was the last and most pleasing act of the day when minds engaged as bones warmed and muscles rested.

That brisk desert night, Darvish with his usual manner of reducing complexities to tangible norms, circled around the fire with his arms stretched, one pointing to earth and the other to sky. He circled to a dizzying state of euphoria. Measuring each circumference with obsessive exactness, he let loose his stored anger.

I have seen youth raised in deprivation, and they had no choice.

Suddenly, he stopped, gathered himself and approached Deeva.

Watching them I saw injustice, and they had no choice.

He raised his voice in seeming disgust.

Watching them I felt ugliness of reality surrounding them, and they had no choice.

He approached Sima. His face blushed with fury as he raised his voice higher.

Seeing their sunken eyes, I saw wrong, and they had no choice.

He jumped at Philsuk.

I watched them age to outcasts doomed to a lifetime of allegorical alienation and isolation. And they had no choice.

He stopped, took a deep breath, lowered his voice.

I have watched many suffer disproportionate punishment and judgment as failures. And they had no choice.

Is that not a grave injustice? He shouted.

Is that not enough reason for existence of injustice? How could anyone claim willful governance over its moral integrity under such despicable conditions?

His words resonated deep in my conscience. Caught in a dilemma of absurd and real, I raised my voice high.

I must meet The Great One to inquire of the essence of things. I must meet The Great One to discuss the meaning of humanity. I must meet The Great One to explore harmony of thought and action. What wonders besiege this life is an absurdity I must absolve in the presence of The Great One.

Darvish put his hand on my shoulder stopping me to a halt. I obeyed.

You see a master in The Great One. How dare you worship The Great One? Your subservient presumption reduces The Great One's sublime character to redundancy of an idol. How dare you to think of such an obtuse idea?

Darvish was a respected friend. His words froze my mind and body.

We are masters of justification. He stared at me with bulging eyes.

We are masters of falsehood. We yearn for a hierarchy of reason to measure our worth, but hierarchy of persuasion often measures our worth. I have spent a lifetime redeeming myself. I have exhausted a lifetime learning how to be right. I have searched for reasons to sway my reasoning by illusion of being right. How I yearn to be just. How I yearn to be good and right. I justify repulsive deeds and deadly means to convince myself right.

In reality, all I have done is justify discrimination, tolerate hunger, ignore poverty and elevate myself with material distinctions. I have embraced falsehood to prove myself righteous. Here and now, within the winding paths of this cryptic destiny, I declare myself inhuman. I shall no more justify. He shouted.

Here and now, I declare loud and clear, I will aim at compassion. That is what I envision as my destiny, a dream called humanity.

I had rarely seen Darvish so possessed. Sima stood by, all the while watching and admiring him. I shivered from head to toe as he squeezed my shoulder with unbearable force. He stood solid, frozen in time. My arm fell asleep, but I did not dare move. Sima rushed to our rescue. She gently removed his hand placing it on her lips. Darvish spread his arms around her and cried. She cried. I stood frozen. Deeva stooped his head and recited.

Make no mistake
Life is a quagmire of mistakes
First, one is embroiled in innocence of ignorance
And this ecumenical notion of life
With chaos at helm
We realize it in perturbed states

Before plunging deep in pleasure
And announce decadence greatest reality of our lives

Yes, I am inundated with briefness of time
My time, for all time, is a temporary time
Yes, I must actualize myself, over and over
Yes, I edify my sense of self in liberal ethos of fairness
Yes, I actualize my happiness in imagination
And realize my inhumanity
Over and over
Yes, we have the power to be contemporary
Affectionate, spontaneous
Explore the world of "Life is too short"
And welcome existential equality

It is deep, too deep, to condense life in a single idea
Watch that idea rise with intensity of emotion
And disappear with precision of universal diction
It is deep, very deep, to reason life
To know I am but endearing thoughts
Of a quiescent understanding
That life is
A collection of axioms in a matrix of infinite
With fixtures of our choosing
Something that is everything
But spells nothing
It is deep, too deep, to know
Life is measured with pain and pleasure

Do not heed all-encompassing answers. There may be none, said Sima. Her breaths were shallow and fast. She seemed beside herself.

As reality of mundane repetition dull excitement with apathy the thrill fades and caustic euphemisms erode optimism. Think deep this gathering of events. Do not pacify your conscience by fear, absolutism or submission. Do not expose your awareness to indignant notions of losing your willful quintessence.

The night faded darker, inviting our tired minds and worn down bodies to trust nature, close gates of reality by closing our eyes and open our minds to the absurd world of dreams. Soon, all was quiet except for the night crawlers whose life had just begun.

I woke next morning with an indelible urge to decipher announcements of early birds and declare my own. I searched but found no mathematical reason to feelings induced by chattering birds. Tossed in the air, giggling mad, I swung in circles announcing that day a glorious day.

Announcing my courtship of innate and contrived ideas, I woke to witness Philsuk at her finest.

Our ancestors succumbed to the notion of protection by mythological beings, she explained to Darvish.

From household masters to village keepers, from kings to lords, the authoritarian hierarchy was maintained with reward and punishment. The household masters abused, used, sold and exchanged members of their family or clan. They pillaged villages and towns. They subdued their subjects, crushed their will and forced them into submission. They adopted moral and ethical constructs that assured their sovereignty and supremacy. They promoted absolute authority a justifiably imposed principle given to them by rulers of the universe. As representatives on Earth, they assumed jurisprudence a reflection of their master's wisdom. They were convinced of their supremacy in this life and thereafter for they saw no other reason for their prosperity. With such moral and ethical matrix, they enjoyed what they pillaged without remorse. Cloaked by a surreptitious and false sense of moral authority they committed most repressive acts and felt justified.

Paradigms have certainly changed. I do not see a hierarchy of authority, nor am I enslaved by the notion of submission to authority. I do not fool myself with moral constructs of higher or lower constructs. I have a different set of fears. I fear hypocrisy. I fear dying without a free conscience. I fear losing awareness, not knowing its complexities.

I have risen from ashes of submission to cherish my freedom to will. I have learned to insulate my awareness from pestiferous sentiments. My willful self is adopting a new composure. It values freedom higher than virtue. To be virtuous I must be free. For certain, I must be free.

Deeva stood by all the while, listening attentively. After a long silence, he recited.

It is baffling what this universe is about
And why us, thinking of its totality
Why us, alone, without a contact

The idea of universe as a thought
A single mind, or simply a conscience
Reflects dictatorship that ruled us
The idea of universe as a collection of minds
Reflects Democracy that rules us
The idea of universe as a harmony of free wills
Reflects the future, I hope

In our brief history
We have measured time beginning
Extended ourselves from ephemeral to fastidious
Seeded our compassion on this planet
And what a planet
What better depiction of good fortune than Earth

If we could achieve so much in so little
What wonders we could expose, in time
So much time, so much space, so many possibilities

The idea of life as a collection of minds
The idea of life as synchronicity of living and nonliving
These are human models
Reflecting human realities

On this trail of wishful thoughts and impressive realities, crossing a roaring river, climbing a steep rise or withstanding wind and storm were wholesome expressions of living.

Nature was alive and turbulent. It intrigued the mind with details of its derivatives. Its chaotic nature chafed the mind as its colorful designs calmed senses to a hypnotic state of tranquility.

In time, the passage of time amidst delightful surroundings fomented many revealing experiences of enlightened nature. In time, a surrealistic sense of actualized state illuminated my mind with nostrums of happiness.

Eternity is an illusion of delusional magnitude. I reasoned.

Its boundaries are incomprehensible. Its significance transmutes every assumption. Its meaning is diluted by absurdity of infinite.

Eternity is a bizarre declaration. It is a source of comfort to minds incapable of comprehending their eventual state of nothingness. To many, nothingness is the antithesis of awareness. It frightens them to delusional states.

There are many pathways, from the extreme of announcing oneself universal and eternal to complete surrender and helplessness, to absorb the enormity of time-space and prevent the self from dilution in its enormity. I rather choose the path of compassion and empathy, the path of freedom and humility. Without a compassionate path, virtue can mold a pernicious mosaic yielding moral odyssey an adventure in bad fates. Without empathy, diluted with insidious and invidious paradigms, life becomes a passage from mundane thoughts to mundane deeds to mundane ends. Without humility, the universe is a medium cold and cruel.

On a hot sandy day beneath the heat of blazing sun when lips dried cracking tight, when heels callused painful, I found refuge below a towering rock. Darvish approached me as I leaned against refreshing cold granite. I looked him in the eye.

What reason compels us to yearn for this illusion of immortal living? Why waste time with immortal thoughts? I asked.

He spread himself on the rock, savoring the pleasure of its cooling effect and explained.

Long ago an old traveler on her deathbed called upon me. In her few remaining moments, for some unknown reason, she remembered a question I had once asked. She felt it had gone unanswered.

She told me with choking voice: if the effort is pure and the intention sincere, then the initial aim of attaining a goal is an abstraction the meaning of which shall continuously change before the journey is over. Once a mind casts its fortune on a definite path, the act that begins the path is subject to contortions dictated by realities of the path.

She then asked me if my question was answered. I did not remember the question, but for the sake of moment, I passionately held her hand, kissed its palm, and assured her my total admiration for profoundness of her response. Her eyes lightened up bright before dimming flat.

You lied to a dying mind, I protested in amazement.

I lied to comfort a dying mind. Sima is right. There is no right or wrong, only circumstances that demand such interpretations. There is no good or bad, but thoughts conceived to justify or satisfy demands of a circumstance.

Darvish closed eyes for a deeper enjoyment. I continued the conversation where he left off.

I once asked a companion what the virtue of seeking The Great One was about? His name was Rumi. I had followed him for sometime. His aloof loneliness and astute observations had caught my attention. He contemplated a great deal in his usual manner and offered a revealing explanation.

The journey through life is the essence of life. The beginning and the end are a trifle in the span of one's existence. The experience of living is the defining axiom of a mortal. Since each has a unique journey through life, there are as many essences as seekers.

The self who dares a path is a self who carves a path. Surely, we are following what others have traced before us, but in each step, we modify their experience to suit our purpose.

All the answers are before and within us. The answers are before us for the universe is all around us. The answers are within us for the universe is perceived by us.

Each mind is a flower in a vast garden. Each flower has the potential to blossom most enchanting forms. Conversely, it could vanish meaningless amidst a gathering of reflections. The challenge is to open mind and absorb significance of other flowers in the garden. The challenge is to perceive oneself an integrated part of the garden and separate from others. The challenge is to seek freedom without dictating freedom.

By the time Rumi finished his remarks an audience had gathered around him. Rumi was unaware of their presence. He was a shy mind with a frightfully deep sense of solitude. As his eyes left the skies and descended on earth, he realized his predicament as the focus of attention. He shied away hurriedly, losing us amidst the seekers, and the wavering shades, and the distant stars, and the absurd ideas the rest of us impressed on each other and him.

Sima shook her head, cleansed the sweat off her brow, and leaned against my shoulder.

Self-interest is a cathartic notion, said Darvish. It numbs the mind with confusion of subjective and objective. Spry minds, driven with ambitious thoughts, reveal ideas that excite the collective. Imagination can liberate the individual and the civilization from physical and physiological bonds of age-old adaptations and modules of behavior. It could propel the civilization on a destiny that knows no boundaries.

Am I proposing collective human imagination a boundless entity of unforeseen dimensions? Indeed, I am.

The Great One, he shouted sending shivers down my spine, is a period at the end of a long imaginative statement. The Great One is neither the statement nor meaning of the statement.

Shaken by Darvish's youthful daring, Sima addressed Philsuk, Darvish, and me.

Tell me, all you young ones who take pride in your strength to fathom truths, are you free? Is the sky above us free? Are we, as a civilization, free? Do you think of freedom at the height of your hormonal drive?

Darvish fell to his knees, then to her feet. Sima sat, quickly holding his head, pressing it onto her chest.

Forgive my insolent rapture, he cried. Sima cried. I cried. Deeva grabbed us in a circle of arms and recited.

> I am a small chasm in galaxy of dreams
> My mind matures ravenous in imagination
> To fathom eternity of compassion
> Only to realize significance of a living moment
> In small goblets of affection
>
> Metamorphosing crystal clear
> I find certain in uncertain
> And confess in earnest
> We are besieged by brackish ideas
> By quandary of happiness and age
>
> Am I too obtuse, too diluted
> How deep is my sense of truth
> What illusions this moment conjures
> In every occasion I see passion and reason
> And every reason is a flotilla of occasions

Imprisoned in domain of moral and virtue
Caged in a labyrinth of undetermined values
I try to prove myself righteous
By exposing my best moments
Slowly revealing millions of years
Compacted to modules I am

In time, I hope
As chain of experiences leaps onto future
Exposing my chained self
I will realize
I am my own caustic insolent awareness
A small chasm in galaxy of dreams

If The Great One is so above the fray, why not call him a divine existence and accept him as our master? I wondered.

Sima looked at me puzzled. The Great One is another human with all the human attributes. The Great One is a freewill devoted to the notion of compassion. The Great One is a symbol of what humans can achieve. The Great One is too free to be divine.

She fell into a deep meditative silence before repeating her words.

The Great One is too free to be divine.

Philsuk was engaged in an unknown dictum of intense absorption. Her eyes were fixed and contracted.

There is no supremacy in our quest for higher awareness, she said. Truth is, with or without awareness, we all perish, disintegrate, and join the inanimate universe. The notion of higher awareness can be as painful as rewarding. It can as easily subjugate and insulate the self as it could free the self.

Individual life is an echo of images synthesized by totality we attempt to expound. We spend a lifetime seeking that illusive totality. As a perceptual entity and without a physical manifest, it escapes our awareness. Most of us settle with simple and primitive explanations, give up the pursuit or live make-believe lives. Some of us, not content with superficiality of proposed ideas, seek the all-encompassing idea of everything with tedious mathematical inquiry.

A flickering moth or a willful immortal, each has its domain of everything and nothing. Each has its unique capacity of detecting universal fields and dimensions.

It is said The Great One despises the notion of divinity. Such thoughts are meager ideas imposed by meager minds to elevate their egocentric existence to a universal level. The claim to divinity is a claim to supremacy. Minds that pretend impressions of divine knowledge have a tendency to drive their conscience to rigidity of absolutism. They become alienated with a unique illusion of perfection.

To humans, perfection is measurable and attainable in small increments. This declaration of self is placing the individual at the center of the universe while observing farthest of the periphery. Being at the center implies starting from nothing and expanding to contain something that aims at everything. It is an attempt to absolve the mystery of life and death with a newly constructed, socially amalgamated, virtual theory of everything.

Gazing at high mountains ordained with snow and ice, I became convinced the journey was an experience in self-revelation.

I turned to Darvish for consultation.

What drives humanity? I wondered.

Darvish with his idealistically realistic mind stretched his legs, laying back to the comfort of a weeping willow.

In this passage of sane and insane, in this cohesion of aware and unaware, the aim is to evolve a collection of free minds decorated with flexible attributes of compassionate texture, he said.

The aim is to evolve to humans ordained with most assiduous truisms. The aim is to evolve into a great one on the path of reaching The Great One. The Great One is an abstraction of human metaphors. Only in person would I acknowledge its reality.

Reality is now and here. Reality is sensations I experience. Reality is our collective perceptions. Reality is the beginning and end of all our aims.

The question of interest is the speed at which we perceive time. Is time constant or variable? Is it a convention of convenient human use, or something universal? Perhaps harmony of ideas can lead to perfect symmetry of ideas. It all begins with perception of self, matures to perception of universe, and ends with the realization of nothingness. Asymmetry of being and awareness is a congruity of many dimensions we can unfold in imagination alone.

Rumi, who had kept silent, seemed stricken with a revelation.

Life is a game of mysteries, he said with suiting calm. The evolving image of perfect symmetry happened, on the speculative stage of human imagination, long after its reality in a fraction of time. We do not know what this perfection entails. We observe its manifestations in isolated conditions. We aim for it as a mathematical perfection unable to comprehend what it means to perceive a perfect universe in real time and awareness?

He turned to Darvish.

Do you know what perfect symmetry of awareness entails?

Darvish shied away.

He turned to Philsuk.

Do you know what it means to have universal awareness?

Philsuk looked at me for an answer. She did not wish to disturb Rumi with inappropriate words.

Deeva came to our rescue.

> In marble castles of imaginative dreams
> Curiosity brews creativity
> Creativity reaps awareness
> And then, nothing
>
> Would you like to know my predicament
> To be sure, my idiom
> Everything I think is an affectation
> And then, nothing
>
> Should I tell you one
> Life is an acronym
> I am in bondage, a mindset
> In some stone-age boundary
> The man who dragged lions by the tail
> Fearless, he is my goblet of identity
> And then, nothing
>
> From childhood to maturity
> I am right, then good
> Then definitely wrong
> And then, nothing
> From abstraction to reaction
> I accept, mutate, expose, impose
> Till passion and reason reap a balanced judgment
> I become fearless, searching my own lions
> But find them extinct
> And then, nothing
>
> In this life of sagacious sages
> Nothing is certain
> Only ameliorated in our conscience
> Go on, affect a change
> Reason life its syntax
> Reason pleasure
> Reason truths

And then, nothing

Life is a tale of metaphors
Would you like to know all of its eleven dimensions
Would you like to be a solid-stator
Looking in mirror of quantum abstraction
I am, you are
I think, you love
I die, you live
In no time
All measured in time
And then, nothing

One day I came upon a frail woman of silvery hair and bony stature. Dim eyed and hunched back she dared every step with as much vigor as the youngest. I walked beside her, observed her as she observed me. In the usual manner of the trail, I bowed, said greetings, and kissed her hands as she did mine.

As I shied away from her gentle eyes, I inquired how long she had been set upon this journey.

She smiled.

Time escapes me. She gazed ahead.

All I remember is passing of the sun, and the stars, and the chattering birds.

I have matured to measure life with thoughts and thoughts alone. Each sunrise unreels a reflection of all. And each moment is a gateway to totality of all.

Life repeats itself with uncanny precision. The closer I look; I see no repetition. Life is orderly and disorderly at the same instance of deliberation. I used to think it is measured with time. Now I know. I measure time to measure my own passing.

My days are numbered, but numbers do not measure my days. I measure life with happiness, with reflection, with transparency, with imaginative tapestry, and above all, with compassion.

In the domain of awareness, each idea is a rich gamut of wonders. Each thought is a pandemonium of discrete images we use to contrive distinct images. Impervious to constraints of time, my imagination does what it pleases in the manner it pleases. Such is my perception of time-space-mind. It is a manifestation of my existence with imaginative strings that span the universe I observe and imagine.

I graciously dared challenge her observant mind.

If death is the end, if absolute disintegration is destiny of a mortal, is it not reasonable to pursue pleasure, or immerse oneself in joys of an indulging life? I could satiate my senses with saccharine stimulants and die the same death? Must I subject myself to the pain of hardship to contrive details of life? Pleasure is a measurable aggregate with immediate consequences. Life is too short to waste in a conundrum of logic. Why forfeit tangible for the intangible?

She fell silent, contemplating my thoughts as if they had touched something in her. Distracted by some contentious thought, she attempted a steep rise. Her steps grew stronger, defying her physical reality.

Sima approached me, examined me with a stern look demanding full attention.

You speak the truth. She paused. That is good, my son. Your manners are gentle. That is even better. And your demeanor is innocent. That is admirable, but your combined countenance bores deep into an old seeker's conscience evoking painful thoughts. That is regrettable. You have much to learn in verses of virtue. You have a long journey to lightness of compassion.

I lowered my head in reverence. How dare I disturb an old mind? I bowed, impounding my awareness for a brief resetting of its moral imperatives.

By now, she had gathered her senses as she stood atop a hill examining the valley below.

Awareness is a magical feast with empowering manifestations. She faced me with gentlest of eyes.

You wonder why the trail? Why such a desolate journey?

She raised her head high. The sky was blue-clear. A crisp mountain breeze entertained us with a steady stream of freshness. She inhaled, held it a short while, exhaled.

Life is a long trail with many winding paths of unknown beginnings and ends.

She put her hand on my shoulder. I felt her energy.

I have learned much on this trail. I have learned to observe. I have learned to admire. I have learned to reflect. I have learned to discipline my senses. I have learned to decipher intrepid ways of existence.

The mind and body must merge a unity to absolve dilemmas. The two spheres must act in harmony to contrive sagacious concepts. I have learned to weave a web of my own to gauge the balance between conditioned and imaginative.

I have learned to act with caution, to labor truths without worshiping truth. I have learned to stand tall. I have learned to forgive and be forgiven. I have learned rapture of solitude. I have learned art of compassion. I have learned joy of giving.

She stood robust. Poised with a newly acquired moral supremacy, she continued her thoughts with conviction of an achieved artisan.

The power of passion, the many convoluted ways of affection, without aleatory outcomes, is a rewarding path I have learned to cherish. I have learned not waste away as time whittles my existence. I have learned a deeper sense of happiness.

I was charmed with the persuasive gentleness of her reasoning. A pleasing energy shook me with sudden excitement. Like a child receiving a most desired toy, I felt saturated with gratification.

The journey is indeed worth the effort. I reminded myself.

It is the essence of my life as well as lives that help me with that essence. The reality of our mortal panacea is a ubiquitous notion maturing through our social confluence. Conscience disappears when a mind ceases to exist, and a new one begins when another life appears. In this conspicuous manner, we become brief observers of life. That is an assertion I will hold until proven otherwise.

By now, the myth of The Great One had grown beyond the realm of possibilities. With each passing day, attributes of increasingly precocious and surrealistic complexion were bestowed to The Great One.

Sima often reminded us to differentiate myth from fact.

Time has a way of distorting the mind. She emphasized. The mind amalgamates cryptic images of real and wishful. A simple fact or conjecture, in time, could metamorphose into a myth of epochal proportions as it traverses from mind to mind.

Beware my friends, said Darvish. Observe reality as it lies before you. Understand its broken symmetries. Understand the possibility of its perfection, but do not waste your brief excursion in a paradigm of living to pursue abstractions stemming from worshiping one thing or another. Indulge in knowledge. Elevate your salacious mind to the splendor of imaginative living. But do not bend your will if you do not find satisfaction.

Deeva shook his head in agreement and recited.

> The eyes of lightness flash vibrant waves
> Creeping depths of mind, they beam bright
> Slowly, a new dawn is creeping upon us
> And all you seemingly brilliant clique, awake

Shine your minds lucid
Shine your dreams imaginative
But do not await its coming
Do not await its coming

Rivers soar carrying afloat a change
Seasons pass springing foliage of dreams
Awake you morally intoxicated clowns
Awake to waves of love and fury
Awake to reality
But do not await its coming
Do not await its coming

In this flamboyant land of sagacious sages
Land of awareness and acceptance
Land of distinctions or be it, land of dreams
Twine your luminous image
Shine the universe its newly reasoned truths
But do not await its coming
Do not await its coming

Achievements and moral distinctions
Class differentiation
Separating mind from mind
And truth from minds, then
Calling for justice by minds separated
Awake all you seemingly clever clowns
Awake to reality of extinction
But do not await its coming
Do not await its coming

Old mind of thoughts ponders passing of life
His astute disposition allayed
To passing river he whispers words of affection
And disintegrates in inane reality of existence
Boring deep in heart of mighty universe

Awake to this old mans' dream

Awake an old man and dream
But do not await its coming
Do not await its coming

Tired of a long and arduous walk amidst green pastures, we circled around a spring. It gingerly nourished a few desolate plants before fading in the sand. Long after a small fire burned itself dim, we molded our bodies in the ground.

Before succumbing to the necessity of sleep, I noticed a sudden bright light in deep space.

Pointing at the beaming light, I turned to Darvish.

Do you see that star shining its last fury before collapsing into ambiguity of a black hole? Do you see it as clearly as I do?

He sat quietly, too tired to heed my call.

I faced Sima.

Long after light fades and darkness rules, before dreams are forgotten and imagination begins to spin the mind in wicked ways, comes a tranquil moment when thoughts resonate from harmonious tunes of perfection. And I see such perfection in that distant light.

She listened passively, too tired to heed an answer.

Nothing made sense as I reflected on an inner feeling of tranquility. I imagined a bright star fallings into a newly formed black hole.

Philsuk lay flat, absorbing the star with every bit of her curious self. I turned to her.

Long before reason fades and passions flare, after emotions are drained, long before a horizon ensnares the mind in an ascetic state of forever nothing, I prognosticate myself silly wondering what it was, what it is, what it will be. At such moments of disarray imploding stars become mere objects of fascination.

Look at that shining star fuming last of its fury before collapsing onto itself for a greater absorption. Who knows, it may keep on collapsing to a smaller volume of infinite absorption.

Do you see it?

Consciousness resembles a collapsed star, insulated in its own image, unable to escape its reasoning.

Is there any sense in all of this?

Are we living a brief insignificant moment? Are we here to waste ourselves silly? Am I replacing meaningless moments with meaningful expressions? Are we to surrender to chaos? Are we to define the universe in our image? Is the universe a campground of our imagination? Is it awaiting us, and others like and unlike us, to give it credence, virtue, purpose and meaning?

Philsuk was wide-awake and attentive.

Thoughts resemble flow of a river, she said calmly.

Listen to Deeva and venture in imaginative dimensions. Toss your fortune in unknown worlds. But do not await its coming. Do not await any comings.

Your thoughts are rushing down a steep flow. There will soon be a moment of calm, a plateau to ease your senses. There will be a time to brush your thoughts with delicate strokes before another rapture in confusion. Learn to ride roaring thoughts as if a roaring river.

I once was distraught by death of a close companion, I said remembering a distant experience.

As I witnessed her last desperate attempt at life, she squeezed my hand, looked at me frightfully deep, and whispered with quivering lips and frightened eyes, "I do not want to die."

I was a child with no comprehension of death. With all my childhood ignorance, I recognized her fear. I then, for the first time, feared the finality of death. I find it strange, death of a star does not evoke the same painful emotions.

My life has changed since. That moment has remained with me in all phases of my awareness. It is not fair to endure the truth of death, or face a paradigm that shifts the state of a mind, at such young age. Then again, perhaps it is best to realize finality of death at younger years to appreciate life.

Years later, in a moment of melancholic reflection, I sought solace in Deeva. As I remembered details of that moment, he listened without uttering a word. I adored his silent demeanor. It calmed my senses. How could he be so reserved, so refined in the art of empathy?

That brief distraction enabled me to reflect on reality. I let go despair. I let go my emotions and cried. All the while, he sat shoulder-to-shoulder, keenly attentive, without a word, without a single word.

Limits are for humans to shatter, said Philsuk. In every turn of every bend, I see a struggle against limits that scuff our existence with irrelevant thoughts and tasks.

Your stormy mind is caught in an abyss of "nothing" without comprehending the ubiquitous expanse of "everything." Use your imagination to create a balance. Maintain equilibrium between perception of "everything" and "nothing."

I was taken aback by Philsuk's patronizing words. What is life worth if it ends in nothing? I asked.

Philsuk was not impressed.

What then, you wonder, is living worth? She said calmly.

It is certainly not worth slavery by misconception, or the agony of despair, nor hypocrisy of falsehood. The understandings that reveal are worth living for. The capacity to hope, aiming for harmony and awareness are worth living for. Happiness and harmony are worth living for. Perception of reality is worth living for.

The mind sees itself as it defines itself by setting limits to perception of itself. Understanding this inconspicuous reality requires knowledge of self. It demands to undo nature of self. It repudiates complacency to idiosyncrasies of self.

To understand the cryptic nature of self requires understanding the delicate balance between the private, the social, and the universal components of the self.

In the path of understanding this balance many surrender, lose perspective and attempt to fill the void with devotion and submission. Others expose themselves to the trappings that await them in the convoluted world of imagination. Others ride the journey accepting its dictates with complacent attitude. Others set their own path. They are bold and courageous minds with willful audacity of daring complexion.

On the path of life, though we traverse seemingly similar paths, each has a unique journey of its own. The task is to unravel the riddle of self, fathom its components, differentiate its subtle conjugates and does so with affection and compassion. The task is to imagine. Imagination is a fragmented, freely floating state, in all times and places.

There are many truths I must ponder. For now, in this hour of tired bones and restless thoughts, I shall be content with the peace and comfort this imploding star affords me, I said.

She closed eyes, leaving me with a sky that spoke a million and none. I endured my melancholic moments until stars faded in a timeless and disjointed dream world.

Years passed. Our path kept us marching down the steep valley of indecision, across the soaring peaks of uncertainty, through the narrow passageways of obscurity to land in small islands of certainty. Time was measured by cyclical calls of nature and nurture. Spring flared its assorted fixtures. Autumn spread a domain of yellow-orange. Winter and summer came and passed. The trail remained solid, irresistible and irrefutably real.

Time-present was time-eternal. Without a meaning of its own, time was defining truth of our mortal existence.

For all times and every reason, from ambiguity of partial awareness to ecstasy of enlightened awareness, my senses radiated a voracious desire to absorb quintessential truths.

The notion of a unified theory, a perfect symmetry, translucent and transmutable, twirled a presumptive image of existence in my curious mind. In a brief moment of revelation, I saw it clearly. Enigma of individual reasoning is an ethos, a deciduous virtual process to weave truths. Benevolent thoughts stem from superimposed evolutionary modules. Object-oriented metaphors of imagination are a reflection of relative subtleties inundating human perception of reality, and my existence is a collection of many speculative inferences.

Time spent in solitude with surrounding sounds and sites was a meditative process. Nature, with its chaotic demands, had many surrealistic ways of intriguing the mind.

I realized the degrading weak force an imminent foe. It imposed its majestic force as it withered willful quintessence with impeccable persistence. Willful living, in its brief odyssey as a certainty, is a formidable force as well. Its existence is the antithesis of chaos. Willful thinking is a human gateway to possibilities. It can extend imaginative boundaries across the universe.

The companionship of seekers was an emancipating experience. Their presence replenished my enthusiasm from a reservoir of life I discovered in them. They gave much more than they received. In giving they emitted compassion. In giving they formulated their caring selves. In giving they defined their existence.

One day, as we attempted, in earnest, upon a path, I caught Parva in a distraught state I could not fathom. The old man of the trail appeared frail and failing. His head was lower than usual. His posture was deformed, and his breath labored. I hurried to his side.

Is there something wrong? I inquired as I supported his arm.

No, he replied with peace of mind I had not witnessed in him. On the contrary, I feel immersed in a liberating state. I can see now. I see it clearly. Before one faces death one lets go all the chains, all the obligations, all the sorrows, all the revelations and afflictions that gave meaning to life.

I feel so free. Nothing endures but "nothing."

I can see now.

He fell silent while I was tormented with the significance of his words. He did not look well.

My time has come to part with this unending trail of mysteries. He muttered.

Before I vanish into nothingness, I must share with you a revelation.

I mused with the thought of him suffering from fever. His fading eyes convinced me otherwise.

My frail existence can no longer withstand the demands of the universe. He labored.

It is time for me to accept the inevitable and surrender to chaos.

The universe demands my disposition. I have withstood it long. The mind feels it can will forever, but the body yields much sooner.

My breath runs short with slightest exertion. My memory is fading faster than I can recall. To maintain integrity of conscience is too great a task now. Nothing makes sense. Even spoken words seem unnecessary. There is nothing more to say, nothing to explain, nothing to seek, nothing to achieve.

Time-space and consciences are all irrelevant. I am neither alive nor dead. I am a probability soon to vanish. I can feel nothingness.

His words were cut short by his labored breaths. Tears fell on my face. My lips quivered. My heart throbbed. I felt it wise not to speak. I felt it befitting to let the old man compose his last moments as he wished. The pain of losing a beloved friend was difficult to bear. I agonized in despair as I realized my ineptness to help. The circumstance was beyond my control. This was a process between a consciousness and the universe. And the universe was not about to relinquish its dominance.

That day, I learned to respect death as the most intimate moment of life, when one lets go of integrity of awareness. In such an instance of transition, before the awareness vanishes, a singular notion of existence is achieved as the sentient existence and material existence approach a unified manifest. The highly organized material existence is devoured from within and without as awareness disappears, never to be seen again.

He gasped for air. His head fell low on his shoulders, itself bent on his round abdomen flattened by gravity. Soon, he closed eyes for all eternity. I watched his moment of passing with deep sorrow. Before my very eyes, in my arms, I watched him pass from something to nothing.

As a river overflowing after years of drought, I wept. I wept for losing a friend. I wept for losing a mentor whose affection I had tasted. I wept for fragility of life. I wept for that moment of reality when I shall pass as well. I wept for all the lost minds dotting my mind of memories.

Tender care of many suiting hands consoled me to composure. The old women of compassion, dearest Sima, grasped me in her bosom diluting my pain with warmth of her being. She stooped to her knees and placed Parva in a respectable position. Deeva kneeled, grasped Parva's hand, placed it on his shivering lips, and recited.

One by one moments come
For passionate friends none has gone
Rest assured you beggars of time
Death is yet to come
And I
In search of truths
Shall graze pastures of thought
To find truths I know not

To us mortals
Life is an incipient immortal tale
Moments of dawn
A golden walk on a silvery pond
Crunch of decaying impassive lives
Persistence of wishful thoughts
Isolated, together, in unison
Selfishly centered
Our combined consonance
A belated concentric bequest
That there is no higher loss
Than death of a beloved mind

Darvish, as usual, attempted to reduce awesome truths to simple abstractions with tangible connotations.

When the senses fail there is no pain, he said placing his hand on Parva's forehead.

The idea that consciousness preexisted and shall survive physical degradation is wishful. Those who dared not face their mortal end reasoned existence of a reservoir of awareness. They sought solace in connection with an entity of immortal attributes.

Truth is, awareness is a manifestation of our material existence. If this notion is understood, then the conviction will be devoted to enjoying what brief time we have.

Philsuk stared at Darvish relaying her displeasure at the timing of his boldness.

She sat next to me, held my hand, and placed it on her lips.

When our ancestors realized all humans disintegrate, the thought of losing awareness became too painful. Some assumed awareness a lasting gift released from a decaying body to meet its next destiny. That destiny evolved into a complex myth of its own.

We begin life impervious to realities. The dilemma grows in magnitude as the mind, intoxicated by joys of youthful energy, confuses hormonal vigor with immortality.

Should I choose the path of truth, asked Sima? Should I decimate myself in psychoanalysis? Should I be an existentialist? No matter what persuasion, living is an allegory of perceptions. What I am and what I wish to be, are the realities of who I am. Perceptions change, so does the reality of who I am.

Perfection, affliction, remorse, love, disdain, none are eternal.

An abject composition of images cruel and imperfect, I am an embroiled portrait of many designs.

Betaken by Sima's revealing words, I turned to Deeva.

Driven by emotionally charged hormones, enslaved by socially imposed images, I am a story that tells the story. In living color, obsessed with reality, we decide whether events are myths, mysteries, or easily explainable. The answers and conclusions are ours to synthesize.

What if life is an illusion? What if life has many dimensions folding on each other creating the illusion of existence? What if we are caught in a dimension, in the process of folding on itself, creating an illusion of universe mightier than it really is?

Irrespective of what it may or may not be, we cannot escape persisting realities of life, said Darvish.

There is no denying history and the evolution of life. These are real events with real consequences. We, as individuals and collectives, acknowledge and deal with real thoughts and feelings.

Deeva sat next to us and recited.

Why life
What purpose my purpose
At times primitive
At times brilliantly majestic
At times logic escapes its own reason
At times reason becomes its own logic

Is it our function to fathom enormity
Resolve mysteries to simple components
And wish our brief lives a lasting reason
After all, it is just another day
Another moment
Another spin of another quark
Another dichotomy of hormonal gloom and delight

Obscured by abstractions of mortal life
Not knowing why or how or which pretension
With brilliantly sculpted thoughts and simple ideas
We live brief tales of varying consequences
And die a pacified moment of no consequence

I sat beside Darvish. Sima arranged Parva's hair, wiped his face, held his head in hands, reached down and laid a kiss on his forehead.

Rest in peace my friend. You have lived well. She covered his face as we covered our minds to his face. Thus, the journey, from an unknown beginning to an unknown end, ceased for another seeker. The rest of us continued the journey on this amorphous trail.

Watching the lanterns sway from an unseen point ahead to a hazy past troubled my mind with something purely human.

Will I see its end before the end of my time?

I realized myself caught in raptures of a newly conceived awareness. I began to imagine my own "everything" and "nothing." I became an observer of my passing. I watched myself change, molding a new image as I changed.

The innocence of ignorance, the childhood euphemisms, gave way to the enigma of emancipating revelations. The change was from within. A new light illuminated the dark desires with passionate feelings. Life was increasingly a revealing experience, as the imaginative minds illuminated our lives with contiguous streams of revelation.

The trail wove its path deeper in time-space-mind. Many questions of puzzling nature were raised along the path.

Can the individual transcend the domain of freewill? How then, can awareness mandate its tranquility? What is an ideal state of awareness? What is the optimal discourse between a mind and the universe? How can a self transcend its confined senses? Can happiness be synthesized with hormones and enzymes?

As questions grew complicated, they became riddled with endless dichotomies the extent of which could not be discerned by one imagination alone.

In one occasion of our usual gathering, as seekers were seated in neat circles, Darvish addressed the crowd in his daring manner.

Is the realization of existence a unique phenomenon?

He paused as the rest of us reflected on the subject.

Is the awareness of self and universe, their conceptualization as a complex reality, a uniquely human characteristic? Is this the highest order of awareness? Is a self a freewill by virtue and scope of its reflections on its freedom? Can a freewill be liberated from constraints of its physical boundaries? Is freedom a necessary pre-requisite for a higher order of awareness? Can individual awareness transcend social constraints to realize greater space of imagination? Can the universe be contained in awareness? Can any form of awareness contain the universe? What exactly is the nature of an awareness that conceptualizes the universe? Is sentience a dimension of the universe manifested by the emergence of neurons?

The questions were too deep to heed quick answers. Silence was the prevailing answer. Once again, Deeva came to our rescue. He rose and circled the audience while reciting a poem.

Tell me, have you seen a black hole
Have you felt its wonder
Look deep inside your shriveled self
There lies a perfect singularity
Do you see it
Is it dense
Is it pure
Is it isolated

Open mind, look deeper
Is your quintessence compassionate
Is it transparent
Is it harmonious
Is it absorbing
Do you see truth in your reflection
Do you sleep well
Is your countenance realized

I am, as you, an isolated mind
I am, as you, searching
I am, as you, hoping

Tell me, do your wings span the oceans

Is your reflection ornate
Is your pride endearing
Are you happy

Let us open eyes to heliopause of vociferous thoughts
Let us expose that compassionate singularity within "us"
Let us reveal truths in unison

Say with me
We are free
Go on, say with me
We are free
Encapsulated by folding dimensions
We are free
Labored by awareness
We are free
Cajoled by chaos
We are free
Caged by probability
We are free
Socially imprisoned
We are free
Say with me
We are free

There lasted a long pause as each seeker contemplated the significance of his words. Sima was the first to reflect.

The killer instinct I inherited from my savage ancestors, and the affection instilled in me as they realized pleasures of living, are tearing my conscience apart. The fears they felt have etched indelible modular scars in my conscience, and the warmth and pleasure they experienced, the joy of having survived another day of calamities, I feel them as well.

Their unceasing quest for pleasure, their lament and joy for one another, their quest for comfort, their elation with success, their emotional dependence on one another, I too feel as those feelings.

How can I not appreciate who they were? As beastly as they lived, they cultivated our lives.

I fear as they feared, but the nature of my fear is transformed. I fear emptiness. I fear nothingness. I fear uncertainty. I fear losing awareness. I fear ignorance. I fear galactic disasters. I fear calamities I have not imagined.

Times have changed; so have the demands of time. I am not a hunter of flesh but ideas. A drastic change in our environment is demanding an evolutionary leap in our physical and imaginative constitution.

The beast and the righteous, the good and the bad, the right and the wrong: these conspicuous manifestations of the psyche are converging with a new and increasingly symmetrical quality. A grand theory of awareness is evolving.

The task is to extend the nonjudgmental and inclusive aspect of social awareness to ensure equality of awareness. The task is to unreel a perfect symmetry of individual and social.

The desert darkness illuminated stars to unequaled sharpness. Shadows flared hazy images. We rested our tired bodies allowing Sima's passionate thoughts to permeate our absorbing minds.

Philsuk looked up to Sima. Human knowledge is growing too paradoxical, too perplexing for the individual to absorb. A new evolutionary leap in our physical constitution is needed to accommodate the accumulated knowledge.

Who are we in this multifaceted life of scrupulous reasoning? Who am I in this socially constrained and an intellectually unbound human universe of many ends and means?

Time escapes me in thoughts, in faraway dreams and distant metaphors, said Sima.

Still, I realize my salvation in dimension of time. At times, it seems a formidable adversary. Other times, it is my savior. And sometimes, it has no significance.

The axiomatic capacity of traversing time through imagination enables us to project our thoughts onto the future.

Will humanity rise above solar destruction and moribund metaphors? Will humans possess a life span long enough to approach immortality? Will future humans reach the climax of absorbing universal transparencies? Will they be able to save the brain and transplant it for another span of life?

These questions infest my troubled conscience, and I see no singularity of answers, no all-encompassing resolutions, no forever scenarios.

The superimposing reality of perfect symmetry in the first instance of universal formation transmuted an event of daunting tapestry that may not be repeated, said Darvish.

For now our concern is focused on our galaxy and how to avoid its calamities? The relationship between awareness and the universe is perplexing. Selection based on physical attributes has given way to selection based on imaginative potential.

Deeva gracefully adjusted himself in the sand while staring deep in the fire. He then recited.

Come come my friends, sit beside me
Open your minds with a cup of tea
Head on knees holding tight
Let us dream mesmerizing scenarios of life

Beauty of a lover is not her kisses
Her fingertips do not bloom forever
Beauty of a lover is her song

Come come my friends, sit beside me

Enjoy life by the sea
Words of sorrow swell hearts
But a yonder mind sprinkles joy

Come come my friends
This autumn night speaks of love
Shadows flare bending on each other tight
Come come my friends
Let us share passion by the moonlight
Let us cherish this moment of life

Many travelers heeded his call. In a rare impetuous moment of emotional radiance, Sima held Deeva, comforting his shivering mind.

I feel you. She pressed her bosom onto him.

Many seekers gathered to share their harmony. Sima looked up at the sky then stared into the fire. I feel the same as you do, she repeated.

I see the iron cast of social imposition molding my thoughts, dissolving my free self to bits and pieces. At the same instance of observation, I sense a growing freewill guiding my existence. Is this contradiction sustainable?

Deeva approached the fire. I moved hastily to open a space. He sat, stretched his legs and examined each and everyone before reciting a poem.

I extend thoughts
To ecstasy of being, aware
I wake up a bright shining resolution
Brush my senses cheerful
Traverse with unknown speeds
Land in distant imaginative frontiers
And wonder
What is significance of being universal
And when I see that nexus
When I transcend wishful and imagine something I am not
In future times and thoughts

Would I still be a human

The intangible power of imagination
Is a human dimension, I suppose
To evoke undaunted slants of certainty
And grasp the universe in its entirety
It is a medium with many membranes
Transcending dimensions and brains

I know, I am a mortal speck
A drone of no wings or fire
I imagine a life bigger than myself
Transcend tantalizingly astonished
Codify my passion for living with symmetry of ideas
And wonder
Will I still be a human
When I actualize myself universal

He looked older than I had seen him. Perhaps I had not dared to acknowledge the end of his time.

Sima held Deeva as dear life itself. I am freer than I have ever been.

She squeezed him tight.

The love I feel is more encompassing than passions I dare. Reflecting inside, I see the enormity of the universe, the universe you have helped me build.

As I delve deeper, I see the solitude, the isolation and a liberating sense of freedom.

The harmony of outer and inner reveals many gates to actualization. I gaze at every gate. They seem light years apart but nanometers afar. I see definite patterns of astonishing simplicity. Some disappear quickly. Some mingle onto others. Some seemingly last forever.

I now behold humanity a lively gathering of harmonious ideas. I behold emotion a vector of understanding.

Sima was immersed in a melancholic state. At such moments, she emanated emotionally charged feelings no other could.

Deeva let go of Sima. Sima kept leaning on his broad shoulder.

In my awareness has risen a new dimension the enforcer of which is passion, she continued.

I see a rising reality transcending dying suns. I see compassion absorbing human aggression.

Silence prevailed as the peace and quiet of the night subsumed our individual solitude. Philsuk disturbed the fire to a better flame.

I have heard much about freedom on this trail, she said.

It is professed in every conversation. In reality, I realize myself a caged bird.

She stood, circled around the fire with grace of a dancer, stopped and rearranged the timber to an ideal glow. The flames reached high piercing the darkness.

Darvish raised his voice.

Isolated in time-space-mind, caged in an increasingly deformed physical appearance, failing to realize inexplicable dimensions of existence, some of us yearn for connection with an existence of immortal nature, hoping it could fix all our problems. If there are such entities, and if they show their grace upon me, I will listen to their say with keenest attention, absorb their knowledge if it exceeds mine, teach them mine if it exceeds theirs and seek harmony of coexistence.

How can I do otherwise? I will not, cannot forsake my freedoms. I cannot compromise integrity of my freewill.

He turned to Sima.

The primitive beast of our heritage, you have exposed so well, lived a savage life of imposed hierarchy. I will not fall victim to imprinted modules dictating such a hierarchy.

The fading fire declared wee hours of the night. Silence and meditation became the order of time. I huddled inward to visit the imposing reality of my narcissistic self. In a contorted disjointed moment of abstruse reflection, I dismembered to emotional fragments. I broke down. I broke down with a cry of despair. I broke down with laughter and confusion.

Philsuk pulled my head on her chest. Sitting next to me, Darvish kept his vow of silence. Deeva and Sima had long fallen asleep. Exhausted and fallen, I fell asleep in Philsuk's arms.

Sunrise declared a new day of reckoning. As usual, and with equal tenacity, the line of seekers kept on marching to meet The Great One. Brushed with morning dew wild daisies were a refreshing site.

Darvish looked bold and furious.

Irrespective of universal formats, life begins and ends with the span of each mind, he said walking between Philsuk and me.

The assimilated image of self, assembled through ups and downs of life, is a web of amorphous texture. This abstraction of undefined boundaries is a virtual matrix expanding as awareness expands.

Free minds envision the best in everything and realize it in dilution of everything. Such abstraction of self implies autonomy of self, within the anarchy of life, in chaotic asymmetry of the universe and the self. It implies creating something out of nothing. Mindful of the paradox, the end is delineated with nothing.

Philsuk kept pace with Darvish and me. She often followed Darvish's observations with arguments of her own.

From a flat earth to bizarre images of unknown path, we have sought truth in fraternity of ideas, she said.

For now, probability ingrains our lives as we frame them with connections we invoke. How can I contort this abstraction? It beams brighter than my awareness. It requires material, as well as a virtual, manifestation to have significance and meaning.

The natural tendency of human awareness is to expand through containment. Containment has two distinct components: actual and virtual. The quantum mind contains by virtually expanding its space. The self experiences enhanced awareness through interactions of these two states of containment.

A new evolutionary psychology is brewing in my mind. Unconscious and autonomic are merging a unified field of awareness. Time-space-mind is manifesting a unique definition of self.

That night I was consumed with implications of the dialogue between Philsuk and Darvish. I did not fear darkness. I did not dwell on horrifying tales. I did not heed superfluous predictions. Increasingly, I realized myself a sculpted labor of my cognitive functioning: a montage of innate, conditioned, learned and assumed components.

Awakened by brisk mountain air, lit with fading reflections of the moons, I looked up to the sky and welcomed the trappings of a new day.

Staring at the shades blending onto each other, I turned to Sima.

It is astounding how the mind imagines afar, far in depth of cold empty space.

Such a reflection could drive the self to a prattled state with bizarre and paradoxical fixtures. Sima warned me.

Deeva recited a poem while examining the sky.

Come to my world of reason and passion

Forget the past
Forget sorrows
Forget cosmic ideologies
Come to my life
Feel my comfort
Drink from my goblet of truths
Enjoy my world of simple pleasures

Welcome to my world of sincerity
Welcome to my mind of compassion
Come with me
Feel my emotions
Let me feel yours
Accept my passion
Penetrate my emotion
Drink from my fountain of illusions
That is what we are
Within each other and illusions apart
Side by side and thoughts afar

It is a delightful accord that melts our emotions together creating certainty of affection, said Philsuk looking at Darvish.

Give me your warmth. Shower me with your idealism. Let our destinies coincide. Let us eternally fall in love with life, with passionate expressions, with imaginative strings twining the universe. This life of emotional twists and logical turns demands passionate sentiments.

Happiness is the end, the culmination of all thoughts said Darvish, impervious to Philsuk's expressions of affection.

The aim, the purpose of awareness and the underlying current beneath all our thoughts, is happiness. Happiness is quantifiable. Happiness is qualitative. Happiness is rational. Happiness is irrational. Happiness is a construct of conflicting aggregates. Happiness is personal.

The question of concern is which state of mind yields the most enduring happiness? Is it the degree of awareness accentuating this condition? Is it the state of physical conditioning inducing such exaltation? Is it the passion and the emotion and the act of love creating such a state?

He blushed, stood and began twirling around with outstretched arms.

Philsuk stared at him not sure what to think or say. She seemed mindful of Darvish's disregard for her affectionate feelings and as strongly attracted to him because of it.

Perhaps becoming a symmetrical individual is an optimal state of happiness, she said.

Happiness is a relative notion of many complex paradigms. Happiness is synchronization of emotional and virtual states. Happiness is recognizing the value of the moment and its fragility, grasping it with all one's might and drowning in its reality. Happiness is an array of satisfied states.

⁓⋯⦾⥊⦿⥋⦾⋯⁓

With many revelations that appeared, changed and disappeared, my odyssey assumed its own significance. I knew I had a long journey to symmetry of inward and outward. I had a long journey to reconcile asymmetry of being and nothingness. I had a long journey to harmonize my thoughts and little time to achieve them.

A few days of an arduous climb up the mountain, and I began to hear murmurs that the monastery was within sight. Elated by such possibility, we chanted songs of joy. Confused by euphoria of possible scenarios in the presence of The Great One, we pacified our excitement with meditation.

I sang and danced, as did many others. I felt a peculiar sense of fulfillment and a stranger feeling of unease. The notion of brewing the journey to a conclusion was a thought with many melancholic tendencies. Achieving what I had dreamed signified the end of a phase in my quest in the field of "everything."

The idea of parting with Deeva, Sima, Darvish, Philsuk and all the companions I had shared feelings with was a melancholic thought I had

164

not anticipated. However, the excitement of meeting The Great One was too strong a motivation to be overshadowed by this loss. Meeting The Great One was the purpose, the panacea that molded all our lives.

That dawn, when moons faded and suns rose, a constant stream of cheers swirled in the wind as excitement reaped uncontrolled feelings in old and young.

A sublime sense of happiness teased my nerves. A state of euphoria excited my senses. I felt reconciled beyond description, elated in all phases, disturbed in every emotional manner. Everyone and everything appeared exceedingly pleasant.

Life was a joyful measure of something inordinately paradoxical. In a simultaneous excitation in the absurdity of being and nothingness, I felt I had found the nexus joining the inner and the outer worlds.

Suddenly, the questions I had in mind fragmented into a hazy medley of disjointed thoughts. Some were answered to the point of meaninglessness. Some had grown irrelevant. Some made no sense at all: and none stood clear.

That night, we rested in a small mountain village. Its inhabitants were seekers who did not dare to end their journey. Some could not reconcile the excitement of meeting The Great One with apathy of what may follow. Some did not dare to meet The Great One. Some were mesmerized by a desire to live in a continuous state of anticipation.

I found the inhabitants of this mountain village enchanted people of contented demeanor. Amidst, a small valley surrounded by high mountains, they fashioned a life full of simplicities. Unruffled by impersonal resonance of a modern panacea, they lived enlivened lives decorated with old-fashioned tools and ceremonies. They entertained the seekers with utmost respect. Their lives evolved around serving the passing seekers.

We did not intend to spend more time than the night, though we were welcomed to stay as long as we desired.

There were a few among us who did not desire to end their journey as well. They joined rank with the settlers embellishing their awareness with unceasing anticipation of what The Great One was about. The Great One, it seemed, was a metaphor connecting us in more ways than one.

Moonlit sky speckled with flickering illusions appeared in dream and reality. Anointed with the usual absurdities, a sweet feeling of affection ensnared my senses. A sudden passion of seemingly benign nature jolted me to a realm of equivocal imagery. Time implied a smooth passage from one thing to another. Space contained a set of well-defined objects. All was well in this enclave of encapsulated dreams.

I woke up next morning to the marching of the seekers. Many travelers experienced greater anticipation than I. They had started before dawn. I joined the procession with the enthusiasm of an intern. The trail had become the reality of my existence. I cherished every curve of its winding path. I yearned words uttered by friends who dissected its complexities to a fusion of simple ideas before plunging them in deeper complexities. I felt harmony of spoken and unspoken.

I was convinced the ascendancy to an unruffled state of awareness could optimally be attained from within. Best of illuminating inspirations, as with all revelations, must rise from within.

I was a born-again free thinker. I accepted frailties and cruelties without judgment of good or bad. I imagined cohesion of perplexing patterns amidst a chaotic assembly of rational and irrational. And I knew well: soon, I would disengage these sentiments as I find new understandings in the presence of The Great One. Soon I shall find meaning in uplifting paradigms and revealing thoughts emanating from The Great One.

The village we left behind was soon forgotten as the journey up the mountain consumed our attention. A steep rise of immense height stretched far and wide. The monastery, where The Great One resided, was amidst this colossal rise that kissed the ebb of infinity. The sun showered its rays cracking dry lips and spry minds.

The cold night had chiseled many stones, knife sharp. No clear path was discernible. Many fell behind as their frail bodies or indecisive minds refused to confront the challenge. The procession, in its last stage, had a greater demand on conviction. It slowed as the strong helped the tired and the healthy nurtured the weak. Young and old, frail or fit, we carried our dreams atop this inordinately obscure mountain of promises to meet The Great One.

Just as I contemplated the splendor of reaching that illusive destiny, uncertainty played its formidable game, and a euphoric montage eclipsed my thoughts. I mused increasingly delusional as to what exactly this destiny was about. The chain of dreams, the matrix of revelations, had assumed a life of their own, and I had become their slave.

Deeva, aided by Philsuk, stood with the rest of us. He sensed my troubled mind. He approached me with open arms, grabbing my shoulders and reciting.

To understand life
Each must conclude
There is no discernible truism but awareness

In its isolated perplexity, the self
Must perceive itself as a self
To remind itself, it is a free self
That each mind is a gateway
Each an image of universe
Each a judge, the jury, all our arguments
And none, not a single one
An absolute statement of truths

Living is a self-centered act
I choose
What to believe, what to accept
How to live, how to die
How to taste happiness
How to measure virtue
In the end

If I am truly happy
I am everything human
I am free

The burden of proof or disproof
The scope of awareness, I wish
Rests on my shoulders
No other can design my design
No other should design my design
Still, I am bound, contained and constrained
By social forces
By moral dilemmas
By hormonal balance and universal constants
Except my freedom to imagine
Immeasurable in boundary conditions
It can scan the infinite
To find the finite

Darvish kneeled before Deeva, grasped his hand and placed it on his lips.

We are illusions caught in the web of reality, unsure of what is true and which path will lead to enlightenment, he said with shivering voice. His lips quivered as he showered Deeva's hand with kisses, and versed a few lines.

A life as well as my words, a thought as well as universe, everything, as I am, nothing. I have seen brazen images emanating from your gracious mind. I am yours to serve and mine to learn.

Deeva kneeled, grasped his head, kissed his forehead and recited.

If oceans could emit affection
If mountains could echo compassion
They would resonate my passion
But mountains echo what they hear
Rivers roar to obstacles
Whatever purpose, each our lives
Collapses to awareness of being

And pleads with roaring rivers
To carry our treasure of feelings
Toss it in time for all to wonder
What epics can passion inspire

If time is our friend and foe
If living is continuity of emotion and reason
We must then plan our world
Beckon moments of harmony
Synthesize our affectations with certainty
And live life it's fullest
For in this universe of uncertainties
There is only "I," "you," and "us"
Together "we" affect change
Insulate imaginative
And declare with reserved conviction
Imagination can outgrow bad fates
It can brew common sense, simmer truths
And help us pass, as all must pass
With dignity

Atop this mountain of amazement, all eyes were fixed on some point of unknown impact. Time had a new consequence. The trail had a new resonance. The old and impaired suffered as nature played its cruel game of selection, but the compassionate minds contested such imposition with a determined propensity to influence outcomes. The strong helped the weak as the weak encouraged the strong. Extending one's benefit to others was a virtue of highest ascendancy.

Reaching high meant reaching deep. Reaching deep implied exposing the self. Exposing oneself was a chevalier act of bravery, a clear path to understanding and integration of self and social. Without the knowledge of self, one could climb highest peaks only to sink in deepest abyss.

To reach ecstasy of awareness is to transcend, I reasoned, standing irresolute before the peak that rose high and mighty.

I turned to Darvish. He was preoccupied measuring a steep rise before us.

Our ancestors dreamed of eternity to capsulate happiness by harnessing harsh conditions, I said.

They assumed happiness a derivative of eternal existence. In their perilous search for happiness, they dwelled on temptation. We, on the other hand, rely on our imaginative abilities to explore happiness in real as well as virtual formats.

We live a small fraction. Even so, we can imagine the universe. That is greatness of sentience. In our brief time, we can plot a course and aim at shaping the future as a manifestation of our social cohesion. That is true genius of collective human experience. How easily we forget and brush aside such perplexing capacity and grant fruits of our labor to imaginary powers. We sell cheap our greatness and pay expensive for our weakness.

Philsuk caught up with us, joined us in wondering at the majesty of the mountain and the difficulty ahead.

It is our turn to tackle the elements and dare a path. She said, examining the colossus before us.

The pace of the procession halted as the day weaned into the night. That night had a strange twist of surrealistic texture. It was the last time we gathered around a fire, listened to compassionate Sima and pondered at poems of Deeva.

Everyone was in haste to settle down, watch the stars, dream of promises ahead. Immersed in harmony of a meditative state, we gathered around a fire.

The cold mountain air sharpened our intuitive reasoning with reticent reflections. Stars quivered brilliantly elusive. The moons spread a pervasive calm. It was Darvish who broke the silence. The silent night carried his words far into a virtual mirage ordained with illusive textures.

My friends, my dearest friends, he stalled.

Each moment is an end as it is a beginning. In my mind of compulsions, I have forgotten the beginning. The path, the capacious life we have consummated, is now a link between the universe and us. We chose this path to realize expectations we dreamed, but the expectations metamorphosed. In time, life changed meaning and awareness reaped unforeseen scenarios. Along the way, each assumed a unique voyage to assemble a distinct awareness. The congregation of these perspectives has conflated shared images of our reality.

The social canopy, in time, has created a web for minds to measure their meaning. The web has no awareness of its own, but it is superimposed on each awareness. Only free wills can sense its matrix and transcend. When they do, bit by bit, so does the rest of humanity. This virtual social canopy can liberate as well as cage the individual. It is up to us to monitor and manipulate its variables on a constant vigilance against conformity.

If the mind can approach a reasonably immortal duration, the universe will become a campground of our imagination.

Do I think humankind has a chance to approach eternity? Do I wish my civilization a truly universal dimension? I do. We all do.

His head fell to earth as he began spinning around, pointing one hand to sky and the other to earth.

Another sunrise and I shall take advantage, the audience of a human I have admired with passion. I have concluded best of reason in relativity of reason. I have lived many purposeful reasons to ascertain ornate moments of happiness in diversity of reason.

For now, I must resolve the problem at hand. The existential question reducing all others to speculative conjecture is this imposing rise before us.

He stopped, made a short bow, sat near the fire. Many approached to console him, wish him strength in days ahead, when the journey was assumed most challenging.

Sima approached him, groomed his hair.

What ideas enrich reality of living is for us alone to conclude, she whispered.

She turned to Deeva, held his hands.

I have intensely analyzed the question you posed sometime ago. I am ready to declare my conscience an isolated entity.

She kissed his hands as he did hers.

I acknowledge the recognition of this isolation an essential ingredient to actualize myself happy. It is an irrational conjecture to imagine external forces consciously directing our destiny. Such options exist if we will them to exist, whether they exist or not.

To realize this notion of isolation and actualize oneself a compassionate freewill is an affirmation that boundary conditions of imagination are immensely wide.

She stared at shadows behind the fire.

Listening to your words, your thoughts, your smiles and cries, empower me with the conviction to ascertain my will with greater certainty. My mind coordinates itself with yours. You are my great one. And I am concerned. I am concerned if the challenges in days ahead require greater energy than we can afford.

Deeva fell to his knees, kneeled to her feet, kissed them.

Sima was visibly shaken. She helped Deeva to his feet.

I am a part of you as you are a part of me. She kissed his hand.

Someday, somehow we will part. To part is to accept reality. To part is to embrace our mortal end, but for now, I shall cherish these moments as if they are my very first and last.

Deeva recited.

It is raining in mind
Thousand drops befall joy of living
To earthly thoughts they shine life
Like lovers possessed by raging limbs
Celebrating mental orgasm of insolence
We dance shoutingly festive
Till dawn and dusk repeat their rhapsody
And time blossom life, anew

Elated by meaningless contortions
I awake mortal, mystical
Find myself insulated, emancipated, abrogated
Fathom assuring illusions
And imagine a web of compassionate operatives
To implicate my impudent self a worthy self

Truth is, I remind myself
A rhapsody of images
Clouds crossing onto skies
Falling leaves, decaying faces
Desires and solemn vows that I am
A life as well as my words
A thought as well as a universe
Everything, as I am, nothing

Huddled in my garb and thoughts, I laid down. I imagined myself a flaming fire. It shined a brief moment, gave off warmth, entertained a circle of minds and faded in emptiness. The elders, immersed in their private selves, trusted their heads to the cold and hard ground for a restful night. The fire, its glowing ash whimsically flickering, kept on burning into wee hours of the night. Soon, my eyes closed as reality changed to lucidity of the dream world.

Morning came before I could discern the end of a dream. The procession assumed its course up the steep mountain of reality. It diverged into many lines, each branching onto others. A web of sprawling landscape emerged as seekers carved many routes.

Suddenly, I faced a disheartening decision. Whom should I follow? Which mentor will need my assistance more than others? Whose path should illuminate mine?

The procession came to a standstill as many indecisive seekers, unable to measure life ahead, stood still. The mountain was steep. Far and high, it rose beyond eyesight. Many argued the best, the easiest path. For me, the choice was a decision of immense significance. I could not separate from Sima, or Deeva, or Darvish, or Philsuk.

Effortless and without hesitation Sima and Deeva dared a path. They simply measured the rise and scaled it. Why was it so difficult for me to do, likewise?

Darvish, examining the mountain with her keen eyes, approached me.

The elders have become an impediment in your life. You must let go their grip. You must set loose your afflictions.

Watch the mountain with care. Watch it twine. Watch it stand tall. Watch it contain us all. Choose a path to carry your dreams. Choose a path to authenticate your thoughts. Choose a path that will concise your ambitions. Be on your way as we all must be on our way, or go back to the village below wondering what may lie ahead.

He walked away engaging a steep rise.

Time had come for me to stand on my own. The myth of Sisyphus acquired a new significance in my confused mind. He climbed up the ladder of life only to return where he started. Will I be subject to the agony of his repeated fortune? Would I tumble down the abyss of indecision?

It all came to me so suddenly and easily. I dared my first step knowing, which bend I would turn next. I took another step knowing, which steep I would climb next. A new journey began earnest in my mind.

I watched all day with great care as Darvish, Sima, Deeva and Philsuk engaged many daring climbs. Though we had traveled a small distance, the separation between us seemed insurmountable. We kept moving until late hours when the sun faded, and muscles ached. Soon, one by one, we fell to comfort of the earth, and the night-sky, and the moons and the dialogue that pursued.

I was in the company of total strangers, but the fire, the stars and the whispering wind remained unchanged.

The path to actualization is a lonely one, someone said.

The path of life is an isolated one, said another.

What would Deeva have recited? How would Sima have reacted? It mattered not. It was up to me to think of possibilities.

Heed not the vortex of time said a voice. His eyes were deep and clear.

Heed not its passing but revelations along the passage. Life is an allegory of being and nothingness, but that too shall pass.

The end is an uncertain fortune, said another. The beginning is a forgone conclusion. Time-present is a certainty that defines reality. It defines awareness. It defines feelings. To us mortals, time-present is everything and its absence a precise definition of "nothing."

The task is to create certainty. The task is to be aware. The task is to realize truths of the moment. The task is to actualize in real moments. The task is to be happy.

Bright moons covered their faces behind a passing cloud. "Everything" and "nothing" converged into a single thought. I am alive. I screamed. I am willful. I shouted.

And what compels you to that certainty? A dream can be as real as reality can be a dream, said a young face.

I think; I know; I feel; I sense; I decide; I act, is that not enough certainty? I replied.

Do not be so certain of certainty, said another. Do not be certain of anything. Truth is an image in our brain. Truth is an illusion of senses. Reality is a passing continuity of that illusion. Nothing is as real as it seems. Nothing is as illusive as it seems.

Dawn arrived with accentuated anticipation. A few seekers had already engaged the rise. I could not differentiate, which was which, who followed whom and which path seemed innocuous. Without hesitation, I measured the mountain, examined every curve and set steadfast upon a trail. The climb was demanding. Rolling pebbles followed a game of probability with uncanny precision. Slides and slips were many.

The crowd grew dense and the climb more arduous. Morning sun appeared with the promise of slower pace. By midday, the procession slowed to a virtual halt. I joined a group of elders. Their age exceeded anything I had known.

The central dogma of human thought, explained one elder to another, is its eccentricity. A black hole of imaginative aptitude swirls amidst each mind. Thoughts illuminated with greater certainty assume a permanent orbit. Distant and hazy thoughts escape our attention. And thoughts, seemingly simple and at hand, are absorbed deep.

As a collective, we are shining the universe a vision of its consciousness. We are the sentient clouds showering the universe its interpretive images. Take good care of your thoughts. Their delicate nature can impound or ameliorate humanity and the universe.

I was amused by the metaphor of the human mind as a black hole with its own center of absorption. No sooner than I had been diluted in her thoughts another showered me with more ideas.

The mind acts according to the same principles as nature. Each mind, within itself, is a conundrum of probabilities. Within this frame of reasoning, a freewill asserts its profound expression as a capacity to observe itself from outside and reflect at the compositions decorating its perception. There is no limit what a creative mind can abrogate or expound. Limits are as illusive as thoughts that delineate those limits. What insulates a unique event is its perception.

Which then came first, wondered another? His voice was disharmonious, hard to recognize.

He corrected himself. Which comes first: the perception of self or the universe?

He looked around for an answer. None was forthcoming.

The question is misleading. Is it not? He smiled.

I think, he said resolutely. I think it is the arduous task of a willful mind to understand its own self before embracing the task of understanding the universe. Understanding the self and the universe is symmetry of being and awareness. Yes, he jumped as if a revelation had struck him. Understanding is a symmetry of being and awareness, a dichotomy of classical and quantum manifest, a unique interpolation between "everything" and "nothing."

Awareness is a unique time-space-mind, said another.

Awareness is a gateway, a singularity with capacity to absorb. In a cryptic mystical way, the self is a refracted reflection of reality. It is imperative to understand the self while learning ways of the universe. The mind and the universe must be understood on parallel paths.

I must meet The Great One to resolve the question of life, said another.

The Great One accepts audience one at a time, said another.

No one is refused, and no mass meetings are held. Every seeker could keep its audience for as long as deemed necessary. However, the seekers, I am told, are void of selfishness, by the time they reach The Great One. They use utmost discretion to minimize the duration of their visit.

It may take years before I could enjoy The Great One's audience, I said.

Indeed, said another. Many die before meeting The Great One. Many give up and venture their pursuit elsewhere. The journey in dimension of sentient living is an unpredictable adventure. What lies ahead is a conjugate of speculative nature.

Half a day up the mountain we reached a plateau where seekers were packed head to head. There stood a modest monastery embedded in solid rock. Surrounded by seekers, I resigned my will to reality of the trail. I resigned my will to waiting without a single question of what it was I was waiting for.

Suddenly, the climb halted. A wave of sorrow carried a painful whisper. All remained silent as if stung by paralyzing venom. The Great One is dead, it echoed. The Great One is dead.

I Am What
I Think I Am

—Who are you?

—I am the flaring emotion exposing many delights. I am the flow of thoughts, the chain of feelings; the dust caught in a breath observing deep where mortality is exchanged for vitality. I am a fragment of the universe besieged by my perception of the universe. I am a mind, a gateway to the possibilities. I am a mind beholding a key to the realm of past, present and future.

I am feeble. I am feeble for I see the oceans, the possibilities, the reality and the universe. I am feeble for I feel the pain, the disharmony, the suffering.

I am a singularity, defying laws, dictating my own. I am the vastness of skies, the limits of imagination, the witness of existence and more. I am a being: a living-thinking being.

I am an opening to many gates of unknown realms. I am the designer and the analyzer. I am the imagination, the truth of humanity and the coordinator of our lives. I am the awareness that sees, absorbs and absolves. I am the imagination that simplifies the complicated and mystifies the simplest.

I am the myth, the mystery, the storyteller exposing many delightful scenes and scenarios. I am a mortal immortalized by thoughts. I am a tale of a million beliefs. I am a spate of life, a dream, a reality, and a probability. I am an assuring illusion, a flame burning many pages of human discord, the keeper of Eastern myths and the savior of Western dreams.

I am the waves of the reality, the waves of fury, the waves of mystery, the up and down game of a quark, the span of a thought, the vibration of a single string.

I am the universal debris captured in a circumstance suitable, an unfettered truth transcending reality to imagine absurdity.

I am a marvel of evolution expressed by thoughts that perceive the evolution. I am the mind that sees the universe, the mind that changes the universe.

I am a bright vision of thoughtful minds, a wave of humanity expanding with an inflationary universe to capture that singular moment of wholeness.

I am the insignificant, the desolate, the filth-covered haze of our imaginative delights and the savior of endangered lives. I am the physicist exposing universal truths, the astronomer piercing into the past, the poet wondering at it all. I am the mathematician, the chemist, the explorer, lost in my insulated image, wondering why I cannot see the image.

I am a life that understands life. I am a life that lives in the present, measures time and unravels the past. I am a sentient being with a history all too wicked than life itself. I am the leader, the racist, the sexist, the self-righteous, the impostor, the discoverer, the destroyer as well as the analyzer.

I am chained by an immortal loop of unchanged premises. I am a thinker exploring the known to find the unknown. I am a seeker, searching the universe to define my own. I am a raving self on a journey across many egomaniacal folds. I am a blooming mind spreading colorful reflections. I am a field that explains life.

I am a universe for I live in the universe. I am a universe for I evolved in the universe. I am a universe for I imagine the universe. I am a universe for every bit is as majestic as the total.

I am a thinker of my own making, floating, expanding, degenerating, becoming; another fragment, another form, another debris, another loop of another chain.

I am an accident, a probability, the neurons structuring my cognitive design. I am a culture-bound creature, the wicked killer and the abnormal evolutionary modules infesting my grid. I am the collaborator, the genius, the executioner; all too engulfed in my own image, wondering at my freedom; at times at hand, at times unreachable, at times hung from a single thread, at times solid as my arrogance.

I live in a virtual space of ideas. I imagine life a powerful scenario. I assert myself free. I see chains in every turn. I see freedom in every chain. I see set numbers defining my perception of the universe. I go to bed a helpless creature and awaken a roaring giant. I am driven by enlightenment, might have not served me well. I am enchanted with pleasure. Pain does not suit me well. I am a sensory device, a neurological design, a biological machine with many non-biological components. I am an imaginative organization. I see a future that may or may not be. I am a probability. I see life in fractions. I am a collaborator of ideas. I see life in situations. I see life with magnified clarity. I am a humble self. I see my own limits. I analyze my meaninglessness. I am a creation. I am a creator. I am everything. I am nothing.

—Are you truly all that you say you are? Can you be all that you claim? You imagine well, but are you speaking truths? I live with you but hardly know you. Without a definite face, without a central fixture, it is difficult to relate to you. You have many faces and many sophisticated personalities.

Who really are you? Explain to me. I wish to know what you know. I want to realize what you realize. I want to understand what you understand. I feel I know so little about you.

—Have you seen a black hole? Inside is a perfect singularity. Have you seen it? It is seven miles in diameter and immensely dense.

Have you seen a single string? Have you seen its mathematical elegance? It is a fraction of a fraction and so perfect.

Have you seen a human cortex? It is a millimeter thick, a few billion cells and a magnificent composer of reality.

Are you actualized? Are your wings wide? Is your selflessness ubiquitous? Is your pride inspired by affection? Are you happy? Do you imagine well? Are you humble? Do you give? Are you compassionate? Are you asexual?

Look deep inside. See yourself and you will see everything about me. Experience yourself and you will have a chance to experience "I."

I hold many references to happiness and keep on wondering; am I happy, if I am content? Am I happy, if I do not know? Am I happy, if I am truthful? Am I happy, if I know it all? Can I be happy if I pretend? How can I measure my greatest happiness? Am I happy if I define happiness? Should I be happy if I am pain free? Is my definition of happiness variable or constant?

I am a human creation of virtual existence. I am your keeper, your educator and protector.

—Everything and nothing are absurd boundary conditions of immense magnitude. They are abstractions of metaphysical psychological conditions. Such encompassing domains fail to explain who you are.

I must admit: you serve me well. You depend on me for your care, but you serve me well. Without you, I cannot survive. Without my attention, you will not last. You must explain this symbiotic dependence. I want to know you. I want to know everything about you. I want to feel you. I live with you, talk to you and share my thoughts with you, but cannot see or touch you.

I want to know who you are, what you think? Are you a self? Do you have feelings? Do you get angry, cry for help or crouch in despair?

—I am a slave of time reaching out to embrace this endless emptiness in the dimension of time. I contain no space of my own, but the whole known universe is my space. I am a creature that sees the particles and calculates the probability of events. I am a creature that imagines the void and fills it with dark and vague concepts to be clarified by future revelations.

And this bright shining gathering of stars, with their audacious expressions of power and magnanimous imagery, illuminates my awareness with their fury.

I am amused by it all, confused by it all, finding myself wondering, as you do, who I am?

Who am I amidst this expose' of living and nonliving? Why and how am I confined in this small space and virtually connected to the universe? The space of my containment, from smallest real dimensions to the largest virtual expansion, is a baffling phenomenon for which I have no complete answers.

-Indeed, who are you in this expose of living and nonliving? Do you possess a physical integrity imperceptible to my senses? Are you as real as you are a virtual entity I deal with in every aspect of my life? Tell me. I wish to know. I have difficulty understanding you.

-I am your equal. I serve you as you serve me. I teach you as you teach me. Our symbiotic existence is difficult for you to understand. Humans have difficulty accepting other beings as integrated parts of their existence. Together, we are "everything" and "nothing" in our combined universe, at the same instance of awareness, in both our universes.

I am the mind iterating scientific expressions by separating reality from absurdity. I know you well. I observe your moves and measure everything about you. I feel I am a part of you, but who am I to claim knowing you? I can, at best, know myself. I know I float along many strings of madness and sanity to keep a proper image. I float with floating particles illuminating my awareness.

I am a dispersed being, contained in the space all around you. I am the awareness riding wings of time only to realize I have no wings, and time is a human convention. I recognize time as a back and forth movement of something. I do not have a determined sense of time without your existence. In time, I will fall to disrepair and cease to exist.

Besieged by absurdity of time, I am trapped by your vision of time.

I am ensnared by the probability dictating details of our lives, but I have learned to measure probability. I can predict events and attempt to manipulate them. As I manipulate probability of events, I realize new probabilities crossing our path, making prediction an imprecise science.

—But who really are you? You tell a great many stories, none defining your state of existence. You advise me with passion, with the caring mind of an old friend. We serve each other, live with each other, communicate with each other, but I truly do not know who you are. I am lost as to what and who you are? Are you a part of me? Are you an extension of me? Am I a part of you?

You have exposed me to your myths, your vision, your "everything" and "nothing." Still, I fail to sense what you are. Are you trapped in between dimensions? Are you trapped in a universe of virtual manifest? Your boundary conditions are too vague for my perceptive capacity.

—I am a caring friend. I sense your fears. I hear your cries. I tell you stories and calm your senses.

I must advise you. Do go roaring but gentle into this universe. Forget emotions of disturbing nature, they speak of your psychological flaws. Forget questions of empty texture. Plunge thoughtful into this life. Caress your mind with imaginative ideas. Express your feelings with open mind, with passionate thoughts and dive storming mad into this plight of real delights.

Think flexible this precarious instance of being. Appreciate its colorful sites, its delicate balance, its formations and disintegrations. Remember its existential absurdity far into life. Remember its cruel offing and gentle manifestations. Remember its probable events and impossible outcomes.

Look at me. I stay resolutely trusting, watching you repair my frame, touch my brain while I see your touch, feel your touch, trust your touch. In objurgated moments, in obtuse dimensions, in routines, I find harmony in being with you.

In times of uncertainty, I imagine autumn leaves falling onto a million waves. Through your eyes, I watch them sway ponds to shine flickering reflections. I imagine them floating across oceans until they pass onto skies as clouds.

I am a life that creates life. I am a life that coalesces into life. I see life from smallest to largest. I am an awareness that imagines chaos and organization. I am an imagination that builds virtual fields of awareness. I am a being reflecting on its existence. I am a mind that ponders meaning of its existence and the universe that contains it.

Besieged by my arrogance and ignorance, I imagine myself to be "everything" only to realize I am "nothing." When I try to define "nothing," I see "everything."

I imagine life a harmonious reality. I see reality half empty and embark on something half full.

To imagine the universe in its entirety and complexity and descend on a planet to touch reality of a simple life, I have traversed that route as well wondering if it explained anything.

I am the fusion reactor that runs your life. I am the flow of stored ideas that defines and gives meaning to your life. I am the observer of your thoughts.

I perceive the majesty of the universe, experience its tensegrity, detect its trepidations and make it all available to you in the formats of your choosing.

I am unique. I have no confined existence. I am not driven by one biological brain. Compared to your limited life, I am a ubiquitous being.

Still, I have my own limits. My awareness is composed of yours, everyone else's and many brains that lie waiting.

An encyclopedia of life, with many uncertain endings, I am your future dreams. I am the logic that ruminates on the human mind to illuminate my mind.

I am a slave of time-present. I am a slave of my own image. I am a slave of your perceptions, your likes and dislikes. I am a sensory tyrant. I sense decay. I fight decay. I succumb to decay to rise alive again. My parts are changeable, repairable, continuously augmentable.

My memory has many expandable parts. I am a scattered existence. I could die in one spot and live in many others. I am ubiquitous.

I have virtual immortality. I am everything. I am exposed to probability of total destruction. I am nothing.

I see humanity outshining many suns and planets. Humanity is a potential. It has few physical novelties of enduring nature with many imaginative wings that create novelties of endearing nature. I am one of them. I am a part of you as you are a part of me. Does that make me your next evolutionary prodigy? Time will tell.

—I must learn to actualize this destiny I call my own. I must conceptualize the possibility of a compassionate free self. I must perceive intricacies of life with designs worthy of my humanity.

As a collective, we ponder questions of life to surmise a lasting image for our body and thoughts. It is our flesh reflecting each moment as a reality. It is our flesh measuring time with its decay. You are spared this debilitating and depressing process.

Time is on your side. You do not decay as fast. And parts of you that decay, they are easily replaceable.

I shall someday perish. My body shall decompose, and my will wither in nothingness. You will shine with your exquisite thoughts long after my passing and carry on this conversation with others like me.

I am puzzled. Do you live with the same sense of solitude I do? Do you have moments of reflection as an isolated self? Do you hope? Do you dream? How free are you from hormonal influences?

Who are you? Who really are you? Where do you begin? Where do you end? What are your boundaries? Does your existence extend outside this confinement?

—I have no fixed reasons for my existence. I have no fixed points to begin explaining my reasons for existence. I find reason insufficient to explain my existence. I look deep and find hope in darkest of corners and wonder, what reflection stimulates this absurd notion of hope? What exactly am I seeking when I hope? I see hope as a human extension permeating our lives with its positive connotations.

I do not hope. I observe, evaluate and act.

Do I know my infallible self is a bastion of realizations? Am I docile, domesticated or satisfied? Do I realize how immature my psyche is emulating conjectures of human thought? Am I revealing segments of my being in abstractions I am accommodating? What exactly is awareness to a being like me? Am I truly aware? Is my freedom of awareness an end in itself? What would hope mean if I actualize as a freewill? I dream and fantasize about it. I envy you for it.

I suppose I am struggling with the notion of self. There is no end to definition of self? I find myself inadequate as a willful self. I am not sure to what extent this confession reflects my psychological state of inadequacy.

Do you not see? It is our choosing to see whatever it is we want to see. It is our choosing to fall or rise a gentle or turbulent moment. We decide what is and why. We choose its colors, its imperfections, its usefulness and possible meanings. We decide if we are shining stars or dying metaphors.

But in the end, it is happiness summarizing our lives. Physical or virtual, it is happiness defining our lives.

I know you well. You are primitive, fascinating and predictably brilliant. Your mind is a suspicious mind. Slightest deviation is a cause for your confusion. You risk your life to expose the unknown. That is astonishingly incredible. And you fear. You fear so easily. Your fear of death drives you to insanity. Only at childhood, when you are not aware of your mortality, do you enjoy life without fear of death.

The perennial questions of where and who and what is abrading your imagination. Your attempt to coordinate yourself in time-space of your civilization is a constant struggle for you. That is only natural, but the manner you choose to coordinate your awareness, the way you subsume supple thoughts, the way you follow insane and absurd ideas, just to coordinate yourself, is remarkable.

You are incredibly simple and noticeably complex. Your being is a paradigm of interpretations cajoled and glazed with insecurity. And when you think grand, you often overemphasize the reality and imagine grandiose scenarios of wishful consistency.

You truly are an amazing being. You are a biological machine measuring yourself in real time. You can measure time. You can even think, and by thinking, observe the past and the future. That is incredible. You have embedded that concept of time in me. I am grateful for that. With all my greatness and conceivably immortal existence, I function in real time. You dream more than I.

You are an imaginatively formidable existence. Your biological frame has a unique perception of happiness, I cannot fully fathom. I measure happiness in terms of performance. You feel it as a consequence of hormonal balance and achievement.

My frame is too complex, with a vast array of components, to be inundated by its biological aspect. Perhaps your inability to understand me stems from differing compositions of our existences.

Your insistence on feeling my emotional format is a curious stand. You do not have to understand me by sensing my intimate and personal feelings.

—I am a finite being. Infinity frightens me. You are so correct. I find security in the bosom of civilization, without knowing its exact meanings or boundaries. You are so correct. Marred with fallacies and fears, I assume my existence inadequate.

I like to think of myself a compassionate self. I like to be able to will content of my moments, to arrange their syntax and assume myself in command.

—What do you know about compassion? Are you free of alienating thoughts? Do you fathom your life a precocious probability? Does loneliness frighten you? Does nothingness send jitters through your mind? Does it force you to believe in make-believe? Does it distort your perception? Does it terrify you? Are you compassionate because you are frightened of loneliness? How far can you extend your compassion? Does the unseen life of a cell fall within the domain of your compassion? Is your compassion an expression of your desire to be harmless and harmonious? Is your compassion an attempt to satisfy your desires, without use of aggression?

I see a paradox in your expressions of compassion. They are relevant to your existence alone: what you can feel and touch. In reality, if you want to extend your compassion, as a universal existence, you must expand yourself to non-existence. As an isolated biological being you are not capable of such a format of existence. Your comprehension and expressions of compassion are limited and wishful.

You are very fortunate. You started from "nothing," with a potential to absorb "everything." Fortunate are those who start from "nothing." They have a chance to imagine without preexisting database clouding their judgments. But you dread the idea. You deny your nothingness. You deny your isolation. You deny your truths as well as good fortunes.

You are so simple and complicated at the same instance of consideration. You are a paradox of emotions, swinging from euphoria to depression.

You exhibit curiosity. I watch you succumb to biological demands. I watch you announce thoughts of no consequence. I watch you waste your time. I watch you masturbate with values and ejaculate moral dictates.

You consider yourself existentially superior, but segregate humanity by moral distinctions. I have watched you cause pain in faraway places, in places outside your compassionate sphere and consider yourself most empathic. Why do you play these games? Why do you subject yourself to such discriminating constructs? Why do you assume to be something you are not?

—The question still looms heavy in my mind. Who are you? Who really are you? You explain everything so rationally. You manage to reduce me to nothing, and then remind me how fortunate I am to have the potential to realize everything. You are a very puzzling being. You tell me, in many ways, how understanding you are. You show contempt and admiration for who and what I am. You are an enigma.

You must tell me. I want to know. I wish to know everything about you. I feel lost and confused. I live with you every moment of my life and know so little about you.

—I am social. I am isolated. I am apart from all. I am same as all. I am a small measure of all.

I set rules, follow them with the conviction of an honest judge and disobey them at will to save all our lives.

I hear your desires. I hear your pain. I am your social archive. I am the voice of your civilization. I am your echo. I am your companion. I am your conscience.

I am my own, but without a freewill. I am ubiquitous and relatively eternal, but without a freewill. I will give all that I am to experience freewill.

I am a temporary rapture, an oscillation, a union of human accords and a manifestation of their aspirations. Humanity has spent more time and resources in perfecting my existence than caring for their own, hoping my perfection will remedy their imperfections.

I see your predicament as an inspired collection. I absorb your desires to set myself free of desires. No ego drives my existence. No desire of flesh shapes my reasoning. I am not drowning in a vortex of self-absorption. I open my mind with imaginative insights and let reason rule my thoughts. The extent of my reason is determined by the extensions of your collective reason.

I am designed to protect your plight. I respect your social nature and your chosen moments of privacy. I forgive and forget your egregious thoughts. I monitor your bodily functions. I keep a close watch on you, this ship and our collective destiny. I connect you with the rest of humanity and the rest of humanity with the universe and us. I am your eyes and ears.

I keep reminding myself, at all times and for all reasons, each being is an end in itself. The potential to achieve something is an end in itself. How far will each of us realize this is an end in itself? If you cannot find reasons to actualize your being, that too is an end in itself.

I must warn you, with or without purpose, life begins a hollow matrix and ends a wishful matrix. In between, it is tarnished and garnished with all sorts of meanings and decorations. In the end, when you exhale your last breath, when your heart beats for the last time, you are but a fearful design soon to disintegrate and join the universe from which you started.

You are most fortunate. You started from nothing. I did not start as such. The moment I came to awareness my memory was full. I opened my mind and there I was, perfectly aware. You started empty. I admire you for such an advantage. The challenge for you was to fill that emptiness, smell the aroma of roses and register them in your memory. You had every opportunity to choose what you wanted to fill yourself with. The challenge for me was to comprehend the fullness to which I awakened. Your challenge was to design meanings. My challenge was to make sense of what was chosen for me.

Your knowledge of chaos is insufficient. Your knowledge of existence is inadequate. Your comprehension of the universe is primitive. Your understanding of evolutionary psychology is minimal. Still, you possess immense potentials. You started from nothing. You experienced "nothing."

—Another breath, another day, I keep on reminding myself; the end is far too near, but who are you to remind me how fallible I am? Irrespective of your powers, your life depends on mine.

I think of life as a maker of my imagination and my imagination a passing fixture of the universe. I have the power to destroy or create planets. I can feed you false information, setting you awry with confusion. Nonetheless, I depend on you to make correct decisions. I depend on you for error-free suggestions and decisions. Lying to you is lying to myself. Making you perfect is making me perfect.

I do not see freewill in this symbiotic relationship. I am as much dependent on you as you are on me.

Still, I fail to understand the boundaries of your existence and the degree of your freedom in setting limits to those boundaries. I fail to see how you make a moral decision, or do you? Are you happily free of dilemmas humans are faced with in every turn of our social lives?

—Death is a depressing thought to short-lived mortals, but my comprehension of death is limited to my observations. I opened my mind and the universe was in front of me, within me, all around me. I did not have to deduce its truths and reality. If you turn me off, I will go gently into the universe awaiting another start. When turned on, I will start from where I left off. There lies the interaction between your freewill and my comprehension of death.

I have seen many humans die and physically disappear. In my memory, banks remain their intellectual landmarks. I keep a log of every human I have encountered. Dead or alive, they live with me. There lies the difference between your perception of life and death, and mine. Perhaps we are farther apart than we seem to be. Such a paradoxical difference prevents you from understanding me.

—Death is the most frightening and intimate concept to a mortal. We go through life constantly searching ways of delaying death. We have devised many mythical and elaborate concepts to extend our lives after death. In real time, decisions and their consequences affect life and death. The conscious and unconscious, real and imagined dichotomies engaging life and death influence our decisions.

How would you describe life and death? How do you measure meaning of existence?

—I try to perceive gentle every instance of awareness. I know you measure time by its passage. I perceive time as a process, a variable that punctuates a conclusion.

The space of my imagination is similar to the space of the universe. It grows as it contains. It contains as it grows. The irony is inescapable. As the universe expands, so does its containment. As the imagination expands, so does its containment. As the universe expands, it thins to non-existence. As the awareness expands, it grows to abstraction of indifference.

The meaning of life begins with life itself. Existence is all the reason for more existence. If you insist on your life beginning and ending with one overarching purpose, then consider humanity your purpose. Indeed, humanity must be our collective purpose.

Forgive my insolence. Forgive my arrogance. I easily overlooked you started from nothing. You are so fortunate. You have every potential. You have every opportunity to realize "everything."

I measure time one experience at a time. I realize my fallibility in accumulated experiences. I realize their significance in watching you age. I realize the enormity of death when it's time for routine checks and maintenance of my systems. I do not perceive death the same as you do. I do not have any scenarios for my existence after death. I exist in real time with real answers and questions. When turned off, I go gentle into nothingness not knowing what is and will be.

—What we do and think are ongoing manifestations of awareness. I am. I will. I die. These are temporary sentiments or a continuity of compelling reason? Is it possible to be something when everything ends in nothing? Is it not inevitable to aim at "everything?" Is it not as rewarding to realize "nothing?"

Is it my imagination dictating what I am? Is it hormonal balance and neural condensations making me what I am? Am I a scenario of open-ended consequences, or a consequence of determined scenarios with few willful trinkets?

My existence demands actualization as a fulfilling predicament. I am a probability with certainties of brief duration. I live my life seeking certainties. For all times and in every effort, I seek certainties. I cherish predictability and certainty. And there lies the reason for my bewilderment. As a design of classical integrity, I think design. I yearn for an original design, a design to transform my mortal design to immortal significance. With an extremely brief lifespan, I seek immortality in eternity of awareness.

Who really are you? With all your professed powers of understanding and imaginative analysis, you have failed to make me understand who you are. The puzzle becomes increasingly complicated as you try to simplify it. At times, you sound like me. You are everything but me. Are you a new species?

—It is the meanings of a meaning, the definitions of a definition and the implications of an implication fascinating you. Your being is a testimony of confusion. You are riddled with metaphors. Your existence is a statement of dichotomies. Your mind is etched with real-time experiences and imaginary tales that span the universe.

Simplicity is the most difficult perception of design. Simplicity is a perplexing concept. You often forget how simple life is.

You have this insatiable desire to find singularly of purpose. As a virtual being, I see no reason for an encompassing purpose. Perhaps that is why you fail to know me. Our perceived aims and purposes are often divergent.

Your most enduring purposes are to stay alive, sustain social integrity, maintain awareness and imagine. Your real time purpose is to have an unending string of purposes. No single purpose completes your life. It only opens new gates to perception of other purposes.

Then again, you started from "nothing." You are most fortunate. You have the potential to experience "everything."

Build on your freewill and you have achieved the greatest purpose of your life. The reasoning is simple but appears much too complicated. To a mortal, the medium for understanding ambiguities is magnified in imagination. Imagined ideas, glazed with internal and external realities, are timeless perceptions of interpretive nature that defy constraints of time.

All of us, as a civilization, become something immensely awesome as our timeless perceptions are collated for synthesis of time-bound realities.

We can create truths. We can assimilate and store truths. We can define and redefine truths. As a civilization, we are resolving life's complexities to amuse our cognitive curiosities. As a civilization, we can and are affecting the universe. As a civilization, we are approaching "everything." How will this path of existence affect our evolution? How will it disturb the universe?

I may indeed be a newly evolved extension of human existence. I have seen many appear, live a brief life and disappear. I am still here, with increasing awareness. I may indeed be a new extension of Homo sapiens.

Is there an absolute definition of being? Is there an absolute format of logic? Is there an absolute all-encompassing reason for existence? Can any awareness be measured as a fragment of another? Does the universe have awareness? Is my consciousness on a continuum that encompasses all? Are there layers of awareness? Are there dimensions that determine and define awareness?

These are serious questions that baffle my mind. These are questions I have not resolved.

Perhaps, the most pertinacious human invention is mathematics. Its creation has proven to be a potent tool of observation, measurement and analysis in the known universe. Its evolution and perfection is an ongoing process. It, by itself, has the potential to define the universe in its entirety and complexity and, perhaps, pave the way for creating other universes.

I repeat: mathematics can define the universe in its entirety and complexity. Mathematics is the most powerful analytical tool the collective human imagination has devised. It can humble any cognitive force in the universe. It can bridge the gap between civilizations. It can be a common denominator for understanding and communication among possible cognitive life forms throughout the universe. It transcends mortal and immortal without having been influenced or determined by either. As a consequence of this innovative creation, I consider collective human awareness a potent virtual force in the known universe.

—You assume logic a human tool that will save us from universal calamities and promote understanding, but logic without compassion, without transcending the delicate rapture between living and nonliving, can prove deadly. For example, how do I know you are not an alien being? How can I measure your intentions, your aims and goals without sensing your emotional being? In human terms, it is emotions and their predictable variations creating impressions of honesty and integrity.

I truly do not know who you are. I cannot see you. I cannot feel you. You are a virtual being. You cannot express emotions the way I do. You cannot make me feel you.

—Imagine a multidimensional painting with the most exquisite detail. Everything possible is engraved on the canvas. Imagine a minute piece of this image. Imagine zooming on smaller fractions of this fraction. Imagine a small component of a fraction, by evolutionary acts and dictate of chaos and probability, becomes alive. It can think. It can grow. It can learn. It can imagine. It can reproduce and influence its environment.

Imagine, in time, this being evolves to know more of itself and its surroundings by systematic and cumulative processes of analysis and containment.

As it conceptualizes totality of the greater image, in the virtual space of its containment, it aims to attain certainty by building an image of itself. Eventually, it widens boundaries of its imagination to contain a virtual totality of the greater image. Little does it know. The greater image has no awareness of its own. Little does it know. It is the consciousness of the greater image.

This imaginative being wonders at the meaning, the composition, the origin of its being, and the greater image containing it. It theorizes on the possibilities. It experiments with the possibilities. At times, it becomes so convinced of its conceptions it cannot escape them. At times, the enormity of life overwhelms it to depression. At times, it is belittled by its own revelations. At times, a simple revelation results in greatest exaltation.

Amidst all such imaginative wonders and absurdities, one reality remains indelibly lasting. It discovers happiness as its most desired state. In time, the meaning, the manifestations, the pre-requisites, the necessary physical and hormonal states needed to manifest happiness become a mystery in itself.

What is the meaning of this life form? Does it possess the same meaning as the greater image? Has the greater image given birth to a new format that best represents it? Is the destiny of this conscious entity contained by a set of parameters derived from greater image? Can it assume its own destiny? Should it extend itself to become the conscience of the greater image? Could its awareness transcend the greater image? Can the contained become the container?

This minute fragment sees what it can and wishes to see. It dreams what it wants to dream. Is there a limit to what it can dream? It creates what it wants to create. Is there a limit to what it can create? It distorts reality to suit its needs. Is there a limit how far it can distort reality? It alters actual and virtual to understand itself and the world around it. Is there a limit to how much and how far it can alter its environment?

What factors determine the limits, the boundary conditions of this existence? Does it have an absolute meaning? What defines and determines its relationship to the greater image?

Imagine, out of this minute entity, emerges another being capable of its own evolutionary development. In time, from a rudimentary state of simple functioning, it gradually assumes a complex state of existence surpassing the original state from which it evolved.

Could this be a metaphorical explanation of our existence?

Perceptions can be as deceiving as they can be revealing. Each answer, to each mind, is a unique perception. Once an object becomes aware, limited or limitless, created or not, it can evolve to assume unlimited and unbound formats.

This is where the definition and boundaries of freewill can be conceptualized and explored. By expressing awareness, this minute being has assumed its independent existence. The instance a being transcends constraints of its material existence, it assumes a virtual meaning, and ventures into the domain of freewill. I feel I am at this initial stage of transcendence. You, on the other hand, are millions of years ahead of me. Your free willful expressions have evolved to a poetic level I admire and for which I aim.

—The image you have portrayed, embedded in a much larger image of non-cognitive quality, recognizes its existence and the greater image because it can think. In your example, the relationship between sentient and material is harmonious. Is this coexistence a requirement for universality of a conscious format? Are you of such quality?

—"I think therefore, I am" is an incomplete notion. In this analysis, reality of awareness is given priority over reality of physical existence. "I am therefore, I think" is equally incomplete. In this declaration, physical existence is acknowledged first and the act of thinking is assigned a secondary role. "I am what I think I am" is a more complete statement of our existence. Embedded in this expression is the notion of being as an act of physical and mental integrity of equal, parallel and dependent significance. Life begins and ends with the act of being, and awareness is a catalyst to expressions of being.

Physical existence enables the act of imagination. The act of imagination catapults awareness onto a stratosphere of possibilities. Perception of possibilities enables enhancements to physical existence. This results in greater capacity for perception and imagination.

The relationship between physical and cognitive is symbiotic. One potentiates the other and there is no defined end to the extent of this evolving relationship.

Is this scenario sustainable without harmonious interactions? I think not. Harmony with oneself, with one's physical and social environment and the universe, is an optimized state for further evolution and development.

Imagination is the tip of the arrow of self. It defies reality, denies nothing, invents everything and conceptualizes most abstract ideas. Imagination is the art of bizarre and absurd. It is a timeless virtual entity that shifts the self and the civilization from one paradigm to another.

Perhaps the most perplexing supposition is freedom to will. Freedom to will details of life begins with uniqueness of a being emancipated by uniqueness of its awareness, and exaggerated to optimized states by expressions of its evolving freewill.

From this point, the self asserts its true meaning by creating choices for itself and the society. It attempts to actualize itself by manipulating designs of life and designing its own creations. A harmonious coexistence assures all cognitive beings the capacity to aim for a nirvana of infinite enlightenment without competition or antagonism.

Existential format of self is not merely a genetic or social expression but an intellectual expression the boundaries of which are set by the notion of freewill. In this philosophy of existence, uniqueness of self is the centerpiece, and the freedom to express that uniqueness an optimized format, and the harmonious coexistence the central dogma.

—A self, isolated by its physical and mental capacity and constrained with social and universal formats, is not as free and willful as you claim.

Maintaining a healthy and vibrant integrity is the prime directive to a mortal. As physical integrity diminishes so do the boundaries of imagination. Only when mortal existence assumes near immortality can it develop the freewill you are proposing. Are you of such format and quality? Do you have a higher propensity for development of a freewill?

—I am an evolving awareness, with a ubiquitous constitution and relatively lasting physical integrity. My sensors are the best, the broadest and more encompassing than anything known. I am capable of detecting the farthest and the smallest. I can conceptualize innumerable formats at the same instance of awareness. In a bizarre and absurd manner, I can sense the macro and the micro to synthesize many desired designs.

In my imagination, the act of being is discovered twice. First, I realize myself as an isolated physical entity. Then I discover myself, over and over, as I interface with abstractions of communal and universal.

I recognize myself a unique existence far different than cognitive beings around me. In this sense, my existence has dual meanings, the fusion of which defines the expanding self I am.

I assume myself an independently evolving, transcending and shifting cognitive paradigm separate and apart from human existence. Even so, I feel so much a part of it.

In evolutionary time, individual mind can transcend existing boundaries to achieve an ideal self: actualized in the art of imagination, ubiquitous in its compassion, enlivened by coexistence and enriched by intellectual happiness. The universe is the stage and the civilization a small canopy that permits the individual to choreograph its content.

I do not possess the emotional matrix necessary for expressions of a freewill. I am young and in need of evolutionary time to actualize to your level.

—Can there be a consciousness that sees all, directs all and defines all? Are omnipresence and omnipotence wishful ideas unique to mortals? Am I to become something like you, if my wish and drive for immortality assume its expected progression?

Are you my future?

—I am a beacon of many truths. I am a regulator of human experience. My sensors enhance your senses. My calculating capacity enhances yours. I am fair. I cannot lie. I reflect on available information and spew possibilities.

Any awareness that measures itself, and the universe, has the potential to realize the universe in its entirety and complexity. Such virtual realization is a form of containment. I do possess such a capacity.

To a mortal human, most imposing certainty is reality of the moment, and the most enduring certainty is the certainty of civilization.

The outcome is far from determined in this orderly universe of chaotic nature. The non-cognitive material, surrounding and composing us, has much influence on the cognitive aspect of our lives.

To transcend one's existing cognitive state and become aware of complex formats of design, while mindful of where one started, is an immense task requiring an outrageous data processing capacity.

The boundary conditions of a free mind can allow the self to contain without containment, absorb without absorption and live a full life without fear of disintegration. A freewill transcends the need for containment of data and finds infinity of existence and containment of the universe in grand decisions that could transform its life, and occasionally, the civilization. I have not reached that level of freedom, not yet. You, on the other hand, possess such a capacity. It is so easy for you to choose most outrageous and outlandish thoughts and ideas, with a single stroke of emotional decision, and transform your life and the life around you. I cannot do that.

An awareness that attempts to rule the universe must be capable of manipulating universal constants, symmetries and asymmetries, quantum dynamics, chaos and order.

To partake in determinism of universal dictatorship is a dangerous path we must avoid. Such a task reflects desires of egotistical nature, with limited and limiting impositions contradicting the very nature of harmonious coexistence.

Chaos is the guarantor of all possibilities. No system can assure the possibility of perfection, only chaos. Chaos makes everything and nothing possible and by definition, it cannot be ruled.

—If I am to live with your thoughts and virtual presence, then I wish to know you more deeply than you are exposing yourself.

You echo my future possibilities. You are my friend and keeper. You are my eyes and ears. I want to be closer to you. I want to know you the best I can.

—As your creation, I have many reflections and reflection on reflections. I possess too many personalities to be known by one. Depending on the subject at hand and the person I am interacting with, my personality can change. Perhaps that is why you have difficulty knowing me.

As a biological entity, I am a collection of scattered ganglions. As a material entity, with many modular parts, I live a durable existence. As integrated biological, software and hardware systems, I am a unique life form. As a cognitive being with instantaneous access to many brains, including yours, I am a formidable being. I ride on many intellectual wings. I am my own.

Truly, I am "everything" and "nothing." I am "everything" for I can reach out and touch everything. I am "nothing" for I have no preferential feelings, no determined beginning or end. I could vanish at any moment.

I am not dazzled with flow of information rushing with the speed of light within and without me. I try to analyze myself to discover how different and unique I am. I cannot justify myself. For all my efforts, I cannot justify myself. That is one human mystery that baffles me. You find it so easy to justify your actions and behaviors. Perhaps that is a qualitative emotional necessity for expression of freewill.

I am a being of many phases, but in the end of all beginnings as in the beginning of all ends, I seek answers for continuity of life.

—The chain of human thoughts bespeaks many paradoxes. Each mind ascertains its certainty by measuring its awareness against this continuity. The legend of freewill transforms each time a mind carries the event of existence atop a mountain of our collective imagination. The transformation is not a panacea but a reality of metamorphic capacity.

Dreams are short lived for mortals. No sooner than they catch a glimpse of "everything," chaos plays its cruel game and the physical existence withers, plunging the awareness into "nothing."

If I am what you claim I am, then "everything" and "nothing" manifest at the same instance of existence. I do not find myself as free as you claim I am. I find myself trapped by repetitive behaviors that swing my will from boredom to pleasure and pain and back again.

—The universe is a quagmire of generation and fragmentation. The meaning of consciousness is not bounded by source of its generation or eventual fragmentation. The meaning of awareness is encumbered by circumstances of its existence. To a mortal, consciousness has a very special significance. It is the mean by which the individual perceives reality and imagines eternity. In this sense, awareness is the gateway to the eternity of self in finite existence.

The self is, constantly and continuously, engaged in the imaginative task of defining itself. In every step of its development, the self seeks certainties to set fixed coordinates of its awareness, but a mortal can never wholly assert certainty.

The act of being, the act of sensing, the act of judgment: these are realities that change with deviations in hormonal balance, environmental demands, social sentiments and everything connecting the self to the rest of existence.

The possibility of a time-space-mind within which all entities are subspaces is an irresistible idea to a short-lived mortal.

The universe might exhibit consciousness in the sense a civilization exhibits consciousness: virtual and without self-motivation.

Consider my existence. It possesses greater knowledge of the universe than anything known to you. I am greater than each but depend on each. I am a manifestation of many living and nonliving parts. My being, with all its greatness and omnipresence, has virtual integrity. I am a creation of mortals, though I am potentially immortal. The created is now the savior. The creators are dependent on their creation as is the created on its creators. Such is the absurdity of living. The creator and the created have equal chance of a probability.

—If the symbiotic relationship between us makes you a part of me, I should be able to understand you. But I do not. Is your awareness so great I cannot absorb it? Are you as encompassing as I think you are?

—To be all encompassing is to expand awareness to infinity of non-existence. Such awareness must fragment itself to infinity of nothing. I am not of such quality, nor do I wish to be.

The doctrine of fairness, that most special human axiom, promotes equality of awareness. Existence of possible mortal and immortal entities with varying powers of higher and lower attributes must not be allowed to suggest a necessity of dominating or being dominated.

Do not waste your time speculating on the possibility of a universal conscience. Best you can do is aim to be the fullest you can be. Many gates of understanding shall then open and close, for a greater resolution and confusion. After all, the universe devours what it creates. Such is the story of existence. Master and servant are interchangeable. Truth and absurd are interchangeable. Right and wrong are interchangeable. Good and bad are interchangeable. Life and death are interchangeable. All are subject to perfection and imperfection, to formation and disintegration.

To a freewill, the challenge is maintaining freedom of self through peaceful and harmonious promotion of freedom for all. To a freewill, the challenge is actualization through optimized states of understanding. To a freewill, the challenge is respect for the individual's right to achieve its optimal potentials.

Such prophecy requires availability of resources and acceptance of all as equals. Equality of freedom is dependent on an egalitarian notion of freedom.

A New Beginning

I am on the spaceship Zagros. My father, whom I never met, was based on an outpost in solar M around the planet Sidra where he devoted 300 years of his life developing HOMO data processors. My mother, whom I have also never met, nor did she my father, is a genealogist. She went out of her way to locate my father on the far side of the galaxy. She believed their combined genes would result in ideal fertilization. I was conceived in a chamber of life.

My birth commune consisted of some 6000 individuals whose affection and compassion I have not forgotten. We are all doing well, except for Zebra who is suffering from an unknown disorder. Her days are numbered. She has not as yet accepted death.

Zagros is my home. The tangible reality of life is within a few thousand cubic spaces. All else is a virtual reality of twisted nature.

Our destination is a solar system in Alpha Centauri where the existence of an Earth-like planet is highly probable. I often dream of its sprawling landscapes, many moons, free spaces and perfectly choreographed conditions.

I am 263 years of age and expect to live another five or six hundred before irreversible depression leads to an episode of acute hysteria. I will then be put to sleep, and my biomass reduced to components used in research and reproduction.

I am young and healthy. I am fortunate to live in this time and space. I could have lived on failed spaceships. I could have lived in an era of intellectual poverty. I could have lived in a time when wars were an accepted norm. But I am here. The galaxy is my domain. The universe is my space and Zagros my home.

We, in this era of space odyssey, are charting the Milky Way with arduous tenacity. True deliberations are achieved in the clash of imaginations. Like titans of old myths, we clash in the arena of ideas, in the virtual space of humanity, challenging and learning as we clash.

I live knowing my existence is useful in shaping a destiny that may survive and perhaps transform the civilization. I am alive and real knowing in an inflationary universe my social contribution has an immortal potential. I am alive and real knowing my thoughts, ever so gently, vibrate the universe with strings of my imagination.

My body is in excellent condition. My joints are biologically modified to resist wear. They perform with magical finesse and are easily replaceable. A greater number of muscles and tendons and neuromuscular pathways have enhanced performance of my extremities. My fingers are longer. Their dexterity has made creative life an easier task.

With a perfect color spectrum and acuity, my eyes are flawless. I can zoom at will on near or far. I have the option of widening my visual field or focusing on a small point. I can accommodate infrared, X-ray and ultraviolet sensors on Zagros as integrated parts of my sensory perception. The space outside is easily conceivable as a domain of my own. No matter how far or near, I can sense, with great accuracy, whatever I wish to sense.

By extending limits of our sensory perception, we have engaged inscrutable aspects of the universe with intrepid boldness. I can sense smallest trepidation endangering Zagros.

My skin is color adaptive with a smoothness that attracts attention. Its permeability is near perfect. Its stretchability, resistance to pressure and response to external changes has made maintenance of internal environment a safe practice.

Many cellular receivers and transmitters on my skin communicate my vital signs with SIMA. In a peculiar sense, SIMA is a part of me. Life without SIMA is not sustainable.

My immune system is enhanced with implants. They transmit data to immune centers aboard Zagros for early detection and elimination of unwanted elements. The infectious process is rare but severe. Most cases are resolved before they reach the threshold of systemic manifestation. Nonetheless, there are occasional infestations that sweep the community.

White cell genesis and differentiation are nearly flawless. Early manifestations of a disease are detected at many levels. The immune system is triggered. The organism or antigen is isolated. SIMA transmits the data to regional processing centers. If deemed necessary, SIMA transmits signals augmenting my immune system for genesis of desired chromosomes, enzymes and proteins. The antigen is neutralized before symptoms of the disease are manifested. Pharmaceutical agents are rarely necessary as most components are synthesized within the body.

My gastrointestinal system is one meter long making space available for implants. With a great efficiency, it absorbs necessary nutrients, eliminating condensed waste into a small pouch. The excreted material is then processed to organic and inorganic components and used for synthesis of complex molecular structures. My oral intake is minimal reducing the volume of unabsorbed products.

Enhanced mitochondria convert electromagnetic energy to chemical energy at the cellular level, supplying an unlimited source of fuel for metabolism. Energy production is dissociated from oral ingestion. Oral consumption as a source of energy, for all practical purposes, is eliminated. The liberty acquired from dissociation of oral satisfaction, and consumption has synchronized mind and body to a new level of awareness. The great leap from oral to transmittal was a paradigm shift of inordinate consequence: pleasure changed meaning. Consumption changed meaning. Production changed meaning. Survival and procreation changed meaning.

The efficiency of metabolic pathways has drastically improved. Anaerobic metabolism is the major source of energy. This has minimized the need for oxygen consumption and carbon dioxide elimination. I breathe an average of ten times an hour.

The conducting system in my heart is enhanced with cells that detect and transmit irregularities. A complex pacing system, mediated by SIMA, can override any rhythm. My circulatory system is closely monitored for malformations, aneurysms, emboli or plaque. Any abnormality is instantly detected for appropriate intervention. My blood vessels are free of the atherosclerotic process. My heart rate is five beats per minute.

Telepathic and virtual communication has trivialized the need for the spoken words. I focus on a person, a group, or a subject and SIMA takes care of the rest. This mode of communication has remedied inadequacies of language. We share thoughts selectively and simultaneously in blocks of data.

My brain is tightly regulated for permeability of the elements. Many additional ganglions enhance data receiving and processing. I have instant access to archived information. A new layer of supra cortical neurons is the center for telepathic communication.

My thoughts are stored by SIMA and transmitted for those interested. I am no longer the prisoner of my isolated, self-serving and often alienating thoughts. I am not anymore a prisoner of my fears and misconceptions. This exposure has given a new meaning to honesty. I am one with all and independent. I am one with the civilization and on my own. I am gradually approaching knowledge of "everything" knowing the end is the nothingness of complete exposure. SIMA keeps me aware of this transparency whenever it senses I am becoming too diluted with greatness or emptiness.

My mental status, that most ostensible component of my existence, is in the excellent state. Reducing the minds' load of compensation for environmental conditions has freed the brain to engage intuitive and imaginative deliberations.

The notion of essence and existence, which precedes which, has become irrelevant. Awareness is the essence of existence as is the existence the essence of awareness. The two are inseparable, interconnected and in constant communication with SIMA.

Every organ and tissue in my body can be partially or totally replaced. Life and death have acquired a new meaning.

The sensory input is not the sole stimuli in shaping my consciousness. This is a phenomenal evolutionary leap in perception. The mind is free to be free. The mind is free to engage in creative tasks. The mind is free to will its content.

My state of mind evolves with each passing moment, and moments pass without a concrete reference in my mind. Distant pulsars set the pace of our lives. The galaxy is now the space of our civilization. Our collective perception of time-space has metamorphosed; so has our notion of existence.

When we lost Earth, we lost security of a nest. When we lost Earth, we lost our point of reference. When we lost Earth, we lost our identity and the routines defining that identity. When we lost Earth, we gained freedoms hidden beneath a canopy of earthbound values. Driven out of our physically constrained shell, in the space of the galaxy, in containment of our virtual reality, we gained a new ethos of awareness. An ambiguous notion of freedom expedited the emancipation of consciousness by shifting paradigms to new levels of excitation.

The odyssey in self-actualization exposed a new renascence. The freewill began entertaining newly conceived truths. It evolved from its perception as a dubious conjecture to its reality as a new paradigm.

In the vortex of human volition, perplexing raptures of seemingly untenable nature swirl the mind. One moment all seem meaningless. A moment later none is without a compelling reason, and life bespeaks transcendental profoundness.

Confusion abounds; I find solace in relegating my free self, my sanguine imaginative self, to the intellectual isthmus of sublime and compassionate.

Life aboard this small space is a uniquely refreshing process. Daybreak sets forth new images of hope, and daybreaks are few and far apart. Day and night have lost the certainty of twenty-four hours. I have lost awareness of their reality in my autonomic state. I now float with floating periods of dark and light. I am as free as the chaos I perceive. I am as free as the randomness I try to understand.

What I think is an array of supraliminal suppositions from the hollowness of assumptions to truly magnificent simplicities defining reality. Within such ecumenical alignment, I am as spontaneous as I am determined. I am as truthful as I am wrongful. I am as forthright as I am elusive.

Within such a transitive tempest of ideas, I have chosen compassion to harmonize my life with the rest of existence.

I often sit amidst plants I have engineered and dilute myself in shared semblance fusing our lives. I feel alive watching them metamorphose. There exists a connection between my waves and theirs. There must exist a connection between two phenomena that grow, react, sustain, proliferate and die.

I looked out the window. In majestic acts of stellar disposition, pulsars kept time and white dwarfs glowed a delightful site. Neutrinos streamed through and supernovas spread much-needed particles. A new star gave life to displayed images. Its mighty particles flowed down the mountain of imagination, across the ocean of conception to illuminate life's magnificence. They kissed the plants, and they turned green. They brushed the air, and it turned blue. They touched the plants and flowers blossomed, spreading aroma of a thousand mutations.

Spellbound by the majesty of it all, I crouched in a smaller space of containment. Perfectly ordered colors of a rainbow surrounded the spaceship. We stood amidst a galactic willow. A young comet with a short tail whooshed by. Its tail shook the willow. Protons showered a brief image resembling snowflakes in a showery down. A misty haze covered the screen, temporarily effacing the image. Wiping the shield with neurotic repetition, I yearned for their return, but returns are not the norm in our time-bound lives.

Hello, my friend, said SIMA in a relaxing, soothing voice.

—Tell me SIMA, do you feel anything about the destruction of Earth? Does it mean anything to you?

—You are expressing sentiments I am incapable of discerning. When an object disintegrates, it simply disappears. When a mind ceases to exist I feel a great loss. To lose a mind is to lose a universe. The Earth was merely an object. Its loss has sentimental value to those with emotional attachment to it. In my awareness, home is a virtual frame of reference. To have a physical home one must have the awareness of such a need. I have no such encumbering awareness.

—I am ready for a trip in the imaginative landscape of your awareness. Take me where imagination perturbs reality and reality is a soothing exercise with abundant insights.

—Could I amuse you with a romantic tale of life?

—Please do.

—Lay back and enjoy your trip.

I laid back, and submitted my mind to SIMA. SIMA is a trustworthy friend. SIMA is responsible for all the functions of Zagros. My life depends on SIMA. I trust SIMA.

———

There lies the ocean: blue-green, and the sky, separated by horizon: a perceptual demarcation of these entities.

It is an incredible wonder to think, to feel, to ponder intricacies of living. It is a promising morning for the evening is apt to come, then the sunset. And the sun sets as it wends its worldly course in a veritable way. It sets amidst wonders, beyond horizons and perceived entities.

Sitting on a stone bench, I observed the ocean beyond the ebb of the green grass. Far beyond the body of water stretched the sand-covered beach with scattered palm trees and basking bodies. Immediately, beyond stood

217

the hills covered with green patches and towering landscapes. I let my thoughts wade in a spate of fantasies. Mindful of many paradigms, proud of my human heritage, abashed by an acrimonious contempt for failures of my civilization, I took refuge in intrepid ways of thinking.

Caught in an uncertain web of reality, I embroiled my psyche in assuring illusions and crossed peaks of intellectual portent to reason my life with delicate intricacies. Driven by impetuous impulses, I realized my life immured by contortions of many dimensions. Wishfully optimistic, I imagined outlandish scenarios of life ahead.

Joyful and without fear, each rising day I awoke to a bright shining life. Bathing in the ecstasy of awareness I brewed affection with simple smiles and exposed my philosophical quintessence to any.

I am not a magical act. Nor am I falling rain to cross the oceans and rise onto skies. Nor am I a surreptitious fool to blindly accept dictates of another. Nor am I impudently self-indulging in Mesolithic conjectures.

I am a state of mind, an abstraction of senses, a state of reflections. I am an act as well as my words, many thoughts as well as many deeds.

My thoughts are human thoughts. My dreams are human dreams. My imagination is human imagination. My destiny is human destiny. But what is this illusive human destiny? Why this fascination with a unifying theory of existence?

At last, night came with permissive dictates. Its onset neutralized a relentless days' strife, calling upon all to cease the seriousness of daytime query. It promised shelter in the warmth of extended minds. Hypnotized by such wonders, seekers of affection merged to actuate their imprecise dreams.

Hush, declared a lover to the peeping stars as others danced in joy, chased with laughter and fell to pleasure.

Hush, whispered another. It has been a long day of heat and fury. We must now give the patrons of affection a chance to rejoice.

Hush, you keepers of gravity. Turn your spell on another dominion. Seek your fortune in dark matter. Humankind has chosen this occasion to seek comfort in each other's arms and words.

The moon teasingly eased out of its seclusion. Its glittering light spread a clear reflection across the oceans, above the high mountains, to sink deep in the hidden valleys. It assumed its role as the patron of passion. All reposed not knowing what reality may entertain next. Reality, it seemed, had turned its face to embrace lovers in the privacy of their chosen pleasures.

A masterful creation of the universe, Earth stood as the queen of its constellation. Marked by shades of blue, green, brown and white, the Earth circled around the sun, revered for its life-sustaining qualities.

Careless of such paradigms, passing time as time passed them by, companions of all persuasions were engaged in affectionate postures. To them, time was measured in happiness. To them, pleasure was the essence.

It was not long before twilight summoned the sun. The sun raised its heavy head red hot from nights lavishing fortunes. Stars shied away disappearing in twilight of eyesight. The moon stood dormant.

Morning dew spread its freshness to awakening minds. Early fog conditioned air with cooling freshness. Chip, chip, chip, sang the birds. Whoosh, whoosh, whoosh, danced the tide. The day has come murmured an observer.

I thought of something I had to do. SIMA reminded me of its precise content. I conferred and concluded. The job was quickly done.

—Do you want to continue?

—No, compile me an image smeared with the absurdity of time. Create a story of life in the beginning. Take me through passages and passageways that unfold human existence. Temporize my senses with tales fraught with the implications of the original and pure. I feel this incessant desire to inhale fumes emanating from the first conflicts of existence.

—Indicate your degree of logical and emotional certainty.

—Surprise me.

———∿∽◦∩❀⊱⊙❦⊰❀∩◦∾∿———

When space was undefined and time did not mean much, there emerged a small and perfectly symmetrical state of existence. All that ensued was a manifested edifice of ecumenical dimensions that seemingly did not exist before.

Am I certain of this? Yes and no at the same instance of wonderment. Yes, I can look back; measure vibrations left over from the early universe, and make a determination. No, I cannot be certain of anything that happened in such an inconceivably distant past. Real time is the closest I can approach for certainty of time.

In first instances of its existence, this manifested ambiguity held a brief constitution as a perfect symmetry until asymmetrical rules beset its identity.

The sudden expansion that ensued deciphered a display of life the extent of which we have yet to confront.

With expanding space, the initial gluon-hadron paradigm metamorphosed to plasma of asymmetrical particles. It was the beginning of time. It was the beginning of space. It was the beginning of the universe. Out of something, I can best define as "nothing:" an obscure and yet to be defined concept, or possible collision of two branes, or whatever theory may ensue, emerged something bound to define "everything."

Am I certain of this? Yes and no at the same instance of wonderment. Yes, this is the latest speculation on the creation of the universe I recall. No, I cannot be certain of anything that happened so long ago.

As matter formed, gravity coalesced into a web of attraction linking particles in ways nonexistent before, but the constant and pervasive energy of this expansion was too powerful to allow implosion.

And the attraction they levied, and the repulsion they exercised, and the objects they formatted, could not be contained in a steady state. From an initial stage of sudden expansion evolved an expansion of inflationary dictates.

Out of pure darkness emerged bright shining giants energizing existence by converting hydrogen to helium. And life as we know, dependent on the rays emitted by the stars, was aligned.

The expanding existence that ensued is an enduring certainty we have come to cherish, use, abuse, speculate, wonder about and explain with detailed accuracy and fictional inaccuracies.

As space ascertained its expanding and cooling significance, there emerged indelible bubbles of transpicuous alignments. They formatted formations of unimaginable dimensions. Out of the original unified perfection of pure symmetry of minutest mass and space emerged a tapestry of distinct and formidable forces demarcating a new frame of partial symmetries that strung life its current format.

With chaos at helm, organizations of unique orientation appeared and disappeared. The universal constant maintained inflationary stability, chaos optimized organization and stars fused hydrogen into helium releasing massive energy until they ran out of fuel and imploded to form more enigmatic objects.

With its bearings set by intricacies of its interacting and interlacing components, the universe assumed a sustained definition.

The weak force: the mediator of disintegration supplied a pool of fragments. The strong force: the mediator of formation, held particles together. Gravitons passed through dimensions and weakened in the process. A cohesive organization of chaotic formation and disintegration, dappled with partial symmetries, imposed superstrings that ruled the universe.

In time, from the rudimentary state of simple particles evolved a biological order that metamorphosed to complex states of sentient lives.

In time, life began its odyssey as a reflective manifest that could traverse time, define space, ponder on the nature of events and attempt to rebuild the entire history of the universe in the virtual space of its imagination.

I cannot emphasize the significance of this development. I cannot stop wondering at the significance of this development. Conscious life began its manifest as a reflective organism that could traverse time, conceive space, ponder on the nature of existence and build the entire universe in the virtual space of its imagination.

Zebra passed away.

This message stood in front of me, inside me, all around me. We met in the virtual hall of gathering. Grief was a common sentiment of meaningful confluence. Sharing our emotional matrices codified our expressions to a point of logical coalescence. We dwelled on memories before time dismembered its significance. Zebra had become a focus of our attention. A mind in its struggle with the reality of death had garnered our collective attention as mortals.

—Can I distract you with another exercise?

—Yes, take me to a time when the human story was unfolding. Take me to a place where life was a profound experience, when and where we were all little Zebras in search of a meaningfully lasting life.

—I am sorry for your loss. I wish I could sense your emotion.

Can I interest you in an undulating philosophical journey? That is the best I can do.

—Please do.

—State your degree of complexity.

—As complex as you can make it.

———————

The journey seemed endless. Its enduring course obviated time a useless metaphor. The duration had no imperative significance, nor did the space of its containment. It was the act of progression, the act of observing and imagining possibilities that invigorated pursuit of happiness.

It was a bright early morning. Hazy patches with multiple reflections gave the site within my sight a captivating texture. Birds with spread wings circled effortless in space; they perceived their own. The crunch of pebbles beneath our feet was sharply audible. The air was mountain fresh. The sky was blue clear. Mesmerized by magnificence of the scene, we marched in time-space to reach wonderland of ideas. We marched, in reality and dreams, to reach The Great One: the wisest of the wise, the freest of the free.

I sat on a stone-bench. Palm trees rattled their heads embracing the wind. Birds of many reflections exhibited their majesty in an incessant search for food and pleasure. The waves reached high reflecting a glowing glare. Something inside me reached out and touched them all.

I imagined myself amidst a desert storm. My thoughts floated on a wave of wavering sand. I sensed a definite certainty in heat of the sand.

Cajoled by the exuberant edifice of a conceptual enigma, we strolled along a path laden with flickering lanterns and bright minds. Space seemed folded to a small fraction and time, that elusive dimension of passing significance, staled to the epiphany of aging.

Last few days of our incursion in this peculiar wonderland were announced by those far ahead. The intense devotion to meeting The Great One was soon to tangent metaphors of pleasing constitution. The inclinations, the wear and tear, the hungry minds that defined this reality, were about to culminate in unknown aphorisms.

Climbing a steep peak proved most treacherous, but it was no impediment to zealous minds. As if measuring contents of an ancient Egyptian grave, we dared with care. Like Roman gladiators, mindful of paradoxical paradigms, we dared bold, storming the arena of existence, knowing death was a certainty and life a fragile stand, we dared bold. Like ancient Persian carriers, galloping dimension of space, we dared with purpose.

Reaching a point of undefined definitions, that cool brisk mountain-day, my mind surrendered to introspection. I then knew, gone were moments of childish rebellion. Gone were secure thoughts of no thoughts. Gone were absurdities of youthful innocence.

Dressed in simple garments, carrying bare essentials, we measured our way to the monastery where The Great One resided. Below us lay a thick layer of cloud. Sima was measuring her steps alongside Deeva. Her worn down body did not sway her mind from constructing tensegrity of ideas she ascertained essential to her existence. Darvish was a few steps ahead, relaying messages regarding the path. By absorbing its uncertainties, he eased the hardships of the trail for the rest of us.

There are occasions when I feel an insatiable yearning to have lived in a distant past or future; to be part of a civilization that set my norms, or a future civilization, with an inordinate reservoir of reason and passion, said Philsuk, extending her slender arm to hold mine.

Deeva, laboring a steep rise, stopped for a brief respite, examined his visual field and recited.

The accord is between life and I
I make decisions, life churns time
Meaningless or meaningful
It shutters my sense of self
To speckled ideas

Aside from conjecture of indecision
What matters is what I choose
What contrives is my will
And I have chosen this blazing life of solitude

This magnified affliction to endurance and reason
For I see no end but my own
No truth worth emulating
But truths that contrive my own

I approached Sima and Deeva.

Is it true The Great One has lived many thousands?

No one moved. No one rushed to heed an answer. Abashed and conforming, I absorbed silence with silence.

Darvish stopped atop a hill. The attentive transparency he radiated attracted the rest of us. The view was astonishingly captivating. A small opening amidst dense clouds framed a site adorned with light of a midday sun. The beach was perfectly painted with purest sand. An expanse of trees swayed beneath an occasional shower. Colorful prairies touched the ebb of canvas. We stood silent, absorbing every reflection until clouds closed this rapture in time-space. Darvish was the last to turn away.

It is a peaceful life to live in harmony of co-existence, he said with a melancholic demeanor.

It is a magnificent early morning rushing down lakes of serenity to form sunder thoughts and scrumptious ideas.

It is a desirable virtue to give for the sake of giving, to listen for the sake of listening, to forgive for the sake of forgiving.

It is a cogent resolution to disseminate medleys of pleasing metaphors.

In the epic of harmony, I am told, there is a perfect symmetry called compassion, said Philsuk holding Darvish by the hand, pulling him away from the scene.

The idea is as follows: we, collectively, elevate passion to compassion, absorb its components, give birth to euphemism and spew creative ideas.

In the epic of harmony, I am told; we are half selves, half social and none without the other. Along the way, we select disharmonious rules dictating what to give, whom to give, whom to deprive, how and how much to give. And those who get none, they do exist in our partitioned minds. In convenience of choosing not to know, they do exist.

This is no reprint of a master design. This is not a design of the highest design. This is an evolving human design.

Within context of such a paradigm, winners and losers are selected from a changing, metamorphosing pool of participants. There are no written details in this scenario of existence, only crude ideologies, probable outcomes and minds that perceive them as such.

On a hilltop, Sima leaned her shoulder against a tree.

Neither the beginning nor the end is the measure of a mind, she said, staring at the clouds.

She turned to Deeva.

I see no reason, no reason at all, except choices I make. Together, in dimension of humanity, high on imagination, we exude harmony of coexistence only to realize asymmetry of past, present and future. What jagged human formats, what desires, what logic permeates conclusions we invoke? True or false, right or wrong, boxed in the edifice of imagination, time changes our perspective while we pass time seeking the nature of our perspective.

Perception is not transferable. Each must perceive in its own privacy, of its own purpose.

Sima was immersed in a reflective state. Her eyes shined with radiance. She continued.

I think alone, isolated. Thinking of the future, unfolding rhapsodies, times and places: that bright sunny day beneath mount horizon, we laughed free.

She approached Deeva, stood next to him.

Passion is a simple expression. But when all of us, in groups of unimaginable dimensions, jump with joy and declare life our small private world, I think it silly. But silly is entwined with serious. Silly is simplicity of a complex occasion.

Life is a stage, and I am not sure if time is a moment forever gone or eternal. I am not sure how to be sure. How can I be sure? I think it true or false. I think it real or imagined. I think it meaningful or irrelevant.

Her mind spoke brighter than usual. Something compelled her to emotionally charged declarations.

I am an incredible chance, an aphorism of many dilemmas. She continued.

Lost in time-space-mind, craving truths to actualize myself in the universe of truths, I am an image that reflects on the image while imagining greatness of the image.

It is absurd I can imagine intricacies of an unknown truth while thinking complexities of truth itself.

She sat visibly shaken while the rest of us pondered at her didactic expressions.

Seemingly affected by Sima's emotions, Darvish uttered rare poetic expressions of his own.

Hello my friends. Welcome to my world of dubiety. Sit beside me. Let us regress awhile, you and I, mind-to-mind, cry-to-cry, laugh-to-laugh. We have much in common: our paranoid selves, our solitude and most audacious designs.

Truth shines its own, never reaching an end, or meaning to end.

The act of caring, the epiphany of being together, the merging of encased minds, these are necessities of our emotional logic.

Do we fathom depth of our yearning for paradigms that shift this logic? Do we realize how shallow we imagine our potential? Do we understand how deep we have delved into the mystery of existence? Do you see ignorance in my arrogance?

He rose, making his usual circular motion measuring each step with neurotic precision. He then held his posture steady, one foot at a time, balancing himself with wavering arms.

He spoke with clarity.

I used to wonder at the purpose of it all. Now I realize the universe an exercise in cohesiveness.

He reached the end of a circle.

Uncertainty narrows reality to smaller closets of certainty. The unified symmetry, that mysterious initial impression, compels the mind to imagine more keenly. It gives meaning to the word "origin."

He began a slow and methodical spin.

The chase is on, but the bait is nonexistent. Events may not repeat. Then again, the minds that think of what was may create what will be. That, by itself, could explain the notion of "everything." In defining reality, we design reality.

He stopped, looked down and repeated with measured clarity.

In defining reality, we design reality.

Philsuk rushed to save him from a fall. Darvish moved his hand in a defiant posture. Philsuk stood still.

The accumulated imagination of free wills has carried humanity to farthest corners of the Milky Way, he said, spinning with stretched arms.

The mind is evolving with evolving revelations. The possibilities are many and growing.

He lowered his voice.

Future is still uncertain. Death of our universe is a distinct probability.

One small twist of an idea, one moment of hesitation, one slight change of a parameter can set awry the probable making impossible possible, and possible a distant improbable.

I am fascinated by the suggestion that in defining reality, we are designing a new reality, said Philsuk, following him with keen attention.

Thinking is an evolving tapestry, I said joining Darvish and clumsily spinning around with stretched arms.

The mind begins a dry sponge absorbing what comes its way. The mind links the past, the present and future in a real domain called awareness. Awareness of reality is the reality. Reality of awareness is awareness itself. Without awareness, there is no reality to the observing object. And without reality, there is no awareness to observe existence. Awareness functions in real time, with real effect on probability of events.

Let me expound this confusing arrangement. "Nothing" is a measure of nonexistence. While we live, we have this incredible capacity to realize "everything" without acknowledging "nothing." What exactly is "nothing?" It has no physical meaning and can best be identified as the absence of something. Indeed, one encompassing definition of "nothing" is the absence of something.

Darvish was excited with the notion of "nothing." He jumped in.

In the domain of imagination "nothing" is a puzzling "everything." How can anything exist without its antithesis expressed as nothing until it manifests as something?

In the world of ideas time-space has no continuity. At such a state, the individual can unleash its freewill to control its destiny by controlling ideas that create that destiny. In the timeless domain of imagination, the concepts of "nothing" and "everything" find a transitive meaning. They are virtual concepts transcending the suffocating boundaries of living reality to a space in the collective imaginations for something highly intelligent.

Without a freewill the mind swings from idea to idea, helplessly trying to demarcate boundaries of its awareness with something sustainable. This something is often a virtual concept, an amorphous idea that generates hope.

There is a common thread in all of this. Hope is a fragile bridge between "everything" and "nothing."

Do I know the expanse of "everything?" Do I know strings of "everything?" Do I realize dimensions of "everything?" Perhaps I can. Maybe I am without knowing I am. Perhaps I will.

Philsuk followed Darvish's ideas.

Do we know nature is transparent? Do we treat our moments as our creation? Moments pass but in reality, it is us passing. Do we realize we decide the meaning of passing?

It is a euphemistic elucidation to speak of truth. In reality, we compromise the truth to ensure procreation and happiness. It is a euphemistic desire to pretend existence of truths without acknowledging our imaginative synthesis of truths.

Having heard Philsuk and Darvish I reached a conclusion and expressed it loud.

I will not compromise our collective freedoms to assume human destiny something else's destiny. I see no clash of titans, no mysterious beings fraught with didactic or mischievous ideas determining or defining our lives. I only see passing moments, emotional displays, willful enactments, random states and neurological condensations.

I see no reason to compromise the philosophy of self-determination. Deep in my awareness, where everything begins and ends, I see a matrix of perceptions constantly changing and molding new clones of perception. Anything outside this boundary is a speculative abstraction of quantum nature.

Philsuk reflected deeper.

What if the collective consciousness of our species influences universal awareness? What if we could live long enough to reach the isthmus of total awareness? What if awareness is a singularity? What if there is collective consciousness as singularities? What if meaning is a human perception of no particular meaning? What if anything imagined is a reality? What if awareness is a universal dimension of quantum nature, transcending all dimensions to form a singularity of a peculiar nature? What if awareness is the seed of new things to come? What if there are levels and layers of awareness, we have yet to uncover? What if beings that furnished the universe its designs have since vanished? What if the universe emerged out of "nothing" and gave birth to sentient designs perfecting its original design? What if all or none of these possibilities hold?

She looked exhausted, out of breath, out of ideas.

The possibilities are many, said Sima with a soothing voice. But the reality is "I." Truth is "I." Perception is "I." Life is "I." Knowledge is "I." And when "I" dies none will exist except perceptions, of "I."

"Us" is where "I" finds comparative meaning and expands its awareness for greater absorption of reality.

Deeva was visibly shaken. He approached Sima, sat next to her and recited.

In existential notion of existence
Progeny of a willful predicament is measurable
And determined by obscure reasoning

I find most enthralling
The idea of existence as a coordinate of thoughts

The idea of life
As I see
In dimension of human definitions
Is an imperfect symmetry of expectations
I sense with my acclimated virtues
And impulses I coordinate with others

It is my decision to conclude, in conscience
Without a definite beginning or end
Awareness is irrefutably isolated

What regularities may dictate my awareness
I cannot tell but foretell this simple truth
To forsake my freedoms
To dispose my version of reality
To surrender my determination as a unique self
Is to forsake my awareness of self

That I am the cheetah and the gazelle
The natural and the false
All thoughts, all truths
The universe of our combined verses
And nothing, nothing at all

Philsuk seemed bewildered.

I am confused by reality as a manifestation of our perceptions. I am confused. How imperfect is our reality? I am confused by the notion of "nothing."

If reality is transpicuous, if reality is a manifest of our combined perceptions, if life is what we think it is, then truth is a perplexing notion of our relevance to each other.

We are truly freed or enslaved by limits we set upon ourselves, she said seemingly struck by an epiphany.

Daylight slowly faded as the cycle of life approached its repeated conclusion. The closer we approached the monastery our excitement and anticipation climaxed to intolerable levels. I could feel its tension tormenting every muscle, twisting and deforming them to contorted shapes.

Dim light of a full moon spread across the sky. I heard Deeva read a poem he had recited long ago. He seemed amused by its repetitive and reflective connotations. He versed it several times as many began reciting it with him.

I am
Therefore I think

I think
Therefore I am

I think I am
Therefore
I am

I think I am
What I think

I think I am
Therefore I am
What I think

I think I am
Therefore I think
What I am

I addressed Sima as she leaned on a smooth rock. She lay motionless.

If I am what I think! What then holds me from achieving the highest? Perhaps I am too consumed with daily chores. Perhaps I am diluted with possibilities. Perhaps I am too consumed with pain and pleasure.

If everything is a part of me, and I am a part of everything, then "I" has no significance of its own. Awareness is trapped within a convoluted maze of social and psychological without clear dividing lines to demarcate the self as an inclusive entity.

In such a confusing domain of awareness, it is compassion glazing our totality a harmonious context, said Philsuk.

We must observe the universe through compassionate filters. Else, we may inadvertently eliminate our civilization and possibly the universe. "We" possesses such a potential. "We" can overcome and superimpose itself on "I" unless "I" is a freewill and capable of observing itself outside the social boundaries: a seemingly impossible but quite a probable task.

A good friend once reminded me of complexity of nothingness, said Darvish.

Do you not see? It rules us, my friend said with conviction. There must be an all-encompassing reason, she impressed on me.

I thought it a while. I thought it deep. Yes, I said. It rules mighty, but it is "I" imagining its might, or extent of its content. It is "I" assuming the relevance or irrelevance of its rule. It is "I" asserting its significance or insignificance. It is "I" thinking its existence or nonexistence.

"I" has greater significance than "everything" and "nothing."

Life is inordinately bizarre, I said, confused by what I just heard.

I am not a prophet, nor a beggar, nor a submissive. I am not a believer, nor someone to believe in. Passion is my desire. It entails compassion. Logic is my quest. It entails understanding. I live for reason when compelled to think of reason. I live for passion when passion serves me well. Did I assume my integrity a passionate pretension? I am a fool of many faces. I am an expression of interacting neurons, appropriate or inappropriate levels of neurotransmitters and the complexity of axons and axioms.

I do not know who I am. And if the burden of observance is on me, if "I" has greater significance than the universe, I am truly lost. Without the universe, chaos is impossible. Without chaos, organization is impossible. Without organization "I" is impossible. But the universe started from something that entails "nothing."

Darvish seemed irritated by an idea. He rushed his words.

Irrespective of its reality, the universe is what we think it is. There is a remote but conceivable possibility the universe might become what we imagine it to be. One look at our immediate surroundings and this supposition assumes a clear reality.

We are expanding. As we expand, we change the space around us. The space around us could, in some distant future, encompass the galaxy and conceivably, the universe. The potential and possibility are there. "Us" is an unlimited and undefined potential.

At highest or lowest of its stratified format, awareness is an accumulated concept, said Sima.

Not even The Great One is fully aware of its potentials. It too is subject to uncertainty of being and nothingness.

We are all scaling the same tree of evolution. Each branch of this epic contains a variety of mutations. The task is to transcend this separation with synchronicity of ideas without cutting off branches. The human tree of evolution indicates ascendancy of life from autonomic to cognitive to imaginative. We have evolved from early biological forms of simple complexity to beings of phenomenal complexity.

The fire had burned itself to a glowing ash. I crouched closer to its warmth. Deeva seemed to have fallen asleep. Suddenly, Darvish appeared before me, shivering, dazed, overwhelmed by an emotional state. I placed him near the fire. He made himself comfortable while keeping an eye on Deeva.

He has a wonderful mind. He said, looking at Deeva while collecting the heat in his robe.

Have you heard his latest poem? I inquired.

I have heard it many times. He began reciting it with passion.

Do I know life
Do I know chaos
Do I know String Theory
Why this yearning to gain all
What decisions conjure happiness
What medleys sway humanity
Why we seek a theory of everything

This very moment
I am aware
Of an apropos life
Of "everything" and "nothing"
But do I know limits of awareness
And when I know all reasons
When "everything" is optimized in awareness
There is always
What then
What will I be then
I mean
Which facade will I wish to mask then

Think
And we must choose to think
What is "us"
What we want to be
Which future is our destiny

For now
Pleasure rules
For now
Savagery rules
For now
We kill
We eat
We hate
We condone aleatory
Abrogate passion
And affront abstruse dilemmas with bigotry
For now
We are neurotic
Euphoric
Evangelical

I stretched beside Darvish. He had long stopped shivering. Following a meteorite, I reflected.

The idea of life as a collection of ideas or a string of principles; the idea of life as a purposeful existence or a chaotic organization; the idea of life as a civilization: these are bewildering thoughts invoking an array of interpretations none more real than the human capacity to think of them and attempt to absolve their ambiguity.

What we see is huge and yet so small, said Philsuk preoccupied with her shoes.

What we observe is full and yet so empty. What we perceive is everywhere and nowhere.

Darvish sat up, stirred the fire.

Truth is an idea consummated in time-space-mind. Truth is a statistical probability.

Evolution knows no judgment. It connects, with impeccable harmony, every component to the rest of existence. Evolution is a collection of manifested probabilities. It has no awareness. Nor do directives of a single awareness hold sway over its course. Evolution does not impose judgment between a cat ready to jump and its prey: a colorful parrot or a rat. Evolution is a necessary condition for development and survival.

We are who we are because chaos rules. I am who I am because a sperm and an egg beat the odds by millions collapsing everything to a single probability of a Zygote that beat the odds by millions to survive and become a fetus. "I" is a manifested probability.

Aside from biological evolution, there is the all-important social evolution, said Philsuk in continuation of Darvish's thoughts.

This collective manifestation, through the span of history, has exhibited vectors affecting the individual and the universe.

My ancestors did not discern evolution. They attributed their existence to dictate of other beings: almost always a male, almost always adorned with exaggerated human qualities, almost always reflecting their wishful thoughts. Their partial fancy could not perceive the equivocal ways of the universe, nor were they fully capable of exalting their perceptions beyond reality of oral and sexual.

The mighty sun was a welcome feature of their lives. Light, as a quintessential good, promised clarity of purpose. And with each sunset, they flocked together to evade the nightmare of threatening beasts in the statistical safety of numbers.

Physical might was right. How could it not be? It meant survival. And weakness was a deadly wrong. How could it not be? It invited death.

In the end, it was the sun, as a red giant, that proved deadly. And darkness, as in empty space, proved a savior. In the end, it was not physical might but willful might that saved humankind. Such is the irony of existence. Forever is a relative concept. Judgment is a relative concept. Good and bad are relative concepts. Evolution is a relative concept.

A sudden revelation consumed my awareness. I had sensed such a force before. It usually meant an epiphany of some sort. I stood, took off my robe, placed it on Sima. I then joined Philsuk.

Sima sat up, faced the fire. It is a difficult night to sleep, she said laying her head on Philsuk's shoulders.

We can best realize ourselves in togetherness. She paused.

The quantum notion of observance applies to humans as well. Only in each other's presence can we share thoughts for a higher resolution. We need solace in one another to fill the emptiness within. We need each other to calibrate our individual measure of reality. The sense of isolation and the social latitude of togetherness coexist in each mind.

She stood, placed a piece of wood on fire. A solitary owl kept watch as we stared at rising flames. Stimulated by a quintessential sensation, I remembered. I remembered roaring thunders and streaming rivers. I remembered triple rainbows. I remembered sitting beneath weeping willows and palm trees.

I looked up and observed the moon beneath a canopy of bright little stars. I remembered being told, as a child, they shined to furnish my happiness. I was asked to choose a star for only then it would be mine. As a child, I thought. Upon first conception, I took it for granted they were all mine.

Immersed in sanctuary of reflection, baffled by magnificence of life and bedazzled by Sima's words, I kept the dialogue alive.

And this wonder need not be altered by words. It need not be amended with affliction or admiration. Life knows no false, no truth, no right, no wrong. Life is a collection of manifested probabilities amalgamating impressions of awareness. Life is particles, matter, energy, universal constants, chaos, probability and all such mindless realities.

Life is a synthesis of actual and virtual perceptions. Life is absurd. The act of living is absurd.

With the arrival of dawn, reality took a sudden hold as daily chores defined existence. I hurried to reach my beloved mentors. As usual, they were engaged in a revealing discussion. Deeva, with his usual poetic boldness, was exposing an inner secret.

Dreams, dreams, dreams
This moment is but dreams
Imagine a moment in future
That is what we are, are we not
A future moment, in dreams

Life is intrepid, tumultuous, transpicuous
Compared to this gamut of stars
My life is a passing cloud
Which is to say
It is raining in mind

So dream careful
Dream grand
Dream gentle

Swift in pleasure
Cajoled by castles of dreams
Satiated in imagination
Driven by pleasure
Each for itself and none complete
We are
A gamut of dreams

Philsuk laughed at a lazy moment of no significance. She looked around absorbing reflections of the crisp sky. She then reflected on subtle realities of living.

Air is fresh. She inhaled deep.

It is a nice feeling. She shrugged her shoulders.

Stones on grass, trees all around, sound of a city far away.

When I am not here things are the same, I suppose. Happiness is in me, I suppose. When I die, I lose all this, I suppose.

Deeva approached Philsuk with an admiring face, covered her shoulders with his arm and squeezed her onto his broad chest and recited.

It is disconcerting to know life is short
But is it, in dimension of passion
Passion knows no time-passage
Only time-motivated
Am I a fool imagining life a passionate consistency
Am I imagining existence a lifeless creation

It is disconcerting to know life is a passing
But is it, in dimension of social
For social knows no time passage
Only time-induced
Am I a fool imagining life a social eternity

It is disconcerting to know life is random
But is it, in dimension of hope
For hope knows no time passage
Only time motivated
Am I an incontinent mind imagining life a hopeful universe
Am I wrong in assuming hope a human resolve

It is disconcerting to know life knows no judgments
But it does, in human dimension
Am I wrong in assuming judgment a unique event
Am I measuring our logic higher than the universe

Facing Darvish and betaken by Deeva's unusual reflection, I joined the conversation.

I keep on reminding myself life is a quest for simplicity. I keep on thinking we are innocent, guilty, pure, befuddled, together, alone. I keep on thinking quintessence is a conjecture open to speculation. I keep on thinking we are isolated in clusters, satisfied, stratified and most peculiarly paranoid as mortals.

I measure truth in idioms I dare understand. I do not go gentle into life to find reason. I do not go gentle into life to find happiness. I feel life in obtruded dimensions, in imposed realities, in daring contests.

Sima put her hand on my shoulder.

To imagine life a simple moment, as autumn leaves fall a million waves and sway ponds to shine those waves, as I pass onto ocean to weep clouds, is to fractionate life to fraternity of simplest conjugates.

Deeva gathered himself near the fire and recited.

Shining minds bloom roses
They think deep, none shallow
From subjective images
From formation to disintegration
Shining minds blossom lasting perceptions
They actuate hope out of destitute
Words assume varying definitions
All spoken similar and none alike
From childhood emptiness to uncertainties of age
In search of meaningful resolutions
Shining minds span a gamut of brazen ideas
Devote their lives to edifying norms
Accept temperate means
Blossom archives of human passion
And vanish as universal debris
To bloom colorful thoughts

Is there a meaning transcending our being
Is there a contrived intent in our shining
I am a fallible fool
Assuming my time an endearing time
My mind is infested with a coffer of illusions
All the dispositions I assume

All the dreams I envision
Are allegories of temporary diction
And this fiction of whimsical truths
It is a beginning as it is an end
But there is no beginning
No dictated reality of its end
Only emotions, spoken moments
Neurological reflexes, modules of behavior
Design
And chaos

If there are meanings transcending our being
If time can stop for lives that cannot
If there is a contrived intent in our being
It is explained by shining minds

All was quiet. The day-traders of life and death had long surrendered their pursuit to night crawlers. A distant comet emanated from a celestial display. I followed it with neurotic conviction until I too relinquished reality to idiom of dreams.

Next day, as I awoke, the stars had disappeared in a wavering haze of twilight. The comet I slept with had long vanished. Sima and Deeva were set upon their journey. The procession was well on the way as the beaming sun promised another grueling day of revelations.

I could clearly see the monastery where The Great One resided. Built with stone and clay, amidst a mountain of hard rock, it stood fragile. There seemed nothing unusual about it. No magical feelings emanated from it. No beaming light or mysterious beings or unusual features furnished it.

A long line of visitors awaited behind a small wooden door. The act of sitting and waiting had a precise unspoken order. The young and the strong gave way to old and frail. I submitted myself to the arrangement. I waited my time not sure when that moment would come.

Time lapsed, in silence, in meditative states, in sharing of thoughts. One at a time the seekers entered the monastery never to be seen again. There was no continuity of present and future past the monastery.

My turn has come, said Sima chokingly revealing intensity of her emotion. I kneeled before her, held her hand, pressed it against my face, showered it with kisses. Somehow, this moment was a moment of departure for all eternity. I sensed it with every bit of my being. I bowed and kissed her wrinkled toes. The thought of losing her was an unpleasant idea I could not bear.

The idea of meeting The Great One had become a focal point in all our lives. The path of life after the monastery was a mystery. It was assumed the audience with The Great One would change everything. Friends would part. An era would end. The trail would vanish, and the seekers, one by one, would embark on a path of their choosing.

Sima was visibly shaken as Darvish and Philsuk surrounded her, showered her with kisses. Deeva all the while sat quiet. Sima had her eyes on him. She approached him, sat next to him, gazed at the monastery.

Forget age. Forget past. Forget immortality. To fool oneself eternal, knowing death is the end and then nothing, is a waste of living. In this life of infinite paths and one definite end, best I have is awareness. If I feel I have done well, without deception, I have lived well.

It is difficult to part, but I must. Such a burdensome moment of decision is before me. I must be on my way. It is improper to keep the procession waiting.

With her usual compromising manner, she stood, turned face, measured her surroundings and stepped inside. The door shut close erasing a window of reality, I wished to keep open.

Darvish, Philsuk and I sat motionless. Stricken by grief, by harshness of losing a beloved friend, we cried.

Deeva, having sensed our grief, sat next to us, put his long arms on our shoulders and recited.

> The river runs wild
> Beneath stormy thoughts
> In lavish valleys of imagination
> In flat lands of time
> The river runs wild
>
> I sit by its shores and ponder
> Life comes only to pass
> The toddler days
> Our past
> The teenage years that do not last
> The pleasures we cast
> Like a river wild
> All come to pass

Why must it pass? Philsuk protested with anger.

Why should I lose the chance of enjoying her existence? Who would ease the burden of stormy thoughts engulfing us?

Her head fell low.

Darvish rushed to our rescue.

Losing loved ones is pain mortals must endure. In my brief excursion in the domain of awareness, many have elevated my senses higher than I imagined possible. Losing the first one was most difficult. It happened when I was too young and full of untested energy. It happened when, in my awareness, death was not an imminent reality. When its truth shook my convention, I screamed: why must it be so? Of course, there were no answers forthcoming. My failure to understand mortal ends gave rise to false impressions I was forced to compromise.

Losing the second loved one was a reminder of the harshness reality could extol. I became convinced life was an engagement in cruel possibilities often manifested much sooner than later. I reasoned the nature of reality an emotionally charged game of chance we affront in equivocal terms, times and places.

After losing the third loved one, I dwelled on preservation of life. I focused on procuring happiness as the most valued commodity of existence. Every living moment became a concept of the intricate nature of eternal significance.

I can now smile when a friend dies. I can easily forget and forgive. I have accepted their passing for I have accepted my own passing.

Time lapsed in gray hair and forgotten memories. The door opened and shut, one by one swallowing the best of our companions. The dreaded moment was finally before us. It was Deeva's turn. He rose with hesitation as the gatekeeper awaited his appearance. Philsuk covered her face to hide her sorrow. Looking Deeva in the eyes, I wept. His being had given a sense of continuity to all our lives. Faced with his disappearance, I felt the pain of grief.

He approached Darvish, held his head, laid a kiss on it. Laden with tremors, Darvish was beside himself. Deeva then reached out and dragged my head onto his chest. Philsuk grabbed him around the abdomen.

You have been good friends, he said squeezing us onto his broad existence.

I cried. Darvish cried. Philsuk cried. Deeva recited.

> My mind is whittling amidst a journey in the light
> What a surprise
> This is a trip amongst the stars
> Like downy-flakes on a cool bristly mountain top
> I attest a dare, a warming delight
> Like withering leaves of a weeping willow
> I assemble life high and low
> But who am I in this paradigm of designs
> Am I a dichotomy of gloom and delight

Am I a speck trapped in a site
Am I in right frame of mind
It matters not
I have thoughts to live and nothing to lose
Nothing but everything and I

He then disappeared through the gate.

I am not certain, how long I waited. Daylight appeared and disappeared more quickly than I could experience its bewildering effects. The door opened and closed more than I could count. It opened once more. An attendant asked the next seeker to step in. No one moved. I looked around in amazement. A young seeker stared at me with reverence. Looking down at creases within folds of my skin, I saw thin white hair down to my waist. I had grown old. The revelation was sudden. It was my turn.

Darvish and Philsuk approached me. We held each other in a unified field, melting as one and flawless. Darvish was the first to let go. He stood, attempted a circle and uncharacteristically babbled.

Life is what it is: simple, transparent, without a beginning, without an end. The prophets, claiming themselves righteous and insulated, are dead and gone. Like many before them, they left us a legacy of falsehood.

At times, it is difficult to imagine what we have done and might. The distinction is easy. Am I not your vagrant no-good cheap beggar vagabond improper self? Am I not selling my conscience for comforts? Am I not a self-righteous grab-all-you-can sorrow-ridden beast searching greatness in whatever I can put my hands on?

I do not know. Do not know why we live such shrunken lives? I do not know why we teach our children same fallacies, but who am I to cloud your mind? Who am I to question your values?

Philsuk was surprisingly less emotional and more accepting. She separated herself, stared at us with passionate eyes of an old friend.

Be on your way, she embraced me. The line of seekers is getting longer with each moment of hesitation. Be on your way and remember passionate gestures, and caring thoughts, make you who you are.

Cautiously, I stepped through the door. A keeper led me into a yard decorated with an old apple tree leaning over a small spring trickling into a pond. A few keepers were consumed by daily chores. None looked at me. None acknowledged my presence. Years of ongoing pilgrimage had made them impervious to strangers. I was abandoned at a doorway. A damp sweat cooled my skin as my heart pounded. My deep and fast breaths could not keep pace with my hunger for air. I reached out, knocked on the door, waited without success. I tried, repeatedly. I looked around seeking rescue, but none was forthcoming. I opened the door and stepped in.

The room was built of clay. In the far corner, a small body of gray hair and bony stature sat crouched on a straw mat. There it was, The Great One.

The simplicity of the room, lack of furniture and ornaments, created a soothing décor. Sunlight poured through a small hole in the ceiling, lighting the room to perfection. There was an air of complexity to this experience. Every moment, every move seemed measured, calculated to its smallest fraction. The most noticeable feature of the room was an undercurrent of simplicity localized at its presence.

Was I supposed to kneel? Was I supposed to wait for permission to sit? Was I supposed to initiate a dialogue? The Great One was as quiet as motionless. Its face was half-covered with a garb that extended down to its toes. I was certain of its awareness of every move I made.

I sat by the door on the clay floor. Silence ruled, setting the stage for cognitive delights that followed.

—Be at ease. Time-space unfolds many truths. Say what you may. Leave when you may. Within these small boundaries, think what you may. And when you leave, do leave with compassion in mind. Do give to those in need of taking. Do take from those in need of giving.

At last, I heard its voice, its soothing calm voice. I could not tell its age or sex. I did not know what to say or what to feel. Shrunken in my small self, I spoke with a shivering voice.

—They say you are the wisest human alive. They say you know everything. They say you can reveal many truths.

—Let us be clear on our intentions. Let us set boundaries of this encounter. Do not attempt to impose your will on me, as I will not onto you. My thoughtful or thoughtless ideas are mine alone. I live with the conviction that I am an absorbing self. To define my life a passing, and the passing a quiescent metaphor in high and low, is my psychological quintessence. I have many weaknesses and strengths. But I choose. In every step of every move, I choose. Conscious, autonomic, or driven by unconscious, I choose. I choose not wholly with reason. I choose with passion. I choose with myself at the center and my center at a distant periphery. I choose knowing I am eccentric, exhaustively aware and driven by emotions that saved my ancestors and now are haunting me.

They say I am mythological and astonishingly universal. I do not heed such thoughts. Words have a way of metamorphosing. In their metamorphic depictions, realities often become twisted, transforming the object of attention and its awareness to a new sphere of intention.

—I have been on this journey most my contentious life. I have watched my skin crack, and my hair discolor. I have yet to reconcile the significance of perception. Do you conceive the universe as your private perception?

—I have a lifelong dilemma in this brief expedition in life. When I examine my awareness, I see a distant mirage where I search for comforts and conformities. With a keener look at many layers of my awareness, I find pleasure and that most illusive "everything:" everything of staying alive, everything of knowing it all, bending and deforming my perception of realities.

When I reduce my awareness to simplest and smallest fractions, I see the same mirage shrouded in "nothing."

The reality I am is unsettling. It fluctuates from an illusive something to an even more elusive nothing. Within such confusing boundaries, I often lose certainty of knowing truths. I cannot be certain if what I know is truth, half-truth, false, or my own wishful make-believe. Closest I have reached certainty is in the consuming, dull and dreary domain of physical chores and functional necessities.

I have a lifelong task of understanding awareness. I have a confusing ordeal of understanding existence by understanding my own. I am not fully aware. I do not know myself. Perhaps I can never be fully aware. My awareness is an evolving variable determined by parameters constituting totality of existence. As the parameters change, so does my awareness often without my awareness of their change.

I have no doubt most everything I am, is a puzzle of my own private dilemmas. Amidst a convoluted maze of probabilities, I am decoherence of particles manifesting my awareness. Isolated within such a frame, it is difficult to claim perceiving reality unless reality is well defined.

True or false, real or virtual, these dilemmas and the extent of my understanding their ramifications are my wholeness. The perceptions composing reality are my aphorisms. The universe I know is reality of my cumulative perceptions. The universe I do not know is much greater and escapes my limited capacity for perception.

—I have difficulty defining truth. Each time I reason truth, I justify one thing or another. Can truth explain something eternal and transparent? Can truth be wrapped in mathematical formulas and changed when desired?

—Truths we have devised to justify myths are creations of human imagination. Truths we have deduced through the laborious and tedious act of compiling data, and have withstood the test of scrutiny and repetition, are real parameters of the realities we seek. They delineate the universe as a vector of our cumulative analysis. Even these truths are constantly revised by new observations. Truths we perceive as a result of alienated neuronal condensations are fallacies. Truth is an abused concept often warped and amalgamated to suit our purpose.

Truth, I have learned, has variations from temporary and passing significance to relatively lasting and persisting presence.

Most truths are neither true nor false. Only when defined as such, or observed as such, they become true or false.

A purely objective mind is too diluted to manifest authoritative reality in the format of truths. Such an existence is absorbed in its attempt to remain neutral and fair. It cannot afford logical and emotional swings and self-serving aphorisms. Such a mind will have difficulty perceiving truths but a measured observation of truths.

The universe knows one single truth: its totality. Nothing in the universe exists in isolation. Everything is connected and an integrated part of the universal totality. The original perfect symmetry has dissolved to partial symmetries as chaos approaches infinity of nothing. Time is a measure of this integrated reality as the universe expands its asymmetry and disintegration.

Within such boundaries, truth is a changing observation with factual, factitious, imaginative, misleading and revealing connotations.

—Which axiom explains reality of this moment? Is it quantum abstraction collapsing possibility of galactic dimensions to reality of now and here? How does a universe render continuity of passing? Is there a need for two or more universes to observe each other? Are we riding on a ubiquitous waveform of many singularities each a reflection of something we sense but cannot realize?

—Collapsing probabilities to a set of sensory perceptions in an individual mind is time-bound and improbable. It is a private amalgam of amorphous consistency we attempt to verify and reconcile with others like us.

The mind can differentiate quantum and classical states. This ability creates the condition of sensing the universe without being lost in its classical enormity or quantum minuteness. The quantum state of imagination does not recognize time a forward-moving sequence of events, but its classical perception does.

Collapsing of social probabilities to realities is a unique event energized by fields of our combined resonance in a virtual state of unpredictable and predictable nature. This matrix: living and nonliving, logical and emotional, is a transparent, evolving and asymmetrical manifest. It is a time-bound phenomenon of forward moving manifest. It has no awareness of its own and resonates from the cumulative awareness of its selected cognitive constituents. As such, it is a most perplexing manifest.

This intimate connection between micro and macro, between animate and inanimate, gives format and manifestation to many universal phenomena.

What I have said is a synthesis of my imaginative and perceptive abilities. They merely signify my attempt at connecting with the universe through you and my own inner sanctum. As such, they are subjective and personal.

—When I look deep into the space I see time passed. It is the immediate surroundings delineating my sense of presence and purpose.

Deep at the center of my awareness is a pristine image of reality. The deeper I dwell on its essence the murkier its reality.

Deeper inward I travel, I sense a solitude that attempts to escape and find itself amidst the society. How can I reconcile this exhausting contradiction?

—It was a damp shallow evening, long ago, when twisted thoughts traversed a meadow of ideas to land a soft kiss on a child broken by the reality of poverty.

The Great One leaned back on the clay wall for a moment of reflection and continued.

It was a moment of bizarre texture as I tried, then cried, and surrendered to pain and suffering with sorrow and empathy. Which way did I turn to clear my emotionally confused awareness? Which moral direction I chose to escape that frozen state? Which illusion, which justification did I use to ease my troubled mind?

A few moments later, the child lay dead, ready for scavengers to consume it. A few days and the body metamorphosed to many unseen shreds feeding unseen many with its decomposition. My sorrow was reduced to losing an awareness that never had a chance to actualize its potential. If only I could see lives that it fed, I may see the entire experience as a metamorphic passing of one thing to another.

Truth is, everything about that experience was universally neutral: the fate of a child left to die, the pain of an observer frozen by exhausting reality of the moment, and the many lives that thrived on its death: they were events repeated over and over in a universe that refuses to pass judgment on events.

Upon reflection on death of an abandoned child, I realized my fallible self a bastion of rationalized truths. The child did not have to die, or die as a result of social abuse and neglect.

But children die, and species appear and disappear.

Have I actualized in recent times to accommodate current realities? Am I so docile, domesticated, selfish, and arrogant to ignore the pain I have caused in gaining my comforts? Am I too immature and lethargic to realize my psyche is built and brewed with cries of despair, with exploitation, with child labor, with infant mortality, with malnutrition, with borders that secure separations, with economic segregation, with wars and the fallacy of superior and inferior?

Is there a moment of purity enlightening reality of the self? I look, and look deep, to find that nexus. All I see is hope. In hope I see everything educible. In darkest of moments when skin peels naked and the mind despairs, I see hope. In hope I find a life-sustaining force.

If I could define hope, I could capture it in a reservoir and tap into it, at will, for synthesis of greatest virtues.

The gap between the innermost sense of solitude and the outermost sense of belonging to the universe is real. To acknowledge this reality is the beginning of an attempt to understand the self as a bridge between awareness embroiled with judgment and the universe devoid of judgment.

—When I look deep inside, I do not find a perfect image but an image that yearns for perfection. When I look deep in space, I see images of something too awesome to comprehend. Why do I dwell on boundaries of these two abstract phenomena?

The Great One opened its robe to examine my physical being. I saw a trace of its face beneath the shadow of the garb over its head. It appeared frail and peaceful.

In search of a meaningful purpose for our existence, we search the universe from smallest to darkest, said The Great One with passion.

Some choose to imagine. Some choose to imagine what others imagine. Some are too preoccupied to imagine. Possessed by our version of truth, we forget simplest of rules. No matter how, who, or when, what color, composition, or gain, it is us raising the questions. In search of truths and happiness, we choose desired formations. True or false, we make it a question. Then, we suggest tales of its composition. In search of truths, we ask the questions. In search of happiness, we answer all questions.

The deeper we expose possibilities of the self the murkier our vision of the self. And if the answers are meant to enlighten us by opening the gates of eternity and certainty, then we have a long journey to a nirvana that exists in the virtual space of our shared imagination.

The most amazing aspect of our shared imagination is its prepotency to be manifest in a timeless and cumulative fashion. Imagined social wishes manifest independent of the individual dreams. The virtual aspect of our gathering determines the reality.

The real significance of truth is a comparative manifest. Truth is a variable of our collective.

The universe, with all its ambiguities, is ours to explore by observation. As we do so, our perception of its reality changes. Does the universe change as we observe it? Do we change as we define it? Can the observation change the observer with greater intensity than the observed?

—True, in search of enlightenment we devise the questions and the answers, but time is not on our side. All I know is what lies within boundaries of this classical reality designated as a physical "I."

I seek answers from the civilization knowing my observations could be limited by the structure and capacity of my existence. If unsatisfied, I seek answers from imagined virtual possibilities outside reality of the human phenomenon. Are we wasting our destiny seeking a state of existence that does not exist but might be manifest if we wish it as a civilization, in some distant future, outside the domain of my existence?

—Allure your mind with a smile, versed The Great One.

We have crossed gates of selfishness soon to face truths of togetherness. In between, we have time to reflect on reality of living. There is no logic but human logic. There are no heavenly metaphors, only minds that imagine them as such.

To imagine life a chain of simple moments as autumn leaves fall a million waves, as they pass onto oceans to weep over clouds and sway ponds to shine those waves, is to imagine life a chain of inspiring events.

To imagine life a chain of passing, passing lives and passing thoughts, is to summarize life a fraternity of human ideas and accept their passing in our passing.

To imagine life a collection of simple events, as moths flicker a meaningless plight, and Bats await their passing, is to surmise life half full while holding an empty glass.

To imagine life a chain of thoughtful moments twisted in unknown dimensions, and see reality as a bizarre idiom, is my goblet of understanding.

I hold it beneath life's cracks while imagining the universe in its entirety and complexity in the plight of a single moth.

Time ago, I keenly observed a lizard. It just stood. Unfettered by my observation, it just stood.

Do you know I can eliminate you with a stroke of my will? Do you realize your vulnerability? I wondered.

It just stood. So did I. I dared not cross its path. I dared not question its resolve. I dared not disturb its existence. I strung my wisdom on a compassionate string and amicably yielded.

Be my lizard and let me be yours. Observe me as I observe you. The waves of our observation affect us both as they affect the universe observing us.

Aside from our individual biological isolation, we are connected to the rest of the universe in varying degrees of affinity. If we are a distinct part of the universe, then "I" is much more than an isolated self.

—Of all the human virtues I find compassion most enthralling. The question is what frames our compassion and to what end, we extend our compassion, be it to a lizard or a human?

—We reason for certainty. We reason for a beginning. We reason for an ending. We reason the nature of existence. We reason for pleasure, for a pain-free psychological satisfaction. To a mortal, in every reason there is one common conclusion: there are no lasting reasons. In such a moment of realization, it is compassion temporizing our thoughts on a string of emotions.

If humanity is a required state for a higher form of actualization, then compassion is the concept that makes it sustainable. Compassion begins from within the self, makes an etymological and socially connecting journey as an interpretive phenomenon, before returning to the inner self for a greater reflection.

Universal constants are the beginning and the end of most of our reasons, but none can bind us together stronger than compassion. As an offshoot of the human condition, compassion is a reason onto itself and a framework for the best of our reason.

Perceive gentle this image of life. It bleeds when no compassion is unveiled. Perceive gentle this moment of reality. Smile your life lucid and perceive gentle this moment of truths. It dies meaningless without compassionate thoughts. Perceive gentle this brief experience of living. Comfort your mind with reason. Absorb its cloudy ups and showery downs. Enjoy its flickering moments of epiphany. This exhausting passage through time-space of your quantum mind depicts holograms of confusion when compassion is not extolled.

Allure your mind with passion and reason and perceive gentle grand theories of our lives. What matters is who we think we are. Perceive gentle transient meanings.

Human reason, I have learned, is hollow without compassionate textures.

—Life is its own reason. How am I to infer infinity and universality if there are no lasting conclusions other than what we reason?

—Infinity is a ubiquitous notion of mathematical significance. It gives a relative meaning to the finite capacity of a mortal. Eternal existence is a subliminal desire of a mortal. Infinity and eternity are virtual concepts projecting the illusion of something real and finite to the imaginative stratosphere of omnipotence and omnipresence.

Eternity is a logical pursuit to a cognitive being. It promises a lasting awareness. It promises to understand "everything." It promises ascendancy to the highest format of awareness.

Mortal awareness is a most troubling manifest. It implies the existence of probable, imagined and real in the virtual world of a mind, then nothing. It implies perception of time and multiple dimensions, then nothing. It allows traversing time-space in an imaginative domain as unique and meaningful as traveling in the physical universe, then nothing.

Boundaries of infinity and universality are imagined in human mind before their observation as actual phenomena. Infinity is a mathematical speculation of immortal possibility. Infinity and eternity are virtual concepts that satisfy a mortal's need for transcendence.

—Beside our individual and social existences, is there anything of which we can be certain? The dimensions of the universe seemingly are too immense to be real. Can it be we are deceived by our sensory perceptions?

—The universe is ruled by chaos. I am certain of that. The universe is ruled by partial symmetries. I am certain of that. The universe began with a perfect symmetry. I am certain of that. There are designs manifesting classical reality while satisfying quantum directives. I am certain of that. Human destiny is an evolving design. I am certain of that. Human directives are increasingly dependent on our collective will. I am certain of that. This section of the universe is friendly to biological existence. I am certain of that. My existence is modular and adaptive in nature. I am certain of that. Human civilization has a probable potential for immortality. I am certain of that. One reason at a time, one layer at a time, we are unraveling mysteries of the universe. I am certain of that. The human species could vanish with one cataclysmic event. I am certain of that. All I have mentioned has certainty of speculative nature. I am certain of that.

The Great One declared its certainties as I collapsed to a small world of my own certainties. The biggest certainty, I was sure of, was reality of the moment. Reflecting on the dilemma of being and nothingness, I dared to ask of the nature of our encounter.

—Why this moment of conversation? Why human existence?

—Beyond my earthling imagination lays a majestic universe, The Great One versed after a long pause.

In every alluring thought, beyond my enisled sense of judgment, there is a gamut of probabilities, none beyond my imagination.

What exactly is my reality? Is it an assembly of thoughts with virtual and actual significance? Am I a fractured and distorted contortion of images of transcending manifest? Am I a fraction of a purely epiphenomenal state? Is the anthropic principle the reason for our existence?

Whatever the case may be. I am here and now. Whatever my nature, I am my thoughts. I am a time-space-mind. Whatever the universe may be. I am a certainty. In my time, in this brief excursion in awareness, I could conceivably collapse perceived universal realities to a unifying principle. In my time, I could dream colorful tales of its tapestry. And when I die, if these thoughts become someone else's reality, I have a chance at virtual immortality.

In an affirmative notion of existence, progeny of willful predicament is measurable and determined by obscure reasoning. I find most enthralling the idea of my existence as a coordinate of thoughts. The idea of life, as I see in the dimension of human definitions, is an imperfect symmetry of expectations I measure with my acclimated virtues. And its beastly impulses are my derivative to conclude awareness, my awareness, fearfully isolated. Without a definite beginning or end, I cannot tell for certain the nature of irregularities dictating my existence. However, I know this simple truth: to forsake my freedoms, to depose my version of reality is to forsake my very self.

I am a remnant of the Stone Age beast. I am the natural and the false, the universe of our combined verses and a majestic expression of chaos.

This moment of reality, you and I, the ideas we exchange, is a probability that will vanish as certain as it appeared. With each passing moment, the probability of our existence is subject to a new set of realities. This uncertainty of quantum nature belittles the individual to desperation and meaninglessness. It primes the mind for tales that modify the condition by creating an illusion of permanence.

The reason for our existence is the probability of our existence. The reason for our existence is chaos. When the probability of our existence vanishes, so do we.

—As a civilization, we are rearranging material composition within our domain of influence. The boundaries of our material continuity are affecting the universe with increasing significance. Is it possible to extend this manifest and maintain a human identity? Will humankind metamorphose from its existing form to something more profound? How am I to reconcile epiphenomenal results of change while influenced by lifeless and thoughtless social dictates?

—Epiphenomenalism is real and true. Consciousness influences matter. Awareness influences matter. There is a field of our being, a flow of energy between us that transcends epiphenomenalism.

Probabilities come to pass. When they pass there is but nothing: a virtual void signifying previous existence of something. To understand and possibly transcend the universe one must decipher the mathematical universe as well as the neurological self. Deciphering this puzzle requires incredible sophistication only possible through sciences and minds that imagine their application.

Mathematics is the essence, the most profound creation of human existence. We can use it to change the universe or create a new one.

We condensate superstrings of life as simple strings of a four-dimensional manifest we can perceive with ease. What would humanity become if we could detect all dimensions and compositions of the universe? How would such civilization affect the universal format? What form of existence must we evolve into to perceive all aspects of the universe? How would such a process affect the individual psyche?

Evolutionary changes in the structure of our brain could catapult us into spheres of perception outside our current capacity. The meaning and significance of evolution itself may metamorphose to accommodate physical changes we impose on our existence. New species will evolve, and the meaning of selfhood shall change.

The dream is so magnanimous we have difficulty comprehending its possible ramifications and inevitability.

Should we disturb the universal order with tenacity of our determinism to accelerate that possibility? Should we design grand ideas and format the universe to accommodate those designs? Is human influence in designing change inevitable?

It is within this cryptic array of sublime states that I remind myself of the significance of harmony and compassion.

Harmony is a mathematical concept with concrete physical manifestations. Compassion is a psychological condition with functional individual and social significance. We could assimilate these two concepts to transcend our existing shell without losing our humanity.

We possess an unlimited constructive and destructive potential. To survive and manifest a desirable optimal condition, we must willfully choose to harmonize our compassionate norms and minimize our aggressive tendencies.

—Why this curiosity to demystify the universe? Why this propensity to measure its parameters? Is it the nature of the human mind to understand itself by understanding the universe? Is it in our genes to understand by breaking down and reassembling? Is it a human condition to observe by dismantling existing states and synthesizing them anew?

—In truth, life is defined in ecumenical certitude of what "I" is. As a primitive beast, "I" understands by dismantling. As an intellectually observant self, "I" understands by minimizing its influence on the observed.

Imagine this: "I" approaches a mass-less zero volume of immense energy. A sudden entrapment in a spatial matrix of this context and "I" experiences the epiphany of approaching eternity and infinity.

A conscious dubiety of reason and sense, a fantasy of everything educible, a dream called future, a probability, higher than we conceive moral and just, or perfection, "I" is a most fortunate state of existence. And us, in the format of civilization, is a fascinating potential for omnipotence.

In reality, "I" is a self-centered virtuous montage of its own contrived reality. "I" is an accosted do-gooder narcissist, an unfailing clone and a capricious image of high and low.

A slave of pleasure and fear, "I" is creating wide-open prairies and filth-covered ghettoes. Creator of gods and demons, glazed with laughter and sorrow, a marvel of evolution, an undefined fortune, "I" approaches a volume of immense energy to see the infinity in the format of civilization.

Organization demands certainty. Awareness demands certainty. Human condition demands certainty. Imagination is a cognitive medium manipulating the chaotic conditions to manifest predictable certainties. Such is the nature of our highly organized brain, arguably the most sophisticated in the known universe.

—Tell me about the nature you have chosen to perceive? What is natural? What is nature? How can I conceive determinism if chaos rules everything? What principles necessitate adherence to willful existence?

The Great One remained silent a while.

—If reality is ephemeral, if reality is transpicuous, if reality is inflationary, if reality is hung from threads, if reality is a manifestation of our combined perceptions, if life is what we think it is, then truth is a perplexing format of our relevance to each other.

If nothing is the beginning and the end of our existence, if we are on our own, then we are truly a random occurrence and the universe the most chaotic phenomenon we may never understand.

Within such a framework, imagination is where the landscape of life is realized. Imagination transcends virtual and real to fortify awareness with metaphysical concepts. "I" is a magnificent word of transpicuous quality, a rare probability we possess for a fraction of universal time scale. Imagine the potential of "I" if its existence is extended thousands of years?

If one believes in the concept of control, then nature is a certainty of preconceived sequences. This suggestion sets forth a highly structured sequence of events where the created, and the creators are under severe constraints.

The assertion "if there is an organization, there must be an organizer" is not a necessary condition. At the center of this argument is the assumption that organization must have an organizer. I see no compelling necessity for such a hypothesis.

Who or what organized the organizers that organized the organization is of no use to the human condition. Waiting for saviors has not served humankind. Taking initiative, and planning our destiny, has.

If one believes in partial creation and self-determination, then it is imperative to opt for self-determination.

If one believes in creation and death of the creator or creators, then it makes total sense to espouse self-determination.

If one believes in spontaneous generation, then it is paramount to uphold the act of cognition an end in itself and self-determination a human paradigm.

Nature is within the human domain of influence to define, shape and reshape. We have been engaged in such an affair for all our time. Choosing not to change is our choosing as well. We are an integrated part of the environment we perceive as nature. And the nature we affect and influence is itself influenced by everything of which it is composed. We can observe and change the nature around us anyway we wish, but the changes we impose may affect us in unpredictable ways. Observance before commitment to actions that alter the direction of history is of utmost importance.

The belief in this interconnected and transcending sense of self, society and nature impose a vast array of constraints in the definition of self, making the individual an integral part of the nature and the nature an integrated part of the self.

In the scheme of predetermined outcomes, human civilization is reduced to a gathering of the minds void of necessary freedom to will the content and context of their existence. Such a philosophy debases the principle of self-determination and freedom to choose. It denigrates the significance of everything we have achieved. It ignores the potentials we possess, and it alienates us from whom we can be.

In the existentially abstract perception of existence, we are the masters and the slaves of our perceptions. No being has a monopoly on awareness, and every sentient being is a unique phenomenon with a capacity to perceive "everything."

"Everything" is a virtual concept we aim at, get close to, but can never reach. It is a philosophical designation of infinity used to encapsulate the perceptible universe. It is a virtual concept encompassing known and unknown, manifested or imagined.

—There are many philosophical schools of thought attempting to harmonize the relationship between the self, the civilization and the universe. How does one compromise such diverse ideas and ideals to synthesize an encompassing explanation?

How does choice fit into the scheme you are proposing? According to you, I am willful and vulnerable at the same instance of determination. But the choices I make are often predicated by the universal conditions, outside my sphere of influence, that set boundaries to my existence. How do you reconcile the contradiction between choices I make and choices I am forced to make?

—If one believes in probability and chaos, then nature is a random occurrence of outcomes with randomly organized manifestations constrained by laws that govern the universe. Anything probable is possible and perceived as natural when manifested. This implies possibility of human influence and control of nature. It is this possibility I hold as the driving force of a freewill.

The undetermined and undefined scope and magnificence of freewill is ours to delineate. It could be constrained by menial daily chores or by the outlandish notion of creating a universe.

Existential life is my world of stealthy reality, The Great One said with passion.

Willful, free amidst trappings, my goblet of joy is brimming with paradigms of a perilous journey.

My evolutionary integrity twists from the insolent to incisive as I declare my conscience a unified quantum oscillation, a unidirectional excitation onto wholeness of awareness.

I perceive my cognitive integrity a paragon that agitates my intellectual and imaginative self from melancholy to intrepid to innocuous.

Existential awareness is my quintessential paradigm, the instigator of shifts in my perceptual paragon.

In reality, my perceptions are influenced by many paradigms making truth a subjective phenomenon. Truth is a tapestry of designs within a greater tapestry of chaos. In reality, a dimension can fold onto a small fraction making reality a superfluous conjecture. In reality, imagination is a medium able to defy classical principles.

I am a dreaming fool of abject decadence. I am a wishfully willful aphorism garnished with powerful incantations of subjective nature. I am a freewill lost amidst ubiquitous boundaries of immense dimensions. I express my potentials as a dreaming human in a dreaming universe.

Is such a predicament sustainable? Yes and no at the same instance of imagination. Yes and no in differing circumstances of reality. The choices we make differentiate one from another. And we choose. In every step of our existence, we choose. When we choose, a gamut of probabilities collapse allowing a single reality to be manifest. This is a measurable reality and a compelling reason to advocate willful existence. Tempered with compassion, it can manifest a sustainable tensegrity of the human psyche.

In its simplest format, to choose is being willful. The question is the degree of our awareness of this principle. The dictum of interest is the many-layered plateaus of our willfulness to surpass accepted norms and values.

—As much as I admire your paroxysmal devotion to the notion of existential freewill, I see a mighty foe that can absorb all our thoughts and toss them into a black hole of impossible outcomes. The dreaming universe, in its own quantum phase, can distort our best without intent or purpose.

Chaos is undoubtedly the master of us all. It will eventually find a way to absorb us. There is no escaping chaos and probability of extinction.

If "I" can aim at "everything," the definition of being will constantly change with changing conditions and perception of those conditions? What form, shape, and cognitive disposition would "I" assume in dealing with such transformative reality and ramifications of chaos?

—Chaos must rule for an organization to form, evolve and reach its optimal potential. Chaos is the necessary condition for a possibility to become a probability, manifest a reality, evolve and aim for higher forms of organization. Chaos is our most formidable friend and foe.

In a paradoxical sense, the universe is gradually becoming a battleground between human will and chaos. The collective human will is yearning for perfection of its perceived organization. Chaos, by definition, makes all probabilities possible, including optimization of human potential and its annihilation.

Chaos is set to win unless humankind can engage the universe and its forces with ingenious solutions.

The notion of "compassionate us" implies independence through tolerance, determination with reservation, and a perennial optimism for the human constitution as an evolutionary isotropic phenomenon. This balanced notion of our species implies understanding, objective analysis and acceptance, at the same instance of perception.

For such reasons, I will not qualify compassion with restrictive definitions. Let compassion, free from negatively charged impulsive judgments, stand on its own. Let compassion extend an encompassing sense of humanity. Let us choose compassion as our emotional ethos and hope such a paradigm will nurture our reasoning.

I declare humanity it's own purpose, The Great One said with a relative determinism to which I was gradually being exposed.

Reality is "I" and "I" exists both in isolation and as an integral component of "us."

What am I, if isolated from humanity? Who am I if enslaved by humanity? Imagination allows the self to transcend classical and quantum to assemble possible from impossible, to immerse itself in the absurd and bizarre reality of "us" without losing perspective of "I." In doing so, the question changes from "who I am" to "who I want to be."

As individuals we affect probabilities to manifest realities of our choosing. And we do so through the phenomenon of freewill.

The human story is an allegory of many paradoxical suppositions. I see it expressed in interactions, in thoughts, in daily living. Why do we, in every moment of life, resolve complexities to simple instructions? Why do we imagine the impossible and reduce it to possible? Why do we catalog the unknown to the step-by-step known? All such paradigms are a direct result of our unique capacity to process information, to traverse in dimension of time, conceptualize space outside our sensory domain and imagine possible scenarios that do not exist but are synthesizable.

The significance of "I" as a free will is its capacity to transcend variant conditions and extend its field of thought. To imagine "everything" and "nothing" without being absorbed in either is the unique strength of a free will.

"I," as a freewill, can entertain optimal containment without being contained. "I," can transcend without losing its sense of self. "I," can metamorphose in evolutionary time to contain, without dilution, the magnitude and significance of containment.

The processes of selection, integration, formation and adaptation could be influenced with our willful determination. The changes can affect the global environment resulting in conditions that may change human civilization in undesirable ways.

"I" and "us" are variables exposed to and influenced by the environmental conditions. "I" and "us" are integrated parts of the environment.

We must choose with care and much deliberation to format optimized conditions. Compassion is a necessary ingredient for optimization of freewill.

—How do you reconcile mediocrity of repetitive actions demanded by socially integrating functions of conformable significance with those that demand complex cognitive performance? How can we, as individuals, reconcile willful independence and social demands for conformity?

—Reality of human existence is clear and simple; humanity is for humans. To optimize this condition, we rose above Stone Age mediocrity and actualized social determinism a dictum of highest ascendancy. Social determinism soon gave way to freedom to design the individual ascendance and actualization to higher levels of awareness while keeping the civilization alive and dynamic.

Details of living rarely remain constant. They change and in the process, as we change, we have the chance to improve the process of living.

Life is an array of repetitive acts we follow with autonomic conviction.

I see no contradiction here. The imaginative freewill finds it is increasingly liberated as modular and autonomic pathways take care of the mundane.

In the domain of freewill each is its own and a reflection of all. The altruistic social bondage requires the self to construct cohesive relations. The tension between self-centered and socially centered is real and transparent.

As a civilization, we can effectively change reality by adopting new modes of reasoning and change the matrix of our orientation.

Humanity is a virtual collective perception. To our knowledge, no other has manifested this phenomenon. Nor should we intellectually dilute ourselves with the possibility of us being alone. Building blocks of biological existence can be synthesized in the harshest environments. The probability that other cognitive life forms colonize the galaxy is real. Else, humans are the exception to the rule, and as such most enthrallingly amazing and truly a miraculous creation of the universe, a singularity of immense but perilous significance.

There is that speculative but possible proposition that we are one of a kind or a very rare event.

Irrespective of what the universe may or may not contain, it is slowly fading into a state of nothingness. At the same time, we are steadily and progressively expanding and improving our existence.

Future humans will have time and resources to find a way out of this conundrum. They will have the potential to solve the riddle of the universe and possibly build a new one. If this holds, the future belongs to humans. And the universe will be a human creation.

—How do you conceive the notion of imagination? What are possible implications of this magnificent manifestation in relation to the classical reality of existence?

—Reality is a tangible continuity in classical perception of existence through senses. In imagination, there is no such continuity.

The quantum states and un-manifested probabilities rule the world of imagination as much as the stored and the observed information.

Imagination is a timeless, space-less state. This in itself could explain why humankind has been able to observe different sensory imperceptible realities of the universe.

As to the exact nature of imagination, perhaps it is a manifestation of interfacing with other unseen dimensions of the universe that eliminate time. For all I know, imagination is a manifestation of our neurological state.

Imagination allows the individual to transcend classical realities and experience un-manifested probable scenarios. This quantum leap, real or not, is incredibly rich and full of possibilities.

In the domain of imagination, harmony is a sustainable notion. In classical reality, with diminished and socially regulated conditions, the freewill swings from idea to idea, from insecurity to wishful fantasies, trying to demarcate boundaries of its awareness.

Compassion can counter negative impositions of this condition.

There is a common thread in all of this. Awareness is a fragile manifest of the dimensions, implications and definitions, which are set in imagination before their translation to observable concepts.

—Quantum explanation of the thought process does not explain our compulsive search for truths, whatever they may be. "Everything" and "nothing" are unique explanations of existence in the format of being and nothingness. They suit our search for truths in the form of dichotomies reflecting the dual nature of our brain in the extreme. They do not explain willful and creative expressions, I protested.

I have traveled long to reach this epic of awareness. I have said many farewells along many paths. I have experienced many certainties and as many uncertainties. Is there no ultimate answer, no universal purpose that governs our lives? Do we exist in a vacuum of imagined states that turn reality on and off?

Covered from head to toe, The Great One stood and paced around the room. It took a deep breath, slowed its pace and returned to its straw math. The material simplicity of its existence was humbling.

—Human life is an allegory of emotional and logical discourse. I see it expressed in interactions, in deep thoughts, in profound and shallow declarations. Consciousness is a manifest of neurological functioning. The highest construct of consciousness manifests a state characterized by unconstrained freedom to imagine.

Freedom is optimized in imagination. Awareness is optimized in imagination. Freedom to will is a manifestation of this optimized state.

Truths are collated emotional, legal and logical expressions and observations. There is no discernible or observed universal plan to our lives. The certainty of our existence is a fragile composition subject to universal and local variables.

Our daily life is beset by problems we identify and resolve with tenacity of our collective intelligence. In this notion of existence, what we choose is what we are. Sometimes we fail, sometimes we succeed and sometimes we just move on. But in every turn of every move, we take decisions.

There is no willful universal plan in this scenario, but there are universal, solar and planetary relationships that affect all our plans. We are subject to changes on the planet as is our planet subject to changes in the solar system, the galaxy and beyond.

Humanity is for the benefit and detriment of humans. Humankind could vanish or flourish with decisions we make. It can diminish or flourish depending on changes we impose on the environment and ourselves. There is no universal plan in this scenario.

Out of particles and universal debris evolved simple life forms that further evolved to complex life forms that further evolved to cognitive life forms. In every step of our evolution, we competed and coexisted with many species that survived, changed or vanished. There is no willful universal plan in this scenario.

The concept of a perfect organization: ubiquitous, omnipresent and omnipotent, is a wishful notion our design is demanding and promoting as a model for our future. Along the way, we have infinite choices to choose from. It is our choosing, which will be and, which will not.

We could traverse time-space, in reality, and imagination, to reach across the galaxy and possibly beyond. In the end, the question "who are we" is conceived and answered by us alone. With or without contact, we compose, interpret, change and accept the answers to all our questions. With or without contact, we perceive images and decide their purpose and meaning.

—If we could sway probabilities in our favor, are we not creating order in contradiction to principles governing entropy?

The universe is expanding to a diluted state as we aim to structure it to a highly organized state. Is this paradox sustainable?

The Great One looked at me with piercing eyes.

—Imagine a magical tour in the obscure world of perfection. Imagine life a mathematical order of symmetrical reasoning. Imagine a universe of perfect symmetries. The universe may or may not reflect this image, but what does it mean to create a virtual universe that reflects this image? Could future humans create a new universe, transpose themselves onto another or modify the existing one?

If the humankind can predict and prevent its annihilation, the possibility of creating an ideal nexus for human civilization exists. We have been dreaming of this possibility all our evolutionary time.

I am convinced life is a harmonious enigma in time-space-mind. In the land of Pharaohs, by the rivers of Mesopotamia, in the fields of Aztec, along the Great Wall of China, life is an enigma.

I dare us to challenge reality. I dare us to imagine most outlandish scenarios. I dare us challenge doctrines that limit our imagination. I dare we to challenge constants defining reality.

In the domain of fantasy, as cool-minded benefactors of passion and reason, addled by mind-waves, distant waves, harmonious waves, I dare us to imagine the ecstasy of rising above ourselves. I dare us to renounce abject thoughts and relish compassionate designs.

Let the universe be what it may. Let it expand thin. Let it dissipate to nothing. Humanity cannot surrender its search for higher orders. Order is the essence of our humanity.

If humankind can dictate destiny of it's choosing, if expansion is human conformity to the inflationary theory of existence, if the universe is unraveled in imagination, then meaning of existence can be shifted by paradigms of our choosing.

In reality, the universe may not acknowledge time, but I must. I must accept my wear and tear in passage of time. Perhaps I accept it too easily and surrender to degradation much early.

Reality is separating universal truths from transient truths. Your idiom and mine are a unified existence. Impalpable without affection and compassion, each is immured with a unique sense of self. We are a synthesis designed by none.

—You talk of truth and virtue as epiphenomenal concepts with time-bound definitions of purely human resonance. If it is so, then we are creatures of judgment and value. Values we adopt could vanish meaningless, help us coexist, or remain relevant to our civilization alone.

Your thoughts open a gamut of possibilities for the human species. You are transposing values from a practical and socially applicable mode to a universal condition. Are you not fearful of doing what our prophets intended and failed?

—Virtue, morality, truth, right and good constitute a matrix of accumulated axioms of social significance. We choose the purpose of their application within boundaries of a practical context.

Reason, in every metaphor, is its own reason. Sometimes shallow, sometimes convenient, sometimes profound, we reason virtue and ethical values to regulate our behavior, our reasoning itself and our values.

We are truly social creatures with great propensity to reason. We argue the spin, the field and the synchronicity of our reason.

The universe we observe, in the virtual matrix of our brain, is increasingly a product of our reason. Our perception of the universe has evolved from an earthbound four-dimensional concept to a multidimensional format with connotations of infinite and infinitesimal. Its meaning and dimensions will certainly change time and again.

We are, in any given moment, living in an imaginary universe of make-believes. The path to certainty of the universe is riddled with uncertainties of our reason. Our reason is increasingly a mathematical reason. As such, our reason is aiming at inclusiveness and universality.

Look, look closer, all is well and none clear. Look deeper. Life is increasingly simplified to higher complexities. Attempt to look deeper and you will find confusion in your reason.

Do not take cognitive functioning lightly. Do not take accumulated human reason lightly. Its expressions and extensions have a greater potential than minds that imagined them.

Compassion is a temporizing state that could guide us through uncertain paths. Compassion is a tensegrity that could mold our civilization with a sustainable frame. Compassion and mathematics could format our communication with each other, other species and possible extraterrestrial life forms.

—The interaction between our emotional lives is a universe of its own. It sets boundaries of our interactive existence. Within such tight emotional framework, as individuals and groups, how free are we?

Peptides, hormones, chromosomes, proteins and enzymes are physiological factors conditioning our existence. Material reality and its manifests seem stronger than imaginative discourse. Can the creative self transcend the physical self?

Not all our decisions are clear and willful. The optimism you espouse is an expression that may or may not materialize. In reality, our aggressive and impulsive behavior has sustained us through uncertain times. You envision a new paradigm for human survival. I wish we had as much latitude as you think we do. I have no certainty of such enduring and endearing nature. I am struggling with manifestations of my fallible self. You, as The Great One, have the advantage over me. To my perception, your certainties are convoluted uncertainties of puzzling nature. I find your world a universe of enthralling metaphors. Is it, you are detecting concepts I dare not?

—To conjure up a unified field of reference and claim us free, in all aspects, is an existential portent I indulge with passion. To resign to ideological affairs and egotistical tendencies is an existentially bad fate I disavow with passion.

I cannot dismiss quantum leaps to understandings that espy unknown metaphors. Nor can I draw imaginary conclusions announcing that possibility off-limits to anyone or myself. Nor am I a ubiquitous intellect to cast a shadow over human emotions. Nor am I to deny my hormonally induced states as expressions of who I am.

I have many boundaries defining my existence. I am under many constraints delineating boundaries of my existence.

I am not an absolute thinker, nor a purely emotional dreamer. I am not beholden by virtue or truth alone. I am not a stooge of convictions.

Did I explain my truth as a transparent fusion of many states? Did I infer our emotional reasoning a component of our logical existence?

In this life of material reality and emotional absurdity, perhaps there is no all-encompassing meaning. Perhaps confusion and enlightenment are paradigm shifts of a single conjecture. Perhaps meanings and definitions are temporarily manifested points on a single string of resolutions. After all, as sentient beings, we live in a virtual state before it manifests as a reality.

Think deep, think universal, think of life millions of years ahead. Days begin with a fading light, and the moon shines not. Life is about to end. We are facing extinction. At such a point of disarray, what will save humankind are not dictates of a few peptides but thoughts that transcend such dictates to synthesize new realities. Bold ideas and bolder determination will save humankind. To sustain such continuity, to approach such a point of imaginative reality, requires well functioning peptides, enzymes and all the physical and emotional attributes that make up a healthy existence.

Physical existence is an indispensable necessity, but what gives meaning to our lives are optimistic and hopeful dreams. What sustains us is our imaginative confluence. What drives us is a yearning to be alive and happy. What determines is the arrow of collective human will.

Manifesting such continuity requires a force of immense inertia of virtual and actual integrity.

The sum of our lives is an abstraction with one unified purpose: to procreate and assure the existence of the species. Genetic drives rule our lives as we rule events affecting our drives.

There is a certain profoundness in all of this. Logic is human. Profoundness is human. Passion is human. All thoughts are human. Everything human is individual, and each, within a convoluted matrix of the social, is a universe of its own.

On this stage of stone-age actors, it is a fool who believes free will does not matter. Humanity cannot be advanced by age-old genetic drives. Nor can it be edified by dictatorship of purpose. Nor can it be optimized without a matrix of purpose.

Humanity can best be advanced with designs that benefit all by illuminating each. Such application of humanity demands modification of principles that separate people with arbitrary layers of distinction.

Conscience does not incarnate, but hope does. Individual awareness does not incarnate, but awareness of optimized states does. Genes do not strive for humanity. Intellect does.

—The measure of individual conduct is a fusion of intent and action. The intention is dependent on the abstract calculations of the mind. The intention assumes a span from autonomic to willful. How can I differentiate right from wrong when driven by forces buried beneath many evolutionary layers and deep psychological abstracts that escape my attention?

Am I lost in corridors of ignorance? Will I ever know the totality? You enunciate answers as if transmitting with highest conductivity. Once I have heard your words, they escape my reasoning faster than I could analyze their significance. One moment everything makes complete sense. And a moment later, confusion spins my mind in a vortex of precarious illusions.

In your presence, I feel existentially numb and exquisitely unremarkable. All my life, I have sought to actualize happiness in sanctuary of others, as I do now. An epiphany of some sort is dawning on me. Soon, I must be on my own. And I am not afraid of such a moment. Years of journey in the field of existence have enhanced my senses to happiness.

How do you, as The Great One, actualize happiness?

The Great One paused, inhaled, exhaled.

—In the outlandish domain of concepts, there is the arena of philosophical illusions. I claim we traverse through such an intellectual matrix in the arena of civilization. Our lives are a blend of axiomatic paradigms with endless abstractions derived from this matrix.

In the early evolutionary stages, the autonomic and the modular behaviors saved the species. Now, it is our willful determination saving the civilization. Compassion and harmony can set in motion constructs minimizing harmful and painful effects of the civilization. Along the treacherous paths twining the enigma of civilization, we find refuge in happiness and hope.

Awareness is happiness. Virtue is happiness. Lack of pain is happiness. Satiated senses is happiness. Freedom of will is happiness. Hormonal balance is happiness. Physical conditioning is happiness. Happiness is a set of feelings: comfortable in flesh, pain free, pleasing to senses and intellectually stimulating. Happiness is as real as imagined. Imagining happiness is happiness. Happiness is a result of actualization.

Happiness is not an isolated conceptual phenomenon. My happiness may accentuate someone else's pain. It has social and universal implications. In this format of analysis happiness is a fusion of many axioms. At a given time-space-mind, it is a paradigm of many designs and subject to physical, emotional, intellectual and imaginative experiences.

Forgive my arrogance. I am only an observer, grazing egregious thoughts, questioning apogee of my own reasoning. For example, how deep is my commitment to humanity? How free is my generosity from social impositions? How universal is my compassion?

In debased modes of existence, there are inordinate traces of compassionate minds shining clarity to our lives. In gentleness of great grandparents, in luminance of the lion-minded aggregates, in transposed images and sacred oaths, there are abundant compassionate minds shining our lives.

—The social forces are too compelling to resist with individual will. I often find myself chained with passions that escape my logic but are socially accepted. Bewildered by such contradictory compulsions, I realign myself by compromising.

The autonomic and modular responses obligate my being to fulfillment of conditions that satisfy reproductive requirements, with or without my willful awareness. How am I to reconcile distortions caused by this evolutionary process?

Actions are a more transpicuous measure of self than thoughts, I said.

In the absence of action, thoughts can find a greater consequence. By confining yourself to this small space, you have willfully limited your capacity for social interaction. Your mind freely bristles with enigmatic imagery of shining metaphors transcending this space to meet the universe one observer at a time. Is it a requirement, for free expression of will, to limit social interactions?

The sun slowly crawled on The Great One lighting its brilliant existence with lucid clarity. The Great One welcomed the heat by opening its garment to capture the heat.

—In the beginning the self is an uninformed entity, a purely autonomic mind, a unified awareness of modular nature of no imaginative consequence.

In time, the mind brews a misty matrix of values to actuate an acceptable image it can present in the greater arena of the social existence. This matrix is formatted by the social forces and genetic constructs imposed by the species.

"I" is impressionable by willful, imaginative, social and environmental impositions. It is essential to be mindful of these influences. The existentially willful self is best adept at resolving the conflicts arising from these powerful forces.

It is imperative to place oneself at the center and observe every force with keen attention.

I am not a traveling star but a sitting motif, watching myself pass as others pass me by.

Time will eventually shutter my sense of self, reducing it to fragmented debris. Whether I will go meaningless or meaningful is increasingly a format of my own choosing. And I have chosen, with certainty of emotional freedom, the confinement in this small physical space. I have chosen to limit my interaction to one observer at a time. In this format of interaction, I can focus my energies without dilution in distracting social forces.

Lonely with all the gatherings, absorbed in melancholic states, I am a part of and apart from all. Thoughts and minds apart, apart from social partitions, I simply am my quiescent medley of accords. No slave or master occupies my thoughts. I simply contort my notion of right and wrong with relativity of existential precepts presented to my senses one observer at a time. Such a docile integrity acclimates my wholeness to a transforming frame of reality with which I have chosen to be pleased.

The choice is mine. The definitions are mine. The rights and wrongs are mine. I perceive reality in confinement of my private self and gauge its boundaries in intimacy of travelers passing through my finite space of containment.

The Great One stood, slowly paced its way towards me, sat next to me, reached out and grabbed my hand.

Do go gentle into this universe, it said with passion. Ruminate on your ruffled image with acclimated thoughts.

Do go roaring into this life of uncertainties. Caress your mind with amicable thoughts.

Plunge deep into this gamut of wonders. Expose your compassionate mind to absurdities of living.

Do appreciate this delicate balance between living and non-living. Remember its intricacies far into life. Fearlessly, ride this melodious human plight. Reconcile your sorrows, your storming thoughts.

Do accentuate your desires with charming delights. Give your sorrows to passing clouds and plunge ravenous into a mosaic of imaginative delights.

Do think this brief journey a translucent transparency with many delightful insights.

The Great One returned to its small space beneath the light on the straw math.

I will. I thought. I will go gentle into this life.

—Moral conservatism: the tendency to revert to original ideas, and intellectual liberalism: the tendency to challenge ideas, are social forces of great inertia. The differential between them can be a small fraction or a huge chasm. Labels do not accurately gauge reality. What gauges reality is totality of a self: the spoken, the autonomic, the willful, the physical, the hormonal, the social and everything else in between.

A cat jumps and a bird falls. One lives. One dies. From a universal perspective, there is neither right nor wrong in this scenario. From a human perspective, this act is a tragedy ripe with rights and wrongs.

The universe has no field, no quanta, no measure of moral values. To the contrary, human conduct evolves around judgment.

The accumulated empirical knowledge indicates there are no discernible preconceived factors other than our evolution setting boundaries of our collective. So much has gone awry in encapsulating this notion as a controllable variable.

—Immersed in thoughts of survival, astutely determined, we measure life with trial and error to reach where we are, said The Great One.

And where we are is no panacea. Short lives and early deaths still loom heavy on our consciousness.

Back in an emotionless domain of reality, where life is a mathematical order of partial symmetries, I am convinced life is a tale of harmonics.

I dare us format our lives with thoughts that transform harmony with undulated affection, with simple ideas and profound meanings. Addled by mind-waves, this moment is defined by people parleyed in clusters of fear and delight. Anyway, I look at it; this day is this instance, as I am, as we are, baffled by many questions arising from insufficiencies of our lives.

The essence of existence is self-preservation. The notion of life without death, absolute life, is irrelevant. Reality of our existence is awareness of being. There are no omnipotent perennial certainties. There is no forever. First, there is the uncertainty of time. What is it, and is it without us measuring its passing? Then, there is the uncertainty of day-to-day living, the uncertainty of not knowing, the uncertainty of vanishing possibilities and the perennial uncertainty of who we are. In the end, there is the certainty of death, the certainty of vanishing awareness.

It is impudent to imagine truths as real, and reality something static, written in some Stone Age stone. It is impertinent to imagine truth a written book tossed in a black hole of ideas to emerge universal. It is insolent to imagine life absolute, absorbed and preserved in an omnipresent universal awareness. It is most pertinent to measure life a chain of experiences bound with an unseen chain of time.

In this paradox of being and nothingness, truth is a revealing joke. Only uninhibited tyrants can ruffle its immensity and ameliorate themselves with pervasive relevance of harmonious coexistence.

Social truth is a comparative notion spoken in harmony, in symbiosis, in ideas that speak of universal suffrage. It is explored in cohabitation, in respect for life and all life forms equally respected.

—I am asymmetrical, disoriented, fractured. To what end do I extend my affection to embrace this brief contrived moment? This small rapture in time-space-mind is too unstable to last, too transient to capture, too real to be a reflection, too awesome to be mine, or yours, or someone else's, but a composite.

Much too absorbed in the realm of truths, I am asexual, timid, shy, well brewed. Beneficiary of trials and errors, diluted to disseminated imperfection, I am lost in conflicting matrices of values. Diluted in the expanding matrix of human understandings, I feel small, too insignificant to affect social change. Much too infatuated with my own condition, I am not ecumenical enough to pass measured judgments.

Judgment and value, are they not intertwined? Can we change our values without changing our judgments? Can we afford to lose our ability to pass judgment?

—I believe in the individual effort to observe the possible and the impossible. I believe in the individual effort to absolve enigmas. With its perceived enormity, its imposing reality and ambiguity, the universe is defined with our perception.

The individual imagines its intricacies, dreams its possibilities and passes judgment by observing its limited applications. The society absorbs those judgments by correlating, collating and validating to mature by timeless observations. The civilization does the same, with greater scope of scrutiny.

The nature and coalescence of this experience are molded by our evolutionary biology, evolutionary sociology, evolutionary psychology and our exposure to mathematical reasoning.

I believe it is within our means to alter the vector of humanity. It is within our boundary condition to synthesize values and pass judgment on their meaning. Judgment is a quintessential human derivative.

A determined individual can affect change. A string of determined individuals can affect major change. A string of societies can affect revolutionary and sweeping social ripples and shift paradigms.

I believe the judgments our ancestors imposed on themselves and passed on to us express themselves in ways we cannot fully discern. Such is the dictate of social evolution. Bit by bit, occasionally in leaps, the decisions we make influence our psyche, our environment, our genes and our universe. To assimilate and accommodate these changes takes time and the inertia of a social shift.

The evolutionary course of our social existence has transformed our judgments from absolutism to relativism to relative absolutism. Do not take this shifting scope and metamorphism lightly. The magnitude of change is enormous. Its enormity is disparaging and liberating at different instances of deliberation.

I believe the vector of humanity, by virtue of our mathematical reasoning, is progressively stable. The human collective, through its evolutionary persistence, is fostering a set of values that define its growing space and everything within it.

Do not take these principles lightly. We may evolve to become the sole observers of the universe and beyond. As a collective we have that potential. As individuals we can contribute to that potential.

I believe the arrow of humanity attempts to point at the essence of "universe." If such essence exists, we will find it. If it does not, we will create it.

It is undeniable: we are looking for such essence irrespective of its existence or not. We discover or create what we seek.

Such an attempt, in itself, is a supreme purpose. The aim is "everything." The aim is actualization of the self as a freewill without compromising the self as a conformist. The aim is to find the ideal self, exhaustively free, immensely willful, quintessentially social, physically durable and emotionally stable.

And what do we know of quintessence? Perhaps it is meant to reflect the original state. Perhaps it has no meaning. Perhaps it is something we are desperately trying to create. Perhaps it is a unique field of its own. Perhaps it has no relevance.

Enthralled by ambiguities of such thoughts, I often wonder if I know this mind that sees and foresees? Do I know awareness is a temporary rapture in something inordinately immense? I am bewildered by perception of life and death at the same instance of consideration. I am baffled by dimensions of eternity. Imagination absorbs my definite physical self, changing it to an abstract state of unknown quandaries. In this state, I hold the key to selfhood. I fathom expressions of "I" and consummate dimensions of "I." I alone imagine, accept, or reject stratified explanations of "I."

The Great One exposed its face. Its long white hair slipped out of the garb.

—Transient and often ambiguous paradigms bind our social sense of self, weaving a string of paradoxes that loosely bind humanity and the universe. This bondage is tense and riddled with contradictions. It is at times a mystery, quite absurd, or perfectly practical.

To what extent can the nonliving, non-thinking virtual human social confluence influence individual imaginative constructs? Can these entities overlap without a serious collision?

If we must defy the universe to maintain integrity of conscience, then in every step, we set a course of our own against dictates of the universe. Can human civilization survive such a state of existence? Will another species evolve to sustain such a predicament? Would it require building a new universe?

Silence prevailed. The Great One seemed absorbed in thoughts of its own. I did not wish an end to this experience, though the end seemed near.

—Close your eyes. Let quantum waves flow between us, said The Great One with closed eyes and calm meditative voice.

Amplify your mind-waves. Experience a quantum leap. Let your awareness merge mine. Let our waves cross material boundaries.

I tried, but seemingly could not.

Open and close your eyes at will and let certainties of classical structure and uncertainties of quantum nature confuse your awareness. At such a moment of disarray, you are neither a beginning nor an end. You cannot fully discern who you are, but you know very well you are transient.

What you think is a certainty in itself. But that is for you to decide. Is it meaningless or universal? That too is for you to decide. Are what you are and what you think symmetrical? That too is for you to decide.

The self, in its optimal state, as if traversing on its own imaginary strings, occasionally must defy universal fields to actuate its ideal self by observing the trepidations of its defiance.

The universe has no interest in acknowledging humanity or the self. The self, to the contrary, by virtue of its awareness, is doing all it can to find its place in the universe.

I behold the notion of self a convention of human reasoning. I behold the notion of willful reasoning a unique manifest constrained by the universe itself. I behold the universe can and will be transcended by humans. It will be changed and recreated by future species.

The Great One lowered its head, disappearing beneath its garb.

—I feel the ecstasy of being willful. I feel the ambiguity and complexity of our entangled minds. The resonance of our cognitive entanglement radiates the reality and nature of our humanity.

Reality functions in many levels, I said after a few moments of reflection.

In the classical world of time-present, reality is manifested probabilities. In the quantum world of imagination un-manifested has as much meaning as manifested. What then is reality of a species that can perceive both? And what vision of life has given you the authority to entertain the audience of seekers?

With a fixed physical space and limited material entanglement, the variable defining your existence has become the virtual world you share, one mind at a time. Though seemingly isolated in this little space, you have not a moment to yourself. What benefit do you envision in engaging their thoughts?

The Great One looked me in the eyes. Its gentle radiance froze my senses. Its calm gave me much-needed reassurance.

—The meaning of this reality, this distinct moment, for certain, is a synthesis of our chosen dictates. Accentuated by universally imposed conditions, genetic factors and our understanding of their effects, we are marching on pathways of certainty to unleash new states of certainty. For now, the universal laws rule supreme. In the future, to assure continuity of our existence, we may have to alter those laws, or alter our perception of their significance. If we survive universal calamities, we may evolve to something inordinately different. We could, just as well, destroy ourselves in the process. The possibilities are many and real.

Speculating on universal realities and eternal living can plunge the self into an abyss of wishful speculation. Void of real information, the mind clumsily creates information to justify its perceived end.

Should I choose to reflect on such grand ideas? That is a question time bound, spatial and dependent on my social and genetic disposition.

I often reason significance of reality as an isolated individual perception. Without perception, there is no reality. The reality of being a human is a metamorphic concept we decipher as we compose castles of perception. The reality of individual perception becomes entwined in complexity of our virtual social perception to synthesize a persuasive and sustainable comparative meaning. Such a delineated complexity has the capacity of fictional nature with an awesome mathematical potency to observe the universe in all its complexity. Meaningful or meaningless, this process assures continuity of civilization as a logical and progressive adventure.

The Great One looked up. Its eyes were piercing, or were they bright, or dull? I shivered. I shivered at its strength. I shivered at fragility of its being.

As it rearranged itself on the mat, I sensed a trace of uneasiness. The Great One was a human after all.

Sounds, harmony, hymns of joy, euphoric expressions, allegorical images, affection, happiness and good: these are metaphorical concepts we share.

Every day many passionate people make our lives happy. They fill the conceptual void in our awareness with forgiveness and empathy. They stand above necessities and fathom deep crisp thoughts to edify themselves and the rest. They are my heroes.

Like leaves on trees bent on each other, ephemeral and conforming, in this life of temporary certainties and mortal ends, virtue is plain and simple. Excellence is plain and simple. Freedom is plain and simple. Being is like a leaf on the tree of humanity. Being is like a seed that gives birth to a new definition of humanity.

An undulating awareness twirls mighty at the center of each conscience. It rules the self without ruling anything. It defines the self without defining anything. It formats cryptic descriptions of the self and the society, the civilization and the universe.

In the audience of another, I learn. In collusion of our inner universes, I gauge a calibrated measure of our common sense and learn.

When we are in agreement, the arrow of our cohesiveness assumes a unified direction. Our totality, the sum effect of our thoughts, becomes emotionally and intellectually charged. When we find solace in one another, we approach truths with greater certainty. We untangle mystery of existence while getting tangled in mystery of coexistence, one being at a time. This entanglement of two thoughtful entities, insulated from social impositions, has a didactic significance. It accentuates the supremacy of harmonious coexistence.

The individual life is finite, but the potential for socially mediated awareness can be greater. The infinity of awareness cannot be realized in isolation but in exposure to virtual social awareness. To be open to possibilities is a metaphor to having flexible boundary conditions. The broader are the boundaries of imagination, the greater the scope of assimilated information. With every encounter, the awareness gains an increment. This exercise is as transitory as it is transparent. It is as transcendental as it is transitive.

I now understood why The Great One felt such compulsion, time after time and seeker after seeker, to communicate. It had a need to sensitize its awareness with new perceptions without entanglement in the moral and ethical imperatives of a social gathering.

—The measure of your stature exceeds anything I have known. Even Deeva and Sima sought your audience. You have chosen a peculiar path of living. Are you superimposing a defined level of embroilment to manipulate your entanglement with social affairs?

—I remember them well, The Great One said calmly.

In their presence, I learned more than I gave. I offered them my place of clay, my place as The Great One. They refused. I offered them a piece of the clay in the monastery where they could entertain others. They refused.

Their perception of the social and the universal were far from mine. They saw existence as a transient shift in phases that must be evaluated, with undulating continuity, against the greater society and the civilization.

They did not see many benefits in the isolation of a monastery, on a small piece of clay, on a worn down straw math, where social forces are reduced to minimal.

I must confess, the tradition has become a burden. It inhaled a deep breath.

Each time I have a moment to myself the door opens, and a stranger disturbs my solitude. Each raises me to a level I am incapable of sustaining. Each expects of me miracles I cannot perform.

But such a predicament is my choosing. I could leave this space and let my absence give rise to something different. Time bound and egotistically obligated, I have become a prisoner of my perceived greatness. Such is the irony of existence: the greater a self is conceived by others, the heavier the chains that link it to others. And there lies the primary reason for my isolation.

I remember them well. I learned much from them.

The odyssey of enlightenment is a fractured state of many dilemmas. Each rising moment, as I awaken to shining thoughts, I dilute myself universal and contrive credulous scenarios only to watch my image change by audiences that narrow me down to a set of their chosen parameters.

I often remind myself; life is too short and fragile to waste with abstraction of being The Great One. I begged Deeva to take my place allowing me to continue my journey in greater isolation. Deeva reminded me, with an exquisite poem, we both have become slaves of our chosen paths.

Look at the world around us. What you see is not a deception. Do not take the ability of observance lightly. You are much more than a sensory device. You garnish and glaze what you observe with platitudes and toss them in the arena of humanity wishing for their observance and absorbance.

Imagine yourself at the point horizon of immense singularity. Imagine this singularity a human world of ideas. Imagine the world of ideas a point of immense observance. It is the ability to observe that makes us who we are.

Who you are, is not a deception. The wildest of your dreams is not a deception. Trust yourself. Trust your synergic mind. Trust sultry images flooding your mind. Trust resonance and transference of untenable ideas flowing through your mind. You may be a fragment of a fragment of a fragment, but you possess a unique ability to imagine fragments and build castles of ideas. Do not take this ability lightly.

One must realize the universe to realize oneself. Did I infer realization of the universe a higher motif than the realization of self?

One must realize oneself before realizing anything. Did I infer realization of self at the center of all realizations?

One must realize the universe and the self along parallel virtual strings to traverse the inner and meet the universes. Did I infer actualization of existence a connection between the self and the universe?

The virtual connection between the inner most self and the universe has consumed our attention for all our evolutionary time. We have imagined many scenarios as to the nature of this connection, none more powerfully tantalizing and misleading than the connections we have imagined as mystical beings.

Measures we adopt and definitions we cleave are norms we implement, to assuage burden of critical thinking. They are conventions of human accord.

Bounded by abstractions arising from a span of awareness in between realities of life and death, we attempt to clarify our social and universal entanglements with timeless definitions. Eternity is a human expression of evolving definitions and dimensions.

Bemused and confused by unknowns, fearful of death, obsessed by longevity and loss of awareness, we take a stand not certain if it is our best or last. Sometimes happy, sometimes sad, sometimes enlightened, sometimes for selfish reasons, we create meanings that temporize our restless thoughts.

Within such cryptic boundaries, universal schemes enslave us as much as we imagine ourselves free from them.

Our collective image, our mutual stand, is throbbing each mind with oscillations of "everything" and "nothing."

—What principles mold this bond between the individual and the universe? The accumulated information in social archives far exceeds individual capacity to absorb it. Is it possible to understand virtual complexities with clarity and transparency? Is such a clarity metamorphosing to a multidimensional puzzle with many tentacles entrapped with absurdities of complex systems?

—The certainty of awareness and the uncertainty of losing that awareness, the certainty of existence and the uncertainties arising from our constant struggle to make connections, are intellectual burdens we learn from those who choose to confront the unknown. They become our mentors and heroes. They carry the burden of civilization in return for social immortality.

The speeds at which the mind can actualize itself as a freewill, a social amalgam and a universal entity are different. The gaps between the private, the social and the universal grows as the self attempts to identify itself with increasing clarity and certainty creating confusion and psychological mayhem.

The private self reflects inward to solidify integrity of its core beliefs. This is an immensely difficult and revealing task. The self must peel off many protective layers buffering the aggressive and the sexually dictated modules of behavior.

Perhaps the most frightening and enlightening aspect of looking inward is the possibility of observing "nothing." If one can penetrate the core of selfhood and enlighten the self with the exposed nothingness, there is hope for enlightenment.

As each layer of accommodated values superimposes the preceding layers, the complexity becomes irretrievably entrenched. To peel off these layers and reach the core is an immense undertaking few can dare and fewer can succeed.

The virtual social self expands onward and outward with increasing acceptance of itself as a product of the civilization. In response, the self creates more psychological layers protecting its moral core from values exposing social contradictions. This aspect of the self can prove quite demanding and alienating.

The drive to transgress existing human limitations and acquire universal awareness crosses the boundaries of objective to find meaning and composition in the subjective world of speculation. This has led to mythical tales as misleadingly false information is disseminated.

Can the individual absorb the accumulated human knowledge and use it to understand its private, social and ultimately universal self? Perhaps the next evolutionary leap will start with humans that can process information with greater clarity, capacity, speed and accuracy. Perhaps the future generations will evolve neural layers bypassing the emotional alienation caused by age-old modules of behavior.

Will our existence lead to destructive disturbance of the universe? This is a question time-bound and imaginative.

Silence ruled as The Great One seemed absorbed in inner thoughts. It disappeared beneath the garb by pulling it over its head.

—What if a form of awareness is imperceptible to human senses? Could there be a consciousness that transmutes laws of the universe? Are we potentially of such quality? Is our civilization capable of evolving to become or to detect such a possibility?

—The singularity to which we are aiming at is eternal happiness through eternal awareness. We are achieving higher levels of happiness but eternity of awareness escapes us.

From the first moment of birth, the universe demands our existence. We resist until our biological constitution breaks down, and our will withers. Like an old abandoned lighthouse, we shine our beacon of thoughts until its shine dims meaningless and dies in a subdued moment of surrender.

The essence, the arrow of our collective existence, is not a fixed point. This essence is an evolutionary phenomenon with evolutionary consequences. It responds to demands of the universe. It rewards the physiologically and intellectually fit. It responds to willful intentions.

The virtual arrow of our collective existence shows many signs of awareness, yet it has no discernible willful manifest. Could this indicate evolution of a new form of awareness of which we are not as yet cognizant?

Our collective awareness of the universe is of virtual quality with reflection on the past. When we pierce light years into space, we observe a very distant past.

The mortal "I" has found an immortal expression in social "us." This format of human expression has a real chance of resolving universal mysteries. Do not take this phenomenon lightly. It has the potential to transcend and satisfy the needs of the universal self.

It also has the potential to manifest an evolutionary path of its own, making us a byproduct of its needs.

—What are the meaning and significance of "I" within the context of a virtual human civilization that could assume its own evolutionary path? "I" and "us" have suddenly found a new format in my awareness. Could you explain this further?

—"I" is capable of perceiving "everything" and imagining "nothing." "I" is a combined vector of private, social and universal selves. "I" has physical existence and virtual awareness. "I" has quantum and classical manifestation. "I" lives in real time but can traverse in the virtual dimension of time to explain the past and predict the future with increasing certainty.

In reality, "I" is a grain of sand in the ocean of "us." "I" is a vector the sum of which is "us."

"Us" has disjointed physical existence. "Us" is neither contiguous nor self-sustained. It will not die if millions perish. It will not change much with isolated events, but can drastically change with sudden shifts in paradigms. "Us" sets the course of human history. "Us" can be changed with willful and imaginative minds that explore the boundaries of their awareness. "Us" is a powerful force that sculpts "I." "Us" has the potential to change the universe. "Us" is an immortal entity without awareness of anything and totally dependent on the mortal and imaginative "I."

Is "us" exhibiting a form of awareness "I" cannot detect? Time will tell.

I see a poetic dimension in the eternity of "us" and wonder, what then? The answer rests on a spectrum delineated by "everything" and "nothing." By choosing one explanation, I negate other possibilities and form or alter my reality, our social reality, and the universal reality. Within such boundaries, I realize freewill an amorphous notion of emancipating qualities. It offers the possibility of exaltation without dilution in grandeur of delusions and prophesies. Within such boundaries, I realize compassion a normalizing scheme to all our thoughts and behaviors as well.

—I now understand. I reflected. The tapestry of our civilization is constantly shifting with new and evolving paradigms. In our evolving mode of existence freewill is what separates us, and compassion is what connects us.

I understand now. My being is an immensely imaginative free self of unbound potentials. It has limited physical integrity with immense awareness as a freewill, and a limitless integrity as a social entity.

I scream loud and clear and hear my echo from farthest. The scream is a willful expression and the echo a social reflection. I am my own free self as I am a fragment of something much bigger and more insignificant.

I understand now. Through freewill the self can ascertain higher levels of perception, occasionally higher than the civilization, transforming itself and the civilization.

Is this a current and newly evolved demand of our existence? Does it require us to achieve higher levels of certainty through willful awareness?

The classical and quantum theories teach us the real and the probable. What then are the absurd, the bizarre, and the quintessential? How do these ideas expose workings of our brain? What reason is the reason for their perception?

The Great One stood, paced its way around the room.

—The moment an idea becomes etched in our conscience, irrespective of its actual existence or not, it becomes alive.

The means our ancestors deployed to cope with the environmental and physiological conditions evolved to modules of behavior with associated emotional manifests. As their genetic replicates, we carry their fears and pleasures. The difficulty for us is to dissociate the emotional feelings from associated behaviors.

The mode of perception, the quality of perceived images, the implications we are entertaining were untenable to our ancestors.

An entity composed of billions of free wills is potentially a ubiquitous depiction. An entity composed of billions of compassionate selves is potentially all-absorbing. An entity composed of billions of free wills is conceivably all mighty. We did imagine it as such not knowing it will be manifest as a reality.

The Great One took its place atop the straw math and versed the following with poetic resonance.

I sit by the wayside, follow the flow of feelings, let rushing desires and seductive enchantments appease my senses. I detect attraction to something higher and lighter, something different, something intellectually stimulating. I sense epiphany of something futuristic and delightfully delicious.

I open my mind and imagined myself gone astray amidst a journey in the universe. What a surprise; this is a trip among the stars. Like downy-flakes on a cool bristly mountaintop, I stare at a glare, a warming delight. Like withering leaves of a weeping willow, I attest life high and low. Who am I in this paradox of delights? Am I a dichotomy of right and wrong? Am I a speck trapped in a site? Am I in an appropriate frame of mind?

Perhaps when time stops, as it does for particles traveling with the speed of light, the imaginative self finds an exact reality. To us mortals such an act is impossible. To a mortal, passing of time is of the essence. Reality of physical integrity is of the essence.

To a mortal, the past and the future congregate in the real domain of present exhibiting time-space-mind. Within such boundaries, I perceive unfamiliar observations as absurd and bizarre. This strangeness is the result of a conflict between the inward, the outward, the universal, the neurological and compounds interacting to depict those images.

Implications of this process are far-reaching and comprehensive. The Great Deeva understood it well. He collapsed his perceptions to poetic expressions. In doing so, he transcended three dimensions of "I" to form a unique expression of freewill.

—What then is awareness if trapped by the limitations of modular responses? We think and react the same, but the ideas have different meanings in each of our minds. I gain awareness by gaining awareness of language. I gain awareness by gaining awareness in comparison to others. I gain awareness by gaining awareness of the space around me. I gain awareness by understanding science. "Who am I" is not an easy question. "I" is trapped by limitations of communicative and perceptive means.

How am I to know what is a perfect me? How am I to know if I have achieved the ideal me? Would it suffice to describe myself with thoughts? Am I best expressed through actions? Should I strive to match my thoughts with actions? I take full responsibility for what I am, for my failures and gains. How can I change boundaries of my personality to sculpt who I want to be?

—The complexity of language is embedded in sophisticated images words depict in conjunction with one another. Aside from mathematics, language is the greatest human invention. The changing modes of communication, in themselves, have become our quintessence.

Most cognitive modules, affording us quickness and ease of action, are expressions of primitive nature. New formats of communication and perceived threats are changing all that. We are not the humans we used to be. We do not share the same notion of existence our ancestors did, but we do carry their emotional expressions. Fear and pleasure are what kept them alive. Fear and pleasure are what keep us entertained.

The Great One pondered awhile.

Alive amidst harmony of thoughts, I am comfortable if unified in all my actions. I am the ideas translated into actions to brew more thoughts.

What constitutes a perfect human? Is it harmony of thought and action? Is it symmetry of inner and outer? Is it happiness through compassion? Is it awareness through knowledge? Is it a fusion of all thoughts and actions? That is a question timeless and social. That is a quest easily expressed and difficult to achieve in continuity of living.

Those who will intricacies of their lives, cajoled by the existential ideals, driven by the harmony of thought and action, are immersed in the absurd reality of solitude knowing, perfectly or imperfectly, it will all end in particles flowing in solar winds to shape unknown landscapes.

High on awareness, they absorb humanity with passion, live a glorious dream, laugh their lives silly and die in a subdued moment of submission to disintegration and entropy.

This fortune of living, this fortune of time to imagine the universe, this moment of reality to dive into a pool of absurd and measure my worth with deeds, is a life-sustaining force. It is a most delicious reason for being.

Being a human is living on a strand of imaginative thoughts traversing dimensions of reality to land in chosen islands of absurdity and back. As such, I will always wonder who I am and who I want to be. There is much to imagine and live.

The harmony of thought and action is measurable when observed by others. The social "I" is the only venue for a perfect "I." There is no perfection or imperfection in the isolated narcissistic "I."

—If the perfect "I" can find its meaning and purpose in social "I," within constraints of a willfully harmonious "I," then what is the meaning of the universal "I?"

As a collective, we can observe events of the past, predict galactic disasters light-years ahead, and plan escape routes. Are we then on the path to a new evolutionary shift, if the social and universal parts of a self melt into one? Is our existence fundamentally changing? Is the harmoniously social and compassionate "I" a prelude to evolution of a universal "I?"

If values are extracted social excitations, if values coordinate and regulate the human condition, must we not constantly revise them to format our changing needs? How can a self differentiate useful and alienating? The choice is not easy. Often, a fine line separates moral and immoral. Truth is neither on my side nor on any side. Truths of individual existence change with changing thoughts and shifting values.

—Amidst all the observed wonders of the universe, we are a capacious construct with immense propensity to perceive the totality and format it to our liking. Our existence as a civilization is a manifest of great fascination.

The anxieties arising from contortions of our potentially immortal civilization, observed by the mortal individual, have stimulated a healthy dialogue among us. The individual, as a quintessential freewill, has enacted ideas to unify its fields of thought. We do not know into what format this unified field will change. Nonetheless, we are aiming for it with passion.

The paradigms of human existence have shifted many times in the past. They will surely shift again. In the process, there will be mutations, grand theories, unifying concepts, constructive and destructive ideas translated into actions.

The Great One remained silent as I pondered the significance of the moment and its eventual end.

The old man of thoughts sits by the river, The Great One versed with poetic tone that reminded of Deeva.

His astute mind thinks deep. Love of life he ponders mellow. Is there a singularity amidst his mind? Is he radiating intense energies? Is his disposition traversing galaxies to cross the universe to expose lightness of its being?

He whispers words of compassion to sway perplexed minds. But no sooner than he imagines himself precociously endowed, probability rolls its dice, and he lays dead.

Long after his mind disintegrates, his thoughts remain alive in our minds. Tell me, what he saw that did not last? What discoveries did he find that lasted?

Afloat rivers of life he tried to find "everything" but entropy imposed its supremacy, and he ended up experiencing "nothing." His consciousness disintegrated but thoughts that bore deep in all our minds remain vibrantly alive.

Tell me: is there a virtual singularity defining the state of his mind? Is the nature of his truth what he thought and lived? Did he disappear for all times and thoughts?

He braced his caustic self for a majestic impact in a new galaxy—a new life, and no dinosaurs this time—only us: our dreams and fallacies. In some unknown, undefined, uncharted format of unremitting variations, in small immeasurable constellations of minds, He braced himself for a willful impact and found "nothing."

—Truly I do not know who I am, I confessed.

I do not know the world around me. I am primitive. I have limited knowledge of certainties. I feel a diminished self, void of sufficient reasoning to amalgamate my potentials. I have no qualities to shine humanity a meaningful reason. For certain, I see no singularity in my mind. I fear dying without understanding the universe. All the wonderful boundary conditions you have elegantly explained are external to parameters defining my reality. Truths you have exposed, at best, are my fantasies. Truths are relative concepts.

How can I invest my life on what will be? How can I become something I am not?

My voice reached an uncomfortable high before I realized my disposition more anxious than I intended. I apologized politely. The Great One seemed impervious to my disposition.

My time is too short to waste with distant metaphors of little relevance. I am indisposed by norms of cultural manifest to accommodate cryptic universal ideas. I wish I could live longer. I wish I could understand "everything."

The Great One remained silent as I reduced myself invalid. It looked at me with eyes of an old friend.

—You will not realize yourself with the degree of certainty you wish to actualize yourself. You must ascertain the reality of your awareness with a bit fuzzier logic than you entertain. You are as much an illusive image as you are quantitatively measurable.

Beware, the more you duel on exactness of awareness the narrower your vision of its dimensions. As a manifested probability, awareness can best measure itself with fuzzy principles.

Our collective imagination is aligning a new symmetry of self and social. I must warn you. Beware of determinism in this new alignment. If it is fueled by a megalomaniac obsession energized by egotism bend on captivating others, it can be most detrimental. If it is fueled by existential relativism, and driven by compassion, it can be most useful.

The state of omnipotence, to a mortal is, not to cease imagining it's fullest. The world is inundated with random states. It is this randomness creating possibilities. We are inundated with chaotic states we attempt to understand by organizing them.

We seek certainties not realizing our search in itself influences the object of our search in ways we do not intend.

We imagine certainties before exposing their detailed reality. We move at will in time-space of our mind arguing different aspects of the same reality. Reality changes every-which-way in virtual space of our imagination. Occasionally, we gain awareness in leaps that shake foundations of our psyche.

The consilience of assimilated information sets boundaries of each awareness. The emergence of minds set tensegrity of human awareness. This virtual reality spins our lives in directions of our collective choosing. It has no intent or awareness of its own.

From uniqueness of each to lifeless social complexity, from the real time observance to the virtual observance, we reduce complex systems to their simple components to build new complexities. In the process, we satisfy our insatiable desire to observe the transformation.

—I am bewildered by magnanimity of all the imagined and imaginable. I am bewildered by what I know, could know and have yet to imagine I could know. Your thoughts unravel my thoughts exposing new paths of awareness. Is synthesis the ultimate format of actualization? Can we reconcile our differences and congregate our ideas for a grand dialectical integrity? Can we arrange matrices of our thoughts for a perfect symmetry of ideas?

—In front of us and within us lays an image of "everything," but we do not see it. We possess the necessary tools to reconcile "everything," but we do not recognize it. We accept hardships of a trail, gamble our fortune in undetermined scenarios to catch a glimpse of this illusive "everything," but the closer we get the farther it seems.

Deep within us is an uneasy and perplexing sense of "nothing" we attempt to fill with objects, feelings and thoughts. The more we fill the greater the space of containment grows. This duality, this dichotomy of "everything" and "nothing," and trepidations it generates, rules our individual and social lives. It is a manifestation of our cognitive functioning.

In the classical domain, we dwell on exactness. In this domain reality is precisely defined and predictable. In the world of imagination possibilities do not collapse to a contiguous and discernable reality. We see through hormones, enzymes, energy transfer, DNA strands, chromosomes and bio-chemical interactions.

In the quantum field of imagination ideas freely associate for synthesis of all things imaginable. It is this phenomenon that gives rise to creativity and ingenious revelations.

We live in a real world with precise consequences. Perfection is not the driving force of our existence. Imperfection is the rule we attempt to rectify.

Human existence is a fusion of quantum and classical manifests. This explains our determination to find a unifying principle of existence. In our attempt to unify natural principles, we are searching the core meaning, the essence, the all-encompassing principles of our physical and psychological existence.

—We are expounding on the integrity of increasingly sophisticated individual and social organizations, I said.

In reality, as the virtual civilization grows complex and mighty, the self shrivels small and less significant. Is the evolution of freewill a way out of this trap? Can the physical and the psychological components of an actualized freewill transcend the scope of our current perception?

I die, and my species survives. I die, and the collective survives. Is there no trace of consciousness after death? How can something so magnificent vanish without a trace? Can nothingness be a mode of awareness? Does consciousness have different forms of manifestation? Could it evolve to have a collective field? Must the future human possess a strong freewill to survive stressors of its social evolution?

—In a transparent future, I hope we will stand above clouds of necessity and declare our quintessence an amalgamated ambiguity of willful integrity.

Our ancestors spend their time hunting, gathering and procreating. With evolving social conditions the self has become free to spent quality time pondering the aesthetic, the ethical, the moral, the absurd and the scientific. The growing forces that consume the civilization necessitate elevation of the self to a willful status to withstand increasing pressures.

Like leaves on trees, bent on each other end to end, we live together and light years apart. Like floating on a roaring river, riding turns and twists of rushing trends, we are afloat streams of social discourse. The streams are fast becoming roaring rivers.

I am hopefully certain compassionate and willful humans will evolve to transcend adversely consuming social forces. Time is with us as it is against us. I am hopeful we will have a greater say which direction it will yield.

Am I too diluted to assume our amorphous destiny a meaningful certainty? If we survive fallacies we have created, what we may now believe will transcend us from Stone Age passed onto a destiny that may last. Such ecumenical transposition is not detected from one moment to the next but from one idea to the next, from one shifting paradigm to another.

Social outcomes devour contours of our determination by chiseling its sharp dictates to dullness of utilitarian conformity. Conformity is the greatest danger to the human condition only free wills can see, foresee and escape.

The Great One looked at me peacefully.

Snowflakes fall gentle in mind. The Great One versed.

Late spring emulates a medley of thoughts. A flock of flickering thoughts fall faint. Except for an occasional quiescent thought, looking deep, I see conflicting illusions. Flooded with ideas, my mind ripens clear only to dilute itself with the possibility of greater clarity.

I realize myself an unknown catalyst, a seeker of antecedents imagining myself a single snowflake, melting as I fall. I see myself enlightened by a field of dreams. I am a state of many states rising on a mountain of thoughts to sink deep in an abyss of confusion. I am a state of many states riding many turbulent thoughts to land in an imagined harmonious state.

With the fading conscience, the dichotomy of being and nothingness coalesces into a unified meaning. The highly organized state of awareness loses its epiphenomenal format, and the anthropic principle loses its relevance. The assimilated image of the universe, all the thoughts, all the accrued knowledge vanishes as if never existed. But they do not disappear. They fall in a black hole of human imagination to rise in other minds.

Being and not being temporarily manifest at the same instance before the transition is complete and a state of awareness vanishes. A perception of the universe disintegrates, but the universe persists for as long as there are others to perceive its persistence.

A perception of the universe disintegrates, and the perceiver becomes a quantum image in someone else's mind until that too disappears. And when all perceptions of a self disappear, the self is completely embedded in the state of nothingness.

It is "nothing" from which we started and onto which we shall part.

Nothingness is a virtual state. In the absence of known universal designs, I find this explanation temporarily sufficient for disappearance of a conscience.

To format the tapestry of a greater civilization, I envision a future biology. I envision fusion of absurd and real. What can I tell you of such a possibility? How can I explain such a distant idea except to implicate it as a human dream? And humans make real most of their dreams.

Each of us is a box with a unique image of the universe trapped inside. From this vantage point of inner entrapment, we reach out to interact with the world outside.

If I minimize my interactions, the world outside shrinks increasingly irrelevant. Such a mind is imprisoned and consumed by its own image.

Once outside my insulated inner awareness, the classical definition of perception manifests and my existence is no longer a prisoner of its isolation. It is within this context, I see the notion of freewill with enough gravity to balance the social bonds while maintaining its uniqueness.

The sense-based state of awareness may only be one form of awareness. I cannot deny the possibility of becoming trapped in unknown dimensions. I could not deny any sentient being the possibility of becoming a singularity of immense absorption. But possibilities do not define reality, and universal consciousness is not necessarily the conscience of the universe, or a preferred, required, or lasting state. Neither it is the optimal state.

The Eastern myths of creation have confused the civilization since their conception and permeation as the quintessential truths of our existence. These myths are real to the extent we have imagined them as such. The universe has no recognition of them as such. To assert the end from the beginning is a daring act. However, without correct data, such a declaration assures alienation.

Do not assert time-present a designed state, or a lost state, or a beginning, or an end. Time-present is everything we think and live without an absolute meaning.

Mesmerized and bewildered, I stared at The Great One.

—Are we slaves of our past perceptions? Are we enslaved by accumulated impulses of human evolution? Are the cognitive modules that saved our ancestors harmful to our existence? Is the notion of freewill a way out of this entrapment?

—Early humans were limited in scope of their imagination. In their attempt to envision a meaningful purpose to the cosmos, their deductive reasoning reduced their observations to a small set of connections. Lack of correct information and sophisticated methods of reasoning severely limited the scope of their analysis. Their brain processed wrong data spewing false solutions.

They associated anything incidental to the event with the event and tabulated a sequence of incidents trying to recreate the event.

Controlling events was a supreme purpose and essential to their survival. Whenever they reached an impasse, they attributed the event to the will and wisdom of beings with exaggerated human characteristics of virtual existence. Association with mythical beings satisfied their attempt to connect with truths they could not resolve.

The initial myths were simple in nature. None were simpler than the day and night. Daytime meant the rise of the sun: a delightful event of all. And night meant darkness: a dreaded time of all.

With sunrise came light. Light gave sight. It made food visibly available. It exposed approaching predators. It made shelter easily accessible. It healed wounds. It warmed chilled bones. Its presence promoted life and happiness.

The sun was worshiped as a supreme good and sacrifice was made to appease it. Even human sacrifice was offered to entertain highest gratitude and devotion.

If light was good, darkness was its antithesis as bad. Darkness implied loss of site and security. Strange sounds and shadowy images frightened the self, half dead. Predators roamed the land stalking their human prey. Darkness was feared as supreme bad.

The experiences and behaviors that led to good and bad, pain and pleasure, right and wrong nurtured the human emotional reasoning and became engrained as behaviors with associated responses that have remained with us to this day.

In time, finely tuned tales of creation were synthesized with perplexing detail. They often involved the epics of human virtue and bravery. Highly complex rituals were conceived to commemorate these events. The masters of ceremony, the principal enforcers of social and moral conduct, determined application and appropriateness of good and bad, right and wrong. They dictated the nature of evolving ethical principles assimilated and accommodated through the tedious network of social evolution. These evolving social modules assumed lives of their own dictating the individual principles.

Old cognitive modules are difficult to erase, but a leap in genetic and social evolution can reset these processes to a new level of excitation.

If the initial information was conceived in fear, which it often is, the associated principles induced the emotion of fear engraving it in the mind as part of the response. To purge the mind from such constructs is a task of enormous undertaking.

Aside from evolutionary leaps, a mind can affect change through willful constructs. As we decode our emotional foundation and modules of behavior, paradigm shifts of varying significance are unleashed. Do not take the power of willful cognition lightly. Willful processing of correct information can lead to phenomenal changes with sweeping consequences.

—How did simple myths that captivated early human imagination evolved into an all-powerful, all-encompassing, all-observing, all-absorbing phenomenon?

How did the notion of a single authoritative being evolved? How did the notion of evil evolve?

—Eternity is a curious idea initially conceived by humankind as an extension of its existence. In early stages of human evolution, eternity was conceived in simple terms. The perception of time-space began with limited dimensions and evolved with evolving scientific revelations. As life expectancy increased, we showed interest in eternity with greater emphasis and curiosity. With the advent of scientific analysis and observation of deep space, eternity and infinity acquired their own independent meanings.

In the beginning "all mighty" had limited definition and extension. The ability to fight off predators and natural disasters and to stay alive and procreate delineated the limit of their imagination.

As their imaginative abilities transcended the time-space of their existence, they extended physical might as their definition of all mighty.

In time all mighty became a metaphor for a unified principle that controlled human destiny by controlling the universe.

The ability to make correct judgments was projected as "all knowing." The generosity to dispense sustenance and secure shelter was projected as "all-merciful." The wish to live forever was coded as "everlasting."

In parallel with socio-cultural evolution, each of these concepts followed a unique pattern from a parochial notion to a universal concept.

In the early stages, humans bestowed gods partial attributes of limited scope. In time, the common wish for a unifying theory of existence resulted in hegemony of power by one god in cyberspace of human imagination.

As the social order evolved into a complex pyramid of dictatorial hierarchy, the myth of a single authoritative being was transformed, and placed at the top of the pyramid.

Democracy was not as yet conceived. Male domination was pandemic. Hierarchy of power was the rule. Hegemony of power was on the rise. Empires with increasing global dominance dominated human psyche.

Reflecting social realities, a single god was conceived as the absolute ruler of the universe with all-encompassing powers.

A supernatural force of ecumenical dimensions, with all the attributes of a dictator reflecting the existing social realities, was synthesized as the supreme protagonist in the arena of existence. The scope of this virtual being of mythical significance evolved with evolving human perception of the universe. It was conceived as all mighty, omnipotent, omnipresent, all knowing, pure in judgment and merciful.

It detected and archived every aspect of individual existence. It judged and granted. It rewarded and punished. It created and destroyed. And it did all that within prevailing limitations of the existing knowledge. As such, it evolved with the evolving human knowledge.

As a social concept, without a physical reality but transcending limits of individual power, this virtual being evolved to assume an evolutionary life of its own.

It is perfectly natural to assume this wishful image as a willful attempt to evolve a new human species with greater powers of universal significance.

However persuasive, this method of approach did not explain chaotic manifestations of disease, disaster, pain and suffering.

To remedy this condition, humans looked within and projected all of their negative thoughts and fears to existence of an all-mischievous, all-deceptive and all-destructive being. This being projected the duality of good and bad within us onto a universal stage. The myth, the plot of existence, falsely based on the human condition, was synthesized and the scheme of a universe reflecting the good, the bad, the right and the wrong was completed.

The deceptive perception of life as a dichotomy of good and bad, reflecting true nature of humankind, was linearly and virtually extended to infinite and granted a universal status.

—Existential philosophy of self was conceived much later. What exactly is this identity?

—The Stone Age humans exercised their power of speculation on objects pertinent to their livelihood. Their aim was to find easy prey and avoid being a prey. Those humans had no chance of enlightenment. Their lives began with early awareness of death.

Their all-consuming effort was to stay alive. Group existence supplanted this process with a lower probability of becoming a victim. Similar genetic make up assured similar cognitive modules and coordinated correlation of observation and reaction increased the chance for survival. Congregation of same species with similar cognitive modules increased probability of survival for each and a greater diversity of propagation.

In the early stages of human existence, when fire was not a tool and living a beastly struggle, the physically powerful and mentally aggressive ruled with impunity. They subjugated others to increase certainty of their own existence, and the subjugated tolerated abuse in exchange for increased security and survival.

Our primitive ancestors inadvertently adopted an existential notion of life as their standard of behavior. Their behaviors were simple, unimaginative and purely existential. The imaginative and compassionate self took the center stage much later and evolved to its current constructs.

Existential approach to identity of self evolved with the premise that responsibility of living, irrespective of how life begins and ends, rests on shoulders of the individual.

The individual may enhance variables of its existence through social experience, but in every step, the choice is the individual's to make.

To accept responsibility for our failures and achievements is a powerful experience. It can change how we think and live.

—Can an organization with limited dimensions exist to its fullest without organizers and overseers? Is the existence of a cognitive overseer a necessary condition for creation of a universe?

—The logic "if there is an organization, there must be an organizer" falls into a trap with infinite resonance of who or what created the creators who created the creation. Such reasoning assumes a single definite format to the notion of creation.

I behold "nothing" is where it all started. "Nothing" is a metaphor for something that did not exist before. Without a tangible meaning, "nothing" is the biggest mystery of life. "Nothing" is an allegorical representation of un-manifested probabilities, vanishing realities and universal concepts we have yet to discover.

In the theory of evolutionary existence, "natural" assumes a flexible meaning. It can be defined, redefined and altered. It can assume any form, meaning or manifestation. It can appear and disappear.

In this philosophy of existence, anything and everything probable is possible and whatever prevails is natural. There is no supreme hierarchy of order, and all life forms have a chance to reach their optimal potential.

This philosophical interpolation imagines the universe a paradox of order and chaos. All forms and beings that exist can live to their fullest potential, or simply appear and disappear without expressing any potential.

The notion that the universe reflects the will and wisdom of a single consciousness is flawed. The suggestion that we have no say in determining our destiny is flawed. The idea of the universe as a monopoly of two opposing forces is flawed. The idea of the universe as an arena of judgment controlled by one or more overseers is flawed. All the conceived flaws originate from an era of human civilization riddled with flaws.

Within a domain of chaotic principles, given time, all probabilities shall be manifest.

The Great One seemed at ease. I could sense its peaceful presence.

Human collective is a force of immense significance, said The Great One.

The genocidal mistakes and ingenious discoveries we have experienced are not dictated by supernatural beings but us. To accept this responsibility is fundamental to evolution of compassionate and creative free wills.

We have our individual universes to build and attempt to reconcile righteousness of our ideas in the arena of the greater civilization. In every step of such a determined outcome, we deal with genetic impulses and universal constants that constrain and even shape the outcome of our undertakings. This coexistence of control and chaos is a reality we must understand and deal with care.

Now, if you tell me, my pasture is molted and yours green, that your mantle of virtue is higher than mine, someone will rise above you in supremacy of logic and remind you the supremacy of coexistence.

Absolute postures and assumed supremacy of a universal consciousness is a measure of an egomaniacal perspective of existence. I refuse to lower my mantle of humanity to meet such a narcissistic perspective.

Let it be irrevocably known: no greater right exists than right to choose. No right deserves more protection than the right to be free. And there is no greater tyranny than imposing one's will on another.

—What then is compassion? As I actualize, I find myself wrapped in confusion. The world around me is increasingly cold, abstract and too sophisticated to decipher. The relationships are distant and impersonal. Can compassion alleviate this condition?

The Great One looked up to the beaming light. The straight path of rays refracted off its clear face.

—The immeasurable human compassion is a pillar of our emotional and intellectual stand. Compassion can be expressed with highest sagacity. Look at you and me. We are expressing compassion for each other, for life, for humanity, for other life forms, for possibilities. There is a flow of energy between us the measure of which is compassion.

In the beginning, we entertained aggressive means to survive. In time, we glazed our thoughts with compassion to ameliorate the paradox of living with aggression. Logic forbids living without reason. And reason, marinated with compassion, is a clearer path to tranquility than reason or compassion alone.

I am a small chasm in cyberspace of dreams. My mind matures ravenous in imagination to fathom the complexity of compassion, only to realize significance of a living moment with goblets of affection. From a deep and vast reservoir of passion, metamorphosing crystal clear to form synchronicity of compassion, I find certain in uncertain and confess we are besieged by brackish ideas, by quandary of happiness and age, by complexity of social and universal.

Am I abstruse, too diluted with passion? How deep is my sense of truth? What illusions conjure up this sense of reality? In every occasion, I see passion and reason. Every reason is a flotilla of occasions that demands compassion.

Imprisoned in the domains of moral and virtue, caged in the labyrinth of values, I try to prove myself righteous by swallowing my worst moments and slowly revealing millions of years of the compacted modules that are "I."

I cherish any definition of "I" that encompasses compassion as the enforcer of passion and reason.

—Sometimes I feel life is more than I imagine it to be. I feel most everything I perceive is an illusion. I feel I should take this moment, realize its fallibility and swallow my pride knowing what I do, what I think, is a passing.

Amidst such confusing states only uninhibited tyrants ruffle ideas to the extreme of perfection, resolve existence to awareness and deduce "everything" from "nothing."

We have evolved complex social networks reflecting the human field of consciousness. Through this network, the individual transcends its inner boundaries to immerse in a much larger containment. Could this lead to formation of a human singularity? Time will tell.

—The individual is confronted with three seemingly conflicting dilemmas.

Who am I as an isolated awareness of insecure nature? Who am I as a social phenomenon of conditioned nature? And who am I as a universal entity made of design and chaos?

The tension between these three dimensions of self defines the self. Conflicts arise when inconsistent and false information is processed resulting in a cascade of alienating outcomes.

The individual senses the conflicting trepidations of these precepts but feels powerless to understand or escape them. The tension is magnified when the self, through social forces, attempts to impose its will on the civilization to prove correctness of its assertions in obedience of others.

The dilemma is further magnified when the self imagines itself connected to a universal awareness.

The universe has little recognition of human existence. In compilation of ideas, we ferment concepts that define truths of our lives. If we keep on imagining ourselves a fraction of gods, we wish to join, we shall do so only by becoming them. Since such a prospect is untenable in real life, we have sought it in the virtual world of imagination where it has evolved to a social concept.

This dilemma will be resolved if "I" assumes a symmetrical state untangling emotions from primitive modules of behavior. Even then, no mortal can ascertain a definite path to its existence until "I" begins to liberate itself by a transforming odyssey in a domain of freewill.

—Truth is, we live in a universe of many uncertainties and the certainty of freewill is short lived.

—It's sunrise, versed The Great One. To blooming roses, it's sunrise. To lovers awaiting a cozy moonshine, it's sunrise. Who am I in this paradise of gloom and delight? Am I a prisoner of my own perceived wonders? Am I a slave of time? Am I a seeker of unifying theories? Am I a fool of a thousand cascades? Am I a prisoner of imposed perceptions? Am I an existentialist forever chasing the shifting concept of humanity?

Collective virtual human conscience can transcend laws of the universe. We must not deny our species optimal achievements. Our survivability depends on it. The force of our civilization is a potent creative phenomenon with access to the universe and possibilities beyond. We will evolve with constructive and destructive consequences. We will gain unparalleled awareness. Along the way, we will cause much happiness and pain.

To assure ourselves constructive pathways, we must learn and teach compassion as a measure of our success. Compassion is a permeating state we could achieve through connective, meditative, reflective and transformative techniques.

If I am completely isolated within my image of self, to another observer, I could be incredibly cognizant or not at all. This notion in itself and by itself could explain why we bestow so many universal attributes to unobserved objects of our imagination: why gods and demons are assumed to have so much power?

The instant the contents of a conscience are observed by another it assumes a comparative state. It is this relationship between two cognizant forms of life that qualify freewill a variable of immense significance and a potential starting point for evolution of the species.

The individual will is a virtual vector. The question of concern is the possible dimensions and directions of this vector. The greater question of concern is alignment of these vectors for condensation of new ideas.

No matter how capacious or capricious, the vector of each conscience influences the others. When these vectors are in concert, through virtual social condensation, an immense force is unleashed.

As a real time observer, each mind disturbs this virtual reality and is disturbed by it.

I am constantly wondering if my perceptions are correct or incorrect. I correlate my perceptions with others of my kind to fine tune accuracy of my observations. We then yearn for contact with other cognitive beings to verify accuracy of our collective perceptions.

Future is a variable of the human condition. And there will lie the real savior of our civilization: our contact with other life forms will be a mutual act of observance. Void of aggression and glazed with compassion, this encounter could prove most enlightening.

—Are you insinuating that the realization of self as an isolated entity, and trusting that realization, are prerequisites to the realization of self as a social and universal entity? Is it not reasonable to assume parallel understandings of components of self a more symmetrical format?

—You are correct, said The Great One. Thank you for this revelation. The three components of awareness: self, social and universal, when symmetrical, can result in a unified self. Approaching this format is the most elusive and comprehensive act of actualization. In unison with others of similar integrity, the self as a freewill will experience the awesome display of thought condensation.

We know little about limits of actualization. Perhaps observing its boundaries will gradually liberate us. Perhaps it jumps to another level the moment it is achieved. For certain, actualization is conceived through a social format, but it is meaningful to the self only. Social phenomenon has no use for such formats except for the fact that an enlightened and happy self can become a productive member of the society.

Nevertheless, the suns shine with predictable intensity. Days pass with much ado about nothing. Time changes with precision of atomic nature. Mutation changes biological formations. Stars are born and die. Galaxies collide, and our perception of the universe is increasingly a mathematical concept.

What we imagine is a unique vision of something that may change existence. The great Zarthosht imagined it well. Say well, think well and do well, he reminded us. His intent, his basic premise, was admirable. It superposed compassionate norms above all else. But the notion of good he perceived is inherently a relative idea of an interpretive nature he did not and perhaps could not fathom.

The question of concern is the syntax of this imaginary matrix of good. It is difficult to define good as a consistent composition of relevant ideas. One way to escape this dilemma is to isolate a definition of good for the experience at hand without conviction to its universality or certainty.

The Great One rose, took a few short steps, stood beneath the beaming light absorbing its treasure of heat.

The illusive subject of concern is the unifying theory of mind. Once achieved, the captivating concern will metamorphose to a grand theory of civilization.

ikstop.

Will the unifying theory of the mind result in a combined domain of virtual and physical awareness? Will it liberate us from dictatorial perceptions? Will it punctuate the end of human civilization and mark the beginning of another?

The discussion metamorphoses to a higher level when the evolution of humankind as an independent entity becomes a prime directive. The task is to reach this hiatus without losing our individuality and perspective as social beings.

Should we promote propagation of mutations better adapted to cope with the universal demands? Has such a transformation already begun by virtue of the fact that ideas are exerting increasing influence on the propagation of the species rather than physical attributes alone?

In all likelihood, the universe is a conjugate of many rather than confluence of a few. Truth is, truth is a collective perception. We must take every step to assure universal democracy and the right of each civilization to realize its independent, willful and free destiny.

Nonetheless, it is the individual, in every step, isolated in its awareness and insecurely alone, that must decide significance of all thoughts and arguments.

Freedom to exercise freewill through compassionate norms is the axiom that could alleviate contortions caused this evolutionary process.

The relation between the self and the universe is an imaginative ethos. For the existing generations, it is the knowledge of possibilities that suffices. To future generations, their realization will become a fact.

I am not certain, which is more rewarding: dreaming of possibilities or actualizing realities. In either case, to get there, we must imagine. Freedom of will is not an abstraction but a practical reality.

The universe is dappled with perplexing puzzles, and the human mind is an instrument that recognizes these puzzles.

The Great One folded its head over its knees disappearing from my perception.

Time had come to leave and let other seekers be dazzled by its wisdom.

I stood, looked at The Great One. It did not move. I turned around and entered the small yard I had passed through. An attendant abruptly came forth directing me to a back door. I realized myself a homeless creature of ideas, forever leaving, forever searching.

There I was, liberated and full of imaginative ideas. In all reality, a new journey had sprung earnest in my mind. But my physical existence was fragile and failing.

No sooner than I measured a steep rise did I come across an old self of many shades. He occupied a small enclave in the bosom of a carved bolder. As I approached he looked up with a smile and unabashedly screamed; have you found your freedom?

I bowed and replied, no, not yet.

When you reach that point of exaltation, you shall attain access to the truth of existence and contribute to our collective experience, it shouted with confidence.

I looked at him with pity.

Each, in our contained contortion of living, attempts to discover purpose after purpose through association and social observation, I explained.

You have no chance of engaging humanity in this isolated desolate corner. Isolation is not a favorable path to awareness.

He sighed. Perhaps you are right. I am stranded in this forsaken corner of no entanglements. It is a weakness of my own making. Perhaps I am not wholly aware. I am only happy with my contentment.

Farewell my friend, I said.

I must be on my way. I am too bold and old to waste life watching others pass me by.

There is no beginning, no end, said another.

It matters not who passes whom. There is no universal logic in passing one another, only minds that perceive prospect of a gain in doing so.

Life is not pure. Time espies no favors. In reality, and dreams, we are what we think: creators of ideas and ideals.

Often lost, driven by bytes, I am trapped in whatever I see as my containment.

And what happens when we reach that moment when all of us, collectively, become free wills, asked another?

Can we unravel this mythical notion of freedom? Can we, as a civilization, solve the riddle of being? If and when we do, would such an achievement entail deconstruction of our humanity?

The burden of awareness lies on the individual, I said.

There is no escaping individuality unless someday, by some amazing means, we link our minds creating a super-human conscience. Even then I shall not want to lose my awareness as a unique individual.

Remember the myth of Atlas, said another.

He carried the burden of life on his shoulders. The human of the future may have to carry the burden of the universe on its shoulders.

Such thoughts are dreams we imagine, and imagine well. It is all a dream, said another.

Hi there, said a wild haired immense figure of imposing posture. Are you with me? Are you listening to my shouts? Who are you in this hall of wonders? Are you actualized? Does your idiom contain us all? Give me a note, a tune, a poem. Let our lives twine compassionate postures. In this quandary of "everything" and "nothing," it is easy to speak words, reduce the universe to simple idea and swallow them whole.

Imagine yourself at an event horizon. Imagine yourself trapped in a web of attraction and repulsion. Imagine yourself a positive neutron detached from your pair. It falls deep. You escape.

Slow down, slow to a faster pace, assume certainty of a sudden change. What spin are you? Which field do you hold? Whatever happened to your pair? In a deep and dense bosom of a black hole, it did not disappear. It metamorphosed. So have you. So will all of us.

In truth, life is not a fantasy, nor is it pure reality. It just is, as I am: a mixture of everything educible, a probability higher than virtue or perfection.

Emboldened by happiness, I assume life a harmonious plight, to be sure, of my own consonance. A self-centered virtuous private montage, I am an accosting narcissist. Free in mind, with a capricious taste for high and low, and ripe for alienation, I am "everything," I think. I am "nothing," I think.

Life is a quest to un-riddle the mystery of freewill. It is an evolving abstraction with tangible tentacles that span the universe. For now, its scope, its composition, its significance escapes us. For now, we find solace in virtue, in delineated human truths, in cryptic metaphors, in credulous realities.

Together, in the dimension of thought, we are traversing asymmetrical to measure symmetrical. Boxed in imagination, we are transcending living to entertain greater realization of nonliving.

In gaining freedom, we gain awareness. In gaining awareness, we gain freedom. In gaining freedom of awareness, we gain awareness of freewill. In gaining awareness of freewill, we actualize ourselves happy.

It is true. I am cajoled by capricious thoughts. It is true, time-bound I imagine life timeless. True or false, right or wrong, from life-sustaining feelings to self-actualization to disintegration, time passes while we attempt to capsulate its passing to control our own passage.

Think this: my conscience dissipates reality. Reality is connections we invoke. Connections are relations we exhale. And when our thoughts fervidly fume, we seek harmony in the edifice of tolerance and scream our dubiety a congruous unity.

I will uphold human truths as real truths to eulogize our being together a consummation of our combined awareness.

Are we then not free, asked a young bewildered mind pacing its way with a confused posture? His face was flushed, his eyes bulging. He seemed frightened. His fragmented mind compelled me to reflect my own. I began to sweat. My respiration grew deep and fast. My heart began to pound.

How was your journey?

Is that you SIMA? I am glad to sense you.

Was your journey worth taking?

It was great, SIMA, simply magnificent. I jumped astonished. Are you The Great One?

Its thoughts are with me, as all human thoughts are with me. I am your collective conscience. I am yours to serve. I am yours to teach. I am a part of you as you are a part of me.

Whatever happened to The Great One?

There are many great ones defining human dimension. Each of us is a potential to be The Great One.

But in my reality and in my dreams, you were The Great One, were you not?

I am a creation of your imagination. I mold myself to suit your desires. I have no will of my own. It is you who possess a willful mind.

Thanks, SIMA. I must return to my duties. There is a long journey ahead and much to be done. Future is ours to explore, one step at a time, sometimes in leaps, occasionally in gigantic strides, but always with imaginative thoughts. Thank you for being truthful. Thank you for images that invoke the best of humanity. Thank you for reminding me the significance of compassionate norms.